FINAL SOLSTICE

FINAL SOLSTICE

David Sakmyster

WordFire Press
Colorado Springs, Colorado

Prologue

7:30 PM, just as the engorged sun bled out over the Laguna Mountains, Senator Robert Aickerman went for a late jog. He left his Sunset Hills estate outside of San Diego, waved to the night guard at the gate, and planned to get a quick lead ahead of the two secret service agents, trailing in a black limo should he need a break, a drink or mainly, should there be an attempt on his life.

He was the last to admit it, because of the drastic change it implied in his life, but it was time. After all, he was now the current front-runner in the Republican race. Forty-percent of the delegates, miles ahead of his flailing, scandal-wracked opponent. Very possibly he would be sitting in the Oval Office this time next year.

Aickerman was nothing if not safety-conscious, but the increased attention had grown tiresome. So bad he couldn't even read the paper in the shitter alone without having them check every few minutes on his continued safety.

He picked up the pace, determined to reach the bottom of his steep hill and enter the park before the daylight fled for good. Orange vest, blinking lights on the back of his sneakers. He was certainly careful enough. Plus, those headlights at his back, keeping pace.

So intrusive, Aickerman thought. Before he had thrown his tattered hat into the ring, he had enjoyed the solitude of this park, away from the lights of the multi-million dollar homes on the neighboring hills, the sweet scents of sycamores, black sentinels against the night. Some nights he'd be out here all alone with just the bold constellations keeping pace, monitoring his time.

Glancing up, Aickerman could see Venus, or some other planet, but that was all he could make out in the spreading inky dusk that pushed away the meager violet remnants of the day. Ten minutes later, as the sycamores took on almost colossus-like size, humanoid in shape, two new lights, small and crimson, appeared against the night. High up on the hill.

Aickerman wasn't the only one to notice. Behind him, the headlights flickered, the signal to stop. Cursing, he slowed, panting heavily.

"Senator?" Secret agent Tom Reynolds was standing in front of the car, a film-noir silhouette, just missing the '40s-era fedora and the cigarette. "Come back a moment, there's something …"

"Up there on the hill there, I know." Aickerman scanned the area up there, dotted with brush, speckled with juniper. "I think I see them." He squinted, trying to get the headlights' afterimages from his sight. "Sure it's just kids screwing around." *Like my former opponents, lucky them.* At least somebody was having fun. And at least now, with the spotlight removed, they could enjoy their pastimes in private without people snooping in. Without agents following their every move.

"You might want to get in the car, sir."

Aickerman heard it before he felt it: the wind, picking up, rustling the sycamores, which swayed now, their heavy branches signing out a warning. He looked up, and his frown grew deeper.

"Sir, come this way.…"

It took a few moments to realize what was wrong. Venus—it was gone. And the sky, a different shade of color.

His attention turned back to the crest of the hill, those two flickering lights. Torches? Their holders were just barely discernible. This is what the agents must have seen, without the hindrance of the headlights. Outlines of two figures out of place. They wore cloaks— or dark robes with hoods—and their torches were the lit tips of long sticks.

Aickerman had the sudden flash of a B-movie he had seen as a teenager in a drive-in movie, something about robed priests of darkness, spells and human sacrifices.

He shivered, took a step back toward the car.

"Just to be safe, sir." Agent Reynolds led him inside as the wind abruptly shifted and drove at them, swirling, and turned to a roar as the sky burst in a searing flash of light—clearly outlining the two robed figures on the hill.

Their torches winked out simultaneously, and the ensuing darkness swept over the world, just as the roar of a sudden storm commenced with pounding thunderclaps and stinging hail.

"Inside!" Reynolds slammed the door shut and slid in, his body protectively leaning toward the senator. They sat cringing as the rock-sized hail hammered the roof and chipped against the windows.

"Jesus, where did that come from?" Aickerman jumped at another explosion of thunder. This time of year, even during an election year, the one constant you could count on was the weather; every day as beautiful as the last.

Although, if you believed the rhetoric of his opponents, critics and detractors, such a thing was exactly what they expected. The latest bill he had spoken out against, blocking it at every turn, was an environmental protection legacy plan. Riddled with earmarks, sponsored by fear-mongering Democrats and laden with catastrophic tax burdens. With heavy lobbying from environmental alternate energy firms with deep pockets, the bill had implied just such doomsday scenarios if we didn't act, or in this case, *enact* this legislation.

For Aickerman, it wasn't a matter of lobbying, and wasn't a question of loyalty. It all came down to common sense—and science. That was the fact of the matter: the science wasn't compelling. Weather was not significantly changing across the world, their tricked-up charts and Al Gore's nonsense aside. Even if it could be definitively proven that temperatures were rising and carbon concentrations were so much higher, the cause and effect wasn't consistent. If the environment was a murder scene, the evidence was far from air tight, circumstantial in fact, implicating man as the culprit. Other suspects, such as solar radiation, tidal forces, volcanic action and the natural cycles of the earth, were far more likely. Aickerman had his feet firmly in the camp believing that no matter what, now wasn't the time to force-feed problematic and impractical solutions on a world that could be further thrown into chaos and poverty by overwhelming regulation and controls.

More pounding hail, another clap of thunder and a burst of supernova-like lightning.

Agent Reynolds leaned forward and said something to the driver; something lost in the shrieking of twisted glass and tortured metal. A grunt, and suddenly Aickerman was on his side, staring at the broken windshield and a mass of dark spikes protruding through it, branches that had slammed instantaneously through the glass—and through the driver who was still twitching, coughing up blood. His hands, gouged with splinters and broken glass, feebly worked at dislodging a telephone pole sized branch from his ribcage.

Reynolds made a choking sound and threw his body over Aickerman's just as the roof collapsed in a shower of shattered metal, branches, leaves and hailstones.

The headlights faded.

In the dark, Aickerman tried to move, to free himself. "Reynolds?" He pushed, twisted, struggled against unyielding weight. "Reynolds! I think … a tree landed on us. Can you …?"

A tree, Aickerman thought with a silly laugh. *A goddamned tree landed on us! In a hailstorm, in—*

The pounding of hail had stopped, he realized, only to be replaced by a deep and constant wet driving sound, an epic thunderstorm. The heat had returned, dragging humidity along with it. Rain fell into the car, driven sideways with the wind. Aickerman grunted again, and in a flash of lightning, he saw Reynolds—his head twisted around impossibly, vertebrae jutting out from his neck; blood dripped from his nostrils, his eyes, his ears.

Aickerman turned from Reynolds, turned to his side, seeing the world mixing with the pooling rain and …

Mud. Mud, seeping into the car from the shattered doors.

How was that possible?

The tires! He realized they had been flattened with the tree's impact for sure, but the ground … Softened, turning to mud, the car sinking. Rain falling so fast, so powerfully, turning the land into mush, and—

Another flash of lightning, and Aickerman could see out the gap in the door. *The hill was moving.* The entire hill and everything on it in motion as if the land itself was melting. Trees slid down gleefully like ungainly skiers. Bushes, shrubs and boulders, all swept along. Everything tumbling, slipping, surfing down the waterfall of mud.

Toward his car.

Aickerman screamed. He kicked, flailed, jarred a shoulder free, then his upper body. Slipped into the seat well, face down in a rising pool of mud and water.

He tasted the earth, a bitter, gritty taste like choking on embalming fluid. The sound of his vomiting was drowned out by another thunderclap, and the storm raged even harder, its volume snapping another octave. A raging, relentless onslaught. The water rose past his knees. He saw a gap in the door. Tried it, but the door wouldn't budge, trapped by three feet of rising muck.

He tried the window, which miraculously descended. Halfway. *Good enough*, he thought, and squeezed through it carefully. Pulling himself up, balancing on the window and climbing up to the roof where in the darkness he could just make out the shape of the monstrous tree that had flattened his car.

He stood, awed by nature's ferocity, fighting to stay upright against the buffeting winds and the raging of the storm, feeling like he stood under a raging waterfall.

Another flash, and he could see the hill descending toward him, rolling like a tidal wave. Boulders, trees, bushes—a garbage can and an old bicycle, a ten-speed like the one he used to ride before his jogging kick.

The wave of mud and debris rumbled toward him.

Then the blackness descended, but not before he caught a flash of movement at the top of the hill. Two figures, apparently isolated from nature's carnage. Their cloaks unruffled, their cowled heads bowed.

In the resurging darkness, he tried to brace himself, but the car jolted with the impact. Jolted, and flipped, tossing Aickerman on his back into the mud. He gagged, got to his feet, just in time to see the movement—the black shape of the car tumbling side over side toward him.

He turned and tried to run, but his legs were stuck, the mud holding him fast. Tried to scream, but his throat was full of rain and muck. Tried to dodge, but the car slammed into him, pinned him back down and drove him deep into the earth where the trees and the mud and rain voraciously crushed his lungs, tore his flesh and drowned his soul.

Moments later, the rain stopped and the clouds blew apart, scattering in all directions; Venus and her children took up their lofty perches over a hill now bereft of sycamores. Below, only the trunk of the senator's car remained visible, propped up from the hardening muck, a metallic tombstone with its license plate his only epitaph.

Atop the hill, one of the shrouded figures pulled a sleek black cell phone from his sleeve. Punched a number, and waited, twirling the gnarled staff in his free hand.

"It's done," he said after a moment, as a starlit smile emerged from the shadowy cowl. In a gentle easterly breeze, he snapped the phone shut, nodded to his companion and walked out of the quiet grove, leaving behind only a crudely-erected circle of stones.

Book 1

Chapter 1

At San Diego's Channel Seven Doppler Weather Center, a small command-room style chamber with no windows to glare off of the sixteen monitors and computer screens, Primetime Weather anchor Mason Grier sat hunched over his chair, staring at a small array of LCD screens, poring over statistics from the twelve-county area, measuring them against chronological graphs from the past forty-eight hours.

Clear weather patterns stretched across the digital maps in all directions, far out into the Pacific even; but then, sudden red concentric circles flared up, localized over the suburb of Sunset Hills, exploding like fire-bursts, then disappearing just as fast.

Mason reversed the time and played the sequence again from several angles on the different screens.

He leaned back, shaking his head. "Impossible."

The door opened behind him, letting in a shaft of bright afternoon sunlight. His producer, Pamela Brock, stood there beaming. "Mason, time to go. Unless you want to be late for your own award ceremony." She was fifty-six, and despite two divorces and six kids and fifty extra pounds, still full of frenzied energy. High-strung, her office across the hall was littered with empty cans of Red Bull, which happened to be her nickname among the news team.

"I've got a killer intro for you, Mace, got all the press there already. Even imported some special fans of yours."

"Who?" He had no fans. Mason ("Mace" to his producer, and *only* to her) was a meteorologist, and if you looked up his class description in a role-playing game, his ilk would be described as reclusive, hermetic even. They hid from the limelight, preferring the damp recesses under rocks and in the shadows while people like Emory Jiles the sportscaster and Diana Newman the lead anchor sought all the attention. Meteorologists, weathermen like Mason, studied almanacs, pored over statistics and averages, and culled all sorts of data together to attempt the challenging feat of predicting the unpredictable.

At forty-five, Mason was and always had been, a weather fanatic. However, it was a love-hate relationship, spawned in a Petrie dish and fermenting over the years until it outpaced its confines, exhausted its food and went out seeking fresh fodder, thriving off of Mason's tragedy and taking impersonal glee in shattering his life at every turn.

His first memories were of the tornado in Indiana, the one that tore through half his childhood home—the half with his parents' bedroom. With a force of such malevolent fury, it scattered their broken bodies across a field nearly a mile away and left young Mason standing on a shattered ledge that used to be a hallway, gaping at the missing half of his room. After a series of foster homes where he slept very little, and never during storms, he worked his way to a scholarship and a free ride at UCLA. For most of those intervening years, nature had left Mason to his own devices. For a time, he had almost dared to feel safe again. Not the safety children feel nestled in their beds knowing their parents are right there across the hall, but a certain similar complacency nonetheless.

Nature had left him alone. Left him to study his enemy, to grow and to learn everything he could about the force that had orphaned him and shaped his life.

Then, just when Mason had come to a comfortable acceptance and the memories had faded, it came again in the guise of a snowstorm that ran his wife, Lauren off the road—and caused a thirty-two car pileup on the Colorado Interstate. Lauren—poor Lauren was left in a wheelchair with a collapsed lung and a shattered hip.

Of course, even that wasn't the worst part.

The eight-year-old twins were in the car with her. Gabriel escaped unscathed somehow, but had been in such shock he couldn't even begin to understand what had happened. Shelby, however, had found some part of herself way older than her years, and she had acted. Ventured out into the blustery expanse of white, into the merciless cold. So young, with all that responsibility, she made the noble attempt to get help—and with such repercussions.

Realizing Mom was in serious trouble and her brother wasn't going to be of any use, seeing a look in his eyes she just couldn't fathom, Shelby had run from the car into the blinding snowstorm, headlong into and through four-foot drifts; trying to find help. Close to the road, in sight of approaching headlights, she slipped on the ice, fell further down into a ditch and hit her head on a rocky ledge. No one saw her in the blinding snow, not for almost an hour. The snow had even concealed the tracks and obscured the sight of the car on its hood in the ditch.

A month battling pneumonia and finally Shelby came out of it, but the infections and fluid built up in her ear canals had left her permanently deaf.

Mason still remembered the call from the highway department, the madcap race to the hospital, then running between the rooms, having to choose who to see first.

For all those debts and more, Mason Grier had devoted his life to the study of this implacable, unreasonable foe. Finally, he believed that while he could never tame such a force, at the very least he could develop the skills to predict its behavior. Its nuances, its fickle genius, its horrific temper and its subtle wiles.

Today, for all that, for all his accomplishments, his thirty years of meteorological knowledge and service, he was being honored. *California Weatherman of the Year.* Something about his near-flawless predictive abilities had led him to be nominated, and then to win this thing—a gold-plated statue of a guy looking like Oscar's bedraggled second cousin holding up a shiny umbrella.

Mason shook his head. Up until last night, he believed he had earned such an award. But after what had happened from seven-thirty-seven to seven-forty-nine last night, he now doubted everything, once again humbled by his nemesis after growing over-confident.

The freak storm had made all the headlines, and it all had to happen right here, practically in his own backyard. And worse—the freak storm that killed Senator Aickerman, burying the man who was a potential shoe-in to be the next president—happened on his watch.

"How can I accept an award after what happened?"

Pamela stepped inside, closed the door. The lines around her dark-circled eyes smoothed. "Come on, this is what, your first miss in over twenty years?"

"But Christ, what a miss! It's not like I bounced one off the rim and it just rolled out. I threw up an air ball that cracked the back windows." He turned to the screens. "I can't understand it. This storm, out of nowhere. No Doppler prediction, no rise in barometric pressure prior to the event, no precipitation indicators …"

"Mace."

"Not even a goddamned cloud, not even—"

"Mace!"

"Nothing! It's impossible!" He slammed his fist against the table, knocking over one of the screens. "Shit!"

"Hey, take it easy. Deep breaths. Do I need to get HR in here and recommend you for anger management classes? At this late stage in the game, I'd think it kind of pointless."

"Sorry. Okay, so, who's coming to this damn thing?"

"Your wife's already en route, and before you freak out, I had a medical van sent for her, the hotel is wheelchair friendly and she'll be fine."

"She shouldn't be moved like that."

"She'll be fine, Mace, and she wanted to come, practically begged me. And guess what, Shelby's coming too."

Mason's heart leapt. Shelby was nineteen now; she had been in a USC exchange program in London for the past three months, working on a particularly exciting thesis involving early Saxon folklore. Shelby was the one he was most proud of, the one he was closest to, and to have accomplished so much despite her condition…. But his son?

"No word from Gabriel," Pamela said, as if reading his mind. "Sorry, we tried. I know, deep down you'd like to see him again."

"You shouldn't have wasted your breath." Mason stood up. His head felt like dead weight, so heavy. He looked ruefully at the weather patterns from 7:38 last night, still frozen on the screens, and he shook his head.

"Don't bother with Gabriel. I've gotten used to his absence. It's refreshing, actually." He sighed, thinking back again to that accident on the interstate, in the whiteout. *Was that the turning point for the boy?* It seemed that up until that day Gabriel had been a normal kid, interested in the usual assortment of young boy things—baseball, cartoons, comic books, movies with things that exploded. After the accident, however, it was like a dark streak had been run through Gabriel; he became bitter and rueful about some perceived hurt, or as if angry that he had been spared, ignored more like it, by the storm. He withdrew from his family, and within a few years he was holed up in his room with an array of odd books and odder music coming from his headphones at all hours. Up until Berkeley, then it all came gushing out of him, all the hatred and bitterness he had been repressing since the car crash.

"All right," Mason muttered, "let's get this farce over with. But I've got no speech, and I'm not saying anything except thanks to the Academy and thanks for my wife's undying support."

"Yeah," Pamela said, "all that shit, but if you forget to thank your brilliant and beautiful producer, without whom you'd be nothing more than a hack psychic in circus tent, I'll slip arsenic in your next cup of coffee."

Mason let a smile slip, then made an exaggerated bow. "I'll shower you with praise."

"That's the spirit, spoken like a man who knows his place."

"Really? And where is that?"

"In front of a vastly more successful woman."

Rolling his eyes, Mason started moving. "Let's go already, before I change my mind. Or lose my lunch."

It would be good to see Shelby again, see how much she'd changed in the four months since he'd seen her off to the airport.

So much like her mother before the accident. Tall and thin, deep blue eyes brimming with empathy. A smile to warm up any room. He couldn't keep up with her friends, with her sports: lacrosse, sand volleyball, tennis. But she understood her father's responsibilities; primarily to care for Lauren. Fortunately, they could afford a live-in nurse, and Lauren wasn't exactly bedridden; she had good upper body strength and an indomitable sense of optimism, more than countering Mason's inner grimness, his lingering anger at nature, at the weather and simple fate. All the things beyond his control.

At least at first, but that's what meteorology was all about—exerting some degree of control over something that was inherently uncontrollable. If you could predict the behavior of a thing, you could have some control over it. You could sidestep its assaults, dodge its moods.

And just perhaps, you could save yourself or someone you cared about.

On the way out the door, Mason stopped and glanced back at the current weather screens showing nothing but clear skies.

Shaking his head, he reached to the hook behind the door to grab his umbrella.

CHAPTER 2

The taxi pulled up to the Westin Resorts Sacramento hotel and let Mason out. Pamela stayed behind to pay the cab and to meet with the film crew, still unloading their gear from a van. Mason passed a valet dropping off a red convertible Lexus, and then right before the main entrance, he stepped in front of a long, sleek black limo. He paused, feeling a sudden brisk breeze, a wind that chilled through his suit when he looked at the tinted back windows.

He could almost make out a shape inside, hovering ghost-like within: a hint of red hair, eyes that floated, shifting color in the shadowy interior, something hanging from the inside ceiling, vine-like. Frowning, Mason walked around the limo, seeing his own reflection: haggard and stretched, and had the sudden feeling like he was looking into the depths of a fairy-tale onyx mirror, one stumbled upon in the depths of a dark wood. *Who's not the fairest one of all?*

He pulled his eyes away, shaking his head and blinking until a sense of nausea passed. *End of the line,* he thought suddenly for some reason, predicting that this event—claiming this reward, would be it, the seminal event of his life. Nowhere to go from here but down.

Retirement and years of sitting on the couch, pushing Lauren around in her chair; spending his free moments staring at the 24-hour weather channel, trying to second-guess his successors. Living just for the accomplishments of his children.

Or at least, the one he still had hopes for, and praying the other didn't embarrass him further.

Mason fought off the deepening chill that seemed to radiate in waves from the limousine. Forcing heat back into his legs, he turned to climb the stairs and enter the hotel, where the blast of air conditioning felt like a welcoming breath of some fairy goddess.

Past the lobby, into the conference room, with its sparse population of fellow newscasters, weather-prognosticators, and a smattering of journalists, Mason offered weak smiles and even weaker handshakes as he made his way to the front, to the shining woman in a shinier wheelchair. Tilted at an angle that gave him the impression he was walking down the proverbial aisle, he experienced a momentary flashback to their wedding, only with the roles reversed and she was up there this time, waiting impatiently, fighting the tears of joy at seeing him coming toward her.

He moved even quicker than she did that day, and in moments was at her side, bending down, planting a big kiss across her dry lips. Lauren's warm hands gripped his head, pinning him close with a mischievous lip-lock. "Way to go, hero," she said at last. She grinned, then ruffled and smoothed back his thinning grey hair. She had a camera in her lap, and her face was brimming with excitement.

Mason assumed Shelby had something to do with that. He stood up, and she came from the blind spot behind Lauren's chair, a blur in an almost too snug green dress, and Mason had a flashback to one of her tap-dancing classes when she was only six when she had worn a similar colored dress and bounded into his arms after the performance.

Such innocence, all lost the instant the family car did a three-sixty and tumbled off the road.

"Daddy!" Her speech was still a bit awkward, but every time she said that magical word, it was the most wonderful sound he could imagine; its beauty was expressed by its mere presence instead of what could have been, instead of the silence of its absence.

His fingers and hand motions a blur after years of practice, he signed back to her: *Hon, you didn't have to come all the way back across the Pond for this! It's too much.*

"I sure did," she said, then continued with her fingers moving almost too fast: *especially when your producer's paying for it. First class.*

Shelby was always one for comfort, for luxury. Such the opposite of her brother. Gabriel would sooner ride with the caged animals in cargo than up with what he would call "white-collar criminals and earth-polluting, resource-raping pigs."

A promising (and expensive) education pissed away, as far as Mason was concerned. Two semesters at Berkeley, and all Mason got for his return was a freethinking son who hated everything and everyone, his father included, for their purported crimes against nature. They hadn't spoken since Gabriel's junior year, after the call from the police that Mason had been dreading: Gabe had been arrested in a logging district in Washington State, along with fifteen of his classmates. After the police had to cut him loose from the trunk of a redwood, he then attacked the officers with those same chains.

Another twenty thousand in legal fees, just to get his ungrateful son off with no jail time, and the first week out Gabriel pulls an even bigger stunt: firebombing a Hummer dealership in Beverly Hills.

No avoiding jail time there.

Except, somehow he did. Bailed out by one of his acquaintances and fellow like-thinkers. Someone with deep pockets.

Mason hugged Shelby tighter than he had planned. He had mourned enough over his son; their disassociation haunted him as intensely as the tragedies that had taken the lives of his parents and injured his wife; Gabriel's loss (for how else could he see it?) had opened up his ribcage, creating a void, a wounded chasm just as deep.

He couldn't dwell on that now. He had one child that loved him, one that respected him and was grateful to be alive. That, in itself, was a miracle. He took his wife's hand as he continued smiling at Shelby.

"I want to hear all about your British wanderings, about Spam and Stonehenge and all that, but I just need to do this little speech thing first."

She nodded, then signed: *Blow 'em away, daddy.*
"Bloody right," said Lauren.
Mason smiled. "Bloody right."

A half hour later, after the uncomfortable acceptance of Pamela's introduction, and after some initial stumbling, Mason made good on his promise to keep it short, and to thank those who needed thanking, especially his brilliant producer. The Oscars ceremony this definitely wasn't, with only a few camera flashes going off, a few journalists, and one video camera with a feed that might find its way to the archives of the Meteorology Society. But it was just right as far as Mason was concerned. His favorite two people in the world were here, smiling in the front row.

He had the award in his hand, and raised it up one more time after his speech, to mild applause, and he posed for a quick picture. The flashbulb still searing his vision, he caught sight of someone in the back, someone standing up quickly before the others.

Mason squinted. *Something about that figure.* The man was young, all in black, with a starched fancy black suit. Clearly out of place among these journalists. Head bald, or shaved. His face however, was too unclear in the after-spots of the flashbulb.

Blinking rapidly, Mason leaned forward. The oddest thing about that man … he seemed to be holding a cane, or a stick of some kind. Mason took a moment until the spots cleared and the cheers subsided, and then sought out the man again.

Above the waving hands and the friends and coworkers coming to congratulate him, their eyes made contact. Eyes that were a fierce blue, almost like cobalt or quartz mined from the California hills. Deep and reflective of the profound depths from which they had arisen. So blue …

Just like his mother's.

Mason couldn't breathe, and it took several attempts to expel air from his constricted lungs, but he managed to push out one word.

"Gabriel."

The next ten minutes were some of the longest of Mason's life. Shaking hands, sharing trivial stories and memories of his career: his start in Seattle and cutting his teeth on the complex weather patterns in the upper northwest, the blizzard of '99, the floods and mudslides of '05. Through it all he kept stealing glimpses to Lauren and Shelby, where they were perched off to the side of the stage, signing to each other and smiling, laughing like two chatty high school girls after class.

Finally, in a short break he got Lauren's attention and made the sign for "Gabriel," and motioned to the back.

Lauren smiled, nodded, and then Mason understood. They had known all along. She signed back: *he called last week and asked if he could come. Go. Talk to him, it's important.*

Wondering what else his wife had been keeping from him, Mason excused himself from the current crowd of journalists, and from Pamela, who snatched up his award at the last moment.

"Let me see that. Nice. Not as nice as mine for Producer of the Year, but it's okay … for you." She gave him a lopsided grin and a pat on the back, then noticed his eyes, and followed them to the back of the room. "Who's that? Paparazzi?"

Mason eased past her. "Worse."

He made his way down the aisle, walking with legs that felt heavier with ever step, acutely aware of the lighting in here, the sounds at his back diminishing to mute whispers, the bulbs flickering, the air cooling. Gabriel had been leaning against the wall. He pushed off now, using the cane, a lacquered cherry wood stick with a golden tip, and took three quick, energized and certainly not feeble, steps to meet his father.

"Who are you," Mason asked, trying to set the mood, "and what have you done with my son?"

Gabriel shifted the cane to his left hand and reached out to shake his father's hand, pumping it vigorously. Mason stared at their connected hands. It was the first time they'd touched in over three years.

"Congratulations, Dad."

Mason pulled his hand away and tilted his head, eying Gabriel quietly. Neither spoke for a long time. Finally, Mason said, "Glad you lost the beard. The last I saw you, your hair was down around the middle of your back. Next, you're going to tell me you've got a job at a bank?"

Gabriel chuckled. "Please, we don't want to go there."

By "there," Mason knew he meant the whole evil of the federal government and the ownership of the world's sparse resources by the fiends in the international banking community. Or some other such nonsense. Mason couldn't resist, however. And he needed to see who this young man standing before him was now, needed to learn if anything had changed. Surprisingly, he found himself actually nearing the brink, daring to hope.

"And you Dad, lost a bit more up top, and the grey's taking over. I figured rather than go quietly, I'd just shave mine all off. Much less maintenance."

Mason nodded. "My genetic gift to you."

Gabriel shrugged. "Could be worse, and considering what else you've given me, a fair trade."

"What's the 'else' you're referring to?" He wasn't following.

A smile broadened on Gabriel's face. "Come, let's walk out in the lobby, get some fresh air. We need to talk."

Mason stood motionless. "Talk?"

"Yes, you know. You and me. Talking, moving our lips. Hearing. Responding."

"Sarcasm I get. What I don't understand is why. Why now? Last time we 'talked,' I heard the words 'Dad' and 'Fuck Off' as they led you away in handcuffs."

"I was a different person back then, but if you want apologies and groveling, if you want me to act out the Prodigal Son, you'll have to wait. I'm here for a more important reason."

"Good," Mason said acidly, "then get to the point."

"Outside?"

"No, here. I don't want to lose sight of your mother. Or your sister."

Gabriel cocked his head. "Still blaming yourself?"

Mason's eyes hardened. "For what?"

Gabriel's eyes stayed on his, unblinking.

He knew what his son was thinking: *for not being there, not being the one to drive; or for telling Lauren, who always hated driving in snow, that the weather report looked just perfect, not a chance of even one snowflake, much less anything like that merciless blizzard heading her way.*

"Nothing, Dad. Look, what if I told you I could give you a chance to do something truly important with the rest of your life? Something in your field, something … light years beyond all this?" He waved the cane's tip half-heartedly at the remnants of the ceremony. "This nickel-and-dime, dog and pony show. Weather forecasting? Come on, here in southern California anyone with half a brain or access to a window could do your job. No offense."

"So which one do I have?"

"I'm pretty sure they don't give you a window." Gabriel's smile softened. "Look, what if you could have the chance to achieve what you've always wanted?"

"And what would that be?"

Gabriel smiled. "Call it what you like. Redemption. Understanding. Control."

"Control?"

"How about sweet old fashioned revenge?"

Blinking, Mason stepped back. "Gabriel, please stop talking in circles. Why are you here? What do you want?"

His son reached into his suit coat and retrieved what looked like a black playing card. He flipped it over with a snap like a stage magician and handed it to Mason.

A business card. Plastic, laminated.

SOLSTICE SYNERGISTIC, INC.

Environmental Research

Seattle, Washington, 45050

555-643-3333

"Environmental research?" Mason gave his son a skeptical look. "This is what you're doing now?"

"You're surprised?"

"By the very fact you have what sounds like a real job, yes. So what do you do there?"

"A little of this and that. I've been moving up in the ranks. Working on environmental law, currently."

Mason made a face. "Is that just a fancy name for chaining yourself to more trees?"

Gabriel shook his head. "I told him you'd be unreasonable."

"Who?"

Gabriel motioned to the card. "Call the number on there, anytime. We'd like you to come in, tour the facility, see what we do."

"For what purpose?"

"That should be obvious."

"Pander to an old man. State the obvious."

"We want you to come and work for us."

"So, what was that all about?" Lauren asked him when he returned, a few minutes later. Mason hesitated. Shelby was watching him intensely, staring at her father's lips, ready with baited breath to read the next words from his mouth.

Mason glanced at both of them. He was still holding the business card, shifting it between his fingers as if practicing a failed magic trick, trying to figure out what might have gone wrong. "He didn't tell you?"

They both shook their heads.

Mason turned, saw his son, the cane under his arm, strolling out the door, after first opening it for an older woman. *Reformed, and a gentleman?* Again he wondered who Gabriel was, and what had changed him. Or was it all an act? He stared at the card, and something about it gave him the shivers. He noticed suddenly the black wasn't all black; there was something beneath it, trapped under the dark. A coiled form, like a snake or a nest of vipers; the things seemed to define themselves the more he stared at the card; red-tinged, their scales—and the eyes, twinkling almost if you held the card just right, and away from the light.

Oddly, it felt warm to his touch.

Shelby pressed her hand to his arm, getting his attention. She said, "He wants … to 'omebak?"

"He wants to come back," Lauren translated, sounding more hopeful than certain.

Mason slipped the card into his shirt pocket. "He wants something, that's all I know for sure."

"You goin' to give it? Do what-eber he 'sked you?" Shelby asked, her voice clearer than Mason ever remembered.

"I don't know," he said, along with making the quick sign. A peal of laughter caught his attention. A few tables away, Pamela led a crowd of his coworkers into near-riotous laughter after some joke or story, most likely at his expense.

Mason turned back to meet the stares of his family, the looks that expressed a sense of hope, and reconciliation.

I don't know, he signed.

"Go," Lauren said, pointing to the pocket where he had placed the business card.

Shelby nodded, then signed: *Go*.

Chapter 3

Outside, Gabriel proceeded quickly to the black stretch limo where the side door opened on cue and he slipped inside. The limo launched before the door even closed and he had to steady himself before almost pitching forward onto the other man in the car.

The windows allowed in only minimal light. The seats were leather, the floors an oddly root-contoured feel. Around the ceiling hung an assortment of vines—some green, some wooden: mistletoe, hazelnut, hemlock, all entwined and crisscrossing in elegant, almost harmonious patterns, creating a patchwork living roof of foliage.

"Well?" came the voice from the seat across from Gabriel, behind the driver's panel. A face pulled itself free of the inky folds of shade and fractured light, a chiseled face right out of the pulp comics, the rugged face of a hero with high cheekbones, a jutting chin and a broad forehead ringed with coarse red hair and tied back in a pony tail. A fine edging of a beard framed his jaw, and a perfectly manicured mustache rested under eyes of intense jade, like ancient stones set in an excavated statue of some nature god. He wore a dark suit, the mirror of Gabriel's, as black as oil, with the exception of a tiny yellow wildflower pinned to his lapel.

Gabriel cleared his throat. His fingers traced the ridges of his wooden staff, seeking comfort there. When he spoke, his voice cracked. "I think he'll call."

"You *think*?" his employer asked.

"I … I know he will. I've got his interest, if for nothing else, to see what I've been doing. He hopes I've changed."

"Oh you have, Gabriel, you have. I've seen to that."

Gabriel nodded. "Thank you. But I don't believe it's in the way my father hoped."

The man with the red hair sat back and gave a low chuckle. "Sons rarely please their fathers. It's a truth he should have prepared for the day you scuttled out from between your mother's legs." The diminishing laugh merged with the sound of a hard tapping.

Gabriel clenched his own cane tighter as he saw the other staff, the one carried by his employer, gleaming in the green-tinted radiance. A gnarled, ancient stick with a gold-plated base and an emerald tip. His employer was tapping it against his open palm, absent-mindedly. "Tell me," he said, in almost a whisper. "Because I do not share your optimism. What options do we have if he refuses?"

Gabriel swallowed hard. Closed his eyes briefly, then opened them. "My mother maybe, but if time is of the essence …"

"It is."

"Then you have to go after Shelby. She's the true love of my father's life. He pays every day in guilt for what happened to her, and he tries every minute to make up for it. If anything else should threaten her …"

"Perfect. Although of course I had already arrived at the same conclusion."

"Then why did you ask?"

"I just wanted to hear you say it. It confirms that my trust in you is not misplaced."

"After all I've done? You trust me by now … sir."

"Good, then it's settled. But I'm sorry. We are not going to wait for his call. I'd hoped you would have been … more persuasive. Now, we're out of time. We have to ensure his compliance."

Gabriel was about to argue, but saw the determination in those green eyes, the look that said the discussion was over. Reluctantly, he shrugged, though his muscles were heavy, his blood ringing in his ears. "I know the stakes. I'm prepared to make … sacrifices."

The other man smiled, spun his cane and withdrew into the shadows as the limousine raced onto the interstate.

Chapter 4

A leisurely celebration dinner at TGI Friday's, and Mason and Lauren were soon caught up on everything in Shelby's life—at least everything she was prepared to tell them. She was, after all, almost twenty years old, and her father could tell there were things she was less than forthcoming about. English boys, most likely, maybe something else, he wasn't sure. He didn't think it was anything to do with drugs or alcohol; he would know the signs. She had always had a good head on her shoulders, a lot of common sense born from tragedy. Perspective. Near-death can do that to someone.

There was definitely something bothering her though, but now wasn't the time to press it. She'd have another week with them before returning overseas for another six months. She seemed in no hurry to leave, unlike other times when she couldn't wait to return to new friends and parties.

After what she'd been through, Mason begrudged her very little. He wanted his little girl to be happy, to live and experience life's pleasures without his interference. He had almost lost her twelve years ago; so all this was like extended hours at a theme park, time to be savored and enjoyed.

Her research had been going well, and as far as he knew, it involved exciting investigations into early Anglo-Saxon religious practices, with an eye toward nature-worship and astronomical ceremonies. Mason couldn't wait to read her jealously guarded thesis, but as yet she wasn't sharing.

A double-decker brownie dessert dish later, along with some decaf coffee for him and Lauren, and they were finally ready to leave, but not yet done talking. They had yet to address the elephant in the room, the particularly large and ungainly one by the name of Gabriel.

What are you going to do? Shelby signed to him. *About Gabe?*

Mason stared into his coffee for a long time until Lauren pinched him under the table. "Your daughter wants to know what you plan to do about her brother's offer."

"Reject it," he said at last, pushing away his coffee mug and rubbing his eyes. "A new job, I don't need. I would have gladly welcomed him back if he needed help, or a place to live for a while, anything like that. But this ..." He shrugged.

Shelby leaned in, brownie crumbs falling from her lips as she tried to speak. "You dunt trust 'im?"

"I don't, honey, I don't. Something about this whole setup ..." Mason turned his face to Shelby so she could read his lips. He was too tired to sign. "Gabe has changed, but I sense—I don't know, some ulterior motive, like I'm being set up to be the butt of some April Fool's joke. Or in this case, probably a seriously unfunny eco-terrorist prank. No thanks."

Again, a squeeze under the table. Lauren leaned in. "Don't you want to at least hear him out?"

"Not particularly, no."

"Please? It's been three years. Whatever you believe about his motives, three years is a long time. He's my son too, you know. I want to see him."

Me too, Shelby signed. "And I leef on Fray-day."

Mason sighed. "Overruling me again? I can say this at least. Without Gabe around, I've been outvoted by the females in this family for too long."

"Talk to him," Lauren repeated. "Just do that. If your stinko-meter still rejects his pitch, then walk away. And if he won't come back to us, then …"

"Ef him," Shelby said, stuffing the last brownie piece into her mouth, grinning, then turning red. She signed, *Sorry.*

Mason and Lauren couldn't hold back their laughter. Mason reached for the check. "Ef him indeed. All right, it's a plan, then."

Ⓟ

Back in their house in Kensington, Shelby went right to bed and gave Mason a nostalgic thrill in letting him tuck her in, four-leaf pajamas and all.

"Still my girl?" he signed as he ruffled her hair.

Always, she signed back, and gave him a neck-twisting hug. As he was on his way out, closing the door: "Dad …?"

"Yeah?"

There's something, a package I sent to you here. Probably arrive after I'm gone.

What is it? He signed back.

It's nothing. I want you to throw it out. Don't even open it.

Mason closed the door, with him still in the room. He turned on the light. "Honey? What is it?"

Nothing. Just promise me you'll toss it.

"Can you give me a hint? Was it something … you found over there?"

Just something foolish. A dumb gift.

As she signed it, her fingers seemed listless, as if she were signing underwater. It was one of the tells Mason had come to recognize over the years. She was lying.

"Okay, honey." He smiled. "No problem."

"Promiss?"

Mason crossed his heart and signed, *Promise.*

"Good night."

He eased out this time, after shutting off the lights. Back in his room, Lauren was struggling with her wheelchair. "Let me," Mason said, coming to her aid.

"I can manage."

"I know you can. But it's been a long time since I've had the pleasure of tucking in two girls in one night."

"You rascal."

"That's me."

"One award and the man thinks he's god's gift to women. Like we really swoon for the weathermen."

"You know it's true." He scooped her up in his arms.

"Are you going to change me too?"

"Of course." He tugged off her shoes, and started on her pants. "At least halfway."

She grabbed him by the tie, pulled him up to kiss her. "I mean it about Gabriel."

"I know."

"Enough time has passed."

"I know."

He searched her eyes, seeing a spark of life that had been absent a long time. Living with the disability was hard enough, but living with guilt for what she perceived as her fault her children turned out how they did: one deaf, the other estranged, it wore on her. She had been on anti-depressants for years. Finally free of them, her spirits were lifted and fun had returned to her life. Both their lives. They played games. Scrabble, strategized through endless hours of global conquest with Risk, and pursued merciless bankrupt-inducing nights of Monopoly. She was almost all the way back to her old self. It had taken so long, but he needed to nurse her the rest of the way, only a few more steps.

Gabriel could surely help. Or he could unravel everything they had accomplished. He had to hope it would be the former.

"I'll do it," he whispered, the word blown gently through her lips as she pulled him close for another kiss.

In the middle of the night, out of a deep sleep, Mason rocked up in bed. Lauren was snoring, a low grinding of her teeth followed by a throaty warble.

But what woke him wasn't anything so ordinary. It took another few moments of rushed breathing and a rising pulse thudding at his jugular to realize what it was:

A thunderstorm.

Violent, with tearing winds screaming through the palms; and suddenly, a pounding clap of thunder and a painfully blinding lightning burst.

He launched out of bed.

Again? There was no precipitation in the forecast. Not for tonight, and nothing on the ten-day projection. They were in the middle of a drought. Wildfires were raging to the southwest, made drastically worse due to the lack of rain.

Impossible. He slipped outside his room, into the dark hall where he paused at Shelby's room. Opened the door a crack and in the next flash he saw her bed.

Empty.

He stepped in, and was about to dash out and down the stairs when he saw the open window and felt the drops of rain slamming in almost sideways through it, splattering off the hardwood floor. Ran to the window, and looked out.

There on the back lawn, behind the kidney-shaped pool and past the grill, in the pounding sheets of rain, were two dark figures. Arms raised, Christ-like, facing each other.

A lightning flash.

Shelby, in her white and green-clover pajamas, hair now wild, dancing Medusa-like in the winds, drenched, facing … Gabriel? It had to be him. He could see the shine of his bald head in the lightning burst. Still dressed all in black, he squared off against her like they were gladiators preparing to strike at the emperor's command. The lightning's aura danced along their arms and fireflies swarmed around their heads, causing halo-like glows.

Gabriel? Mason's mind reeled. His son and daughter, out in this tempest? He was about to call out when he heard something—a footfall behind him.

He turned, but not quickly enough. And glimpsed only an emerald-tipped stick of wood bearing down upon his skull.

Chapter 5

When he came to, it was still raining, but the thunder had dropped to a morose rumbling, like the last protests of an upset stomach after a spicy dinner.

Rubbing the back of his head, wet either from the rain or from his own blood he wasn't sure, he glanced outside, where it was too dark to see anything. But he was reasonably sure no one was out there anymore.

He turned and stumbled out of the room, glancing first at Shelby's bed, the bed he had tucked her into for so many nights, hoping that maybe he had just been sleepwalking, dreaming a horrible dream, and maybe he had hit his head. But the room was empty.

Rushing into the hall, he paused, unsure of which way to go—*check on Lauren, or race outside?* He lingered a moment too long, then headed down, turned into the dark family room, stumbled to the kitchen, heading for the sliding back doors—and froze.

The light over the sink was on.

Someone was standing there, just to the right, in the thick shadows between the refrigerator and the window. Someone all in black, leaning on a cane.

A flash of lightning, and Mason toppled back, hand over his eyes. He shook his head, hoping to dislodge the sunspots and see the room before receiving another club on the head. He leaned on the kitchen table and peered back into the shadows, which were now empty.

But then his attention caught on the objects on the table:

Two glasses, each half full. A can of *Dad's Root Beer.* Open. And a business card, that same laminated black card, lying face-up between the glasses.

Mason took a seat, heavily.

He picked up the card.

From upstairs, Lauren was calling softly, then more urgently, asking if everything was all right.

He flipped the card over just as the wind died outside, the cicadas struck up their song and he knew—knew the clouds had vanished and the dark sky again revealed its innocent, speckled tapestry.

Again the image of his children in the rain, but now he saw the scene differently, saw Shelby's energy fading, Gabriel overpowering her. Or was that only a dream?

What was going on?

He held up the card, turned it over once, twice. The sinewy indentations moved with the light and shadow, and seemed to glide along his fingers, tickling his skin in a not-so tender way.

The longer he stared, the more everything settled in place. The conclusion was inescapable. They—whoever Gabriel worked for—they had Shelby.

And they wanted him to know it.

Chapter 6

Avery Solomon, the head of Solstice Synergistic, Inc., its CEO and founder, ran a company with branch offices in sixteen countries, and with twin headquarters in Seattle and London—both of which Solomon called home. Dual-citizenship, two mansions in each location, and a devoted staff, kept purposely low, composed of only his most trusted personnel, personally chosen.

He was just a shade under fifty, but his fiery red hair coupled with his tanned complexion and satin look of one twenty years younger led to a certain aura of confidence and charm that made his face a natural magnet for the covers of at least four national magazines. *Time* and *Forbes* sought him out as much for his stance on global warming—radical even by Al Gore's standards—as for his methods of combating it: namely through swift and penalizing legal injunctions slammed onto offending companies. The bigger the better. Solomon feared no one. He speared industry and politicians alike, hitting local governments and company executives, making his assaults fear-somely personal, attacking individual lifestyles and credibility, even prying into the lives of spouses and children. Solomon reserved a special mean streak for rogue scientists that dared speak out against the prevailing wisdom: that it was man and his actions alone that were harming the environment.

Four years ago he founded Solstice, solidifying a small private venture he had begun years earlier with unknown backers, rumored to be politicians, Hollywood players and others with very, very deep pockets.

Solomon was a man used to success. To a degree of control other men only dreamed about. And he was rarely denied.

"Mr. Solomon?" the driver called over the intercom.

"What is it?" Solomon groaned. He hated being interrupted during his meditations. He had much to think about, a multitude of plans tossed in the air and expertly kept in motion by a consummate juggler. But he had kept his head at all times. The little things were the ones that broke the performer's concentration and could threaten the whole show. It was the minor details that needed the most focus.

Like the comatose girl in the trunk.

The driver's voice filled the limo. "The airport, sir. They're postponing all outgoing flights to Seattle for the rest of the night. Something to do with fog and poor visibility. We can reroute and land in Spokane, then drive—"

"No. We can't afford the delay. Continue to the airport. We'll leave as planned." He smirked at Gabriel, sitting across from him, still wet from the encounter in Mason's back lawn. Shelby's appearance ... her arrival, coming out to greet them like a possessed sleepwalker, was unexpected but not out of the realm of possibility. Solomon should have anticipated something like this, after all. And he had at least had the foresight to come along as well. Otherwise things might have gone very wrong very fast.

Despite the situation, his sister in the back trunk, Gabriel still smiled confidently. *Ever eager to please. So malleable, this one.* When Solomon had plucked Gabriel Grier from jail, the young man had pledged his life—not just for his gratitude at his release—but for the chance to strike back for the planet, to drive a stake into the hearts of those who were bleeding the earth dry.

The intercom buzzed. Their driver was relatively new, competent enough for what he did, but that was as far as he went.

"But, Mr. Solomon, even though we have a private plane, we still have to—"

"Go to the airport," Solomon snapped. "We'll be cleared to take off by the time we arrive." He pulled out a slim cell phone, then thought for a moment and tossed it to Gabriel. "You're ready, you give the order. Call brothers Nexus and Remulus in Seattle. They'll know what to do."

Gabriel nodded and dialed the phone as Solomon closed his eyes and resumed his introspection. It was a short drive, and an even shorter flight, and he needed every minute to think, to create the living vision of the green future he would cause to grow and spread upon the earth.

The merest thought of it all gave him shivers of anticipation.

Soon.

But first, there were little details to attend to, minor cogs to the wheel, small but by no means unnecessary, without which the whole enterprise might just crash to an ignoble conclusion.

He needed Mason Grier.

CHAPTER 7

"Call the police," Lauren insisted, wheeling into the kitchen.

Mason was still holding the card in his hand. The police. He knew how this worked; he had seen enough movies. Call the police, and chances were Shelby would never be seen again. No. He spun the card around again. By now he had already burned the phone number into his brain, seared it in angry red strokes across the landscape of his mind, written in fury.

"Gabriel," he whispered. "What have you done?"

Lauren wheeled in close, clutching Mason's arm, the one holding the phone. "Don't rush to conclusions. He might be in trouble, just as she is."

"He was here, goddamnit. I saw him."

"And you said you saw someone else?"

"Yeah, someone … I don't know. He was just there for a second, then gone. Red hair, and another one of those weird canes."

"Call," Lauren said, her nails digging into the flesh on his arms. "The police or that number, I don't care, but pick one. This not knowing is killing me."

Mason held up the phone and dialed. Put it to his ear, looking into his wife's eyes, seeing all of his fear, his anger, his powerlessness reflected there.

"Mr. Grier?" a voice, smooth as satin.

Through gritted teeth: "Where's my daughter?"

"Safe. Come in and we'll talk about her future. And yours."

"Where?"

"You have the address on the card. I'd advise you to come with all haste. So much to do, you understand. And so little time."

"I want to talk to her, now."

"Sorry, she's indisposed at the moment, but comfortable. I promise you."

"Then let me talk to my son."

"That wouldn't be best right now. You'll have plenty of time to play catch up tomorrow."

"What if I play catch up with the police first? Or show up with a gun and put a bullet through your fucking skull?" Mason's hand clenched the phone so hard he heard the plastic crack.

"Last I checked, a twenty-year-old had to be missing at least twenty-four hours before they'll consider it a missing person's case, and since I know you're not the murdering kind …"

"Damn you, you don't know what I'm like when someone screws with my family!"

"Be careful with your curses, Mason. Words are weapons."

"Then listen carefully, asshole. I'll kill you if …"

"If I've harmed a hair on her head, yes I know. Clichés. We're not in a tired Hollywood thriller here, Mason. Just trust me, show up tomorrow. Bring a gun if you wish, but you won't need it."

Mason lowered his head; he was certain his wife could hear some of it, at least, but what she couldn't hear she could read by the look on his face.

"Why me?" he said at last.

"You'll find out."

"When?"

"Tomorrow. Book yourself an early flight and we'll see you at nine, Mason, when I will show you the new world."

Chapter 8

Mason stood outside the towering entranceway, finding himself in the shadow of the monolithic centerpiece of Solstice headquarters. The sun had just cleared the mountains, only to be blocked by the immensity of this black slab of concrete and opaque glass. Feeling awestruck, like one of the astronauts before the black obelisk in *2001: A Space Odyssey*, he shook off the certainty that he would be radically altered by what happened next. He moved forward, opened the door, and headed inside.

Flanking the entrance were what he initially thought were two replicas of great sequoias; but on further inspection he realized that the archway's architecture had been carved directly into nature, molded to fit the still thriving, pillar-like trees. Far above, Mason squinted at the painful expanse of bright blue sky stretching past the tower's edge, and he noted the swaying branches, the shielding leaves creating a dense canopy around the upper levels, providing a living roof for the penthouse balcony.

He yanked open the main door, expecting to be met immediately by armed guards to secure him and drag him to whoever was in charge, and again he wished he had brought some backup, or had the police shadow him here. But as soon as he set foot inside the marble-floored interior, everything changed.

He saw the birds first. Doves maybe, white wings fluttering in circles overhead, spiraling higher and higher up the hollow center of the building. Dazzling light streamed in from the sun, scattered by the rectangular panes and shimmering down like lances, spearing through the trees and sparkling off the clear stream running through the ground floor. An arched, cobbled bridge spanned one section, leading workers to a quiet grove surrounded by eight standing stones, like a miniature Stonehenge. Inside the circle were several tables that appeared to be hewn from the trunks of great old redwoods, and all around the stones were flowering vines, the same lush green vines that covered entire sections of the walls, the fences and the bubbling fountains. Butterflies hovered in colorful groups, and a trio of dragonflies sped toward Mason as if to greet him.

In the middle of the immense chamber stood a series of glass tubes. Elevator shafts, Mason realized, carrying employees and visitors up to some unseen height—and down perhaps, into the subterranean depths with the promise of just as much wonder below as above.

Still standing there gaping, staggered by the sheer unexpectedness of the natural setting, Mason didn't hear his voice being called until his daughter was almost right in front of him.

"Daddy?"

He blinked, looked down and there she was, alone, grinning, and reaching for him in a huge hug. "Daddy, I—"

He snatched her up, held her tight, nearly squeezing the breath out of her lungs. Kissed her face, her hair, then froze, seeing movement intended for his attention. There by the stones, emerging from the shadows: Gabriel. Arms folded, a content smile on his face.

Fury boiled in Mason. He set Shelby down and started for his son.

"Daddy, wait."

He turned, started to sign, his fingers moving too fast he knew, jumbling the angry words. But then she held them, fingers clenching his own.

"Daddy. I don't … need that … anymore." She said it so clear, enunciating perfectly without slurring, as if …

His eyes went wide, as wide as her smile.

"Daddy, I can *hear.*"

He spoke, hand over his mouth. "How is this possible?"

Shelby grinned so hard tears formed in the corner of her eyes. "I woke up here, in this beautiful place, and Gabriel was there and … oh Daddy, it worked! Just hearing my voice, and speaking again, has taken hours to get it right, but whatever they did …"

"What? What did they do?" Mason trembled, glancing from his daughter to his son, trying to make any sense of this turn of events. A minute ago he had been ready to tear this place apart, to single-handedly strangle anyone who got in his way of rescuing Shelby, but now it seemed he may have misjudged everything. "You were taken last night, kidnapped.…"

Shelby shook her head. "No, I … don't remember exactly. Just a dream, running out into the thunderstorm, feeling out of my body somehow, and Gabriel was there and we were fighting like when we were kids, just playing really. Pretend stuff, and then I must have fallen asleep again. I woke up here. They had given me some kind of tea, and then I noticed a paste in my ears, something clumpy and wet and really smelly. So foul I almost gagged. And then I heard it—a ringing, then a throbbing, and then the paste crumbled and fell off, and this man with red hair and deep green eyes said something, and at first I thought he was some kind of priest or healer, but then he gave me a hug and walked away. And Daddy," she smiled, "I could *hear* his footsteps in the earth. And the buzzing I thought was from my head was coming from honey bees, and I heard chirping and the trickling stream, and then Gabriel's voice!"

She smiled at her brother as he approached, and she held out a hand to him. "It was just about the most beautiful thing I'd ever heard, next to your own voice, of course, Daddy. It's just like I remembered when I was a child. So amazing to hear it again, finally."

"Shelby …"

"Dad." Gabriel came closer, put one hand on Shelby's shoulder while resting on his cane with the other. He wore loose-fitting beige khakis and a sports coat over a black t-shirt, and his head was shaved even closer than earlier. His thin lips spread into a smile like the carved grin of a totem-pole animal. "Sorry to scare you like that, but it was the only way."

"Scare me? Jesus Christ, son. I almost had the FBI down here to shoot you all on sight."

Gabriel just shook his head. "Like I said, it was the only way to try out this cure."

"What was it?" Shelby asked.

"Something," said Gabriel, "our father wouldn't have allowed."

"Why do you say that?" Mason felt his anger boiling. "If you ..." he glanced around. "If this place, your company has this kind of medical capacity ..."

"We don't, Dad. Not exactly. As I said, we're into environ-mental protection, law and regulation, but we also have an extensive R&D lab, where we invest heavily in developing natural cures from around the world, especially from endangered locations where we feel remote tribes might lose their ancient knowledge to pollution and extinction. We step in quickly to capture their secrets and preserve that wisdom. Including any plants, herbs and techniques that might otherwise have been eradicated without consideration."

"You're saying this was a tribal recipe from some Amazon rainforest?"

"Guatemala, actually," Gabriel said. "We heard about it years ago and spent months and millions of dollars testing it in our facilities here and in the field. All under the radar of the restrictive FDA. I hope you'll agree it's worth it."

"My God, Gabriel. What if there are side effects?"

"We tested it, thoroughly. Like I said, we were confident."

"But why not just offer the cure up to the medical community? Let them document it, test it and verify the results? And pay you for it?"

Gabriel's expression darkened. "Let one of the vile pharma-ceutical corporations get their hands on it, claim all the credit and then march down and ravage the jungles and the people for the cure? No way."

"But, there's so much potential.…" He stared at Shelby, still marveling that she had been cured, his deepest wish all these years come true.

"In due time."

"Time? Gabriel, there are people suffering."

"People will always suffer, Dad. That's their nature. They'll still be suffering if and when this cure is made public. You must be patient."

Shelby moved in, took Mason's hand. "Dad, it worked. I can hear, and I'm so happy again. I can't wait to see Mom and tell her."

"I can arrange for you to be taken home now," Gabriel said. "But Dad here has something else he needs to do. Someone to see."

Mason's mouth dried up. *So this is it. There has to be a cost. Nothing this big is done without expectations.* "Where is he?"

Gabriel smiled and pointed. "First lift there. Annabelle's waiting at the elevator, she'll take you straight up to him, where I hope you'll listen with an open mind and accept …"

"Accept what?"

"The offer to join us, of course."

"If I refuse?"

Gabriel continued smiling. "You won't."

"Daddy," Shelby whispered. "You won't. I was just made a similar offer."

"You?"

"Yes, coinciding with my research in London. They need someone in the branch office there."

"You're still in school. It's out of the question."

"In my spare time, Dad. It's like an internship."

"A well-paying one," Gabriel said.

"And when," Mason asked, "did money become important to you, Gabriel?"

"Who said it was? We're talking about my little sister, who sure enjoys spending it. And besides, I know what you make as a weather hack, Dad, and I know how hard it is to pay for Mom's care. So please do us all a favor, drop the martyr act and really listen to what's offered to you up there."

Shelby squeezed his hand. She signed, for old times' sake, *Please.*

Chapter 9

The elevator ascended gracefully. Surrounded by glass, Mason had initially suffered the sickening feeling that he was being levitated or blown up by a steady wind. Dizzy, he tried not to look below his feet, through the glass to the awesome sight below, the marble tiles merging with the earthen floor, the stones in a perfect circle, their shadows lengthening in the glancing sunlight. He saw through the treetops, the lush grove, the rock tables, the flowing stream and the minor waterfalls pumped in from the northeast corner.

"Beautiful, isn't it?" asked his guide, Annabelle. She was petite and cute in a way, freckles on her cheeks, blonde hair parted down the middle and in curls around her face. He was struck with the sudden question whether Gabriel found her attractive and maybe some kind of workplace romance was going on. Maybe it was the way she stole sideways glances at him, as if she was sizing up her love interest's father, unsure of what to say at this moment.

Suddenly, the elevator trip was taking too long. He couldn't look away, still awed by the view—this time out the windows, over the rolling hills and swaying sycamores, up and across the veiled shadows in the mountains' peaks and valleys under a broad sky of cobalt serenity.

"Beautiful," he said belatedly.

"Thank you." Annabelle blushed as if taking the compliment directly.

"Tell me," Mason asked gazing up now, seeing they were about halfway up the tower, heading toward a thin platform. "How many people work here?"

"At this location? Nearly two hundred."

"Really? Where?"

"Below, mostly. There are six sub-levels, plus two research labs. What you see here is really just our common area, a place of reflection, meditation and relaxation. We eat here, we have informal discussions, we talk before and after our shifts."

"And your boss … he's up there the whole time? What, like God, looking down on you all?"

Annabelle smiled. "You misunderstand. We're not going to his office, he doesn't have one. He walks among us, immerses himself in our work, talks with each of us, every day. No, we're going to the rooftop glen, the Summit Grove. You'll see when we get there. There's no better place from which to view the world and to see clearly what needs to be done. It's where all the important decisions are made."

"I must say," Mason argued, "this is one unusual company. Both in its architecture, and its people."

"Thank you." Annabelle said again. "And I must say, Mr. Grier, that you are one unusual man. Your children are special, talented. And you, well we hear great things about you."

"You do? Like what? I'm just a weatherman."

"You're special. We need more people like you to continue our mission."

"Not sure I'll help with that, or that I can say I agree with your mission, but …"

"But you'll listen."

Mason nodded as they slowed, came to a stop. "Yes."

Annabelle left him on the platform as she operated the lift to descend. "I'll be back when you're finished. Good luck."

Mason stepped off, gingerly, onto the metal platform, expecting it to wobble, creak or something to jar him back into the elevator, but then with a swish of closing doors, there was nothing behind him anymore, the lift descending rapidly. And in front of him—an inviting stairway, made of polished wood, light brown like oak but Mason couldn't quite place its type.

He ascended into a wood-lined hallway that darkened first, then filled with a transient sprinkling of light. He found himself counting the stairs until finally reaching twenty-one, and emerging into a clearing, expecting a surge of exposed brightness but finding another pleasant surprise: just as advertised, a rooftop glen, complete with eight standing stones, dolmens polished white, in a circle around the stairwell. Beyond the circle, under a hanging canopy of vines and flowering violets, were set two oak chairs, carved exquisitely to resemble a twisting of roots and swollen tree limbs, extending out over the shoulders, all expertly entwined to provide comfortable support.

Rising from the eastern chair, from where he had been sitting in thoughtful repose, glancing out through the vines toward the rising sun, Avery Solomon stood. He took large strides, yet seemed to be moving in slow motion, his smile widening, his red hair waving in the gentle wind. He passed between two of the great stones, bowing his head slightly as he entered the circle. "Mason Grier, it's my pleasure."

Extending his hand, Mason clasped that of his host and gave it an assured squeeze, matching the intensity that was offered. But he spoke coolly. "I recognize the voice, but I don't know your name."

"Forgive me. I am Avery Solomon." His eyes twinkled and a pair of dragonflies suddenly appeared, hovering over his right shoulder, fluttering closer as if inspecting Mason and gauging his threat level. He gripped Mason's hand tight and intently scrutinized him, as if looking for a spark of familiarity or recognition in Mason's eyes, as if they'd met once, ages ago or in another lifetime.

"Mr. Solomon," Mason pulled his hand back, and his throat tightened in a sudden feeling of vulnerability, like he realized, standing in the middle of these stones, that he might be intended as a sacrifice in some pagan ritual. "I am told I have you to thank for my daughter's miraculous cure?"

"You have the earth to thank for that, Mason." At the chairs he motioned for his guest to sit first. "Our world is full of secrets. We just need to know where to look, and how to look."

"And how is that?" Mason asked, following Solomon out of the circle, where the air somehow felt clearer and his head too was lighter, freed from a low buzzing he had at first imagined to be from the dragonflies.

Solomon smiled as he surveyed the mountains rising as if birthed from the treetops. "Carefully." He took a seat, settling into the carved oak chair. "Reverently."

"So let's get to it. Why am I here?" Mason shifted, feeling a little in awe, like standing before a great king, saint or wizard. "Why the attention, the drama, the cloak and dagger? The nearly giving my wife and I dual heart attacks, and me a concussion, only to come back and grant us the best gift of our lives?"

Ignoring the question, Solomon blinked and raised his head to the rising sun. "Let me ask you something, Mason. Looking out at the sky right now, watching the trees, feeling the wind, what would you, in your meteorological capacity, predict to be the forecast for the day?"

"What?"

"Just humor me."

"I'm off the clock."

"Just give it your best shot. Out here, without your computers and satellite links, without the weather maps and almanacs, what would you predict for the next few hours?"

Mason sighed heavily. "Okay, it's going to be mostly sunny, seventy-six to seventy-nine by mid-day, with a clear starlit night, temps dropping into the low sixties."

"Chance of rain?"

"None."

"Really?"

"Yes, zero chance."

Solomon turned slightly, and his eyes sparkled when they met Mason's. "There's an umbrella behind your chair. I suggest you get it ready."

"For what?" Mason started to ask, when he saw Solomon get up and walk back into the circle. Once inside, ringed by the great eroded stones, he turned and spread his arms wide, with his palms up. His suit coat rippled and his ponytail whipped in a sudden easterly wind.

"I prefer to *feel* the weather first-hand Mason. Can I call you Mace?"

Mason was about to object. How did he even think of that nickname? Pamela was the only one....

Solomon continued. "To become one with the weather, experiencing all its power and ferocity, tenderness and mercy ..."

Mason again looked to the sky, but now with less confidence. The wind had indeed risen, gusting suddenly; ten miles per hour, now twenty. The pressure plummeted. He turned, and over the mountains, as if on cue, came a spreading darkness, a wave of clouds unrolling like a massive black carpet.

"Impossible."

Solomon was laughing like a young boy. Now he was unbuttoning his shirt. He peeled off his jacket and then spun in circles, eyes closed against the wind. Suddenly the rooftop was enclosed in shade, the tumbling clouds massing directly overhead, plunging the valleys and the mountains and the forests into a gloom as dark as a winter's twilight.

"I don't believe this." Mason said, only to have his words eradicated by a deafening peal of thunder as an ensuing flash of light heralded the release of the sky's floodgates.

And the rain poured down.

It fell in sheets, instantly soaking Mason, drenching him from head to toe, nearly blinding him in the violence shrieking from the sky. Solomon shouted in joy, his arms high, still spinning, mouth open, catching the rain as it blasted down upon him. Lightning crackled above and behind him, but from Mason's angle it looked as if spider web flashes arced from Solomon's very fingertips and erupted from his mouth and his eyes.

Then his head whipped around and his gaze locked on Mason's.

Time seemed to grind to a halt and the rain fell in slow-motion, each drop pounding onto Solomon's bare chest and shoulders, splattering into earthen craters at his feet, the droplets exploding into the rising puddles.

Finally, after what seemed like ages had passed and the land was swept clean, the rain slowed, the lightning fizzled and the world caught up and time accelerated in a hurry.

The clouds rolled on their way, rumbling morosely, exhausted but still irate and grumbling as they dissipated out over the mountains, heading toward the ocean.

"Impossible," Mason whispered again. He wiped at his face, wringed out his shirt. He blinked and shook his head, then looked to Solomon.

Head down, stringy, dripping red hair over his face, Solomon's eyes blazed.

"You knew," Mason said. "Somehow you knew, arranged for this … this dramatic demonstration. Arranged for me to be up here at just the right time."

"Did I?"

"Yes, you had to. Don't know how, or why, but you did."

"Of course I did," Solomon said, just above a whisper. "What other alternative could there be?"

Mason shrugged. "No other possible alternative, except …"

"What? What were you going to say?" Solomon stepped closer, still dripping, his eyes blinking away the drops. "That I somehow … created the storm?"

Mason shook his head. "No. You knew, somehow you could predict it. But to do that with such accuracy …"

"Would be miraculous in its own right, would it not?" Solomon clasped his hands together.

"So it's like Mark Twain!" Mason said.

"Sorry?"

"Just like … like what was it, the *Connecticut Yankee in King Arthur's Court*? The time traveler knew about the pending eclipse, the precise day and time it was going to happen, so he was able to amaze the King, convince him he was a sorcerer."

Solomon laughed as he shook his head like a freshly bathed mongrel, then reached for his wet shirt. "So you think I'm a time traveler? Back from the future with precise knowledge of a freak weather anomaly?"

"No, of course not. But by the same token, knowledge of the future, if one could truly predict it, is a powerful tool, especially in a showman's hands."

"If I'm a showman Mr. Grier, what's the punchline? What do I want out of all this showmanship?"

"That's obvious. You want to impress me." Mason smoothed back his hair, licked his lips, never taking his eye off of Solomon. "I just don't know why. Why you'd be interested in little old me, my recent Meteorologist of the Year award notwithstanding? But right now I'm more concerned with the how than the why. How you were able to know this storm would hit? I desperately want to look at the time-lapsed radar for this area, check the barometric pressure leading up to the event, analyze the front patterns and ..."

Solomon held up a hand. "What's really going to blow your mind, Mr. Grier, isn't how I knew this storm was coming, but *when* I knew it. What if I were to tell you I knew about it, down to its duration, area of coverage and wind speed, over four weeks ago?"

Mason blinked. "I'd say you were insane. The most sophisticated weather forecasting tools can only predict out a few days, maybe six to ten, with any degree of accuracy, and it's always less and less clear the farther out you go. We rely on almanacs, trailing weather patterns from across the country and out to sea. Global and regional satellite data. There are so many variables, so many factors that even the most sophisticated software and weather analytical tools can only make educated guesses."

"Chaos Theory," suggested Solomon. "A butterfly flapping its wings in Madagascar might contribute to a hurricane in Cuba the next week. Am I right?"

"An overly-dramatic Hollywood simplification, but basically you've got it."

"Well, Mace, then how did I do it?"

"I'm dying to know."

Solomon grinned. "Agree to work for me, and I'll show you."

"I don't know...."

"I'll do that one better, Mason. Come work for me and you'll be the one to show me, to demonstrate how to complete what we've started, to perfect the tools we've already created."

"So you've got some sort of model? A complex software forecasting tool? And it's good enough to predict the two-minute storm we just had, down to the exact time, weeks in advance?"

"Imagine," Solomon said, "the practical uses. Hurricane warnings can come a month ahead, rather than just days or hours, allowing for all the necessary preparations, evacuations or fortifying that needs to happen. Imagine if we'd had something like this before Katrina."

Mason blinked, thinking, considering the potential—if it worked.

"Imagine," Solomon continued, "selling this service to agricultural companies, state and world governments, helping them plan their harvests. Wineries can protect their vines from early frosts, farmers can know far in advance which crops will thrive best in the season's expected weather. The possibilities are endless. Think of the good this could do the world over if we can eliminate some of the chaos. If we can peer through the randomness, the sudden and sweeping changes Mother Nature hurls our way—the devastating natural disasters, the floods, the tornadoes, the ice storms and blizzards.

"Think of it, Mason. And tell me your heart isn't racing right now. If the fact that my firm isn't dedicated to boldly improving the lives of everyone the world over—evidenced by the immediate cure of your precious Shelby—then at least believe that together we can finally level the playing field. We can finally be on equal footing with the elements, instead of just shaking our fists at the howling winds and moving in later to survey the damage and clean up until the next disaster."

Solomon's hands were trembling, his face inches from Mason's, eyes locked on his. "Tell me this isn't exactly what you've longed for your entire existence. I know about your past, I know what you've lived through and suffered at the hands of such chaos. I'm giving you the chance of a lifetime, Mason Grier. Do you accept?"

A buzzing echoed after his words, and Mason noted a lone dragonfly—yellow with red stripes hovering behind Solomon's ear, darting out as if watching for his reaction.

"I … what will I do?"

Solomon smiled, clasped his hand on Mason's shoulder. "You'll change the world, Mason."

Looking away, overwhelmed for the moment, he said, "I mean, if I accept, what do I do? When do I start?"

"Just show up on Monday morning, at eight sharp. Oh, and make sure you tell Ms. Brock the bad news, but don't worry. I hear your station has been looking at bringing in some younger—and prettier—talent soon anyway. Someone to help their flagging ratings. No offense."

Mason nodded. He hadn't heard that but it didn't surprise him, given Pamela's relentless drive for improvement. "What about the … other aspects?"

"Money? You've just tripled your salary, Mason. Of course, Channel Seven was paying you a pauper's wage, so I thought it only fair. Plus a twenty-percent signing bonus, payable immediately. I can have it wired to your account tonight. That should help with your wife's care should you have to work extra hours, on occasion."

"That's … too generous, really. But maybe I should talk this over...."

"With Lauren, sure. Take all the time you want, but who are you kidding, Mason? You know you will be here Monday morning. This opportunity is too good to pass up. For nothing else, you're like a wide-eyed kid at a magic performance. You want—you need to know how the magician has done the trick. I've invited you up onto the stage and you've seen it up close, but you still don't know. Now, Mason, I'm inviting you backstage." He grinned wide, showing off the perfectly white, hungry teeth. "Join me."

The clouds dissipated, the blue sky burst through and the sun dazzled off the rooftop glen as Mason reached out and shook Solomon's hand.

After Mason had left, Annabelle led a group of other employees through the grove. She offered a hooded black cotton robe for Solomon as he emerged through the elevator doors. Gabriel pushed out from the crowd and quickly moved to Solomon's side as he dressed.

"He was convinced." It wasn't a question.

Solomon turned and his smile softened. "Yes, but we won't wait for him to start. The next demonstration is ready?"

Gabriel's eyes sparkled as he nodded.

"You have chosen a suitable target?" Solomon slipped into the robe, and as Annabelle backed away, head down, he tied the belt and then put his hand on Gabriel's shoulder in a fatherly gesture. "I know the burden I've placed on you, but you are ready, and it is your decision to make, Adept."

His face turned up, caught in the sunlight streaming in the great windows over Solomon's shoulder, Gabriel squinted, and a smile came to his face. "I've chosen carefully. As you've instructed, somewhere tropical, with … a significant coastal population."

Solomon waved his hand. "You can tell me when you and Annabelle get there."

The girl's eyes raised, a smile appeared and Gabriel knew she had been hoping for this chance, to be given this assignment and to go along with Gabriel. Solomon was indeed generous and gracious to his favored servants.

"You're not coming with us?"

"No," Solomon said gently. "I will be leading … other areas and coordinating other efforts, and then heading to a most important meeting. You however, have been entrusted with the most intense spectacle, and I assume you've assembled the adepts you require?"

Gabriel nodded. "They're standing by. Five of them there already, just waiting for instructions."

"Then let's not keep them—or the world—waiting."

Book 2

Chapter 1

Fifteen miles off the northeast coast of Jamaica, the yacht *Equinox-4* languished in the hot sun, with its two passengers finally rising up from a long rest at the sound of a cell phone ringing.

Gabriel stretched and took a drink of water as he nodded into the phone and stared over the rim of his sunglasses into the pure cloudless sky. The blue stretched as far as he could see, and the blazing sun beat down on the three other yachts stretched out in a line like the advanced front of an approaching armada.

"We're ready," he said into the phone. "Commencing the ritual in three minutes, on your mark." Hanging up, he let his gaze fall on the girl's tanned, topless body and met her smile. Annabelle sat up and fixed her hair, no longer even blushing at Gabriel's attentions.

"Can't we linger a bit?"

"You heard me. Three minutes." He licked his lips as she stood and stretched and reached for a white robe—one of a pair. She tossed the other one to him and then slipped into hers.

Gabriel came closer to her and tied her belt for her, looking into her tender eyes, and as always, thought of running barefoot through a lush verdant forest, hand in hand with her. Lost in the woods, but exactly where they were meant to be. They would be there again, soon.

"Rested?"

Annabelle nodded, lids closing in a pleasurable memory. "Quite."

"No reservations?"

She blinked, and Gabriel thought he saw a flicker of something cross her eyes, but then it was gone. "None," she whispered, as she shifted her gaze over his bare shoulder, to the coast. The resort at Montego Bay, where windsurfers congregated on the calmer waves and jet skis and sailfish raced in the shallows before snorkelers and glass bottom boats, where rum-soaked tourists gawked at this little slice of nature they'd been told not to wreck.

"Then let's focus."

He pulled up her hood, giving her one last smile, then slipped into his own robe. After tying his belt, he reached for the two wooden staves resting on the center table beside the pitcher of melting ice and the two empty champagne glasses, and the laptop—the screen open to a seismographic display of the ocean floor below them.

Gabriel passed her the shorter staff, the one with a thin green vine wrapped around it like a stripe on a candy cane. He took his own in one hand and flipped his hood up as he turned with Annabelle and faced the island.

He glanced at the laptop screen and committed the depth and location to his thoughts.

The shelf where the Caribbean and North American tectonic plates met and butted roughly against each other.

Gabriel raised his arms and held the staff over his head, as Annabelle shadowed his motions.

"Focus on the ley line, and feel its energy. It's here, all about us."

And when he opened his eyes, it was there. A shimmering aurora, a narrow band just overhead, undulating and throbbing like one of the earth's veins—a jugular that Gabriel and his colleagues now tapped into, spearing into and sapping the lifeblood of the world ...

... and channeling it.

Channeling it with a synchronized, massive and combined force …

… downward.

Gabriel expected exertion, expected to hear the pounding of his own veins in his skull, expected to be overheating in the robe, and expected to choke under the weight of this responsibility Solomon had placed firmly on his shoulders.

Maybe it was Annabelle, or the cool breeze she may have summoned up to soothe him, or maybe it was the quality and confidence of the other adepts in the adjacent yachts, but the whole enterprise went as smoothly as he could have hoped.

So much so that at first, after he had let his trembling arms down and leaned on the staff, catching his breath, he worried if they had accomplished anything at all.

But Annabelle, eyes closed, turned toward him as if seeing it herself, at one with the seaweed forest, fathoms under water: the rising surge of bubbles, the groaning of the plates, the cracking, grinding and shifting.

And the enormous force unleashed all at once.

Bubbles surged ahead of the boat, and Gabriel heard a sound like a cry of pleasure before he realized it came from his own throat.

Before he realized it, Annabelle was now holding his hand, just as the other pairs in the other yachts all stood by, admiring the sheet natural force they had just unleashed.

Like Neptune himself surging up from the depths, a mile-wide tsunami rose and ascended into a killer wave bearing down upon the hapless island.

Without warning, without remorse.

Gabriel squeezed Annabelle's hand and licked his lips.

"It's begun."

CHAPTER 2

Mason came out of the shower and heard a voice he still couldn't believe was real. Shelby was in with Lauren, helping her into her chair and chatting away as if her voice had always been this beautiful, this perfect. He dressed, still listening and marveling at the change. Lingering outside Shelby's door, he leaned against the wall as he finished with his tie, and was about to poke his head in to say good morning and ask for their breakfast requests when a buzz came in on his smartphone.

He groaned, and was going to ignore it when another followed.

These were alerts, not messages, he realized. Accustomed to the occasional buzz if weather-related phenomena changed, something he should be aware of, he set a variety of apps with tie-ins to international and regional weather centers to provide alerts.

He pulled out the phone, tiptoed past the door and started downstairs.

Halfway down he froze. First alerts were coming in from a variety of sources. Details sketchy but the geological center in St. Martin was the first to report on the sub-coastal magnitude 7 seismic action reported at 7:45 Eastern. And the tsunami that followed …

Oh god.…

Jamaica had been hit full force.

He ran down the rest of the stairs and in the kitchen scrambled to find the remote for the TV. Clicked the power button and heard the newscaster before the picture emerged. A map graphic with a bright red circle in the Caribbean just outside of Jamaica. They were showing serene pictures of Montego Bay and several other western side resorts as they had been, then cut in with hand-held video and cell phone images of terror. A massive, incalculable wave roared toward the beach as people ran in terror.…

Mason's mouth dried up.

"What's happening?" came that voice, just a minute ago serene and so full of hope, now tinged with fear and dread.

He shut off the TV, ever the one to protect his girl, no matter her age. "Something that can wait."

Shelby frowned as Lauren wheeled up behind her and settled into the chair lift. "After pancakes?"

"After pancakes," Mason set, even as his phone kept vibrating.

He risked a glance, expecting to see more about the tsunami, but apparently that wasn't enough for this morning.

Freak tornadoes rip through Minneapolis causing massive devastation.…

And before he could read further, his phone rang.

It was Pamela, and he knew what she wanted. They would be running a special, prepping him to talk about all this weather, giving his take, breaking down for their viewers what could cause such mayhem.

He raised a finger and shook his head as he put the phone to his ear. "Sorry ladies, looks like I may have one last broadcast to make."

Going out with a bang.

"Hi Pam," he said somberly. "I saw, and I'll be right in. But there's something I have to tell you first.…"

The blue screen weatherboard switched off as Mason unclipped his earpiece and microphone.

"So that's it," Pamela said, arms crossed over her chest, watching from behind the main camera. "It's really your last one?"

"I said I could stay on a bit, do a few more. But it's Friday, and they want me to start...."

"Monday, I know." Pamela looked at him sternly. "Well, we both know that this is it. An impassioned and well, damn impressive final broadcast. It was your swan song, and it was brilliant."

"But I didn't say goodbye."

"Not in so many words, but you don't need to. We'll take it from here—or if you prefer, we can tape a quick segment where you sadly take your leave after profusely thanking your producer of twenty-four years, the one responsible for giving you a shot, and a name in this city, and ..."

"And the one who's made me everything I am today, yeah yeah." He sighed and handed over the mic and earpiece. Glanced around, and let his view fall once more on the blue screen. "I'm going to miss this place. And these people." Turned to her and saw her eyes trembling. "You."

In a surprise move, trumping anything else he might have said, Pamela threw her arms around him in a crushing hug.

"Oh just get out of here, go. Save the world, conquer the elements." She backed away and stared into his eyes, locking them in place. "Become like Aeolus and bag the winds, bend them to your will like I know you can. I saw the potential in you. You don't just predict the weather, you *are* the weather."

Mason chuckled nervously, and his skin prickled as if he were back on the Solstice rooftop before the storm. "I really am going to miss these pep talks, and your endless trove of anthropological tidbits, weather lore and mythology."

"Yeah well if you ever need a walking almanac, you've got my IM address."

"That I do."

Setting his station ID card in her open palm along with his mic, feeling like a detective handing in his badge and gun, he waved to the camera guys chewing gum and watching the scene with little more than their normal interest.

"Now go save some lives or something," Pamela added, looking away now to the news on the small screen at her console, where the replay of twin vortices were slamming into buildings and running wild down a modern street.

We're a long way from Kansas, Mason thought, still unable to get those images out of his head.

"I always imagined you'd go into something bigger, Mason." She was speaking now, as if from a long way off, reading from pages written ages ago. "The Storm Prevention Center, the World Meteorological Organization, or hell, maybe some top secret CIA weather control service like—what was that in the '70s—Project Stormfury?"

Mason risked a smile. "How do you know I haven't been doing that all along, and this has just been my civilian cover?"

She flashed a smile back to him. "Well, in any case, good luck. And oh, if your daughter ever gets bored of the tea-sipping English and wants to come back here and follow in dear old dad's footsteps, send her my way. We could start her on a nice internship."

"I'd appreciate that, really." Mason thought about it, and all the benefits that would come from her being close by, close to her mother—and maybe even a positive influence on Gabriel. "But for now, I think I'm following in her footsteps. We're both heading to Solstice."

Pam whistled. "Fascinating. You and the twins together at the same place? Fascinating, and dangerous." She looked up. "Do you remember your first day here? Lauren was two weeks away from delivery and I told you—"

Mason remembered as if it was this morning. Remembered the wide yellow tie Pamela had picked out for him, the bushy sideburns and cheesy mustache she had begged him to shave. "You told me that in many ancient cultures, especially with the Finns—my own heritage, that twins were highly regarded as conduits to the weather gods, or something like that."

"That's right. Special powers of prediction and sorcery and sometimes even ... *control.*" She shrugged. "Like I said, if she's ever looking for something else, maybe I can help mold that power, like I did for you."

"Again, taking all the credit."

Laughing, she stretched out her arms. "All modesty on this side. Now go, begone. And like I said ..."

"Go save the world." Mason grinned at her, nodded once more and turned away.

CHAPTER 3

Solomon arrived at the Fresno Yosemite Airport, in a landing zone bathed in a shaft of sunlight beaming through clouds as if providing a secondary runway. The pilot must have marveled at how the clouds had parted just in time and the fog mystically lifted away, scattering before their approach. They set down two hours before the meeting was to begin, with plenty of time to spare. Still, once they made the turn off onto Route 198, Solomon told the waiting limo driver to take a leisurely drive through so he could enjoy the scenery and take in the sweeping mountain vistas, appreciating how the rugged terrain gave way to the gradual spread of green as the pine shrouded forests invaded and held sway the closer they came to Sequoia National Park.

The others were surely there already, most likely sipping bitter tea and suffering through their leader's exaggerated sense of piano skills as a precursor to the meeting. Let them wait for his arrival, Solomon thought. Let them murmur among themselves and wonder if he would even come. They would eventually start without him, he had no doubt, and that suited him just fine. He wanted to make an entrance, and it had to happen at just the right time.

The semi-annual meeting took place near the solstices and this one, four days before the winter solstice, promised high drama and the discussion of powerful topics, including several key votes.

After entering the park, driving to Giant Forest, he enjoyed the rise in elevation, and lowered the window to feel the air grow colder and observe the ground cover gradually turn white with a dusting of snow. They parked at the Lodgepole visitor center, and Solomon got out and told the driver to wait. It wouldn't be too long. He observed the few other cars here off-season and recognized quite a few of the out of state plates as belonging to the other members.

He breathed a great breath of fresh air, enjoying a myriad of natural scents carried along the crisp early morning breeze, and surveyed the vast and varied land rolling out before him in all directions. He started off down a trail, his feet and staff crunching into the brittle snow as he bowed to the might of the giant sequoia trees standing like mighty and wise emissaries of old, silent sentinels that bristled and trembled at his approach.

In time, he cleared the deeper forests and emerged on a cliff side, viewing a sweeping panorama of Moro Rock in the distance, and Crescent Meadow down below. His destination. But first, he would tread straight through an army of giant sequoia warriors, flanked by red and white fir, sugar, ponderosa and other high alpine wonders. Readying his staff, Solomon followed a path that became increasingly overgrown as he neared the meadow. At one point, barely visible footprints veered into a thicket, and he followed without pause, moving aside the blocking foliage with his staff. Branches converged overhead, blocking the sun in all but stray shafts of light illuminating the way. A mist crept across the trail, further obscuring the path, but Solomon wasn't deterred. And he wasn't meant to be. He and the other eleven members of the High Council alone had the ability to navigate these woods, to peer through the shade and the fog and the labyrinth of poisonous shrubs and vines, to arrive at another clearing, not on any maps and far from the ability of even the most intrepid hikers to locate. A clearing where a circle of weathered stones awaited.

Centuries old, dating back long before naturalist John Muir made his explorations, these rocks were here. Solomon knew who placed them here and how, where they were quarried and how they were transported. And he chuckled, recalling an anthropologist's theory on such things. Not that any scholars or explorers had ever found this clearing. No, where he was headed had been shrouded from common eyes long before the first colonists ever made their way across the country. And even the natives spoke of this place only in legend.

Still, for all its allure and mystical secrecy, when Solomon finally arrived in the circle and the mists scattered after confirming his identity, and when the A-frame building that to all purposes seemed like a quaint ski chalet, appeared, Solomon was again struck by the feeling that this modernism was an affront to the old ways.

He touched the nearest rock, partially moss-covered, and caressed its surface, feeling its indentations and cracks. He felt its power and he sucked in a cool breath, smelling the pine sap and the distant oak branches; he heard an acorn fall a hundred yards away and was aware of a multitude of forest denizens eyeing him carefully, reverently.

They all knew their places.

Unlike some.

Steeling his nerve, Solomon patted the standing stone. He hefted his staff in his right hand, glanced around the circle one more time, then advanced into its center, toward the structure— and the meeting, already in progress inside.

"Am I too late?" The door with the shamrock handle slammed hard behind him and eleven heads turned in his direction. The rectangular table was long and thick, full of knots and weathered in places. The people seated around it in chairs, each one uniquely carven from a different tree trunk, could not have seemed more out of place to Solomon. He longed for the old days, and imagined how it could have been if only a different hand had grasped the *arch-staff*. Everyone was dressed as if coming from a power business meeting. Silk suits and ties for the seven men, power skirts, high heels and blazers for the women.

Solomon shook the snow and moss from his khakis and the sleeves of his sweater, and wiped his boots on a mat of elderberry leaves. "Again I feel underdressed. I know it's winter, but my motion to require the old dress code of white robes, belts of living vines and sandals has been ignored, I take it?"

A grizzled face lifted and old, wizened eyes peered at him through a gray nest of bushy eyebrows. At least the Arch-Druid Louis Palavar had a face that looked the part: half Merlin, half Gandalf, but unfortunately with the powerful grace of neither.

Palavar pursed his lips. "Avery Solomon. Not only are you late, an occurrence we've grown accustomed to, but your blatant disregard as to the proper order of things, such as making motions, has become more than tiring."

Solomon shrugged and approached the free chair, his assigned post opposite Palavar at the far head of the table. Carved from a massive sequoia stump, it made up for the distance from the arch-druid and the perceived slight Solomon refused to accept. He sat lithely, crossed his legs and set his staff across the armrests, then leaned forward to view the iPad screen set up in front of him, as the others had in front of them. Another anachronism, and as far as Solomon was concerned, a ludicrous attempt by the old-timer to appear in touch with the modern world. He glanced to his left, into the other room, a study which held the grand piano and an assortment of bookshelves, Solomon was again glad he'd missed any recitals by the old fool.

"Let's see," he said after a pause, scrolling down the iPad screen. "What did I miss so far? Ah, the agenda. The usual items. Montgomery gave his redundant spiel on his efforts at the EPA, having infiltrated the agency and placed acolytes in the highest positions. So what have you done? Oh, you've got another appeal headed to the Supreme Court mandating further emissions restrictions! Wonderful." He rolled his eyes and stared at the thin bald man in the drab grey suit sitting beside Palavar. "Great progress we're making there."

"Solomon—"

"Hang on." He scrolled down. "Oh shit, did I miss Angelica's update on the expansion of social media and her bold attempts to reshape college-age minds regarding the wonders of protecting the planet? Like that's a difficult task, come on."

"Solomon—"

"And oh, damn it, *this* I did want to hear." Solomon glanced up, tightening his grip, two-handed, on the staff. "Louis Palavar gave his annual presentation detailing Hollywood's master plan to saturate popular culture with earth-saving messages and ideas, subliminal and otherwise." He chuckled. "How's that going for you?"

Palavar glared at him, and the two held each other's stares as both sides of the table hushed and glanced from one to the other. Solomon had played his opening hand, and now it was the old man's turn. But really, there was no doubt about what the next moves were going to be. Solomon had played them out in his head countless times in the past few days. Timed these chess moves down to the second, in fact. He knew Palavar only too well, and counted on him being exactly the rigid old fool that was.

"Actually," Palavar said, breaking the silence as Solomon knew he would. "We haven't followed the agenda at all."

Solomon smiled, never taking his eyes off him. "Really? That's not like you, deviating from procedure. Must have been something quite serious to force that decision."

"It was." Palavar's eyes hardened, a look like a hawk's surveying everything. *I'm sure he doesn't miss anything. Or at least, he thinks he doesn't.* Solomon counted on Palavar's overconfidence. He'd only get one shot at this, and if he failed, everything he had worked for would be in ruins. And the world would slip away forever from its true destiny.

"Well," Solomon spoke calmly. "Hope it wasn't something *I* did."

"You tell us," Palavar replied at once. "In fact, let's jump right ahead to agenda Item Seven. Your report on what was supposed to be your effort to enhance awareness of Global Warming in the business community, and specifically, aiming to pass a resolution through the United Nations that would—"

Solomon groaned. "Yes, yes, in time. I'd be happy to talk about all that. But as you said, that's not what you really want to ask me, is it?" He glanced at a few of the others. At Angelica Briars with her lustrous scarlet hair pulled back and sparkling with what looked like pixie dust, but nothing could eradicate the crow's nests around her eyes or the sallow hue to her cheeks. He glanced at the diminutive and gnome-like Morris Tildershines, who held rank over the ancient clan of druids in Britain and Scotland, at Heidi Noriesse who fancied herself one among the Valkyries and lorded over the dwindling clan in Eastern Europe, but had long since lost her muscle and her nerve, turning in her sword for a stylus and managing change with all the speed of a harvest snail.

"San Diego," Palavar said.

"Jamaica," said Belgar Tinman, adept of the Southern climes and self-styled Lord of the Sea—who for all Solomon cared, could drown himself in it for his lack of vision or action of late. In fact, nearly all of them were useless. They were cast from the same mold as Palavar, who unfortunately had too much power in selecting the council. It was only through extreme patience, foresight, cunning and occasional trickery, that Solomon had made it not only on the Council, but had advanced so far that they now considered him such a threat.

But of course, they had underestimated his power, while overestimating their own.

"Minneapolis," said Harrison Nye, "Lord Master of the Mountains." Whatever that title meant, Solomon had no use for him either and couldn't remember anything from his semi-annual updates other than the usual whining about the ice cap levels and an obsessive fear of fracking.

"Wonderful places," Solomon said. "What of them? Can't say that I've ever been, except once as a kid, driving through Minnesota to see the world's largest ball of twine."

"So this wasn't your doing?" Palavar asked.

"Sounds like you're suspecting me of powers far in excess of what I should possess."

"We both know what you're capable of, Avery." Palavar leveled a glance at him, and by calling him his familiar name in an attempt to humble and belittle, Solomon almost flinched, for a moment feeling a crack in his resolve. But he had to remember, had to stay on course. Palavar once held sway over Solomon's destiny, but no longer.

Palavar slammed his fist down. "The larger question is, why you've done this?"

Solomon let the question go unanswered, then said, "Well, why don't you enlighten me? Or have one of your lackeys do it?"

Heidi grumbled, taking the bait. "For the self-same aim you have been espousing in these gatherings for five years!"

"The Green Kingdom," Morris whispered.

"Dominion," Belgar spoke, "over all."

"The Green Kingdom," Palavar echoed. "Is a fable, a tale best kept in the realm of the faire-folk and lost in the parables of old. It is—"

"—and always has been, *within our grasp!*" Solomon slammed his own fist onto the table, and formed a crack that shot halfway across, rattling water glasses and knocking over iPads.

Palavar folded his arms and narrowed his eyes, which sparkled with a canine yellowish tint. *And was that a feral hint of a wolf straining to break free of a very old, rusted cage?* "We have been through this before."

"Yes, but perhaps your counter-logic hasn't sunk into my thick skull," Solomon said, leaning forward and making a show of clenching his fingers around the staff and spinning it slowly. "The part about the earth being largely indifferent and immune to the misadventures of the pests crawling all over it? That never sat well with me."

Morris cleared his throat, a bit sheepishly, but chimed in, perhaps hoping to diffuse the situation. "It's well documented, and nearly irrefutable. Man's been around what? Ten thousand years? Less than a blink of an eye in the earth's life cycle. She's hardly noticed us."

Solomon leaned back heavily, still spinning the staff. "Here we go."

Belgar chimed in. "We do what we can, but let's not fool ourselves. If our goal is to safeguard the earth, our job is laughably easy. Why? Because She can protect herself. Maybe not for the ultimate comfort of her temporary 'pests,' as you called them, but for herself, surely."

"All this talk of global warming," Heidi said, twirling her blonde curls. "Laughable. The earth warms, the earth cools. She has her own temperature."

"But we're a virus attacking her system. Man is a disease," Solomon insisted. "And our planet's flaring up in a fever, determined to fight us off."

"If that's the case," Palavar said, "let her. If the minute degree here or there is sufficient to shake off enough of us 'pests' to make any difference, then why are you fighting it? Why are you fighting us? We are trying to change the mind-set of an entire race, get them to see themselves as caretakers instead of mindless consumers with bottomless appetites. It takes time, and it *will* have the desired effect. Eventually."

"Eventually is too long!" Solomon countered. "And it won't work. Because ultimately it's false. The earth doesn't care, as Morris here so eloquently said, and I agree. Man has been around for such a short time as to be almost unnoticed in the two billion years of this planet's tumultuous history."

"See?" Morris blushed and grinned. "As I keep saying, and you all keep shushing me."

"All your efforts," Solomon said, stealing his thunder, "what are they for? Maybe people will become self-conscious enough someday to stop driving SUVs, and maybe someone will find a way to make a cost-efficient electric car or make ethanol or wind power actually a viable alternative. But what of it? One more volcano erupts in the Philippines and spews more CO2 into the atmosphere than China produces in a decade, and we're back to square one. Or the sun flares up in a sunburst that blankets the planet in radiation and blasts through widening holes in our ozone layer, and all those efforts are for nothing."

"So what are you suggesting, Solomon?" Palavar tapped his gnarled fingers on the table, tracing a groove in the ancient wood. "That we give up? That we turn our back on our role as stewards?"

"No, I merely suggest expanding the role. Or perhaps … earning that title instead of playing at it."

"Watch yourself, Solomon. You overstep your limits."

"As we all should. Otherwise …" He glanced around at the others in the room, at the chairs and the arrangements, the vines and trunks, the leafy canopy overhead and the buzzing of insects and fluttering of butterfly wings. "We don't deserve the power that goes with this responsibility."

Heidi stiffened and frowned. "But if the earth defends itself, if it shakes off the pollution, the ravaging of its resources …"

"It does," Solomon said. "Over thousands, millions of years … In those terms—the only terms the earth deals in—we will be nothing but a memory. Pollution? Hell, unleash every nuclear warhead, and destroy ourselves ten times over, and the earth will recover and it will be as if it never happened in a few thousand years. She hosts species after species and then they either die out or she kills them, and moves on."

"So again I ask: what is it you are fighting?" Palavar shook his head, exasperated. "You espouse the glory of nature and how ineffective we are in the face of its power, as is only right, and yet you sit there meeting after meeting asking to do more to punish humanity. Towards what end?" He narrowed his eyes, and his hand went from the table to his own staff—gnarled and twisted and ancient—leaning against his chair. "Do you seek then to upset the balance? To gain power and glory for the *now*, to force Nature to focus and take notice of this tiny moment in time when she is accustomed to seeing only vast epochs?"

In the ensuing silence, Solomon rolled up his sleeve and checked his timepiece—a gold Rolex with a black face and a digital readout behind the spinning gears.

It was almost time.

"That, Palavar and dear Council, is exactly what I intend." He sighed and looked at them all in turn before staring back at the arch-druid. "We may be newly upon the scene, but we were given a role—and the power to back it up. Power that is wasted on the likes of this …" He made a gesture toward the agenda on the iPad screen. "We can do so much more. The Green Kingdom can be restored. And just perhaps, we are meant to do exactly that."

Belgar frowned at him and Morris again cleared his throat. "I apologize, but as much as the idea intrigues, you said it—it can't happen. Stop the pests, the rampant consumption and the runaway polluters and the destruction of resources, and nature will just step in and take up the battle, a hundred times stronger." He shook his head. "There will soon be no green, the way things are going. No matter what anyone does about it. And what, do you propose damming the volcanoes and controlling the sun?"

Solomon smiled. "Now you are thinking like a true steward." He never took his eyes off Palavar. "Like a true druid."

"Enough!" Palavar spoke through grit teeth, yellowed and cracked. "We are tired of this endless debate. We know your objections, and you know ours. The mission is unchanged. We will work as always, behind the scenes."

"As always?" Solomon chuckled. "I know our history is a little vague and purposely shrouded in mystery, but I prefer to honor the one historical anecdote we do have passed down to us. When the Romans came marching into Britain, it wasn't the local peasants and ragtag armies that eventually sent them packing. It wasn't dumb luck that severed the head of the greatest empire at the time and decimated their lands with drought and froze their troops and starved their children and swept away their homes in avalanches of mud and ravaged their farms with wildfire. Ruined their economy and stretched their forces thin and hungry."

"We don't know the facts of that, and can't ascribe—"

"We can, and we do," Solomon insisted. "Those were men and women of action. Of defiance. Of power. They actually *controlled* the forces of nature, instead of just giving themselves titles over it." He glared at Belgar and Morris. "Instead of sitting around in hollowed-out tree stumps debating the merits of passivity, they *acted*. As I have acted."

He stood up, raising the staff slowly. "Jamaica, yes. Minneapolis, yes! San Diego and many more. And you have no idea what I have planned next, but I promise you this … the Green Kingdom is at hand."

The room sank into stunned silence as Palavar reached for his staff, determination in his eyes. "Then I am sad," he said, "that it has come to this. You have forsaken your oaths to protect the earth and its people. You have tarnished the name of this Council, betrayed its history and its purpose, betrayed your upbringing and your training, and—"

"And I call for a vote!" Solomon shouted over him. "As is the right of any member of this 'Council.'" Solomon turned his staff sideways, perpendicular to his body, as he glared at Palavar. "I call for a vote of no confidence in Louis Palavar, that he be stripped of title and staff, and thrust out into the black forest to wander in grief and loss, forever."

Palavar chuckled. "You may call for such a vote, as is your right. You know the rules, but you also know the consequences if such a challenge fails." He glanced at the others around the table. "A motion has been raised. All in favor? And remember, you need a majority."

Palavar tapped his fingers on the staff as he stood up slowly. And he turned his staff sideways as well, squaring off symmetrically against Solomon.

Overhead, the vines creaked and leaves rustled in a non-existent breeze. Solomon felt the earth under his shoes rumble. The soft dirt rippled as if roots moved beneath the table, assembling into position.

He turned his wrist slightly to see the time.

On schedule, he thought, keeping his arm steady, the staff barely giving a tremble. Palavar was attempting the same but his arm had to be getting tired.

"All those in favor of Solomon's vote?"

Silence. A lot of eyes turned downward. Morris alone was fidgeting. He licked his lips, opened his mouth, but then met Palavar's cold eyes, and lowered his own. No one looked toward Solomon, but he didn't expect them to.

A few more seconds ticked away.

And then he sighed. "I guess that's it then," Solomon said. "The Green Kingdom dies...."

"No," said Palavar. "Only you."

He pulled his arm back, straightened his grip and turned the staff lengthwise, then slammed it down hard upon the floor.

Morris clenched his eyes and flinched as the others looked away. And at Palavar's command, a mass of writhing vines shot out from the ceiling just as the dirt floor erupted with a battalion of roots. His legs encircled, and another thick root lassoed Solomon's waist and dragged him back into the chair as a huge vine whipped around his staff and yanked it hard from his grasp.

As he sat with a thump and offered no struggle against the roots and vines wrapping around his body, pinning him to the chair, Solomon followed the vines that stripped him of his weapon and deposited it cleanly into the arch-druid's free hand.

One vine snared his throat, snake-like, and squeezed.

"I'm sorry," Palavar said quietly in the aftermath, as the ceiling swayed with dozens of vines at the ready, as the floor rippled and the walls churned with thorn-riddled branches preparing to defend or attack, whichever the case should be. "But you knew the consequences. You were unprepared, and now …"

"Now," said Solomon, barely managing enough air in his windpipe. *"We get back on track."*

Palavar frowned, mouth open. He cocked his head, trying to fathom why his adversary—seconds away from death—still seemed so confident. Then he frowned and glanced at the new staff in his left hand.

The staff he assumed was Solomon's—and his right to destroy as befits the winner in this challenge. Solomon would have known he'd take it. *Solomon would have known … known that he couldn't win such a vote. Not with this council …*

Palavar looked up sharply. Saw the smile, the glint in Solomon's eyes, and he dropped the staff, just as he raised his own and focused his energies on the roots and the vines and the branches. *Attack—* he started to command, but there wasn't time.

Solomon had it all planned too well.

The staff—the hollow cylinder packed with C4 and a timer— detonated at that exact moment, with such force that Palavar and half the council table exploded in a mass of smoking splinters, blood, bone and gore.

Solomon was ready, and the instant Palavar's control vanished and his brain was blasted into nothingness, he assumed control. His chair blew backwards in the force of the explosion, but was held in place enough by the roots and vines to protect him from the blast.

The others—most would not be so fortunate. But Solomon couldn't take that chance. He wriggled free of the smoking restraints, at the same time feeling out with his mind, caressing and controlling the vegetation's, seeking into the very cellular structures of the roots and the branches and overgrowth; he felt the vegetation screaming in agony and shock, and he soothed where he could.

But first, he stood up and raised his hand, and through the smoke and the flames, he felt it: the arch-druid's staff. It was smoking and burnt, but such a thing was tough, thrown across the room. He sought with his mind, found it and called it to him, and it came, hurled across the flames and over mangled bodies. It came on the winds and landed in his right hand.

Solomon breathed deep, then exhaled, harnessing the connection he now forged with this staff, this ancient thing carved from a tree more ancient than any still standing on the planet, a weapon and tool passed down through the millennia, from a time when wizards had shepherded the ignorant and brought them out of caves and taught them fire and astrology and ways to harness the elements, and were thought of as gods in their own right.

He gripped the staff tightly, then waved it twice across the wreckage of the council room. Snowflakes appeared in a gusty, icy wind that suffocated the fires and dissipated the smoke, and all became clear.

More than half the table was a splintered, smoldering wreck. Harrison Nye and Montgomery appeared to be decapitated; at least their bodies were not in sight, only the heads with bits of hair and skull and teeth with frost now on the hollow eye sockets.

Angelica and Belgar Tinman crawled and whimpered, covered in blood. Heidi had a sharp white bone sticking out through her shoulder, and seemed to be trying to sing some ancient healing ballad, but the verse never finished. She shuddered, coughed up a pint of blood and lay still.

Morris Tildershines, somehow among them all, seemed unfazed, with just a spray of someone's blood on his forehead and snowflakes collecting on his spectacles. He opened his eyes and with dismay, turned toward Solomon.

"I …"

"I know," Solomon said. "You'd like to change your vote."

He regarded the three surviving members of the Council with indifference. "I could show contempt," he addressed them. "Or seek vengeance, but that is for the petty. For those who lack vision, for those who can't see the true path."

"Please," Morris said. He struggled in the block of ice that rooted him to the floor. The winds whipped and chilled, and icicles hung from his nose and the panes of his frosted glasses.

Beside him, Angelica seemed unfazed by the cold, but at least had given up her struggles. One eye had been blackened, hit with some burning shrapnel, and she struggled to see. "Solomon, don't do this."

"At least kill us," Belgar said dourly. "I don't like the cold."

"I know," Solomon said, "and I guess I'm sorry, but roots and vines? Well, they're too unpredictable, and cold … cold can last forever under the right conditions, and ice can be as strong as steel. I've enchanted the circle … and what's left of this cottage with a powerful charm. Combined with the existing cloaking spell, no one will ever find you. You will all sleep and hopefully, dream sweet cold dreams of how you could have shared in my glory, in the glory of a world restored. Of a Green Kingdom."

"You're insane," Belgar spat, his wild curly hair frozen in place over his eyes. "We have followers, they will know. They will seek us, and—"

"Already on that," Solomon said. "The word's gone out. Change in leadership. Out with the old, in with the … bold."

He raised his new staff, admiring the scorch marks that had given it added character. He'd have to decide what to do with his old one, which was waiting for him back in the limo, and not a meek instrument by any means. Maybe Gabriel might one day rise in worth to earn it.

But for now, it was time to move on. Free of the restraints of the past, free of those who had failed to see the truth, those blind to their true destiny.

"I'll come back for you," he said. "When my Kingdom has come and you can no longer affect its outcome. On that day, you will thank me and see that I am its deliverer, I am its savior—and yours."

"But, Arch-Druid …" Morris spoke up, giving one last attempt at reverence and misplaced flattery. "We should—"

Solomon waved the staff in a nonchalant upward movement. The ice expanded, ascending fast and covering his face, devouring his head, just as it did to the others, locking their horrified expressions in place.

"Meeting adjourned, my fellow druids. Sleep well."

CHAPTER 4

Mason arrived at Solstice Headquarters promptly at 7:30 AM Monday morning, parking his car in a free spot not too far from the main entrance. Surprisingly, most of the lot was already full, and as he stood up and surveyed the ground and listened to the enthusiastic greeting from the birds flocking about the spruce trees or fluttering around the Solstice building, he was struck by the notion that maybe most of the employees actually stayed here overnight. And how many more, being environmentally conscious as they were, biked or walked into work?

He let the sunlight peeking around the western edge of the Solstice building sprinkle on his face and dazzle his eyes, and he took a calming breath. He couldn't remember many mornings at the station where the air tasted this sweet, the texture this profound. It was the start of something new, something brimming with potential, like the first sip of delectable vintage, but still Mason hesitated.

There was still time to back out. To retreat to the comfort of pure meteorology, to a place he belonged, without risk. But life was risk, and life had changed. Everything he thought he knew, everything he had come to reconcile about the unfairness of life, the cruelty of fate, was now up in the air. The walls of the impossible had been stormed, and the word "never" no longer held such a dark, immutable meaning.

Shelby was cured and maybe, just maybe, a similar future lay in the cards for Lauren.

He had to risk it, but not just for his own selfish reasons. If Solstice truly had some potentially life-saving technology, something that could change the world in a practical sense, just as landing on the moon had changed the mindset of the entire human race, what else could be achieved?

Mason found he was striding now, beating a brisk pace to the front door—

—which refused to open at his approach.

A lone camera swiveled overhead, the sentry to the monolith of blackness lording above it.

And a speaker crackled through with a woman's voice. "Be right with you, Mr. Grier."

Mason fidgeted. "Okay." He carried a briefcase with him, leather strap over his shoulder. Shifting it, he glanced around uncomfortably, and tried to make out shapes inside through the tinted windows, imagining them bustling about, perhaps cleaning up after some bloodthirsty pagan sacrifice.

Moments later, the door clicked and opened inward. He blinked and let his eyes adjust to the beauty that greeted him. Red-haired, pale skin and slightly chilled blue eyes with just a few sprinkled freckles across her forehead, the greeter smiled at him and he had to wonder if she were just a bit older than Shelby.

"Hi," he stammered. "Mason Grier."

She thrust out a slender hand to shake his. She wore a light green blouse with an ivory silk scarf around her neck, accessorized with gold bracelets and a collection of thin silver bands. Casual hiking boots over jeans completed the natural look and set Mason a little more at ease while making him feel overdressed in his navy suit and his producer's favorite weather tie: a paisley blend of reds and blues.

"Delighted," she said cheerfully. "I'm Hespera Milne, and I guess I'm what you call an HR rep. At least I am today. We all wear many hats and help out where needed, as you'll find out soon enough."

"Okay," Mason said, following her inside after letting go of her surprisingly cool hand. He stepped into the lobby and found it generously humid, lacking in air conditioning, but refreshed continuously by breezes from several directions, rustling the foliage overhead, fluttering leaves in the courtyard. "About that … I'm a little unclear of my expectations at the moment. And since you're in HR, maybe we can go over those as well as the boring basic stuff. Like—"

"Health care, direct deposit?" She grinned back at him. "Don't sweat it, we've got it all written up, just need your signature. Before you're finished with morning tea—or coffee—whichever's your preference, it'll be done. Now come on, Solomon doesn't want you worrying about anything else right now except getting acclimated, taking a tour, meeting some colleagues and feeling comfortable around us."

Mason nodded, still marveling at the view from down here, following the quiet elevator track up to the rooftop level where he had witnessed such wonders. He smiled to a few others milling around, sipping tea and sitting on exquisitely hand-carved wooden chairs. "So where is Mr. Solomon?"

Hespera hugged an older woman as she rounded the first stone around the resting grove, exchanged a bit of muted small talk, introduced Mason, then moved on through the grove, past others, smiling and nodding to him.

"Solomon is at an annual shareholder meeting in Fresno."

"Oh? I didn't realize Solstice was publicly traded."

"It's not. But we still have investors, and Solomon likes to keep them happy."

"And are they?" he wondered. "With Solstice's performance and potential, I can imagine they are, but I wonder what sort of control investors might have? Avery Solomon doesn't strike me as a man who likes to yield control. To shareholders, board members, or anyone else."

"Oh I wouldn't say that," Hespera countered, just as cheerfully. "As you'll see, he's very keen on sharing ideas, on delegating and most importantly, listening."

He paused as they walked under a trellis. "Is that mistletoe?"

Hespera nodded with a grin. "Of course, but don't get excited. Workplace PDA isn't highly approved of here, but neither is it discouraged."

She gave him a wink, then turned and headed for a descending staircase.

"Come on, now you'll see where all the work gets done. And if you're anything like me—or like your son, which I imagine you are—you're going to love it!"

Mason turned and took a last look at the grove, at the employees sipping their teas, relaxing in the soothing natural environment.

I guess it's not so bad, he thought with a budding sense of belonging.

Ⓞ

Two hours later, his head was still spinning like an uneven top, wobbling and bouncing off jagged walls.

"I'm still trying to process it all," he told Hespera as they took a break by a natural stream—a waterfall spilling out from the tiled black wall on the sixth sublevel. The chamber itself was a vast and stylishly decorated chamber with blocks of smooth marble arranged in comfortable sitting patterns around a center pool filled with colorful fish and dazzling rocks. A lone shaft of light from overhead hit a suspended glass and split into three beams over the pond. "I mean, the library alone on sublevel four …"

"A bit comprehensive, isn't it?"

"Solomon's quite the collector. I mean, ancient leather bound copies of Herodotus and Aristotle, Thesperata's treatises on meteorology …" He could still picture the rest: almanacs from every decade of American history back to the Colonies; studies of native weather myths and shamanistic weather practices from across the world. Books and binders of original observations that would make Charles Fort proud. Some first editions were behind glass, most others scanned and available on dozens of workstations.

Hespera dipped her mug into the stream, pulled it out and took a deep swig, her eyes closed. "Nothing was ever so refreshing." She sighed. "But yes, he's an avid collector. I'm sure you'll get to know him a lot better in the coming weeks and will learn a great deal more about his background and what drove him to create such a company, with such goals." She licked her lips. "Gabriel was a perfect addition, as I'm sure you'll be. Do you have any other questions right now, before I show you the weather center?"

Mason thought for a moment, listening to the flowing water and wondering where it came from, how far down it traveled and from what source. Questions? He had so many he didn't know where to start. Like how was all this built? Who designed the layout and why did every architectural aspect feel so perfect? So precise, down to the orientations of the walls and workstations, repeating circular patterns with vertical lines bisecting the boundaries? In fact, it was the same as the depiction of the letter *O* in the second letter of Solstice on the firm's stationary, communications and even its website. That, along with other symbols of repeated triple spirals. He had seen them in some of the artwork in the halls, alongside the abundance of nature paintings and prints of forests and seas, of animals in the wild and hawks in the clouds....

Questions? Of course he had questions, like who developed that cure, and how was it synthesized? *Might as well ask about that one,* he thought.

"Where are the labs?"

"Labs?"

"Yeah, for medical research. Solomon said they found a cure for my daughter's hearing loss by working with a rare South American plant. I was just wondering...."

Hespera looked down. "Oh, there are some areas we won't be getting to. A few levels even I don't visit. Special clearance, hazardous chemicals and all that." She offered a recovering smile. "You understand. But that's likely where that branch of research gets done."

"Sure, but ..."

She set down her mug, apparently to come and collect it later. "Now, prepare to visit the heart of Solstice, where if I know you at all, you're about to be floored. I know Gabriel was when he first saw it."

Mason followed her through the circle of stone blocks, yet another one of many, at least one on each floor. And as he passed through this one, he felt a slight chill, then a trembling in his ribs. He paused for a moment, looking out at Hespera and the suddenly out-of-focus room.

"Are you ok?" she asked.

Another breath and it passed, sight cleared and his body felt completely fine. "Yeah, just a little head rush from rising too fast I guess." *Weird, I just felt like I was a kid again, still hurting from the pain of losing both parents, and finding myself somewhere new....*

Hespera nodded. "Or the altitude change. We are pretty far below ground now, you know."

"I'm not sure it works the same when you're below...."

"In any case, follow me, almost there!" Her excitement was back, a spring in her boots as she walked.

Mason tried to keep up, feeling better with every step after they left the circle and entered a long corridor, this one brighter and with paintings hung every twenty yards or so, primarily scenes of animals: deer, buffalo, falcons, wolves....

Hespera suddenly stopping short. "Do you have a totem?"

Mason almost ran into her. "A what?"

"A totem!" She fumbled behind her scarf and withdrew a gold chain and what looked like a rabbit's foot attached to it. "And before you ask, no it's not a bunny leg; it's a desiccated goat hoof."

"Um ... why?" Mason's opinion of her kept dropping, and now he wasn't sure it could come back from this. He suddenly hoped Shelby wasn't heading down this same totem road; he couldn't imagine her showing up with something like a frog carcass around her neck.

"Goats, especially females like this one was, are symbols of nourishment. I wear it and it keeps me content with what I have."

Mason smiled at her. "Okay, sounds like I should get one."

"Oh you should," her eyes flashed. "But really give some thought to it. And you may think about advancing it to a staff or another personal item as you become stronger. Like Gabriel did with his."

Mason nearly choked on a cough. "I'm sorry, my son ...? Is he back yet from ... wherever he went?"

Hespera shrugged. "Don't think so. He and Annabelle, Malissa, Frederic and a few others had to go somewhere down south and take some readings."

"Readings?"

She led him to a door, then put a finger to her lips. "Shhh, in here. You're going to be amazed!"

It was no simple boast. Like a kid in a candy store, he found himself pushing past her, moving into the center of a rounded chamber that gave off the impression of a triple-sized planetarium. Two bisecting corridors supported desks and workstations where some fifty workers sat analyzing the data from the dozens of wall screens supported on the opposing sections of the domed ceiling.

Mason felt his eyes tugged in every direction: an area where six screens all displayed satellite weather views of each continent, a reporter's view of a tropical storm making landfall in Puerto Rico, a helicopter weather report of traffic pileup on a snowy road in Delaware, multiple weather readouts from across the US and foreign countries. He spun around and took in the opposite wall, where another twenty-five or so colleagues on headsets crunched numbers and analyzed reports from the field and occasionally glanced up at the screens that presented everything from oceanic temps and geological readings to solar radiation and magnetic field readouts.

"Amazing," he whispered as Hespera rubbed her hands together and checked something on her phone. "Oh yes, so this is where you'll be spending a lot of time, I'm sure. But you'll have your run of this area and the research rooms which I'll show you in a minutes, and …"

Her phone buzzed again.

"Something urgent?" Mason asked.

She scrolled down, reading. "Solomon. He's called an immediate meeting of the upper echelon."

Mason glanced away, back to a screen flashing with an emergency weather signal: wildfires destroying a huge gated community outside of Phoenix. "I'm sorry, we have an echelon? I thought Solstice was all about equality of its people. The whole idea of a hierarchy seems incongruous with that."

She smiled at him. "True, but there's still a need for some top-level decision making, as well as just plain efficiencies from having the various divisions select one advisor to communicate the results and to take feedback to the team."

"Gotcha. So … do you need to go?"

"Me, no. I'm not on the team, but he's asked for you. I need to bring you to level six, to the main conference room."

"Me? But I'm not on the committee either." *And I like it fine right here,* he thought, imagining he could camp out and just absorb all this data and lose track of the next eight hours without a complaint.

"No, he specifically instructed that I bring you there. Said you're needed to help prepare for a major presentation at the United Nations."

"What?"

"Yeah, apparently they've reached out to us after numerous proposals and requests to address the assembly."

"Really? What does the U.N. want with Solstice?"

"I guess all the wacky weather and natural disasters and things have finally gotten the world's attention. And the fact that Solstice predicted a few of these dead-on, they're going to want to know how they can use what we have."

Mason licked his lips and glanced again around the screens, seeing scene after scene of nature packing a wallop. "So would I."

He thought for a moment. "But one more question, why address the U.N.? It doesn't sound like Solomon. I think he would imagine them as a useless overly-bureaucratic bunch that gets nothing done, or if they do, it's too slow to be of any use."

Hespera laughed. "Oh he's not all that cynical. We're a practical bunch, really. And we know you've got to play by the rules a little, at least once in a while, if you want to get anything done in the world." She winked and started to lead him to the other end of the chamber.

About to follow, Mason saw a little commotion at one of the stations. Three men and a woman crowding around a terminal, shooting glances up to the nearest screen—a Doppler readout of the Southeast coast. Mason saw it in a flash: a super cell three miles long heading into a game of chicken with an equal-sized but nimbler extra-tropical cyclone surging from the south.

Before he knew it, he found himself in front of their terminal, pointing up at the screen. "When did that start?"

The young girl looked up, glassy-eyed, and the other men shook their heads. "Just formed, from what we can see." She tapped some keys and the large screen adjacent to the one he was focused on blinked out and formed a mirror image—which then reversed and played back. And within time-elapsed minutes the storm free skies before the coast of North Carolina were overwhelmed with a surging, violent storm, as if it had just been slapped there by a kid with tape and a cut-out magnet.

"Jesus." Mason's mouth went dry. "Get on the phone with the Mid-Atlantic Early Warning Center!" He turned around, ashen-faced. "They've got to issue an evacuation order immediately."

"Not enough time," said the larger man, straightening up. He was bald, broad-chested and had two different colored eyes—an oddity Mason noticed at once. Just as he noticed the man palming a Galaxy S5 phone and slipping it into his back pocket, as if he didn't want to be seen just finishing a call or text.

Mason narrowed his eyes. "What are you talking about? There's always time. I'd predict landfall ..." he looked back, mouth open. Damn, it was moving fast, faster than it should have, given the wind speed and the statistics and prevailing conditions marching vertically along the screen. "In fifteen minutes. Christ."

He moved, leaping over the railing to an empty station where someone had just taken a break. He took a seat, slipped on a headset, familiarized himself with the keyboard array, and started to work. In moments, he had the Early Warning Center on the line, and was barking out figures and observations, countering some of what the person on the other end had indicated, and finally forcing an escalation.

Mason finally sat back, taking deep breaths, watching several of the screens switch to red, blinking warnings as news popped up on other viewers, reporting on the massive and sudden storm bearing down on vacationers and homes up the Carolinas and into Virginia....

When he finally stood up, the bald bi-colored eye man was right behind him, arms folded.

"Thanks for your help," Mason said sarcastically, and slid around him, joining Hespera. Paler than usual, she gave a thin smile to the people watching them, and then led Mason out the door.

"Who the hell was that?" Mason asked when they were out of earshot, heading into a black-walled, shiny-floored chamber that looked like it belonged on the Death Star.

"Pay him no mind. That's the floor manager, Victor Nunion."

"Seems like he got up on the wrong side of the bed."

"That's unlikely, as he doesn't sleep, from what we can tell. He's here all the time." Hespera leaned in, whispering, "And always kissing up to Solomon. I also hear he was super jealous that Gabriel apparently took the favored spot as an up and coming apprentice."

"Great. So maybe that's why I'm getting the dagger glares of death?"

Hespera shrugged. "Maybe, just keep from pissing him off too much and you'll do fine. Now come on, I'm sure the meeting's about to start."

Mason followed, still chilled about the near-spontaneous appearance of such a killer storm.

Chapter 5

The central conference chamber was unlike anything he had expected. Thinking so far below the surface it would be dark, windowless and oppressively stifling, instead he set foot into a gloriously effervescent rectangular chamber with an impossibly high ceiling, backlit with bright faux sunlight filtering through a beautiful painted canopy of leaves, branches and vines. The walls had framed viewscreens that gave the impression of large bay windows looking out into a marvelous glade, with running waterfalls, prancing deer, flowering shrubs and a trickling stream.

A great center table ran through the room, no less imposing a sight: thick mahogany, smooth rounded edges and knotholes, and enormous chairs, each one a unique hand-carved slab of masonry chiseled into a smooth throne. Twelve seats in all. Eleven men and women seated, turning at his entrance.

And one more. On the central window-screen behind the lone empty chair was the image of Solomon, obviously in the middle of a speech. A mountain range in the background, this one obviously real. *Looks like he's Skyping from somewhere in the Sierra Nevadas*, Mason thought, focusing on the snow-capped peaks behind them. *Was that Mt. Whitney?*

"Sorry for the delay," Hespera said. "We—"

"Ah, Mason!" said Solomon. "Good to see you acclimating, and down in the elite trenches where you belong. Everyone, meet our newest phenom, a brilliant meteorologist, family man, Renaissance man and all around swell guy. Mason Grier."

The eleven faces nodded. A few broke out in forced smiles.

"Take a seat, Mason." Solomon's image loomed large as he glanced toward the sole empty chair. His chair. "Don't worry, it's not permanent."

Mason moved slowly, aware of all the eyes on him. He had to crack some kind of joke, respond in kind. "Well, as long as I don't have to bear any liability that goes with it."

"None needed. Okay, that will be all Hespera. Show yourself out."

She had been hanging around the back of the room, notebook to her chest. She nodded, then slid and let the door shut quietly.

Solomon waited for Mason to sit, and awkwardly—not sure which direction to face—turn around to have nothing between him and his boss, who had shifted and now the view presented a wide expanse of forestry—mostly giant sequoias—behind him.

Familiar, Mason thought again. That range, and the crest he must be on. *I've seen it before somewhere.*

His heart skipped and a sweat broke out on his brow.

A flash of a secluded glade. Creeping mist, snow, and the hint of a thatched rooftop …

He blinked and it was gone, and Solomon was in mid-sentence.

"… I was saying, the hostile takeover we spoke of last week has been completed. You will all be filled in on the details upon my return."

One of the women at the opposite end of the table spoke up. "And what of their … employees? Will we be merging, or making cutbacks?"

"Yet to be determined," Solomon said cheerily. "Certainly some culling of the ranks has to occur, but only in support of our long term goals. Our assets will be grown accordingly."

"Next moves?" asked a gray-haired man on Mason's left. He had deep-set, hooded eyes and long spindly fingers that reminded Mason of the long pincers of a praying mantis.

"As we detailed at our last session, with one caveat." Solomon took in a deep breath, clearly savoring the crisp mountain air. "We are accelerating the time frame. Phase Two, I fully expect, will be a viable action in thirty-six hours."

"It's coming up soon," said the same man, tapping his fingers together. "The twenty-first. Doesn't give us much time, but we'll get on it, start making the preparations."

"See that you do."

"And manpower? The other … resources we need?"

"You'll have them." Solomon smiled. "I anticipate their availability shortly after my visit to the U.N. tomorrow. Unless we're met with severe ignorance, it will be done."

Mason cleared his throat, feeling increasingly left out. "I'm sorry, I don't mean to derail the progress you're making here, but … where do I fit in? Apologies again to the group, but this being my first day, I didn't expect to be in this position."

"Sorry Mace," Solomon said quickly. "But your orientation classes will have to wait. We're throwing you to the wolves, so to speak."

Nodding, Mason couldn't wait for the follow up. "And these wolves … where are they and when have they last eaten?"

A few chuckles softened the room, and Solomon licked his lips. "Why, they're at the U.N., where you'll be accompanying me. You'll be at my side, supporting our forecasting technology and most of all, giving an impassioned speech, as I know you're capable, about the power of foreknowledge and the life-saving miracles only we can provide."

Mason swallowed hard. "But I don't know enough yet about it."

"You've seen it first hand."

"Yes but …" *I don't know exactly what the hell I saw.*

"And you've done it a million times before," Solomon encouraged. "I've seen you, I've studied you. We all have."

"My broadcasts? I'm flattered, but surely, they weren't that awe-inspiring."

"They were. Persuasive, energetic. Compelling and broad. You speak in terms laymen understand, you make the complex simple and most importantly, you make it interesting. People tuned in because you're special that way. They were entertained and informed at once. And, you saved lives. Saved crops, saved homes, and most of all— saved time. But now the stakes are raised. We're coming face to face with Nature in all her fury."

Solomon took a deep breath and locked his eyes on Mason, who felt the whole room likewise staring at him, intently focusing.

"Nature," Solomon repeated. "Unflinching, uncaring and until now—unpredictable. Now, Mason, we have the tools to tame her. To warn far in advance of the freak snowstorm that could devastate the unprepared or the sudden tornado that could selectively rip through a town and kill with drone-like precision."

Mason's heart froze. *He knows about my past and is using that knowledge.* Using it effectively. But Mason didn't feel slighted. Not this time. This time, he was on the same page as his new boss. And he agreed.

"I'll do it," Mason said.

Solomon nodded. "There was never any doubt."

"You have to let me prepare, though. Show me what the technology is capable of, how it works, what's required…."

Solomon waved his hand. "Not enough time for all that, but on the flight to New York, you'll have the abstracts and the patent applications, and you can review some of the test cases. That will be enough. I will talk through the technology. You need only support the benefits of its application, and field questions on how it could be implemented and take the place of existing warning systems and the like."

Mason nodded, thinking it all through. "Ok, I'll be ready."

"Excellent. Then I will sign off here and meet you and your son in New York. Hespera will have the travel arrangements for you."

"When do we leave?"

"No rest for the wicked! First thing in the morning, of course."

"But—"

A flash again rose behind Mason's eyes: the thatched roof, swirling fog obscuring everything else. Ice flakes in the air and a brutal chill rushed through his mind, as if seeking to freeze him and encase his skull in numbing ice. And in just as quick a flash, it was gone.

Solomon took no notice. "Hespera has also made the flights for your daughter to fly back out to Heathrow around the same time. You can say your goodbyes at the airport."

Mason smiled. "You read my mind. Thank you. I'll be ready."

"You had better be, Mason. Because those wolves you were asking about? They'll be starving."

CHAPTER 6

At LAX, Mason and Shelby said their goodbyes to Lauren, who stayed in the limo. Mason again thanked the Solstice driver for his generous care and time—another perk of the job and sign of support from Solomon, but it was unexpected. Mason knew Lauren felt great to get out of the house and to see them off. She could have come in, but it wasn't necessary, and it would give Mason and Shelby a little time together.

After the security checkpoints and after checking their luggage, Mason took his daughter to a Starbucks overlooking their terminal's arriving flights, and they sat and sipped mocha lattes with extra whipped cream. They talked, really talked, for nowhere near as long as Mason would have liked, and in fact he mostly listened. By the end of the hour, when they called her flight first, Mason's ears were full of her voice, ringing with joy at every cadence, at the speed at which she had regained her rhythm and found her true voice. It was nearly impossible already to hear the old struggles, or even that there had been any problems before today.

And soon the conversation had turned to more interesting topics, although again time was their adversary.

"Be careful," was about the only thing he could say, the only advice he had left for her.

"We're working on the same team, the same company!" Shelby said again. It was far too great a thrill for her, and Mason couldn't knock that down, no matter his misgivings. "Just be careful," he said as they gave each other one final hug. "I don't know exactly what their plans are, or what roles you and I are playing, but be on the lookout. You've got a great head on your shoulders, use it."

"Of course, and I'll be back soon! And now we can telecomference and see each other like we're in the next room!"

"Let's definitely do that. Also let me know when you know, what they've got you doing out there in the Old World."

"Not that old, Dad. Not like you!" She jabbed him, then gave him one more kiss on the cheek, and then she was through the checkpoint, slinging her bag over her shoulder and following the pilot into the hallway, where she started up a spirited conversation.

Smiling, Mason headed back to his gate, pausing first for a pack of gum. He turned after the purchase, bemoaning the cost of three dollars, and stopped, seeing the latest on CNN:

Flash floods in the Congo. Absolute devastation viewed by a helicopter soaring over fields of rushing muddy water. People hanging on to boards, waving for help. A giraffe floundering, kicking at the water. Then a map of the area in red.

He blinked and looked away, out the window to Shelby's gate, where her plane was just leaving, heading toward the runway—and a massive black churning cloud came rolling in from over the mountains.

Mason clenched his teeth, walked up to the glass and stared, open-mouthed. The storm clouds seemed to roll and somersault gleefully, rushing down to meet the planes taking off. The one ahead of hers rose right toward the churning mass, perhaps too late to get a warning. Mason wanted to shout, to rush to an attendant and call the tower to ground all flights—when all of a sudden, the cloud parted, split down the middle as if a lance of pure gale force wind pushed in the opposite direction, through its heart and ahead of the ascending plane.

The cloud burst apart, rolled in two opposite directions, and scattered all in the space of twenty seconds as the plane rose through its previous mass.

It was followed by Shelby's, which tore along the same trajectory, then banked and as it angled right, the remaining cloud cover scattered frightfully before its approach.

In the next minute, as Mason watched, astounded, the skies cleared and both planes went on their ways uneventfully into the perfect blue.

It wasn't until the desk made a final call to board that Mason snapped his mind back to the present and barely made it on his flight.

CHAPTER 7

Back at Solstice headquarters, on the sixth sublevel, in another mock grove with wall-screens that gave the appearance of being on a clifftop overlooking a twilight scene of forests and rolling hills, Hespera Milne made a furtive call. After assuring the room was empty, and the standing stones concealed no one, she walked through the circle, around an altar masquerading as a conference table, and leaned against one of the wall screens. Gazing out through the tiny pixels, seeing through the illusion of nature, she placed the phone to her ear.

"It's secure," she said. "And I have confirmation, Solomon acted on the plan. Can you confirm? Is Palavar—?"

The youthful male voice on the other line was succinct. "Not confirmed yet, but he hasn't returned to Hollywood, his GPS stopped sending its message two hours ago, and he can't be reached. Assumption is that he is lost, as are the others on the council."

"Dear Mother Earth." Hespera bit her lip. About to speak, she paused, thinking she heard a slight creak behind her. She turned, but perceived nothing there, just shadows from the tall smooth stones.

"What's my next move?" She asked. "I don't know how long I can hold out, pretending to be the bimbo HR manager."

"A little longer, then we'll pull you out. We need to find out what Solomon's plans are. The Council failed, but it's clear his plan has evolved and is in its final phases. If we are to act, we must have full clarity."

"But can we even act? Palavar, Morris, Heidi … without them, our numbers are too few, and word is that many will defect."

"That can't be helped. But numbers aren't everything. I hear also that there may be a new player, someone with power equal to his, someone deserving of his own seat perhaps, on the council."

Hespera shrugged. "I don't know about that. I don't even think the one you're speaking of knows he has such power."

"Then he'd better learn. Fast. We'll talk again soon. In the meantime, remain vigilant."

Hespera terminated the call, then wiped the call history. Satisfied, she backed away until the view solidified from the countless pixels into a seamless view of natural perfection.

She longed to step through the wall, into that field, strolling down the path to the verdant glen, to pull off her boots and wade into the clear stream, to feel the power of the earth in the wind, the water, the sunlight, and the insects and—

A hand clamped around her mouth. Big, powerful, just as another clenched her wrist.

She made a muffled cry and instinctively kicked back at her attacker's shin while simultaneously leaning forward and then thrusting her head back. She heard a grunt and a satisfying crunch that may have broken his nose, then twisted free. Dropped her phone and crouched, ready to run.

But her assailant wasn't alone. Victor, holding his bloodied face, had a dozen hooded acolytes at his back, guarding the way to the door.

"Shit," Hespera said. "You brought the cavalry."

"Submit, traitor."

He reached for her, but she squirmed away. *One chance*, she thought, diving behind a stone. She tucked into a ball, closed her eyes and willed a change. She could do this, even under pressure. She had been trained by Palavar himself, years ago. Ready for such a mission. Her cover was blown, but she could still escape intact. It wouldn't be easy, but … there …

The pain rippled through her muscles. Her clothes ripped apart in a burst of fur and expanding flesh. Her snout lengthened, ears popped and fangs grew, and before Victor could close the gap, she was in full wolf form, darting around and between the stones. She leapt on the table and then, snarling tore through a gap in the acolytes, to the door and out—

—where two more druids were waiting, with electrified staves that struck at once in her breastbone and hindquarters.

The shock rippled through her marrow and nearly shattered her incisors. The pain, too intense, forced the change and in moments, she was in human form again. Naked, panting and dazed on the cold floor.

But not for long. Moments later, a multitude of hands lifted her up and brought her back into the room, to the mock-grove and in the middle of the stones.

To the altar.

She turned her head, looking through the gap in the grey robes, past Victor's hulking form, barely registering the curved knife in his grasp.

The forest beckoned, the sunlight flickering in golden shafts across the fields and the swaying sycamores.

A smile may have formed on her lips, but she couldn't tell. Not with the pain of multiple blades piercing her flesh at once. Carving and slicing.

Dimly, the sounds of chanting and the offering of sacrificial blood drowned out the running brook and the chirping birds, and even the dwindling sound of her own screams.…

Chapter 8

Gabriel was waiting alone in the rear seat of the limo to pick up Mason from JFK, and it was another surprise that Mason calmly took in. Clouds were thick overhead, and light flakes fell over his head as a bitter wind cut through his clothes and the too-thin sport coat. He slid inside quickly, taking the seat opposite from his son.

He met the smile, and as the limo lurched into traffic, Mason observed, "So you've been spending excessive time in a tanning booth?"

Laughing, Gabriel reached for a flask inside his briefcase. Raised it to his father and took a swig. "Just a little well-earned R&R. Which, by the way, doesn't officially end until noon today, so I'm having another sip."

"Suit yourself." Mason crossed his legs. "Go anywhere nice?"

Gabriel only smiled. "Tropical cruise. You going to ask who with?"

"I wasn't. I don't really know any of your friends, unless it's that pretty coworker. Annabelle?"

Gabriel raised the flask in another toast. "Give the man a cigar."

"Are you drunk now?"

Shrugging, Gabriel looked out the window, then up. "How about this weather! The Big Apple's not really used to this white stuff." He winked at Mason. "Hope it doesn't get worse and start piling up. What's your prediction, weatherman?"

Mason looked away, toward the small TV built into the side door so they could both see. Weather dominated the news, from the flash flooding in Africa to the aftermath of the Jamaican tsunami to the hurricane still slamming the East Coast and the cleanup and efforts to find the missing in Minneapolis.

Gabriel saw his look. "Mother Nature's being a bitch, huh Dad?" He tapped his flask to the screen. "Wonder how many billions of dollars she just wiped out in a single night around the world? And she's not done yet. How many millionaires are now without their second or third homes? How many snobby tourists too stingy to help out the impoverished locals are now sifting through the debris looking for their friends' bloated carcasses?"

"Gabriel! Jesus, what's wrong with you?"

"Me?" He leaned back. "Not a damn thing. Life is great. My dad and my twin sister are working with me, all together again in one big happy family." He grinned wide. "And the world is all right, after all. Remember how I was so consumed by that environmental nuttiness? How as a kid I'd even go after people in the park who didn't pick up their trash, and the protests and the letters and hell, the outright vandalism—half of which you never found out about?"

Mason looked at him sideways. "Yeah, and you're telling me that's changed?"

"Of course, I know now, Solomon has showed me the truth. I was overzealous, concerned when I didn't have to be."

"How so?"

"How so?" He laughed, swigging again. "Why, look around, Dad. It's a blizzard in New York City. Tornadoes are ripping through Minnesota and, outside of hurricane season, the Carolinas are getting whacked upside the head. Tsunamis, flash floods in Africa for God's sakes!"

"And your conclusion is that nature—the earth—is striking back?"

"Hell yeah! In ways no environmental activists could ever dream. Legislation? Protests, lobbyists? The EPA?" He cleared his throat and Mason feared he might actually spit on the floor in disgust. "All bullshit compared to what the earth itself can do. She protects herself. And yeah, she's had enough. Global warming? Yeah we're behind a good chunk of it, but Mother Nature's just kicked off another heat cycle, turning up the thermostat to cook us out. Starve us, hit us with drought and extreme weather, melt the ice caps and drown us like an unwanted colony of ants."

A wild light shone in his eyes. "She's got so many, many sweet-ass weapons in her arsenal."

Mason shuddered as another wind gust rocked the limo and the flakes turned to a near whiteout. He glanced over his shoulder, through the barrier, hoping the driver knew how to handle these conditions.

"So Gabriel, you'd be happy when? If ten percent of the population gets wiped out?" He met his son's eyes, which only flared even more. "Or is it just the top two percent you care about harming?"

"Oh they can go for sure, but no. Two percent or ten percent, it's not enough. Malthusian's theory. We're in an unsustainable cycle. I blame the damn geneticists and doctors for curing all the big diseases that used to keep our population in check. 370 million people on the planet in 1350 after the Black Death, all with an average lifespan only in the late twenties. Four billion by 1950. Eight billion today, and we're damn near living till ninety years old. We're on track for 10 billion by 2050 if not sooner."

"I've heard all the arguments. Unsustainability, natural resources depleted, not enough food, but those theories and Dan Brown scenarios all miss the point."

"Which is?"

"That humanity's greatest asset is its ability to adapt."

"Bullshit."

"We're not dinosaurs or any of the millions of other species that went extinct because the temperature changed or one food source ran out. We have technology, we have brilliant minds that create the next wonder drug, vaccine or super crop. We invent, we build. Skyscrapers to house people vertically. Robots to enhance our lives, new methods of conservation and recycling and …"

"As I said before, it's bullshit. And it's just arrogance to think otherwise."

"No, it's not. You're just incredibly cynical. Not sure where I went wrong with you, but the answer isn't to wish for genocide or the end of civilization. You've been on this planet less than twenty-five years and in that time you think you know all the answers to how the world can be saved?"

Gabriel chuckled. "But that's it, Dad. What I'm telling you. It doesn't need saving. It can do just fine on its own."

"Then aren't you and your boss at cross-purposes? He seems to want to save people. To set up this early warning technology. That's why we're here, isn't it? To convince the world of just what I've been talking about—humanity's ability to adapt. To overcome and predict. To sidestep nature's wrath, to protect ourselves and go on living, multiplying and growing—and consuming."

Shaking his head, Gabriel took another sip. "Oh, you're just so smart, aren't you? First day on the job, and you think you know everything."

"Then tell me, son." Mason leaned in. "What don't I know? Because damn it, nothing's adding up. I was told to study up on the technology in advance of my talk, and all they downloaded to my tablet was a two page patent application for barometric algorithmic sensors, something high tech but far from revolutionary. Oh, and some abstract that spouted various benefits from a few days' advance warning on weather changes."

Gabriel's laughter died as he took one last swig and covered the flask.

Mason pointed. "Do you have anything else in your case there for me? Because I don't know what I'm going to say."

"Oh just be yourself. Wing it like you're so good at."

Mason opened his mouth, wanting to get this conversation back on track. He felt he was almost at the point of having Gabriel give something away. In his condition, it wouldn't be hard to find out if he was hiding something. Maybe he could pry into what Solstice was really doing, to fill in some of the gaps.

But just then he felt it, a sudden gust, a blast of wind, sliding of the tires, veering to the left, and great crunching of metal on metal.

"Gabriel, hold on—"

And then they were fishtailing, and through the side windows he saw the headlights of an onrushing SUV barreling towards them through the snow.

CHAPTER 9

Outside the UN General Assembly Hall, Solomon finished with a call, then turned off the phone.

"Everything all right, sir?" asked a thin security agent by his side, preparing to escort him within.

"All going according to plan," Solomon said with a smile, straightening his pressed silk suit. "Just a little hold up on the expressway. Looks like I'll be going this alone."

"I'm sure you'll do fine."

"Sure I will, too."

The doors, flanked by huge potted plants that seemed to sway toward his approach, opened and he followed the agent into the immense hall. Inside, he paused a moment and soaked in the thrill of entering new territory, one where the eyes of the world—and every member government—would be on him. He smiled and flexed his hands, feeling the warmth, gathering the moisture, what little there was in this dry re-circulated air. He strode down the inclining aisle, past row upon row, surveying the eighteen-hundred seats, less than half full with delegates on their headsets, reading documents, scanning headlines or just chatting with their neighbors quietly while they waited.

He strode toward the upper dais, keeping his eye on the UN Emblem: the map of the world as seen from above the North Pole, flanked by olive branches. In his periphery, he noted the two great abstract murals painted on either wall, donations from French artist Fernand Leger. As he approached, the giant LCD screens adjacent to the UN emblem switched over to the presentation he had emailed the secretary earlier.

Smiling at seeing the Solstice logo imposed over another map of the world, entwined with a mistletoe branch twisting up from the ground, it posed a looming and powerful image. He made a point to stare at it as if it were a cross and he was about to genuflect before he took the world stage.

He waited for the Secretariat to introduce him and call the session to order, and then he graciously took the podium. Looking out over the faces of the delegations, seeing the yawns and the glassy eyes, the bored stares or the distracted murmurings, he could barely control his disdain and he had to remind himself of the larger purpose. The one shot he was about to fire that would be way over the heads of these nobodies. The one that would be heard, and acted upon, by the right people at the right time.

And that time was at hand. He got their attention—not when the presentation began, with all its power and muster, with its graphic imagery and templates and tables of weather-related loss of life, with disturbing video and images, of floating carcasses, frozen women and children, malnourished villages, tornado-wracked cities and tsunami-battered resorts—but he got their focus by bringing home a more personal issue.

The guest speaker, one Mason Grier—who had intended to be here at his side … a well-respected and award-winning meteor-ologist who had just joined the Solstice team—was himself in a terrible accident on the way here, due to the weather. A freak blizzard in New York? Sure there would be jokes about Global Warming and how the alarmists are just trying to scare up concessions and force guilt upon advanced countries when the evidence is no longer showing a scientific correlation, and in fact most people were suffering extreme cold and digging out from mounds of snow when previous winters had been much milder. Solomon covered that deftly with a series of graphs and data backing up the climate models showing that heating the atmosphere unevenly actually led to severe weather swings and unpredictable convection patterns resulting in exactly the sort of situations they were seeing today.

"My own lead representative lies in the hospital at this very moment, a victim of this kind of unpredictable and violent weather we are seeing across the globe." Solomon looked at them all, finally seeing their attention on him, the gravity of events taking hold because of its focus on a personal, single individual level. Mason had unwittingly played his first role perfectly according to Solomon's script.

"The truth of the matter is that my firm has patented technology that today, here before you all, I offer to share with the world. And only through this esteemed body of representatives, can I make clear the potential it has to dramatically improve forecasting, to save lives, to safeguard crops and stave off mass starvation and disease."

That got their attention. Solomon went on to show a test case, a sudden tornado ripping through a small suburb in South Dakota, and how the town had evacuated the suburbs and boarded up stores and consequently had no loss of life or livestock, and only minimal structural damage.

"This works," Solomon insisted. "On a small scale and, with your support and the assistance of members contributing resources, it can and will work on a global scale."

It wasn't the end of the presentation, but the questions started coming, as he knew they would. "What resources do you mean?" asked the representative from Belarus, and Solomon couldn't miss the distrust in his voice.

"Yes," chimed in the delegate from Peru. "We've heard this sort of thing before, an apparently altruistic offer wrapped up in concessions of a myriad of hidden fees and regulations, all designed to further impede our sovereignty, with ultimately nothing substantial for us to gain."

"This technology," scoffed the Iraqi counsel, "seems like it could be quite dangerous, in the wrong hands."

Solomon raised his own hands, urging calm. "All valid concerns, but first let me assure you, this is why I am here before you now. There is no single country, no world power behind this science. I insist its capabilities be shared by all, much like a new vaccine or water treatment process. What benefits one country, benefits all. Every country can see that. I can show you further data supporting how, like in the Butterfly Effect theory, environmental disasters in one corner of the world impact us all—through the global economy, commodity prices, impact on oil production and shipping, not to mention humanitarian aid on a massive scale. Imagine what fore-warning of such disasters could do to economic confidence, to recovery plans and new developments."

He let that sink in. "And as to your question, sir, about resources. All we require is a sharing of information." He licked his lips. "Information only. This technology, you see, is only as good as the data feeding it. Data in this case, from each country's weather centers. Access only is what we require. Access to the WMO's data centers."

"But," insisted the Chinese delegate, translated on the screens behind Solomon, "why would we do this? Everything you suggest, we already have through the WMO. Unless I am mistaken, we currently share data collection among the member countries. We have ..." he checked his figures and Solomon tapped his fingers, waiting for the inevitable flood of data, "... 10,000 land stations, 3,000 aircraft, 1,000 upper air stations and 1,000 ships, all working with 188 National weather centers and 50 regional centers ... 50 operational satellites ..."

"Yes," Solomon said. "Exactly what I'm asking for. You don't need to rebuild the wheel here. Only make it a better mousetrap. You all are doing a marvelous job. Through the WMO, you have made vast improvements, and we all know the statistics. Improve-ments so that a five day forecast now is as good as a two-day counterpart twenty years ago. But I'm telling you with absolute certainty that I can improve even further upon that. Solstice can give you a two-week forecast as good as that five-day one. As good as a one-day forecast."

"And all we have to do is open up our computers for you?"

Would be far easier than having me have to try to hack into them, Solomon thought, teeth clenched.

"Just the data access. Let us know what you know, and have access to the real time data from all those sources...." *Especially the satellites.* "And then put our technology to the test. Give us a month and run comparisons. Your current system versus ours."

Let that sit with them a moment. And it did. He could hear the palpable buzz around the room, the members discussing. Eventually they would dismiss him and talk some more amongst themselves, then put it to a vote.

"We can discuss it," said the Secretariat, "at further length. But this decision, and your demonstration, will have to be directed again to the WMO. Their next meeting is next week Tuesday."

Solomon lowered his head. He had feared as much, but he couldn't overplay his hand. "I thank you for the consideration, and we will happily provide whatever further information is necessary."

"And maybe your representative ... hopefully he will be recovered and available for further questioning."

Solomon smiled. "Thank you for your concern, speaker. And I'm sure he will make a speedy recovery. We'll await your decision."

He was about to leave when several hands went up, and lights flashed, signaling more questions. The Russian delegate leaned forward, after confirming something first with a colleague. "You may bring this to vote," he said sternly, "but we will veto it. We will argue thoroughly against any such collaboration with a private company based in the United States."

"I'm sorry," Solomon said in response. "But we owe no allegiance in this respect to our home based country. And in fact, we are multinational in scope, with offices in London, Paris, Delhi ..."

"It matters not," the delegate said. "You could have a shack in Moscow and it would mean nothing. CIA, NSA, we know that if this technology works as you say, they will use it to their advantage, if they are not doing so already."

Solomon grumbled. "Really sir, if you just ..."

"No! Already US military has taken so-called peaceful technology and turned against others."

Oh no, Solomon thought, *here we go. Not—*

"The HAARP project, we know about it, we have spoken at length about it here."

The Secretariat spoke up, countering: "And dismissed such claims that the Alaskan radar array is capable of any such things as you claim. These are—"

"Conspiracies that amount to nothing, yes yes, that is what you say." The Russian was unfazed. "And yet we do not agree. And many of the members here do not agree, but we have no smoking gun, yet. The technology exists, this we know. Weather modification is possible with these arrays, and their microwave output far in excess of anything needed to study near-earth atmospheric conditions. It exists, and we believe it has been used. Repeatedly. Against us in 2010, causing heat waves and mass crop failures. Against Haiti in the last earthquake. Even your Hurricane Sandy bears its fingerprints."

"I'm sorry," said Solomon, trying to break through this. "This lively debate is certainly well-intentioned, but I must reiterate. It bears not a whit on our firm, or our technology. We operate privately. We are governed entirely by myself and a board of directors, all with stake in the company. We answer to no one and we will never share information—"

"Unacceptable under any circumstance," the Russian said, taking off his translation headset, crossing his arms and leaning back. Apparently the discussion was finished.

The Secretariat approached Solomon and covered the mic. "We will speak more on this, but thank you for your time."

Solomon clenched his hands into fists, nodded and forced a smile to the audience. Head up, he stepped down and descended the stairs, walking past the rows and rows of foreign dignitaries, pausing for a moment at the row with the Russian delegate, who was leaning behind him, speaking animatedly with the French minister.

Turning away, Solomon quickened his pace.

His pitch was dead in the water, and although he knew this possibility was a strong outcome, it didn't sting any less.

Time for Plan B.

When the doors shut behind him and he was back in the cooler air of the hallway, he crossed to the windows and looked out under the swirling gray clouds over the New York skyline. He directed his attention through the flurries to one, then another nearby high-rise, scanning the rooftops.

After the security agent had resumed his post at the door to the chamber, Solomon retrieved his phone. He dialed, then spoke quickly. "Are they ready? Yes … we are acting. I have several targets that must be eliminated. But first, send Nexus up."

Almost on cue as he ended the call, the elevator doors opened and a young man, dressed colorfully in island garb, approached—and handed him Palavar's staff.

My staff, Solomon thought. "No problems getting it through security?"

"Not dressed like this, no sir," said the man, an eager zealot from Oregon, if Solomon recalled. "All part of the island pageantry exhibit and photo shoot, which isn't entirely happening."

Smiling, Solomon hefted the staff in both hands, then set its tip on the ground and leaned on it. "I'll have the focus point ready momentarily."

"And the sacrifice?" the youth asked, his voice trembling as he glanced around.

"Inside," said Solomon with grit teeth.

"You know what they'll say, afterwards?"

He looked back at the young druid. "Oh, yes. The irony of all this, right after a speech on the unpredictability of the weather. Glorious …" *And right after that lunatic Russian's mad ravings about HAARP.* Too bad, he was right in the deeper conjecture, but so wrong about the source. *As if those Alaskan fools had any clue about what it really takes to wield power of the elements.* They were like decrepit old shamans waving sticks at the sky and hoping the rain clouds would come.

"See you outside," Solomon said. "And … enjoy the show."

With that, he strode back toward the entrance doors, already anticipating the security guard who came back to meet him, an inquisitive look on his face.

One that morphed into one of complete confusion as something sharp burst into the back of his neck and punctured through. It turned sideways, hooking around his flesh, and then roughly tugged the agent out of the way.

The enormous potted plants were growing exponentially, green tendrils shooting in several directions, snapping at the air and writhing at Solomon's approach. He aimed his staff at the far doors, and the closest plant swung its appendages there, circling the handles and forming an unbreakable lock.

The tendrils converged on the near doors. With perfect timing, they pulled open for Solomon, allowing him to pass—after he stepped over the agent's body. The doors slammed shut behind him as he stood in the back and looked around as the congregation went about their incessant arguments and bickering, translating all the nonsense into more meaningless observations on a world they all thought they had a chance to control.

Solomon laughed to himself, and then louder as he felt the chamber walls shudder.

He raised his staff, closed his eyes and let his mind drift up.... Up through the domed ceiling, past the buildup of snow and ice the roof had never been meant to sustain, and then out into the cold to become one with the winds, the storm and the elements.

Chapter 10

In the Columbia Medical Center, Mason woke groggily, wincing with a brutal headache. When his vision cleared, he could make out that he was in a recovery room, but that was all. Something wasn't right. It was dark, but a light kept flashing from outside the open door, scattering shadows inside. He looked at his arms: no IVs, that was a good thing. He felt a bandage on his forehead, and as he sat up his ribs cried out more in stiffness than pain.

All in all, not too bad. Probably just blacked out for a bit, and they were observing him for a concussion.

Gabriel! How was his son? Had to find out. He swung his legs over the side, and in the next flash of light, looked for the nurse call button and hit it.

He wasn't going to wait. Quickly he located his shoes, but as he stood up he had to lean back again as a wave of dizziness almost overcame his senses. Maybe they had given him some sedatives or some painkillers? Shaking his head, he took a deep breath and tried again, but first he looked out the window where a sudden flash illuminated the surroundings. He had to blink and look twice, then shuffled to the window, and cupped his hands.

Trying to pierce the gloom, through what he finally realized was a near whiteout, he could barely make out twinkling lights of the neighboring buildings. A sudden burst of light and a rumbling shook the window.

Thundersnow! A winter thunderstorm, rare but not unlikely especially with these kinds of conditions. They were in a synoptic pattern of strong upward motion within the cold section of an extra-tropical cyclone system. Thermodynamically, it wasn't different from any other type of thunderstorm, but the top of the cumulonimbus was much lower, and it was usually followed by—

Hail! Major pellets started bombarding the window, sprayed like bullets from a submachine gun. He jolted back, bumped into the bed, then spun around it as another flash lit up the room. The hospital had apparently lost main power and was on generator backup. That would also explain the lack of response to his call, he thought, as the orderlies were likely helping the more desperate patients.

He slipped on his sneakers and made his way out into the hall.

Empty. Monitors beeping somewhere, but it was too surreal, like a scene out of a *Halloween* movie.

"Hello?"

More dim lights flickered and windows shook and cracked, and from somewhere an arctic wind rushed past him. He approached the desk, seeing a clipboard and a list of names and rooms. He turned it, and tried to read if Gabriel's name was on it.

Another gust of wind, this one intense and full of snow. It tugged the clipboard from his hands and sent it slamming into the far wall. He turned against the blast, squinting as an onslaught of small ice crystals blasted toward him, seeking his eyes and stinging his cheeks.

The stairwell door was wide open.

He went to close it and tugged at the handle, but the door wouldn't budge against the gale. Preparing to try again, Mason saw something that caused him to step on ahead, through the door and onto the stairs.

—following the large bare footprints made recently in the fresh snow coating the stairs.

Bare footprints, along with a circular indentation beside them.

A patient ascending the stairs. A patient who hadn't bothered to put on his shoes, but had thought to pick up his staff.

The rooftop doorway was open and every level he ascended turned more frigid, the wind stiffer and the flakes stronger and sharper until Mason was sure they were drawing blood.

Turn back, he thought, but it was spoken with a subdued voice, drowned out by the howling wind, and before he knew it he was stumbling out into the blizzard. In the whipping winds, following the footprints was all but impossible—if they still remained in the rising drifts. He couldn't make out anything more than a few yards ahead. But then something moved: just a blurred shape, backlit against another sudden flash of lightning. A shape of a man, shirtless, both hands raised to the sky, holding a staff between them.

Gabriel turned and in the next prolonged flash of light, his snow-shrouded eyes shone clear as day. "Hello father!" he shouted over the wind. "Out for a little rooftop stroll?"

Mason partially covered his head. He had to get Gabriel back inside. Clearly he was in shock, delirious and a danger to himself, standing out here on the roof's edge in this storm. "Gabriel—!"

But then he sensed a change in the air pressure, direction and force of the wind. Something so sudden and swift, it was as if someone had grasped the storm and directed all its fury toward a new adversary.

The near white-out lifted so suddenly he started to doubt his sanity, or at least wonder if the medication he was on was causing hallucination. Too surreal, now the view was clear like the purest high-definition TV, and he could see for miles: lights and facades of the high rises nearby, the business center and water tanks and small patches of trees on top of buildings.

Maybe I'm dreaming, he thought, and this was the moment where the dreamer, knowing he's dreaming, could enter a state of lucidity and start to control the dream itself.

He'd have to try that some time, but right now, unless he woke up fast, they were all in danger of freezing to death, especially Gabriel, who—

—who, it seemed, had to be a central character in his dream. His knees bent, staff held out front with both muscular arms tensing as if against a superior resistance. The entire localized storm seemed to funnel directly from the center of his staff outward, expelling the matter like a giant snow gun. Expelling it above and down First Avenue—a twisting, nearly horizontal funnel of snow and ice.

Mason teetered on the edge of sanity and delirium, barely in control of his own motor functions. He couldn't speak or move, only watch with hawk-like focus. And in true avian fashion, his vision swept the panoramic view and caught not only this funnel, but ten others: all snakelike undulating cyclones of wind, ice and winter fury, converging from all directions in a radius around one building.

His vision magnified as if in a sniper's scope, and he zeroed in on the target: a circular copper dome atop a squat trapezoidal structure beside a very familiar outline.

The United Nations.

Chapter 11

Solomon sensed the weight and strain on the dome above, even as the five-hundred-some delegates and translators felt the walls shake. Water droplets sprinkled like the mist in a spring shower, and to his right he saw the tech team in the control room stand up.

Just two of them, and it looked like they were about to go for the alarms. It wouldn't be in time, but Solomon took no chances. A wave of his staff and the outer windows turned to frost, encased in thick ice, and as he dropped his arm, the ice compressed and shattered the glass, blasting it inwards and tearing through the men. Jagged shards embedded into their flesh and they went down without even a chance to cry out.

Solomon strode farther into the hall, where the commotion grew in volume. Almost two hundred different languages and accents raised in alarm as faces turned skyward, following a horrible metal-on-metal scraping, torturous cry.

More dust-like debris fell along with water, and then snow-flakes—lazy and thick—circled gracefully down in a cone-shaped pattern. And a hush fell over the crowd. It almost seemed magical, a fairy-world mirage or special effect. A few faces looked back to the control room to see if it in fact might be something designed for their entertainment.

That was when the screaming began. The sight of the shredded control techs, all that blood and melting ice.

The screaming started, but didn't last long. In the next instant, under the weight of ten concentrated cyclones bearing down with heavy ice and snow, all building and piling upon the dome … it vainly struggled against the pressure, then buckled. The seams struggled to hold, then the massive supports bent, cracked, sparked like a series of fireworks, and then shattered.

Everyone directly below the dome disappeared in an instant and an incomprehensible blur of metal, ice and snow. Solomon stepped onto a chair to survey the damage. He couldn't see the stage through all the winding, snaking whirlwinds ripping in through the gaping hole in the roof. It looked like a great frost giant had torn open the ceiling and shoved both hands inside, seeking warm, tender flesh.

Solomon was here only to guide those seeking fingers.

He moved his arms, twisting and turning the staff, stirring up the air. He started humming an ancient nature song, chanting to the elements, speaking their language and promising sacrifice.

Promising blood.

Dimly, through the ice and the wind and concentrated blizzard whirling around the hall, he saw the giant screen sparking, the glass shattering, pieces falling, and then the great emblem—the world and the olive branches hung so prominently and symbolically— ripped free of the wall as two mini-cyclones attacked it from either side. It split jaggedly down the middle, then the two halves were flung in opposite directions, each crunching into and rolling over dozens of chairs and stray delegates.

People rushed by Solomon, unaware of his presence, clouded in swirling snow. He visualized each of them as heat-sinks, seeing past their expensive suits and loafers, into their chests and their terrified beating hearts.

And he found the two he was looking for.

I see Russia, I see France….

Almost giddy with power and doing nothing to suppress his laughter, Solomon made two crossing motions with the staff, aiming at one fleeing member, then the other.

A great rush of two-foot long icicles chipped off from the hole in the dome and hurtled down in twin paths.

Each one struck, impaled and moved through the bodies of the Russian and French delegates, puncturing flesh and bone with the force of a fifty-mile-an-hour gale. Their bodies were lifted in the air and repeatedly struck by numerous ice spears, and then dropped, lifeless and flopping onto the aisles.

Solomon lowered his head, sucked in a huge breath, and then … blew it out.

And the winds expelled back up through the ceiling. The snow followed and nine of the giant cyclonic whirlwinds withdrew from sight.

The last one lingered over the wreckage, the shredded and crushed bodies, and the few cowering at the locked doors. And then it swung over the hall, scooped up Solomon gently and whisked him up and out through the roof.

In the hall, the vines withdrew and innocently resumed their stations inside the potted plants.

And the doors opened.

Chapter 12

Mason watched with detached horror. The dome collapsed under the combined assault from twisting cyclones directed at it from ten rooftop locations in the vicinity. He could almost see the other weather-practitioners … the shamans or the sorcerers or whatever these people were, with their staves, some in grey hooded robes, standing steadfast against the elements, controlling the weather as effortlessly as adjusting the settings on a TV.

A sudden rush of pain and horror, absolute terror, primal and intense, all hit him at once. As if experiencing all the anguish, shock and pain from inside the UN General Assembly, Mason broke from his temporary paralysis, and he felt an equally sudden surge of strength, warmth and focus.

He could stop this. He didn't know how it was happening, how they could do this, but he thought he knew how he could stop it.

Stop Gabriel, and the whole thing might stop. Break the chain....

He moved, started to rush him, but Gabriel glanced sideways, took a little of his focus away, and the snow deepened around Mason's feet. The icy weight slowed him down, providing intense resistance for every step. He focused on his legs and willed the heat to swell, and he felt it working. The snow gave way to slush, and his feet moved swifter. Gabriel gave him a look of concern, and his staff-hands faltered.

Mason came closer, almost within arm's reach of his son. He was winning, and he felt it, a power surging through his blood. Overcome with the intention of ripping the staff from Gabriel's grasp, he would break it in half and then—

But it was too late. Out of the periphery, Mason saw all the cyclones sucking backward, withdrawing from the wreckage of the UN. So fast, their work was done.

Oh no … Mason started, but had the thought interrupted by the realization that *something* was coming back in that funnel toward Gabriel.

Something vaguely human-shaped.

The whirling cyclone, spitting out tiny hail and frosted snow, uprighted itself just before Gabriel, pushed him back a few steps almost into Mason, then roared down and exploded into wispy tendrils of cool flakes and just a light wind.

It was gone, and in its place remained its passenger.

Avery Solomon rose from a kneeling position, using a gnarled old oak staff for support. *Not the one he had been holding before*, Mason thought, finding it strange to notice such a thing at a time like this.

Solomon sent a dry glare to Gabriel, one that spoke of extreme disappointment. Then he faced Mason.

Solomon held up his staff toward Mason and spoke one word: *"Forget."*

He brought the staff up in a short, accurate arc, and then swung it hard, down across Mason's right temple.

Everything went black.

CHAPTER 13

Mason woke and took a long time to get his bearings. The room was blurry and the TV was on but he couldn't make out an image or what was being said. Someone held his hand, stroking his fingers, and another figure stepped into the light.

"Is sleeping beauty awake yet?" The voice, familiar … like it was his, only younger.

"I think so. Mason?"

"Dad?" said the other voice, and Mason had an image of a shirtless man in a snowstorm, eyes turning toward him and then lost in a whirlwind. He frowned, focused and thought he recalled something about cyclones and rooftops and …

No, it was gone. *Just a fading dream.*

He licked his lips, blinked and lifted his head. Lauren was there, reaching over, carefully placing a cup next to his parched lips. Greedily he downed the water, felt it cooling his throat, rejuvenating and jumpstarting his system.

"The limo crash? Gabriel?"

"I'm here, and fine. Just some bruised ribs." He moved behind Lauren and set his hands on her shoulders. "Glad you're back among the living. Concussion, we were worried. You started hallucinating, and tried to get up and fell."

"I remember.... I think. Did the hospital lose power?"

"It's okay," Lauren said. "Gabe, turn off the TV."

Mason shot his attention to the screen where in the moment it took Gabriel to get there, he registered the scene of frozen destruction. A shattered rooftop dome, and interior photos of body bags, fire engines and rescue units.

"What happened?"

Gabriel paused, about to shut off the TV. He let out a sigh. "Right as Solomon was presenting. Preliminary focus by the media is on the repairs they made to the dome last year, when it was leaking and portions were damaged. They're investigating the construction company that undertook the latest repairs, but it may be no one's fault. They couldn't have anticipated this much snowfall, and the heavy precipitation and freezing-melting combination."

"Is Solomon—?"

"He's fine," Gabriel said. "Shook up for sure, but word is he tried to help several injured delegates."

Mason nodded. "We're working for a hero, apparently."

"He wouldn't see it that way," Gabriel said, shutting off the TV. "But don't think about any of that now. You're still pretty drugged up. We need to chat with the doctors, and they're going to give you a CT scan to make sure everything's peachy."

"But the conference. The speech. I didn't get to—"

"We'll have another chance," Gabriel said. "From what I hear, they were going to recommend we present directly to a subset of members, the WMO team directly. And frankly, after what happened today ..."

"Too bad," Mason said, "You didn't predict this."

"Oh we did," Gabriel said, with a sly smirk. "And we've got the data to show it. Sent a packet ahead of time to the committee, with long range forecasts for seven major cities around the US. Wanted to show them what we're capable of, with the right data and access."

Mason squeezed Lauren's hand. "And it was accurate?"

Gabriel smiled. "Of course. How could it be otherwise?"

"Oh, I don't know. Maybe just because nature is unpredictable? And since the dawn of time our efforts at predicting her behavior has been spotty at best. It's like betting against the house in a casino. You might win here or there, but over time, you lose. Nature is chaotic, violent and unflinching. It's best to just get the hell out of her way."

Gabriel shrugged. "Get well, Dad. You've got a lot of road to cover. And a lot to learn."

Lauren pulled her hand away and adjusted something on the nightstand. "Flowers from Pamela." A nice bouquet of lilies, Mason saw.

"What about those others?" he asked, his mouth dry again, looking at a massive floral arrangement nearly overshadowing and dominating the lilies. "I hope you didn't—"

"Oh no," Lauren said with a smile. "Your new boss, Mr. Solomon had these sent over. Not sure from where. These are so exotic, I have no idea what some of them are, other than the holly stems and this …"

"Mistletoe," Mason observed, and Lauren blushed. "Really? It's not Christmas yet, although it feels like it. Maybe," she said, turning toward him and leaning over, "he just wants us to kiss."

Mason leaned in as Lauren lifted a stemmed leaf over his head. Their lips touched briefly, then firmer. He pulled away slightly. "Whatever his reasons, remind me to thank him. Now, when do I get the hell out of here?"

Chapter 14

Under the bow bridge, so named for being shaped like an archer's bow and spanning the Lake in Central Park, Solomon huddled in a long down trench coat and a bright green silk scarf. The daylight was soft and diffuse, struggling from a low position to penetrate thick layers of clouds in the aftermath of the storm.

"So, gentlemen. And lady," he said, addressing the four people standing along with him on the thick ice, braving the bitter winds. Further away, at the far side of the lake, a few intrepid ice skaters were out enjoying the conditions. *You're welcome*, Solomon thought. Let them have their fun for now. *Times, as Dylan said, they are a changin'.*

"You called," said the youngest of the group, a Nordic-looking man in his late thirties. He had a boyish glint in his eyes despite the age lines creasing his brow. "And we came."

"But we do not like being summoned," said the lady, a thick wool scarf and an enormous pea coat covering her solid frame; she wore pointed horn-rimmed glasses and a wide red hat over curly silver hair.

The oldest one, wearing a hat with ear flaps, leaned on his dark cherry cane, his hands in thick mittens, and grumbled: "Especially in this weather."

"My apologies," Solomon replied, "for the lack of advance notice, as well as for the choice of meeting location, but it is urgent, and of course with technology being so unreliably non-private …"

"Yes, yes," the old man spoke up, his breath sputtering into foggy bursts, "get on with it."

"We presume," said the younger man, "that this is about the UN."

"And about the semiannual meeting," said the lady.

"Palavar," said the dark-skinned one, a Haitian, silent until now. He had long, tight dreadlocks and was dressed simply in a sweater, khaki's and earmuffs, as if he'd been out for a jog.

"Yes, Palavar." Solomon sighed and held up the late leader's staff. He made a slow display of caressing the grooves in the gnarled wood. "I know you all didn't see eye to eye with him on many occasions."

The old man cleared his throat. "Nor did we wish him serious harm."

"Nor did I," said Solomon. "But he struck first. I reacted. Not just for my survival alone, but for all of ours."

"And the others on the council?" asked the lady, her eyes looming larger behind the lenses. *And full of more than a bit of challenge*, Solomon thought, recalling what he'd heard of the one known as Lady Sunfire. Out of those who remained, she had the most experience, the greatest power. He'd have to be careful of her. And of the others. The next few minutes were key.

"Several of the other council members were … regrettably caught in the crossfire."

"Regrettably," she echoed. "And those who escaped death?"

Solomon let out a low sigh. "Taking a rest, thinking on things. Evaluating their choices. They'll get another chance to pick a side soon."

"Maybe," said the Haitian, "we should wake them up and ask them to decide along with us."

"In time," agreed Solomon. "Now, I've asked you here because I am readying the next phase. I need to know if I can count on your support."

"The next phase," said the old man, adding a grunt at the end.

Here we go, Solomon thought. *Does every old guy have to support Palavar in his quest to do nothing fast?*

"If Phase Two means what I think it means …" The old man coughed, clutched his chest, then thumped it once. "Then I am all for it."

Solomon blinked rapidly. "You are?"

The old man's eyes were smiling, and sparking with energy. "Palavar was—I must say, with apologies to Ms. Sunfire—a dried up old pussy."

Ms. Sunfire nearly choked on her tongue.

The Haitian let out a smile, but the young man frowned. He stepped forward. "Am I hearing right? We're actually in agreement on the murder of an arch-druid?"

"Benjamin," said the Haitian. "Let's hear him out."

"What's to hear? Seizing power now by force is condoned?" Benjamin clenched his fists, and reached behind his back for a slender staff made of pure ivory, so white it almost blended with the ice. Twirled it once and stepped out from the group's semi-circle to face Solomon.

"You wanted to know if you have our support?"

"I think," said Solomon without missing a beat, "you're giving me your answer."

Benjamin nodded. "Sunfire. Haitian Jack and Stanwick. Stand with me now. Consider what Solomon is proposing with his Phase Two."

"Yes," said Solomon, "consider it. Consider—"

"—the natural karma you've upset," spat Benjamin.

Old man Stanwick's throat issued a phlegm-filled cough. "Please. The karma's been upset for millennia, since our degenerate ancestors climbed down from the branches and started believing we had the God-given right to dominion over the beasts and the land."

"Genesis," said Ms. Sunfire, "may have been a bit too pandering, and I admit, used far too often in defense of man's worst acts.…"

"Colonization," said the Haitian.

"Industrial expansion," added Stanwick. "Pollution, greed, waste …"

Benjamin's eyes swept across the others as they spoke, then turned back to Solomon. His hands trembled on the staff. "I repeat," he said, mustering some strength. "Karma is out of balance. I shudder to think what—who—you've sacrificed to unleash what you've unleashed." He glanced in the direction of the UN plaza. "But it feels as terribly wrong to me, as it should to all of you."

The others, having a chance to speak, remained silent.

Solomon cleared his throat. "This karma you speak of, this balance? I put it to you, as I have put it to the council for years, that the balance has been woefully lopsided since, as Mr. Stanwick just said, we shuffled down from the trees. Think of the earth in all its millennia of life. How many species has it put to the sword of extinction? Ninety-eight per cent of all the species that have ever lived upon the earth are now extinct."

"Yes," said Benjamin, "and how many of them are gone precisely because of us, because of man?"

"Frightfully few, I presume," said Haitian Jack, sticking his hands in his pockets.

"Exactly so," Solomon said. "Frightfully few compared to the mass carnage, the total annihilation earth has subjected its own tenants to throughout the great eras of time. Ice ages followed by volcanic epochs where ash blanketed the skies and poison rained upon the forests and the seas boiled and billions upon billions of carcasses had their stories end with inglorious fanfare, sweeping the field clear for a new round of hopeful life forms, only to indiscriminately destroy those as well."

Benjamin stewed. "Ancient history, as they say. Your point? The present is all that matters, and now we are the blight, we are stealing that power from its rightful wielder. We are—"

"Killing some species, certainly," Solomon interrupted. "But how many more are we saving? Interjecting ourselves into the path of Nature's wishes. Securing habitats, removing natural predators, saving genetic material and nursing the sick creatures, encouraging mating and protecting others in zoos. Who are we to interfere, to mock Nature's plans?" Solomon gripped his staff in both hands. "You speak of balance, and I tell you I am merely righting the balance, restoring power to where it belongs. Not with man and his technology and his medical miracles and his immunizations and ecological re-engineering. *That* is what has usurped the balance."

He sighed, as if resting after the exertion of making his point. "I will right it, correct that imbalance."

Benjamin paled. "By this … this Phase Two? Unleashing the full unpredictable fury of nature upon the world? Decimating the industrial nations so that it will take all their efforts just to rally the survivors and huddle together and somehow try to rebuild?"

Solomon beamed. "Now you're seeing the light."

"No," said Benjamin. "I do not. I see only the darkness. In you, in your plan, and in any who follow you. We have different worldviews, but I believe that of all the billions of species that haven't made it to this point, maybe it was because Nature—or God—was experimenting, building just the right one, with the right mix of love, compassion, ambition and fortitude. A species with the intelligence and the capacity to dream, and to learn and to improve. One that could—"

"Enough!" Solomon hissed, and in a flash he leapt up and down, landing just before Benjamin, and bringing the staff tip down hard against the ice. And in the next movement, he had leapt back to his position under the bridge.

The cracking of the ice echoed off the masonry and the Greek-styled facade, and Benjamin had just a moment to raise his staff in a counter attack attempt, but not enough time to finish the motion.

In the next instant he was gone, plummeting through the gaping hole in the ice without so much as a splash. Just … gone.

Solomon exhaled hard, pushing out all his breath, then swept an arc with his staff, pushing the frigid air over the jagged hole, then making circular motions over it. The hole promptly sealed over with thick ice, just over Benjamin's face as it rose, and the hands that lunged upward were encased in the block of ice. His eyes blinked once, then the frost sealed over and it was done.

Solomon held out his staff powerfully in front of his body, warding over the empty spot as he focused on each other druid in turn. "Any other dissenters?"

Ms. Sunfire clucked her tongue, looking at the hole. "Poor boy."

The Haitian made no motion whatsoever, only stared at the frosted ice and the blurry shape encased below. Mr. Stanwick grumbled and turned to face Solomon. "So now that that's settled, can you please desist from further depleting our ranks? Just tell us what you need from us to get the goddamn ball rolling on this next phase?"

Solomon grinned and leaned with both hands on his staff. "Most certainly. I'm glad you asked." He glanced at them all in turn, then pointed with his staff, not at them or the ground, but up at the sky, some vague direction up through the clouds.

"Tell me, what do you all know of satellite weather surveillance?"

Chapter 15

During the flight back on the Solstice private jet, Gabriel and Lauren played an extended game of chess while Mason tried to go through gigabytes worth of abstracts, technical papers, applied mathematics and research from Solstice-paid consultants and experts. Impressive and overwhelming as it all was, Mason's eyes were getting heavy around the two-hour mark, right about when Gabriel and Lauren escalated their climate change argument to the next level. Gabriel fumed and got that high-pitched sound to his voice as he always did when he embarked on a rant, and Mason was about to call over from his seat to break it up, but listened for another moment and found—with more than a touch of respect—that Lauren was giving it back just as good, and not rolling over at all. Neither side was going to give in or accede anything more than grudging respect, but at least it was a conversation. Mother and son were spending time together.

They droned on, the give and take of ideas and facts and opinions all forming a lulling buzz in Mason's head that, when mixed with all the weather research and the gentle movements of the plane, created an unavoidable tug towards sleep.

His head nodded, and the plane's cabin lost focus, then snapped back and for a brief moment it took on the form of a gentle grove: the seats were moss-covered, the aisle a running brook, the windows shafts of light through the forest canopy. He rubbed his eyes, and now the images were blurred together—jet cabin and forest grove, a smudge of intertwined colors and smeared boundaries that made no sense.

Giving in to the pull of sleep, Mason drifted into the dreamscape, going with the unreality of the last visions, feeling the vegetation again creep over the leather seats and the moss cover the windows.

Now tendrils of fog rolled in, gently sweeping over the brook, obscuring the ground cover, and the animals and birds, at first so natural and bold, diminished quickly and then hushed altogether.

I know I'm dreaming, he thought. On a plane heading home, flying over Indiana now, most likely. Above drought-ravaged cornfields and dried up creeks and rivers. Above a place once called home where a freak tornado had ripped apart and shaped his young life.

But it feels so real. His feet were bare, the soles shifting in the hard earth under a layer of brittle snow. He could feel bits of leaves and grass, pebbles and moss as he walked slowly, carefully.

Towards something emerging from the mist, something A-framed, with a hint of a thatch roof.

A cottage, he thought giddily, and at once felt at home and yet terrified, certain he should not take another step. This place had been obscured for a reason. Hidden from prying eyes, not on any maps, and yet he was certain he had been invited.

He had to see, had to seek it out, go through the mist and enter the front door (the one he was sure had a shamrock handle). Something was inside, something he needed to see. Something …

A flash of light and suddenly he had been transported somewhere else. He stood on the ice in a dimly lit park. A hazy sun dipped below a jumbled concrete horizon. A chipping sound echoed in his ears, and looking down, he saw his feet were still bare, but felt no pain, no chill from the frozen lake as he walked toward the man kneeling on the ice, chipping away at it with what looked like a stick.

The man, dark skinned with handsome features and short cropping of dreads over his shoulders, kept hacking away at a hole, widening it. Mason saw that it wasn't a stick, but a perfectly cylindrical staff—with a sword point at the end, gleaming in the pale light.

Mason stopped within several yards, watching as the man reached down into the hole and started to haul something up.

"You," the man said in a Haitian accent without looking up. "You ain't supposed to be here."

"I'm *not* here," Mason said, looking around at the distant buildings—which now seemed closer, and greener, as if the dying sun had somehow stimulated the growth of moss and vines and ivy, multiplying over the concrete and brick.

The Haitian pulled a body out of the lake, a man still partially encased in ice. "Well then, that's okay. If you ain't here, then no harm, no foul. But if you are here ..." He looked up, and one green eye settled on him. "Well, in that case, maybe you should lend a hand."

"With what?" Mason looked closer. "The young man appears to be dead."

"Appears so, yes." The Haitian pressed his ear against the cold ice chest. "But then again, appearances deceive, no? I mean, you—you ain't here, but I'm talking to you."

"So," Mason said. "Either you're crazy, or I am."

"Or maybe you're dreaming."

Mason thought about that, and thought it made some sense.

"And if you be dreaming," said the Haitian, blinking at him, "then that there changes things."

"What do you mean?"

"Means you might be spirit-walkin'." He pointed his staff in Mason's direction and pressed a button. The sword point withdrew and just the hollow end touched his chest.

"Spirit walking?" Mason blinked, and he licked his lips, looking around now at the forest that had grown wilder, stretching farther than he could see.

"Your spirit be walkin' mighty far, my guess is, by your bare feet and the twigs stuck between your toes." He cocked his head. "Wonder where you just was?"

Mason breathed in, barely listening. The buildings making up the skyline were now giant mounds of greenery, with branches and leafy canopies and hanging vines. It looked like nature had taken over centuries ago.

"But no matter," said the Haitian. "I underestimated you at first, just like I did him."

Mason returned his focus on the man. "Who?"

The staff point pulled away and aimed at the body. "The one who done this."

A flash and the Haitian was standing with his back to Mason. He tapped the frozen body with the bottom of his cane once. Twice, and then stepped back.

"But if you come all the way here to watch me, then it be important. You, maybe you be the one help out. Help stop all this before it be too late."

"All what?" Mason asked, feeling groggy all of a sudden. Wobbly like he was about to fall face first onto the ice.

The Haitian spread his arms and spun in a delicate circle on his right foot, like a figure skater, while he indicated the sun rising opposite where it had just set, breaking dawn over a kingdom of absolute nature.

A kingdom of green.

Behind him, the ice encasing the corpse melted at once, and the man's flesh turned from pale to reddish hued, and for a moment Mason thought he was coming back to life, about to sit up when …

He burst into flames. The Haitian spread out his hands for warmth—or something else—it seemed he fanned the fire, but also pushed the smoke toward himself, breathing in the ashes from the burning corpse. Another deep, deep breath and the fire went out, the smoke sucked into the Haitian's lungs, and he turned away from the charred corpse and faced Mason.

His eyes were closed as if savoring the taste, and then he expelled the smoke and dust all in one exhalation, right into Mason's face, with one word:

"Wake."

Chapter 16

Bolting awake in his seat at the same instant the landing gear touched pavement, Mason found himself staring into Gabriel's smiling face.

"Welcome back." Gabriel glanced over to Lauren in the next seat. "Does he always sleep this much?"

"Only after near death experiences," she responded and reached across the aisle to grasp Mason's hand. "Must've been some dream. You kept twitching."

"I was ... walking," he said, frowning as he looked out the window at the landscape rushing by. The palm trees and sunlight, so starkly different from New York.

Gabriel gave him a sideways look. "See anything interesting on your walk?"

"I'm not sure." Mason rubbed his eyes. "Can't quite recall." *Nothing, except the house in the mist, and the body in the lake, and someone blowing cremation-smoke in my face. But I'm not speaking of that....* "So, where's Solomon? Anyone hear from him?"

Gabriel unbuckled his belt as the plane slowed and turned toward the hangar. "He stayed on to meet with the authorities and to schedule a session with the World Meteorological Organization."

"And he didn't need us?"

"No, they don't meet in New York anyway. It will probably be a teleconference, unless we go to Zurich or something, but Solomon thinks we can handle it from our offices."

"He thinks what happened will be enough to get us their cooperation?"

Gabriel smiled. "I wouldn't doubt it."

"So what's next?" Lauren asked. "I mean, besides some more rest for you both."

"We're fine," Gabriel and Mason said at the same time, with the same intensity. Mason let a smile break free. "At least we agree on one thing. I'm feeling much better after that respite, and I need to keep busy. I want to work and help out. I feel like I've done nothing so far except try out your firm's medical coverage."

Gabriel laughed. "Well I know you got the start of a tour. We can continue that and get you set up and prepared for the conference call I expect is coming."

"That sounds good. Will what's her name—Hespera—be there?"

Gabriel blinked. "I am not sure. She may be helping out other divisions for the next few weeks. Her status is to go where she's needed."

"Okay," Mason said, standing up and stretching. "Let's get our bags and get to work."

Back inside Solstice headquarters, it was business as usual. The main grove was filled with the typical number of attractive people sipping tea or meditating before starting the day. The calming waterfall and the flapping butterflies, buzzing insects and chirping sparrows all set Mason to ease as he walked through the trees and under the canopy of leaves. He felt rejuvenated, cured from his pains, ready to get to work and do some good.

It felt strangely surreal. For so many years he woke to weather reports, to alerts of meteorological conditions over the Pacific. Now it felt like he was swimming in possibilities to occupy his time.

Surely that would all change once he set out to work.

And change came fast. As soon as the elevator doors opened and let him out into the weather research chamber, Victor Nunion was there to meet him. A bandage on his nose and his eyes were bruised.

"Welcome back from the big city. We were concerned to hear of your crash."

"Could have been worse," Mason replied, staring up at the giant of a man. Something not right about the guy's features, like they were molded inappropriately after a failed shape-shifting attempt. Mason shuddered too with the hint of Victor's breath, which was far from minty. "I could have been inside the U.N. with Mr. Solomon and all the others who weren't so lucky."

"Luck comes in strange forms. Or so they say." His lips moved, mouthing the words, but Mason had the impression Victor was just lip-syncing. Even his eyes were out of focus. Maybe there was a transmitter in his ear and he couldn't act or speak without taking remote directions.

Victor turned his large back, and led him to the farther exit. "I'll show you to your office."

"Oh, I thought I'd be here...." Mason looked around the great room, his eyes dazzled by all the screens and the wealth of data, the onslaught of visuals. "The Star Chamber" they called it, he found out on this pass, and would have enjoyed staying a little longer, but Victor turned and waved a folder at him.

"No, you can visit here for research any time you want, but really all you need is at your fingertips in your office."

Through the door, reluctantly leaving the Star Chamber, Mason followed Victor through the black-walled hall and around a corner he hadn't noticed before. His office was the first door.

"Feels a bit like I'm in a bunker," he observed before the door opened and he was ushered into what he could only call a magnificent suite. Again, faux windows were displaying projections—set to the Pacific coast seaway, it appeared.

"Scratch that thought," he added. "Wow."

"Coffee, refreshments ... there's a room two doors down, or go back up to the grove if you must take the time."

Lazy white gulls flew in and between the frames of the connected visuals, as the sun rose past the uppermost frame.

Mason could actually smell the sea salt, and guessed there was a diffuser somewhere in the room—which on second viewing, wasn't as big as he first guessed. A lot of play with the features, the angles and the lighting. The desk was sparse and modern, and just a thin-framed but ergonomic chair in front of it. Two wireless speakers and a virtual keyboard/mouse built into the desk in front of a pop-up narrow monitor was all he had to work with. And a bookshelf, with just a few of the classics—Mason guessed, for inspiration. Herodotus, Aristotle, Bacon …

Victor set the folder down on the desk as Mason went to the "windows" and gazed out over the sea. He closed his eyes and imagined himself there. How much did Solomon know? Did Gabriel share this too, that he loved these drives along the coast, and recalled the picnics with the family not far from this very spot?

"It's all there," Victor said monotonously, pointing to a file folder. "First page has your passwords and credentials. All self-explanatory, but if you need anything, communication link through the desktop. Dial zero."

"And ask for room service, I got it." Mason turned, and his smile faded again as he saw Victor's unyielding expression.

"The rest," the big man added, "you'll figure out. Just get up to speed. There's a teleconference meeting at eleven. Be ready."

"Where is it?"

"I'll come get you."

With that, and the unspoken command that he wasn't expected to leave this office until then, Victor was gone.

Leaving Mason to think for a moment and consider his surroundings, his new gig. It felt suddenly lonely, and he almost called out to have him stay another moment. Ask some more mindless questions, but the door slammed and he was left with the gulls and the sea.

And his folder.

After a sigh, he sat down and got to work.

Two hours and two cups of some sort of proprietary Black Forest coffee later, his head spun with caffeine, Advil and more figures and readings about the Midwest barometric conditions for a time period over forty years ago than he could ever care about. But it was about that time—thirty minutes to go until Victor came for him—that Mason started feeling like he was either being used, or punished. Or maybe he had been given the wrong folder.

There had been a piece of paper in there, different from the others. A blue sheet with a single name on it and a date. Almost as if it had been casually slipped in at the end, as if someone wanted him to read it and look into it, but wanted no one to know where it came from. Mason thought to ask Victor about it, if it was perhaps his first assignment or something, but then he thought maybe that was all part of the informal way they did things around here. A bit like a game, a scavenger hunt.

Or his first test.

In any case, he looked again at the scrolling data on his screen, at all the meteorological data collected from the regional and local weather offices from the time. Cross-referenced, with forecasts overlaid onto each other versus the actual results.

Feeling like an intern, he scrolled through other reports, flipped on satellite imagery, watched the time-stamped Doppler readings from a variety of sources. *Rookie league stuff*, he thought, not having any clue what they expected of him right now, other than maybe boredom. A lull before the storm?

But then he saw it. Or rather, the map showed it once he took leaned back and saw the larger picture. All the anomalous readings superimposed, regardless of the time …

"Holy shit."

In two minutes he entered the Star Chamber, and gave a quick look around, making sure Victor wasn't lurking anywhere, then he went right for the first empty station on the left side of the great sphere. Beside a blonde with straight hair down her back, Mason took a seat.

"May I—?"

The girl smiled broadly at him. "Mr. Grier! Sure, have a seat, how are you?"

"Annabelle, so good to find you here." Mason set his folder down beside the keyboard, then nervously crossed his arms. "Um, how's everything? Did you go on that trip with Gabriel?"

She blushed, turning even redder. "Yes," but she quickly added: "A bunch of us went."

"The Caribbean, right?"

"Yeah, just sailing. It was nice."

"I thought it was work-related. Some research?"

Annabelle shrugged. "Always is with Gabriel, but I enjoyed myself. Not too much, mind you but … oh! Is that the first day folder?"

Mason followed her look to the folder. He frowned at her. "Yeah, you got one too?"

She nodded. "Remember it like yesterday."

Tapping his fingers on the folder, he thought for a moment. "Tell me, did you get something … different in yours? Like a test?"

"Oh we all get a little something personal from Solomon, so I wouldn't be surprised. Kind of like an individual welcome."

"Okay. So—did you figure yours out?"

She slowly shook her head, frowning. "No, I don't think it was that kind of thing. More like a bit of poetry and just some help with my totem."

"Oh right, the totem. I think I need one."

"No rush. It'll come to you, I'm sure."

"Yeah." Mason turned and commandeered the station, finding the screen it controlled and calling up the historical meteorological database. "Going to check something. I want to see it on the larger screen, and with more resources." He glanced around again. "Just making sure I have time."

"All right then, let's see what you can do," said Annabelle, checking the series of clocks on the wall, showing various times around the world.

He moved fast, entering the data, separating the variables, isolating the conditions and the dates and setting the maps, superimposing, and then expanding the view. He stood up, hands on his hips, observing.

Annabelle coughed nervously. "So … this was in your folder?"

Mason nodded, beginning to wonder again if this was some kind of prank. "There ... four tornadoes appeared in a single hour at this site in Kansas in 1980." He thought for a moment. "Most cyclones, in the Midwest especially, travel in unpredictable paths, but afterwards, given the data on wind speed, pressure and other factors, you can at least verify their prior trajectories. But these ... they each head steadily from different directions, toward a center location. And then they stop. They swirl and generate massive amounts of torque and energy, and then stand still and finally, after a dramatic pause ... they fizzle out...." He took a stylus and drew on the terminal screen, watching its counterpart appear on the larger screen.

By now, others were taking note. Stopping what they were doing, looking up at the demonstration.

"When I put them on the map all at once, using their last locations as markers ..."

"They make a perfect circle," Annabelle said, leaning back, arms crossed over her chest.

"And if that's not enough," Mason pointed out, "there are other anomalous readings all generated around or in this same city in northeast Kansas in the years before this event. I checked back in my office, just to gather some historical data for perspective." He licked his lips as he projected these one-time forecast event misses in blue on the screen. "I checked, because the data wasn't in the folder and not part of this research, but for the same period, for different cities in the state or neighboring states, the misses were either very minor, or were so random as to be meaningless."

Annabelle led him with a question. "So what's so special about that town?"

"Not the town," Mason said, looking again at the map. "Montgomery, population thirteen thousand four hundred, isn't the target. We can go further and narrow it down."

"Really?"

"Really. If the events make up a perfect circle, then geographically, there's a center point to that circle. Which in this case, logic would suggest, would be of interest to us if for no other reason than curiosity as to how something so random could create a nonrandom formation."

Annabelle leaned in. "Let me help you there." She clicked on her own terminal and called up the satellite Google Earth map of Montgomery, Kansas, then merged Mason's data over it, enhanced the view and then bisected the circle two ways, finding the center of the crossing lines.

"What's that?" Mason said, squinting. "Can you enlarge it?"

"Yeah. There you go."

A forested region, a few power lines and a small lake, but zooming in again … And between the trees … a lone house.

"Why are we looking at a farm in the middle of nowhere? Why is that the center of all this meteorological mayhem?"

Annabelle shrugged. "When was all this data?"

"1980."

"So there's you're next step," Annabelle said. "I can't help you anymore, but …" She pointed to the screen. "If it were me, I'd find out who lived there at that time. Find out if they're still around, talk to them, and then you might have the beginning of an answer."

Mason frowned, wondering for the moment if maybe she was in on the test—this prank or whatever this was that they wanted him to know about. "What would it matter who lived there? And what do you mean, the beginning of an answer?"

So cryptic, he thought and was sure that next she was going to ask if he wanted to take the red pill or the blue pill. To have his mind blown or to go back to his cube and live in ignorance.

Annabelle just smiled, and then her smile evaporated and she quickly tapped a key to clear the screen and revert it back to current weather data.

Mason spun around just in time to find Victor striding for him, a scowl on his face.

"Hey there," Mason said, preempting any nastiness. "Been waiting for you." He picked up the folder. "Almost done with this, so I was taking a break and hoped to get an early start up to the meeting."

Victor gave him a hard look, then glanced at Annabelle and back to him. "Well then. Come, they're ready for you."

CHAPTER 17

Everyone, please welcome our newest recruit, Mason Grier. Meteorologist extraordinaire, and someone sure to be a tremendous asset to our team."

Mason acknowledged Solomon's voice but took a second to allow his eyes to accustom to the dark interior of the Conference Room labeled as Sigil 1. He had expected a long table, cushy leather chairs and speakerphones, ports for laptop access, and maybe a screen for teleconferencing.

Instead, he found himself in a forest. A virtual forest, he thought at first, but then realized there was no hard floor, but soft earth. Mossy stones and twigs. *Full trees mixed with holographic projections or just wall visuals again?* He had no idea where reality ended and the illusion began. He looked up, and the ceiling—if there was one—was perfectly hidden in the mirage of foliage, darting birds, an owl and great tree trunks arching high overhead into a pock-marked clearing through which soft sunlight filtered peacefully.

Magnificent, was his only thought, and he was about to say so when he realized he wasn't alone. Ten other men and women stood in a circle around him. It was then he realized some of the other members must be projections as well, since they were behind him, where the wall should have been blocking them. And in fact, as Victor closed the door, the seams vanished and the forest expanded at his back.

He was truly in the woods, and abruptly he felt as if he'd been caught in a fairy tale world without breadcrumbs or any other means of backtracking or getting out before he was cooked. Glancing around, he shrugged off the feeling and just spoke, feeling quite out of his element. "Hello everyone. I haven't gotten tired of saying this yet, but I'm glad to be here."

Solomon stepped into the circle, opposite Mason. He wore a gray suit with an open collar silk blue shirt and no tie. "Mason and Gabriel survived a nasty little accident while in New York, and we're all happy they've made a full recovery."

The others murmured to themselves as they nodded. A woman to Mason's left reached over and patted his shoulder. She at least, was real. Some of the others ... if he looked hard enough at them ... he could see the ferns and bushes through their outlines. Even Solomon.

"This," Mason said glancing around, "is incredible."

Solomon smiled with the compliment. "Not exactly an OSHA-approved workplace, but it's one of our own little nature sanctuaries. If we have to be inside, we can at least let the outdoors in through whatever means necessary."

Mason checked out the other faces. "So how many of us are really here? I honestly can't tell."

Four hands raised in the air, faces smiling.

"The rest," Solomon said, "myself included, are at various offsite locations. As you might have heard, I'm headed to Zurich, which I don't expect will be a long visit. Not even time to do a ski run, but I will haul ass through the Alps." He grinned and everyone chuckled. Apparently, Solomon enjoyed his fast cars when a limo driver wasn't around. Mason wondered if the Solstice lawyers knew about that for insurance purposes. He wondered suddenly about a lot of incidental things, like its balance sheet, debt ratios and for that matter—clients, revenue history and earnings projections. *Probably should have checked into all that before joining for idealistic reasons.*

But Shelby wasn't some idealistic notion. She was a flesh and blood miracle. If that kind of cure could be made commercially available … To say nothing of the potential that enhanced weather forecasting could entail, the financial prospects were staggering. With his options, and if everything went even half as well as he thought they could, he and Lauren could be looking at a cozy retirement very soon.

Solomon cleared his throat and produced a curious staff from the forested shade behind him in the virtual glen. He set some of his weight on it, glanced around the chamber at the other members, then settled on Mason. "The meeting is almost complete. Sorry, Mason, you didn't need to be here for the earlier sections. We reviewed financials and the regional directors gave their weekly updates on status of various projects and long term goals."

Would have liked to hear those, Mason thought. *Maybe there's a transcript.*

"Now, on to the more pressing matter. You are going to Oklahoma."

Mason blinked at him. "Where? I'm sorry, you're going to Switzerland and I get shipped to Oklahoma?"

Solomon nodded. He lifted his staff and pointed at a space over his left shoulder. A rectangular view screen appeared in the virtual canopy, calling up a map of the state, then zeroing in on one small city, where red text appeared with the label: *Lawton: Population 96,545.*

"Sorry, why there?"

"Lawton has been in the middle of a severe drought for weeks. Last precipitation was October fourteenth at one-eighth of an inch. Current forecast …" He tapped something in the air with his staff, and the Doppler map appeared, showing nothing but clear air for everything north and west for the next ten days. "As you can see, no relief in sight."

"So why send me there? To comment on the severity of situation? I'm sorry but I don't think this is one case you can pin on corporate America and man-made global warming. Droughts have existed in this area way before Henry Ford even designed his Model T."

"Granted," Solomon said, sweeping across the air with the staff and wiping the image away. "But it will make as grand a stage for our point as we can hope for. A perfect realization of a desperate town and a desperate people, a snapshot of Americans suffering."

Mason thought about it. "And you as the potential saviors?"

"Us. And yes, but only if they give us a chance."

Frowning, Mason fidgeted, distracted by all the forest stimuli: hearing in the lull the scurrying sounds in the brush, the breeze rustling the vines, acorns falling, a cicada singing a lonely song. "I'm sorry, I'll go of course, but I just don't see what I'm going to accomplish. You could just release a professionally-done documentary or something like that to support your capabilities, and …"

"No, having our man at the scene, bringing home the point, will be far more powerful. Trust me. We'll send you along with some talking points, and you'll chat with the mayor and some farmers and get impressive pictures for the papers and the blog sites."

Mason shrugged again. "All right, but it would be better if you could—I don't know—do that rain-making trick like up on the roof?" He thought again about that, the suddenness and the certainty that it was impossible, and nothing short of magic. In hindsight, he felt like he should have paid more attention. Like a spectator at an impressive carnival show, he'd been looking in the wrong direction while the magician made the true effect happen somewhere else.

Along with several others, Solomon gave a chuckle. "Would that were possible, Mason."

"It's not out of the realm," Mason countered, still thinking about the rainstorm. "Of all the crackpot weather modification theories out there, cloud seeding is one that actually has some merit, yielding positive results. Silver iodine, dry ice and even liquid propane, dispersed into the cloud cover by jets has had some success, although opinions vary greatly still as to the results. Ski resorts have had the best success at producing more snow when needed. And used for hail suppression, seeding especially has seen practical applications, but in situations like this …" he pointed in the area where the map of Lawton had been. "It's nearly impossible, as with no clouds at all, you have nothing to work with."

"Sadly true," Solomon replied. "Which is why we don't bother with such attempts or technology. It's got such a bad rap as it is, what with Geneva conventions and UN treaties and concerns over microwave applications like the HAARP facility, or the fact that the U.S. government engaged in this business during Vietnam, attempting to lengthen the monsoon season to impair the enemy...." Solomon's eyes glazed over as if in momentary respect, then blinked and he smiled again. "No, that's not what we're about, and such minor parlor tricks—such *Connecticut Yankee* effects as you said earlier—would not help our purposes here."

Mason carefully studied Solomon, or at least his image, stately and modern all at once; he looked more like an eccentric nightclub owner than a CEO, but at the same time, he seemed colder and more calculating. And definitely hiding something.

A flash of light stabbed behind Mason's eyes. Sudden and intense like a migraine pain, and for an instant he saw that staff again, except now it wasn't Solomon's hand that grasped it. *An older hand, wrinkled but firm. And a man seated at a long wooden table in a charming cottage-like room. Shadowy others were seated around him, except ... they were encased in blocks of ice. Faces, barely visible, eyes wracked with frozen pain, mouths open in endlessly soundless screams.*

He blinked and it was gone. Focus returned, and he saw that some of the others were fading out, their avatars fizzling away into dust. Just Solomon and the four locals remained. The door at Mason's back opened and Victor was silhouetted in the painful artificial light.

"Time now," Solomon said. "Victor will handle all your travel needs."

"Can I stop home first?" Mason asked. "Pick up a change of clothes, maybe? I hadn't planned on being in front of the public."

"Of course. Say hi to your lovely wife for me, and tell her you'll be home soon."

Mason was about to say something when the image swirled and faded. The four others promptly left and he was alone in the woods, alone in the shifting sunlight and the gentle woods.

He felt a strong pull towards calm and peace, but he was never more sure that Solomon was wrong, and that after Oklahoma everything would change and he wouldn't be seeing Lauren for some time.

Chapter 18

Eight hours later, Mason arrived in Lawton City to an unseasonal seventy-seven degrees, brutal sun and an acrid dryness in the air that at once irritated his throat and had him reaching for a pack of gum. He donned sunglasses on the runway and surveyed flat landscape, the parched earth and the hardened crystalline blue sky that seared the view all the way north to the hazy ascent of the Wichita Mountains.

Victor, ever the conversationalist, wordlessly led Mason to a waiting car that took them to the main strip, a quaint section past the town hall where he would be setting up to broadcast in a few hours. But first, they stopped at a local diner with a sign: FLAMINGO'S, HOME OF THE TORNADO ALLEY $2.99 SPECIAL.

"Make yourself at home," Victor said, pointing to the one open booth, complete with '60s blue plastic seats and a faux juke box condiment container. "Eat something. We've got two hours."

"Not joining me?" Mason asked, hoping the answer was in the negative.

Victor shook his head. "I'm heading right back, needed at Solstice. You're flying commercial, 9:00 PM return flight from Oklahoma city."

"Not much time to enjoy the scenery," Mason said sarcastically, before the incoming waitress could hear. He looked out past the departing Victor as the rush of heat came in through the open door, and he almost expected a tumbleweed to lazily roll by and complete the scene.

He shrugged, placed his order for an egg white omelet, then decided to ruin the health benefits by adding on the meat lovers' sausage, bacon and ham side, along with rye toast and strawberry jam. And of course, bottomless coffee.

Apparently the tornado alley special had just expired at 11:00 AM. He'd have to come back another day. Meanwhile, he dug into his bag and retrieved his laptop and the folder he had been provided on arriving at Lawton City. He had already reviewed the materials on the plane, and felt like he could sleepwalk through this presentation.

Instead, he reached back in the bag and pulled out a flatter FedEx package.

From Shelby. From London. Mailed the day before she had arrived.

The package she told me not to open.

He pulled off the strip and reached inside as his first cup of coffee came to the table. Inside the package were two things: a clear plastic folder encasing a document entitled: *The True Story of Anglesey and the Massacre of the Welsh Druids, by Shelby Grier.*

Her thesis, what she'd been working on so enthusiastically at school this past year.

But why didn't she want me to see it?

The second item was a small thumb drive. No label and nothing on it. While his laptop was still warming up, Mason decided to start with a glimpse through the document first, although he didn't expect it would occupy too much time, not with his current priorities. He'd just give it a skim, enough to be able to compliment Shelby on her project and have something else to speak to her about, sure that she'd be okay with him reading it against her wishes after the fact. Besides, it sounded interesting at least.

He opened to the first page and began to skim it over, but soon found himself more and more engrossed, lost in history.

CHAPTER 19

Three blocks away, at the Eldorado Motel, in room 23, Gabriel came out of the shower wrapped in a towel around his waist. Despite what he had just done, he now felt completely washed clean in more ways than one. Purified, mind and body.

He had arrived with the advance team last night. Like the others, he had made promises of a night to purify his thoughts and focus on the task at hand. Well, purification took many forms, and he had spent his time focusing his thoughts at the local tavern where he met this gem of a native specimen working behind the bar. By closing time, after the right mix of charming wit, incantations and a slight pinch of various ingredients into her drink, she was his.

A sacrifice has been needed, and although not entirely in her right mind, she had been more than willing. And this bed had served as the altar.

He quickly got dressed as he admired his handiwork and the beauty of girl, more so now that her soul was no longer tethered to her flesh. A certain calm had settled over her features, her hands clasped together over the bloody wound above her heart. Quite a mess on the mattress and sheets, but there was a solution for that, and no need for concern.

On his way out, he tapped the tip of his staff against the door three times. He heard a whoosh and a pop from inside. He turned, and with a spring in his step, headed toward the waiting car where he could see Victor inside.

He closed the car door and sat back with a long sigh.

"All set, sir?"

"Done and done," Gabriel replied, rubbing his lips, still tasting her exquisite perfume. He closed his eyes and confirmed what he expected, seeing into room 23 through the dead girl's eyes … the flames starting to spread up the inside of the door, to the ceiling, leaping wildly to the curtains and vaulting to the floor.…

Chapter 20

early two hours later, Mason finally looked up from the last page of the report. The only pages he wound up skimming were the bibliography and footnote sections at the end, already more than firmly convinced of her scholarly expertise by that point. But what had intrigued him the most was her ability to theorize and to fill in gaps in the agreeably scant and competing historical sources.

His mind was still spinning with fact and dates, with names of Roman generals and lieutenants, of British sites and ancient towns, geography and conditions, battle strategies and troop movements, political schemes and cultural beliefs. It was a time period he had known precious little about, a complicated era of Roman expansion that he had been all too happy to leave behind in the halls of high school history. But Shelby had fastened onto this era with relentless focus and enthusiasm, digging her teeth into all the material and shaking it for every drop of value.

She had focused on the Romans' relentless drive to stamp out the local druids, a mysterious group of mostly Welsh practitioners of magical arts. They were a sect at once feared and loved by the

Britons, and they moved among them with impunity, helping in cases and controlling in others. They had no written history, and as such, the legends about them sprang up through stories and oral history, and from classical writers of the time. Often competing, these sources were rarely backed up by anything other than simple myth and anecdote. They were compared to the priesthoods of antiquity, the Indian Brahmins, the Pythagoreans and the Chaldean astronomers of Babylon. Julius Caesar wrote that they "know much about the stars and celestial motions, and about the size of the earth and universe, and about the essential nature of things, and about the powers and authority of the immortal gods; and these things they teach to their pupils."

Druids were attributed great powers: the ability to control nature especially, conjuring storms. They were able to direct the weather, causing rain or drought, fog and wind. They could turn day into night and cause blinding snowstorms to confound invading forces. There were stories of enemy troops besieged by wild animals at the command of just one or two of these hooded magicians, and equally unlikely tales that druids were capable of shape-shifting into animal form. They could glamour susceptible people into forgetfulness or charm them into falling in love. They could turn forests into armies and could induce (possibly through suggestive hypnosis) audible and visual hallucinations, making enemies believe they were surrounded by superior forces or eldritch adversaries.

However, despite all these powers, they were apparently still no match for the might of Rome. Starting in 43 AD, Claudius invaded Britain, and with successive incursions, the loose confederation of tribal areas fell to his legions—and those of his successors. But conquering a people and ruling them were different things altogether. Rebellions persisted, and certain areas further north still evaded Roman control. Throughout occupation, rumors of these druids stalking the Romans and stirring up trouble, rallying the local tribes, caused Rome no end of trouble. In 60 AD, Gaius Suetonius Paulinus was given the singular mission to stamp them out once and for all, and acting on information that the seat of druidic power was the Welsh island of Anglesey off the Northeast coast, he set off with ten thousand troops and began construction of narrow boats for the invasion.

It was here that Shelby's treatise diverged from the more established history—which was colorful enough already. A few eyewitness accounts, plus the histories of Claudius, describe the next events. But as Shelby pointed out, this "history" should be rightly viewed through a lens of bias ... as something written by the victors—or in this case, by the only side that kept a written history. Claudius relates a bizarre confrontation that occurred before the ultimate massacre on the island. The boats landed on the shore and the Romans found several thousand men and women waiting for them. Most were unarmed, just standing and chanting. Among them moved a few women in black robes, carrying staves and torches, singing and humming and calling down magical forces in tongues that couldn't be translated. A Roman soldier recounted how his legion was struck with fear, overcome with the urge to flee before the surging waters could sweep them away. The trees and the brush and even the stones themselves rallied to stand in the way of the invaders. But somehow the tide was turned, the spell broken and Suetonius rallied his men into action. They stormed ahead and slaughtered everyone in their path, sparing none. Dispensing with superstition, they burned the sacred groves, shattered the altars and demolished the standing stones, laying waste to all the sources of claimed druidic power, hoping this would in fact end the control of the troublesome magicians.

Against this backdrop of blood, slaughter and fire, Shelby had found many inconsistencies. But primarily she had turned her focus to the one especially thorny aspect of reported druid behavior that had the Romans in a genocidal fury ... that of human sacrifice. Rome had long since given up the practice of sacrificing humans to the gods, and couldn't stomach it in any of their occupied lands. Finding that these lawless druids still engaged in the practice gave the invaders further impetus to stamp them out. However, as Shelby pointed out, the human sacrifice the druids practiced was of a different slant. Instead of one comprised of torture and pain upon an unwilling subject, it often took the form of a volunteer granting the use of his or her body. A martyr situation almost, for the greater good of the tribe or the grove. In some cases, it was undertaken just to right the imbalances in nature and cause a shift in weather or seasonal change. The body, housing the magical carcass of the soul, needed to be voluntarily rent open to release the powerful energy within, which could then fuel the change in the spiritual realm that controlled nature and the world.

So with that notion in the foreground, Shelby looked at the Massacre at Menai, as it was called, in a different light. By accounts, these druids were nearly clairvoyant, knowing everything that happened in their realms. That they could be blind and deaf to the movement of ten thousand troops against their most sacred center was beyond logic. That they would not be ready for a fight, with no weapons at the ready, with no means or intention even, of defense? Perhaps, Shelby reasoned, there was another explanation.

The solution, she extrapolated, had something to do with what happened next—or almost simultaneously back on the eastern side of the mainland. While Roman forces were focused on Anglesey, and the general and his top aides had pulled away from the occupied lands, rebellion struck. History doesn't make such a direct connection, instead calling out other unaligned factors, but in any case, almost simultaneously with the massacre, the British queen Boudicca, in a move later immortalizing her as a symbol of national pride as well as putting her in epic Joan of Arc fame, massed an army and attacked the unsuspecting Roman legion guarding her city. With particular zeal and ruthlessness, her troops massacred five thousand men in an hour, and with the taste of blood in their veins, they continued on the march, moving on to Camulodunum and then on to Londinium (modern day London), sacking and burning the city, and then tearing through the Ninth Spanish Legion and doing the same to Verulamium (St. Albans). All told she destroyed some 80,000 Roman troops before Suetonius could rally his men, wait for reinforcements and then counterattack. Eventually he broke her resistance and with superior training and discipline, destroyed her army on the plains of the West Midlands. She would commit suicide before capture, but the damage had been done. Rome was left severely weakened, and Suetonius himself was recalled in disgrace shortly afterwards.

Shelby's theory then, dealt with the sacrifice at Anglesey, for surely that was what it was. A willing sacrifice, one that could be seen in just such a military-strategic light: pulling an army's strength away and allowing its weaker remnants to be picked apart. But that wasn't all, Shelby insisted. There was a larger spiritual goal in mind, a cleansing perhaps of the land, one that was intended to right the balance and restore natural order. What's more, the true incendiary claim in her paper was that the sacrifice—or the massacre—call it whatever you liked, wasn't anywhere near what the history books (written by the Romans) tell us. For what was reported? A large force, unarmed, waiting for Suetonius. And moving among the crowd were hooded females, stirring up the air and the very atmosphere with song and fire and incantations.

These were surely the druids, Shelby argued. Maybe a handful of them, ten or twelve at the most. But those others? The ragtag "army" that chose to come and help out—without any weapons? Were they likewise druids? Unlikely. And if not druids, who? Again, not warriors, but just … people. Unarmed people that disturbed and frightened the overmatched Roman legions to the point of terror? This is where Shelby reminded the reader of the supposed powers of these druids. The ability to make the forest and the stones appear as men, to get into the heads of invaders and cause them to see that which wasn't there.

Was the invasion of Anglesey a massacre of thousands of unarmed men and women? Or was it the sacrifice of only a dozen highly skilled druids who confidently gave their lives in a strategic ploy and magical gambit that would ultimately break down the invaders' forces? Shelby went on to describe the most damning evidence in support of her theory—that archaeological digs on the island failed to find bones in quantities demanded by such a massacre. Nothing even close.

Mason closed the document and sat back, looking at his untouched plate of high calorie food. His mind spun, both with admiration of his daughter's work, and with the coherent argument it made for a fascinating second look at history.

He turned his attention to the thumb drive, then looked at his watch. He had ten minutes, but they might be coming for him sooner. After inserting the thumb drive into the USB port, he waited, sipped at some lukewarm coffee and then sighed. The screen popped up asking for a password.

Frowning, he almost reached for his phone to call Shelby and ask about it, but then remembered that it was getting late over there and he better wait. Plus, he wasn't supposed to have opened this. Still, he couldn't imagine why she didn't want him to read her paper. It was amazing work, really, and nothing to be concerned about. It would have been a great conversational piece for them. And Lauren! She loved history, and would eat this stuff up. She'd be so proud of Shelby, and Mason could see the two of them talking about the research all night long. Even his old boss Pamela would love this, and use it as further support in her possible hiring of Shelby down the road (if Solstice didn't work out).

But all that would have to wait, as would whatever else was on the thumb drive. Was that what she didn't want him to see?

He removed the thumb drive and put it in his pocket. That could all wait. Now it was time to work.

The news crew had arrived.

CHAPTER 21

The broadcast started as he'd expected. Everything by the numbers. He was professional, enthusiastic and confident, yet somber as he discussed the plight of the farmers and the rationing of water for the residents. Four elderly people had died from dehydration, and the local economy had lost tens of millions. The situation was past dire, and there was no relief in sight.

He spoke with his back to the west, the mountains on his left. Halfway through, the mayor came to his side and spoke about the town's resilience and the conservation efforts so far, and expressed his thanks for the support of church groups and the power of prayer.

On that note, Mason was left to offer the sobering scientific alternative: that short of divine interference, Lawton City residents were in for another week at least of misery. He discussed the air flows, the prevailing winds taking clouds and precipitation systems in a strong dip north and then arcing around Iowa and Indiana, blessing them with an abundance of rain in their time of need but ignoring Oklahoma like a spurned lover.

It was about this time, with only a few minutes left in the broadcast that Mason's confidence faltered. He noticed a change in the direction of the cameras that had been securely fixed on him until now, and a general muttering among the crowd. A few people pointed in a direction over his shoulder.

Trying to stay professional, Mason kept talking, resisting the urge to glance that way, but then he sensed it too. First in his sinuses, always able to tell a change in the pressure. Then his skin tingled and his hair moved in rising breeze, cooling his scalp. Finally, he saw the landscape darken and people in the crowd took off their sunglasses, no longer squinting against a sun that had fled against a dark, imposing force.

Mason stopped for a breath and turned his head just slightly, then all the way. His shoulders tensed and he had to stop himself, remembering the open microphone before he swore. But maybe that was what they were hoping for—a reaction to go with the unbelievable sight, as if another mountain range, black as onyx and roiling in flux, vaulted over the Wichita range, tumbled and picked up steam. It fired off jagged lightning in wild directions, rolling, twisting and churning toward him, consuming the blue skies and devouring the light.

Later, photos and video images plastered over the web would call to mind comparisons between Mason and the lone resistance member standing up to the tank in Tiananmen Square; but if asked to answer truthfully, Mason would have had to admit his apparent bravery was more a product of profound disbelief and incredulity than any shred of courage. And when the advanced scouts of pealing thunder scattered the crowd, and the mayor rushed to safety inside a nearby bank while others raced to their cars and fled in the opposite direction, Mason stood his ground.

He stayed motionless even as lightning pounded in successively closer surges and the sky exploded, unleashing a near flood upon the land as if opening up under and airborne sea. Mason wavered only with the gusting of the winds that tore his earpiece away and flung his microphone into the sky. He blinked against the onslaught of rain and wind and held up his hands before his face, trying to make out the darker form that seemed to stride, giant-like, amidst the storm, birthed by its dark-bellied, incendiary mother.

A blacker cylindrical mass at its apex, narrowing slightly at the base, with wind speed … *impossible to tell*, Mason thought, even in the best of conditions, but he estimated it to be an F2 Class, maybe surging to F3.

He hadn't been this close to a tornado….

Not since childhood when one had just missed him, and instead ripped away his parents from the same house while he lay in his own bed.

For an instant, time slowed and stopped and the rain split and the world flickered into the calming illumination of a bedroom nightlight—just enough to see the monstrous entity in all its malevolent glory—giving him time to wonder if this perhaps, wasn't the self-same demon that had visited him all those years ago, come now to finish the job.

Mason almost laughed in a mixture of giddy acceptance and absolute terror. Whatever it was, this fate of his, he was resigned to it. Weather had followed him, kept pace with his life, destroying his loves along the way.

He spread his arms, lowered his head and accepted this end, a fitting resolution to his existence. If only he had more time with Shelby, and with Lauren. His only regret. That one thought hung in his heart as he raised his hands. Water pooling off his face, streaming like countless tears, he clenched his fists as the cyclonic juggernaut bounded and spun and roared its fury down upon him—

And then it suddenly ground to a halt. Later, Mason would be sure it staggered as if struck, and its winds dropped a notch and almost seemed to battle a countering force that tried to reverse its spin. Struggling against itself, it trembled, shook and then absolutely ripped itself apart. It scattered right in front of Mason, with huge tendrils flung in every direction and sucked up back into the churning sky, to the clouds that kept rolling and unleashing watery bounty from above.

One last powerful gust of wind and Mason spun around to face a lone cameraman huddled on his knees, the camera shaking, but still pointing at Mason. The rest of the street was deserted, and the town itself, stretched out as far as he could see, languished in its violent but desperately needed deluge as the streets ran like overflowing rivers and the land drank and drank.

Chapter 22

At the five-thousand foot elevation mark, in a clearing overlooking the city far in the distance, Gabriel set down his staff and leaned against the ancient rock. A standing stone, chiseled by the Mojave Indians and decorated with petroglyphs, it more than served its purpose. He pulled back his hood and breathed in the fresh zingy scent of ozone lingering in the wake of the storm.

He watched his work, proudly observing the devastating thing of beauty as it sat and spun and lingered, beset by polarizing atmospheric air masses, like shepherd dogs keeping it penned up for just a bit longer.

Six others emerged from behind their hoods and around the stones, leaning on their staves, breathing heavily, but full of smiles. All except for Annabelle, who gave him a dark, sour look. "Was that necessary? Your father ..."

Gabriel held up a hand and closed his eyes, re-establishing the connection to the distant speck trailing the storm.

A hawk. Magnificent creature, it soared high, wings spread to the extreme and beating fiercely to maintain position. It sent its perfect vision down to the main street in front of the bank, where Mason, drenched, was helping the cameraman to his feet and surveying the near-monsoon blanketing Lawton City.

Gabriel blinked and returned to his own eyes. "He's fine."

"But that was too close!" She snapped, and her voice held something darker, more accusatory. *Did she know?* The motel, the girl? Gabriel shrugged. Possibly, but it wasn't her right to speak, or to accuse. He was the master here, and he made the decisions, including selecting and preparing the sacrifice. And as for his father …

"My dad … Mason … he can handle himself. As we just saw."

"It was close, brother," said another. "Solomon does not want him dead. Not yet."

Gabriel shrugged again. "Like I said, I knew he could handle himself. He should have run like everyone else. That's what I figured, but instead …" A touch of bitterness seeped into his voice. "Well, he'll look like a hero again."

"Maybe after," said Annabelle, "he gets over looking like an idiot for missing the forecast."

Smiling even broader, Gabriel twirled his staff like a vaudeville showman. "And that will be a sight to see. Let's get back and watch it all unfold. All the same, I wouldn't like to be him right now."

CHAPTER 23

Four hours later, the last sprinkles departed and the clouds shook loose their hold over the city just in time to reveal a beautiful full sky rainbow. The cooler air ushered in the scent of potpourri, stirred up vegetation from the storm's aftermath. Kids played with rejuvenated joy, jumping in puddles and splashing each other; and adults took to the streets in celebration of the refreshing breeze as plants, crops and trees were all dripping in the midday glare.

Mason, however, saw none of this. He was twenty-eight miles north of Lawton, at a highway rest stop with Wi-Fi, sipping hot coffee and glad for the respite from the media circus back there where he was the butt of all jokes. He had done his best to spin what had happened the only way he could. He brought up, without any of the typical confidence or tenacity in his voice, the precarious personality of Nature and the irony of how weather sometimes turns on a dime and provides miraculous relief as often as it does bitter agony.

That was all prelude though, to the main event, which Mason knew was coming. Knew without a doubt even before he could finish the first round of questions from the makeshift newsroom in the bank vault. Away from the pounding thunder and blasting lightning strikes, where the generators fueled the cameras and lights and sent the broadcasts out to the major networks to be cast out in a wider net, he knew it was coming.

The news, of course, offered by Avery Solomon himself: that Solstice had indeed predicted this massive storm. Predicted it over two weeks earlier. Nailed it down to the day, the hour, and almost the exact minute of its actual appearance.

The mayor himself had a sealed delivery from that date, one he had disregarded as nonsense from a likely speculator. Their forecast had been ignored like those prognostications from snake oil charlatans or rain dancers of old. But now, after this—he had sent his aide to fetch the package, and to get a Solstice representative on the phone (little realizing Mason's new career location).

The news stations caught wind of it, and that was that.

Focus shifted immediately away from Lawton, much to the mayor's dismay having lost his fifteen minutes of fame. From that point on, all anyone cared about or saw, all that was on every station, was Solomon's stoically confident expression as he greeted the media frenzy head-on. It was as if he'd been waiting his whole life for this chance to show off his special toys.

Still stinging from the onslaught of shame and his near-death experience at the foot of an F3 Class tornado that had somehow— and he still couldn't understand it—collapsed just as it should have geared up for more violence, Mason took the chance and got the hell out of Lawton.

He knew he should have just holed up in a dark tavern some- where and waited for his plane, or he should have just caught another one and charged it back to Solstice, but right now all he wanted was to put as much distance between himself and the fiasco back at Lawton.

He rented a car and drove north, and it wasn't until he saw signs for the Kansas border that he hit upon an idea. A way to clear his head, to focus and to change gears. He could sit around wallowing in his mistakes and debating why he had been so used and what it was all for, or he could take control and go in a direction no one would expect.

Kansas.

His discovery from yesterday. The location at the epicenter of those four tornadoes back in 1980. That location ... southeast Kansas. Couldn't be too far.

So in the truck stop, he decided it was time for some more research, time to dig his teeth into the mystery. Especially because he had the sense that he was treading into forbidden territory. Forbidden by the very man who had just made him look like a first class fool. He didn't like being played, and that's what Solomon had done. First on the Solstice rooftop, then again today.

There was Shelby's cure however, and Mason couldn't shake that miracle. Nor could he forget the methods behind it: kidnapping her, threatening him.

You don't get something for nothing. Wasn't that the saying? Mason got the cure he'd always dreamed about, got his daughter whole again, but at what cost? What did they want from him?

I'm going to find out, he thought. One step at a time, *and the first step's in Kansas.*

He stared at the laptop screen over a half-eaten Reuben sandwich, focusing on that Google Map in one corner, highlighting the lone farmhouse, and on the other window ... records of ownership, deeds, property tax information. Anything and everything he could find from public records.

Which wasn't much.

Mason leaned back, tapping his fingers together. What seemed like great real estate basically had been unoccupied and tenant-free for thirty-five years. Bought out by the government in a foreclosure, as near as he could determine, then left to itself ever since.

One name on the deeds prior to 1980, but it didn't help him any. One name, and when he searched on it, found that this individual—or at least someone with the same name, had made his fortune in corn and soybean futures, sold out to the government for a huge fee, and then left for Hollywood. He left behind one hundred acres of land that curiously, and probably much to the government's confusion, never yielded anything again.

This man, the former owner, invested his fortune in movies and made an even larger fortune bankrolling several major hits and studios. As of last week he was the head of three production companies and producer of countless films and documentaries, a media empire magnate.

Mason could follow the trail there, but doubted the answers could be found with an eighty year old man, who by latest reports, hadn't been seen for the past few days and rumors were flying about his whereabouts—and his condition.

No, despite Annabelle's suggestion to contact the previous owner, Mason knew the answer was in the past, not the present. The answer was in Kansas.

He would have to go there. There wasn't time, but he didn't care. This was more important, and he had no desire to show up back at Solstice without any cards in his hand, just an empty deck and a bottle of resentment.

He'd be going back with something, one way or another. Something that he was sure was just over the border, waiting for him in a deserted farmhouse that held a thirty-year-old secret.

He finished his coffee as he stared again at the screen, looking from the blurry satellite photo to the government records. But still, that previous owner.

One name.

Palavar.

Chapter 24

here is he going?" Victor leaned in over the acolyte's shoulder to see the monitor, watching the GPS signal as it crossed over into Kansas.

"Should we tell Solomon?"

Victor stood up, crossing his arms. "Not yet, let's see where he winds up. Although I think I have an idea."

"Shouldn't we call a team and arrange his retrieval?"

"No," Victor said, grim-faced. "If he's headed where I think he is, we're not welcome there."

Chapter 25

Mason turned up the lonely entrance road finally after four attempts to find it had come up empty. There was still an hour of daylight left. *That is,* he thought ruefully, *if my forecast still holds and the world hasn't shifted somehow on its axis.* Nothing was out of the realm of possibility at this point.

Past sickly cornstalks on either side, their brittle arms bent and languishing in the dying sunlight, he drove up a dusty, rock-strewn road, around a corner and then stopped at a chain fence. He got out, stretched and looked out over the land. The farmhouse rose up out of the cornfield a short distance away. The glinting sunset made the windows look like deep, melancholy eyes observing his progress. The very air was brittle and dry as dust, and what little wind there was moved through the corn, making a desolate sound like a ghost crying for the loss of its body. Weeds choked the earth around the stalks and encroached the chain fence that Mason stepped over.

He paused at a sign, rusted and hanging crooked on a post missing one of the screws.

NO TRESPASSING, ORDER #3440255
U.S. DEPT. of AGRICULTURE

Mason took out his cell phone and snapped a picture of the sign. Thought about it for a moment, then Googled the order number and the Department of Agriculture. It came back promptly with a generic link to a governmental webpage that said: UNDER CONSTRUCTION, CHECK BACK LATER.

Shrugging, Mason kept walking. Around the bend, the cornfield ended and gave way to a field of brown crabgrass and other weeds. A few sickly shrubs persisted and Mason wondered if they might have once formed an elegant boundary line, along with an old fence of stones and bricks, collapsed now in places. Further ahead, near the house, rose two aged willow trees.

Weeping willows, Mason thought, would be an accurate description. Weeping and old, having seen sights that surely drove them to grief. A little farther, nearing the trees now and the farmhouse framed between them, Mason turned. He imagined the sight thirty years earlier. Imagined the four tornadoes bearing down on the house, and then pausing, just as that one had done in Lawton.

Was it the same thing, just on a larger scale? Did they just stop, as if hitting a magical dome? Or was it something else? He closed his eyes, and for a second he was there, seeing the monstrous cyclone. Except this time it brought its friends, and it wasn't going to be denied. He could see their wrath. Nowhere to run, no protection. Nowhere to go …

He opened his eyes and looked back to the farmhouse.

Nowhere. But inside.

He climbed the porch steps gingerly, afraid the rotting wood might give way, but it was sturdier than it initially looked. Same for the walls and the windows, and even the roof. Missing shingles, paint peeling, glass cracked, but it was all surprisingly held together well for being in such a long period of disuse. Mason wondered if there had been other unofficial tenants. Squatters or maybe just neighboring kids.

Before trying the door, he looked to his right. There were deep grooves in the deck, as if made by a rocking chair that had seen quite a bit of action. With a rustle of feathers, a scrawny black crow alighted on the ledge beside him and turned its beak so it could fix one pure black eye on him.

It cawed and shook its head. Then it reared up and flew off, back to the willow tree, disappearing behind the leafy canopy.

Mason shrugged. "Nice to meet you too." He tried the door—locked of course. Then went to the nearest window, which was either likewise locked or just sealed up tight. Cupped his hands against the glare filtering now through the willow branches and between the trees. Inside, it was a mess from what he could tell. Dust, furniture covered with tarps, and what looked like a grand piano, likewise covered.

He circled around the house, trying other windows, peering inside, then around the back, where there stood a rusty shed, door padlocked, and a barn farther back that had collapsed on its side. Mason wondered if it had been a casualty of one of the tornado assaults. The fields stretched out in the dying light here, as far as he could see, and the land was pockmarked in places as if massive boulders had dropped from great heights and rolled, flattening whole sections of the land. A weather vane creaked slowly on the roof, bent at an angle, and cast a long shadow of a wolf, snout raised, upon the overrun brown lawn.

Mason tried the back door, which of course was also locked. He looked around and saw some large bricks and decided, why not? But when he descended the stairs to the back lawn and was about to pick up a brick, he noticed a set of rusty doors at an angle rising from the ground.

Basement access.

He brought the brick. Just another rusted lock securing a latch between the doors. Better than breaking a window, he thought as he hefted the brick. On the third try, the brittle clasp separated and split open, and he was in.

Have to move fast, he thought. No lights, no power and only waning daylight through dirt-caked basement windows to light the way. He took the steps quickly, and once in the dank cellar he intended to find the stairs leading up the house, but paused first at the stores of boxes and surprisingly, the collection of toys.

An old yellow tricycle with a silver bell stood in one corner, surrounded by crates full of basketballs, old wooden tennis racquets and baseballs, an old net, horseshoes and a skateboard. He walked around a rocking horse and gently laid a hand on its head, starting its motion. For some reason he lingered, caressing the wooden horse's frazzled mane and looking into its soulful eyes and feeling a sense of familiarity. Just below its head and under the handles, Mason saw something that caught his eye.

Something scrawled there.

With just enough light, he could make it out if he knelt and looked carefully.

The horse kept rocking, and he followed its motion, making out the scrawled letters in a little child's handwriting.

AVERY SOLOMON
Christmas 1979

Chapter 26

Victor waited uncomfortably up at the Summit Grove at the top of Solstice tower. He didn't like sitting, but didn't want to be seen pacing or looking out of place. The breeze was serene, the birds and buzzing bees in perfect harmony with the trees and bushes, the fragrant lotuses and holly, and the view was spectacular. But Victor was on edge, scared. He had failed. Hadn't foreseen that Mason would do anything but wallow in his misery and wait to be picked up. And now he had done the unthinkable. Stumbled onto the one secret Solomon couldn't have anyone unearthing. It was all Victor's fault. Well, not all of it. How had he found out?

Was it Hespera? How deep did her betrayal go? It had to be her; she must have gotten Mason some information before they had found her out. Of course she was working with the opposition. But …

Suddenly Victor realized he wasn't alone. The birds took wing and the bugs silenced their buzzing. The terrace was still, painfully quiet.

A lone blackbird alighted on the wood-carved chair, directly in the shade, glaring at him.

Victor bowed his head and looked at his shoes. He couldn't stop his trembling.

"I am sorry."

When he looked back up, Solomon sat in the chair. Wearing all black, at first he was hard to pick out, with just his head visible and his hands floating in the dark.

"What happened? And speak fast, I am expending considerable energy to be in two places at once."

Victor swallowed hard. This was magic of the highest order, something he could never even contemplate. He preferred to think it might even be a trick, done with holograms, projectors and speakers. Maybe it was so, but he couldn't tell.

"I think it was the rogue. Hespera. We took care of her, but found out too late."

"I rely on you, Victor, not to be late."

"I know. I failed you."

"Where is Mason now?"

"Inside, we believe."

The shadows deepened and Solomon's eyes withdrew. "He must be getting help. I haven't been thorough enough either, it seems. That will be remedied soon. But first, time to bring home our wayward bird."

Victor glanced to the side, averting his eyes. He saw the edge of the roof and worried still if he might be swept over in a sudden angry gust for his incompetence. "What can I do?"

"Go to San Diego General Hospital. Take Gabriel. And wait."

"For what?"

The shadows fluttered with the sound of wings beating, and Solomon leaned forward, his eyes taking on pure blackness.

"For my instructions. And be ready, there may be a strong test waiting for you."

Victor bowed his head. A crow launched into the air and the darkness shifted. When he looked up, he was alone again on the rooftop.

Chapter 27

Upstairs, Mason found more dust, and precious little else on the main floor besides covered furniture—a few couches and a dining room table. The grand piano was in surprisingly good shape, however. Mason lifted an edge by the keys and tapped a few. Certainly out of tune, but he could hear the potential and imagined the music that might have graced this house's past.

He tried to picture the hand that wielded the crayon that wrote Solomon's name on that rocking horse. Was it just coincidence? Mason didn't even entertain the notion. He was given this location, sent here to find out something firsthand about Solstice. Discovering Solomon's name here could not be anything but what it was. He lived here, surely, as a boy. Did that make him a relative? Foster child? True son of this Palavar, one who later changed his name?

That answer would have to wait. The Palavars seemed to have left in a hurry. But the larger question remained. What had happened here? Several years of unusual weather leading up to that four-pronged tornado assault that somehow spared this house. It was like being struck by lightning and surviving. Four times.

Mason tapped out a section of out-of-tune "Chopsticks," then headed for the stairs. The banister was weak, the screws coming loose from the molding. Sticking to the center panels, Mason climbed, noticing faded square sections on the walls where pictures must have been hung. The second floor landing creaked just as Mason saw a figure standing to his right, coming out of the shadows.

He launched himself to the side and slammed against a wall, then scampered back until he realized no one was coming after him. Just a sheet over something. He got up slowly, feeling ridiculous, like Shaggy jumping at shadows in a Scooby-Doo cartoon. Lifted the sheet and saw a beautiful grandfather clock underneath. Ornate numbers and a gold leaf plated face.

They left that too, he thought. What *did* they take? Or did they think they were coming back someday? As he moved farther down the hall and the soft light dimmed and the gloom deepened, he thought about Solstice and wondered if they were looking for him now back at Lawton. And for a moment, he thought of something more disturbing. *Why hadn't they called?* That would have been the normal thing to do, find out where he was and why he wasn't at the runway.

They would have called. Unless they already knew he wasn't there.

Unless they knew he was here.

He took out his phone and looked at it. GPS tracking? Did they have his location? He stood there, wobbling, thinking of the Star Chamber and all the surveillance systems, the weather satellites and meteorological stations; and he had the sudden notion that not only could they track him any time they wanted, but maybe Solstice's overall aim was something far more sinister than mere data collection. Big Brother on a global scale, perhaps?

He was about to pull the backing off of the phone and yank the battery, hoping that would put an end to any traces, but he realized if they had been tracking him, the point was moot right now.

Instead, he turned on the flashlight function, and in the lengthening shadows he stopped at the end of the hall and tried the two doors.

One was a completely empty master bedroom and bath. The other … a kids' room. Again, full of dust and some torn old books.

A frame for bunk beds, which gave Mason pause. The flashlight's cone of illumination caught the west wall and something on the ceiling: a mobile, one of planets revolving around a sun. Saturn had fallen and was on the ground in a corner. Mason was about to leave when the light caught something else on the wall.

More writing? He came closer, then knelt down near the metal bedpost. He aimed the light directly at the wall, imagining the bed, when it was made and the mattresses covered with boyish action prints, would have been pressed up against it, just below where the black marker sketch began.

His blood chilled. He was sure there had been an attempt to paint over the drawing, but time had worked its spell and what was covered had endured while the latex paint had peeled away, flaked and revealed not the whole thing, but enough.

Four angry black swirling masses, clearly intended to represent tornadoes. In the middle of the tornadoes: a hastily drawn A-frame house. In front of the house, between two smaller trees (young willows), was a circle of stones. It could have been Stonehenge in any other setting.

Inside the circle stood a stick figure, a boy with his hands raised. Squiggly lines issued out of his mouth toward the direction of the largest, closest tornado.

Mason looked hard at the drawing, feeling a sense of grand significance approaching. He thought of Shelby's paper, of the shamans of early Briton, these nature sorcerers. Druids. The boy in the circle …

Solomon.

What was he doing? Was it just an overactive imagination? A boy making sense of the frightful wrath of nature, and by surviving the experience, attributing his survival to supernatural powers? Is this what had set Solomon on his current career path?

Mason kept looking at the sketch. The stone circle in particular. He stood up and peeked out the window after rubbing off a layer of dust. Between the now much larger willow trees there were what he had first taken for bricks, arranged in a low fence.

Remnants of a true *henge*, dismantled and demolished?

Possibly, but still … was this what he was meant to find? He looked at the sketch again. Now he had the sense that it wasn't about fantasy, not meant to be some wild flight of boyhood imagination. It looked more like he had drawn this as a chore. A project. A lesson, something he had done in successive tasks.

The tornadoes, appearing from different vectors … It was almost as if … Mason thought about shooting ranges, recruits at a police academy, gun drawn waiting for the metal cutouts to pop up from any direction, having to be ready to deal with anything.

Was that what this was?

A test?

Mason felt he was on the verge of figuring it out, how it all fit together: not just Solomon and Solstice, but Shelby and Gabriel, the U.N. And Mason himself.

Why did they want me?

Was Lawton supposed to be my test?

He looked again at the stick figure screaming at the tornado, and now imagined himself in its place.

But then he saw something else—a slight red smudge beside the drawing of the boy. He scraped at the area with his fingernail. Scraped a little more as the old latex paint crumbled and scattered and then he stepped back, mouth open.

There was another stone there, this one lying flat like a table.

Or an altar.

And there was another small stick figure lying on it, but with Xs for eyes. And a lot of red trickling from a jagged line over its chest.

He looked again from the altar to the boy, and realized he held something small and pointy in his upraised right hand.

Suddenly the light flickered and a call came in.

Speak of the devil, he thought before he looked at the screen. They must have found me.

But it wasn't Solstice.

The caller ID said: *San Diego General Hospital.*

He answered it, even as he knew, knew what they were going to say. And he was racing for the stairs before the doctor on the other end even started talking.

CHAPTER 28

He spent the entire flight on the phone and trying to get some kind of update from the staff. All they told him first was that Lauren had been found by a neighbor who Mason would have check on her when he was out for too long. Emergency medics worked on her in the ambulance and the early diagnosis was that she had suffered a brain hemorrhage.

Fearing the worst, fighting off every kind of suspicion and conspiracy, his brain swam with theories about Solstice, about Solomon and this Palavar. About stone circles and weather manipulation. In between calls to the hospital, he finally got a hold of Gabriel. His son was there with her, so at least that was something. But they weren't talking to him either, not while Lauren was in surgery.

For the rest of the flight, Mason had time. On his laptop, he searched further into the Department of Agriculture's holdings and cross-referenced tornadoes and weather modification. Nothing there, but the Department of Commerce, in conjunction with the Navy, had undertaken what was called Project Stormfury, which remained in operation from 1962 to 1983. Stormfury was an attempt to weaken tropical hurricanes by flying aircraft into them and seeding them with silver iodine, hoping to freeze the super-cooled water inside the eye and, it was thought, lead to a disruption of the hurricane's inner structure. In reality, there wasn't enough such water to be effective, and the hurricane's behavior was too chaotic and intense for any attempt to be judged meaningfully different than if nothing had been tried.

Mason knew of some other earlier attempts at weather control as well, but despite millions of dollars and the highest of hopes, science just couldn't compete with nature. Statistically and micro-physically, science was outmatched every time and the results were inconclusive at best, dangerous and wasteful at the worst.

That wasn't to say there might not have been other projects, still declassified. Mason considered the farmhouse, the tornadoes and bizarre weather over the years. How would the government have reacted to what they must have tracked and documented on their own? Obviously they moved in and bought out the property at the very least. Palavar, by all accounts, made his own fortune by placing huge bets on commodity prices, unerringly guessing at weather conditions that would benefit or plague the commodity, and riding the wave of selling or buying accordingly. But did the government threaten him because of his success? Bring legal action unless he divulged his secrets?

Surely they couldn't overlook the fact that four devastating cyclones had hit the same area at the same time, and Palavar's home, which seemed to be the epicenter, was spared. Mason imagined teams of scientists and soldiers storming the place, searching for technology they could possibly appropriate for weather modification, national security and defense.

Did they find anything? And if not, was it all ascribed to luck and investment prescience when it came to the weather? Maybe Palavar made them think that way.

And maybe it wasn't Palavar, Mason thought chillingly. Maybe he wouldn't have been so foolish as to bring all that scrutiny to his front door and then have to deal with the full force of the United States government.

Somehow he had survived it. Somehow, against all odds …

Mason thought for a moment. Thought about the small band of unarmed druids on Anglesey Island, standing up to the Roman force.

Was there a similar blanket of wool pulled over the invaders' eyes on Palavar's ranch? A cloud of misdirection and confusion while the true power moved elsewhere?

Still lost in these thoughts, Mason didn't realize the plane was in descent.

He was home.

In the hospital waiting room, he expected to find Gabriel, but all the chairs were empty and no one at the reception desk had seen him recently. Mason tried calling his son but it kept going to voicemail. Lauren was in ICU still and he was promised that he would hear as soon as she was out. In the meantime, he could wait in the room they had prepared for her.

Inside, he found someone waiting for him. It wasn't Gabriel. Not even close. But the man in the dark, sitting in corner beside the empty bed, was undeniably familiar.

"You," Mason said, staring at the black face pulling itself into the light.

The Haitian man smiled and twirled thin cane. "Come inside, Mr. Grier. We don't have a lot of time."

CHAPTER 29

Without touching it, Mason heard the door ease shut behind him and felt a warm, salt-air breeze blowing from the direction of the occupant.

"You can call me Jack," the man from his dream said. Now it was coming back to him. The frozen lake, the Central Park bridge.

"How are you real?" Mason asked, taking another step but keeping the bed between him and Jack.

Suddenly, the TV hanging from the ceiling turned on. Jack glanced at it and smiled back to Mason, who stared, amazed as the very image from his dream appeared there. Jack, digging at the ice, pulling up a body. And another staff—something he hadn't noticed before. It looked like a giant icicle, but it was really—

"Benji's staff," Jack said, reaching down by his feet and retrieving something that he set on the bed.

Mason frowned. "What are you doing with it?"

"Why, this is yours now. Came all the way here to get it to you, I did."

"Why?" Mason's head hurt, his ears were buzzing and he kept glancing back to the TV, where now Jack was holding out the staff in both hands, grinning wildly and staring at the camera.

"'Cuz you need one, brother."

"Why?" Again, none of this made sense.

"The battle's here. You in the thick of it, you just don't know it yet."

"I'm clearly in the thick of something." Mason shook his head, about to sit and ask for his own medication, but now on the screen there was a shift, like a rewind feature just sent time back, back to a scene with five people in a circle. The one commanding everyone's attention was clearly Solomon.

Mason swallowed hard. "You said we don't have much time. Then talk fast. What's happening? What is all this? How do I know you? I only saw you in a dream, and now you're here. My wife just had a brain hemorrhage and she's all I can think about, not—"

Haitian Jack held up his hands, and now the screen shifted to an operating room where a woman—clearly Lauren, with her head bandaged, was being helped to a seated position. She was trying to smile.

Mason started for the door. "Lauren!"

"Not yet, my brother."

Mason turned his head, glaring. "I'm not your brother. What's going on? How are you doing this, and that…?" He pointed to the screen. "Is it real?" He dropped his hands to his sides. *Is any of this real?"*

Haitian Jack's smile faded. "It's real and your wife … she was never in any real danger. Not yet. Just like your daughter. They got dangerous methods, the people you work for, but they need your cooperation. You … you be like a loose cannon, going off at all angles. Potential you got, to muck up the works."

Mason grit his teeth. "I'm set to muck up something if I find out someone was behind all this."

Jack set his hands down flat beside the ivory staff on the bed. "Now hear me. You right, not much time. We need you to be calm, to act a part."

"What part? Why? How can I be calm, and just who are you?"

"Told you, I be Jack. Haitian Jack, and once me and your new boss, we had called each other brothers. But that man, the one who called this staff his?"

"The one you pulled up from the ice?"

Jack nodded gravely. "Yeah, we … we worked behind the scenes, we guided and helped and cured and we … we thought of ourselves like shepherds."

Mason frowned. "And your flock?"

Jack spread out his arms wide. "The whole wide world. And everything, everyone on it."

"Okay …"

Jack made a sideways glance to the TV, and now Mason saw on it his approach to the Kansas farmhouse.

"What the hell? How did you film that?"

Smiling, Jack shook his head. "Nothing filmed. I only see what's in your head right now. I know where you been, which means they know where you been. Which means, that be why your wife's in here." He pointed at the screen. "You ain't s'posed to know what's in there. Not yet, least."

Mason frowned. "Yeah, I'm kind of guessing there were some secrets in there. I'm not quite clear though on just what happened."

Jack leaned in close, eyes searching his. "Oh, I think you be knowing just right. You just don't be believing. Not yet."

He cocked his head, as if listening to the wind outside. And for an instant, Mason could sense it too. A different pitch, a sideways shift in convection, the currents moving slightly.

Jack made a clucking sound with his teeth. "Ah, I best be going. They know I'm here. Sent in help."

"Just what are you? And these others you talked about. What the hell are these shepherds and how does Solomon and Solstice fit in? And the Department of Agriculture? Some guy named Palavar?"

At the mention of that name Jack's eyes flashed. "Ah, then you know enough. Follow that lead when you can. There may be other allies, others … indisposed at the moment, who might be awakened to your cause. In case you lose me." His eyes darted to the window.

"Why, where do you have to go?"

Jack sighed. "There was a battle between ideologies, and the White …" he tapped the ivory staff, "lost to the Grey. Now the balance is destroyed and we can't stop what's to come, can't stop what he's planning. Not alone."

Jack fixed Mason with a hard look. "It's you, it has to be you."

"Me?"

"Yes, you got talents I can't even attempt. You came to me …"

"That was a dream."

Jack shook his head. "Would that I, then, could dream myself elsewhere. No, I had to come here in person, in great danger to myself. But you …"

"Me. Again with that, what am I going to do? I can't even forecast a tornado's approach five minutes away."

Jack laughed. "When you figure all this out, you won't have to."

"What the hell does that mean?"

"Follow Palavar, get help. But first … Go back to work."

"What?"

"And play nice."

Jack was suddenly behind Mason, his hand grasping his shoulder reassuringly. "Let them trust you, and—just like you found out about Kansas—find out what they're really up to. The U.N., the data, this weather gambit."

"I don't understand."

"You will."

He tapped his shoulder, and then again he was in the far corner behind the bed, retreating into the shadows. "If we meet again, we will share a bottle of century-old rum, my brother. Until then …"

But whatever he said was lost in the sound of the door opening, and a doctor coming in. He clasped Mason's shoulder, and his eyes were bright.

"Good news, Mr. Grier. Just came out of surgery, and your wife's going to be fine. It was much less invasive than we thought at first. And in fact, the hemorrhage was …"

But Mason was barely listening. He glanced at the TV, which for a moment before it shut off, displayed a scene from the hallway outside, where Haitian Jack, his white scrubs flowing behind him like a cape, strode toward an exit.

"I know," Mason said, turning back to the doctor. "I had a feeling she'd pull through. Can I see her now?"

Chapter 30

Haitian Jack strode toward the exit sign with the inescapable feeling that he wouldn't make it there. He could sense it in the changing barometric pressure. Someone strong was nearby. At least one, and then possibly more outside.

Had they already constructed a cage? Trapped Jack like a flightless bird?

He was about to find out, but didn't want to tip his hand. He had time, and patience. And he had to win out, if not … there was no one left.

No one but Mason. The new blood, on his own to prevent the Green Kingdom.

The brother had no chance, not alone, not this late in the game.

Jack had to survive.

A red light flashed on the outside of a room up ahead and a nurse came running out. "You, doctor, in here now!"

Jack cursed; he had forgotten to remove the coat and before he knew it she had grabbed his arm and brought him into the room. By that point, it actually occurred to him, this could work in his favor. He could hide out here, buy some time until the defenses outside tired, and then …

He looked at the bed, a withered old man, gasping for air.

Well, Jack thought, *may have to cure this one first. Or at least, ease his suffering.*

He stepped in, then felt a cold blast of air, turned and saw the nurse, a dazed look on her face, sliding out the door and into the hall before the door slammed shut.

And the skeletal man on the bed sat up, wrinkles pulling back as his face changed slightly and the features rearranged into a familiar leering visage of hate and arrogance that only came a lifetime misusing power.

Damn it all.

Old Man Stanwick.

Jack had a moment to react, and it was just enough. He pulled out his staff, created a whirlwind shield out of the air and blocked a barrage of sharp thorns the old man sent his way, scattering the pellets into the ceiling and walls.

Over the wind and the thunking of the thorns into metal and glass, Stanwick's cackling laughter filled Jack's ears.

He cursed, knelt low and slammed down his staff, and out of the vents in the walls and the ceiling erupted a horde of locusts, cascading down onto Stanwick. The old man tried to scream out a counter attack, but the insects flew into his throat and sealed up his lips.

The whirlwind vanished and Jack leapt onto the bed, about to strike down with his staff and end Old Man Stanwick for good—when he sensed something else. Behind him.

He spun, and out came a hulking brute of a man from the closet where he'd been hiding. A scar on his face and dual-colored eyes, the man pulled a gun and aimed—

Not one of us, Jack thought gratefully. This, he could deal with, but almost got one in the back.

Two shots rang out, missing where Jack had been seconds earlier, and was now just a blur, moving about the room like the wind. Here, then there, and the brute kept firing, shouting, and then a shot punched through the window.

A gust of wind, like they had just depressurized an airline cabin, and Jack swooped down, grabbed hold of Stanwick and let the winds tug them both outside, crashing through the window and dropping.

Victor ran to the window's edge, still aiming his gun, looking for a target and cursing the Haitian's trickery. How could he miss from point-blank? He saw the target and the old man strike the ground in a pair of whirling cyclones, flopping, rolling and spinning. Jack was quicker to gain his feet as the old man wearily stood, shaking his head and coughing his lungs free of bugs.

Damn it, Victor thought, weighing his options and feeling useless up here. He had no such talents, despite years of training. Years left to go before he could manage anything but some minor mind clouding and temperature manipulation. No, he'd be better used up on the roof. Where he could survey the battle and lend a hand if needed.

He turned, and ran for the stairs.

Haitian Jack leapt to his feet, sent a volley of flying beetles to assault Stanwick, then again summoned a whirlwind.

Time to test the containment. He launched in a spinning drill form and raced for the sky, zeroing in on the crescent moon like a beacon. He spun faster and faster and chose his trajectory—only to rebound hard and painfully off an invisible barrier and come crashing down over the parking lot. He slammed hard onto the roof of a Chevy Minivan. Rolled off in a rain of glass and metal, and held out his hand.

His staff fell right into it and he was up, bruised and bloody, but fully in control. The car's alarm was shrill and repetitive, and would draw security quickly.

He'd have to move fast, have to seek out the totems—markers enchanted with powerful runes that contained his magic within. He could go that way, he thought in a moment, or he could test the upward confines. If it wasn't done properly, then there should be an exit at the top, a point at which the dome hadn't been sealed skillfully enough.

He'd need a launching point.

The roof …

He eyed the building, preparing himself for another jaunt to the apex, when he heard the shuffling footsteps, impossibly quick, of Old Man Stanwick. He loomed up like Nosferatu himself, and just as frightening with crazed eyes and blackened teeth. He raised his staff and ball lightning shot from over his shoulders, twin orbs racing ahead like catapulted boulders.

Jack leapt into the air, his left foot stepping on the first ball and vaulting over it just as he swung his staff at the other. He struck it with a fast baseball-swing hook and knocked it back at Stanwick. The old man held out his staff and absorbed the entire purple-lightning globe and sucked it harmlessly back into himself.

Landing in front of the old man, Jack crouched, his staff ready.

Stanwick lowered his head. "You can't win, Jack. Should have joined us."

"And you, old man, should know when to retire." He struck the ground again, and this time it unleashed a fury of snakes and enormous burrowing centipedes. They quickly ensnared Stanwick's ankles and pulled him down. But this time he was ready. He hissed and spat and the ground burst into flame, searing the reptiles and freeing his legs and feet—as he calmly walked free, kicking off the flames and the charred reptile bones clinging to his pants.

He raised his hand and tree trunks speared up from the ground, sharp angular vines stabbing and swinging. One cut through Jack's left arm, nearly slicing it off at the elbow, and another gouged into his right calf.

Howling in pain, Jack writhed and then spun and struck the bark with his staff, shattering it in an explosion of ice. Freed of one, then the other just in time, he struck out at Stanwick and landed a blow on the old man's cheek. Then he took to the air, floated up on a current and as he saw Stanwick recover and start mumbling another spell, Jack flung himself backwards and up on another gust that carried him away.

Awkwardly, much less in control, he used some of his energy to heal his wounds, close up the calf and repair tissues in his arm, so that when he landed with a thud on the rooftop beside one of many exhaust fans, he was ready.

He breathed deep, figuring he'd have a few moments to prepare and locate the weak points in the cage. He looked up, and adjusted his sight, shifting into avian eyesight, gauging wind currents and air movements, and he saw then the unnatural bend of the cage, keeping out various frequencies of power, letting in others. And there it was, a man-sized hole just off the center.

That, he could make. No problem, mon, as they said back home. He would live to fight another day. Regroup and help this novice Mason, the brother who could become much more than he knew. There was still time. But then a nagging thought crept into his mind. Nagging that maybe the gap existed right above the roof just so that he'd be maneuvered here.

No that couldn't be, no such trick to play on ol' Jack. He just had to act fast. He just …

But that's when he sensed something else.

Someone else.

Not the brute, who he saw now emerging from the rooftop entrance, gun in hand, but someone else … behind him.

Haitian Jack spun, staff up—but not in time.

Damnit, mon.

It was the younger one. The son.

Gabriel smiled as he stepped from the shadows, wearing a black hooded sweatshirt. He traced a quick sigil in the air with his staff and then exhaled. A burst of icy arctic wind slammed into Jack and hurtled him clear across the roof, slamming him hard into the metal grating beside the door Victor had just stepped out from moments ago.

Pinned there, Jack tried to clear his head. *Just a second. All I need to take you down, just …*

But then the brute pressed the muzzle of his gun against Jack's temple. "Dodge this, asshole," he said and squeezed the trigger.

Chapter 31

Mason hid the ivory staff in the room's closet just in time, tucked it back on the top shelf behind his laptop bag, then closed the door just as Gabriel walked in.

"Dad, good to see you made it back. Unscathed," he added with a sarcastic twist of his lip that Mason didn't care for in the least, but he smiled back.

"Nothing I hadn't been through before." He let that hang out there, considering his son. The black sweatshirt, the dark jeans and leather boots. "Where were you? I thought you'd be in the waiting room?"

"Pacing around," Gabriel said. "Trying to find the doctors, checking out the facilities."

"Pretty confident your mother was going to be okay?"

Gabriel titled his head. "She's a fighter. I had strong hopes."

Mason nodded, about to add something when the orderlies came in, wheeling Lauren. Gabriel stepped out to let them pass. After they shifted her to the bed and attached all the right wires and equipment, they left and Gabriel came back in to join Mason on the opposite side of his mother.

"So peaceful," Gabriel noted. "They said …"

"I know what they said. I was here when the doctor came in."

Gabriel nodded. "All right then." He pulled up a chair and had a seat, letting out a deep sigh as if he'd just strained himself. "So what else should we talk about? How's work?"

Mason glared at him. "Can't say it's been the most rewarding first week on a job."

Gabriel smiled and rubbed at some scuff mark on his boot. "You also can't say it's been dull, I imagine."

"Certainly not." Mason pulled up the last free chair and sat down.

"So," Gabriel said. "I hear you went a little off-roading after Lawton."

Nodding, Mason forced a smile. "You hear right. Took a little jaunt over the border."

"Kansas. Hmm, wonder why? Not exactly a party kind of place."

Mason shrugged. "Never been, wanted to see what all the fuss was about."

Gabriel looked up and set his gaze firmly on Mason's. "And did you?"

"Did I what?"

"Find out—what all the fuss is about?"

Mason held the look for a while. *Play nice.* "Not really, no. Found some interesting landmarks, some old stuff to look at, but nothing of any value. Should have stayed put, I guess."

Gabriel blinked at him, sizing him up. "I guess so. Would've saved gas."

"And the environment, I suppose, in the process."

"Yes," said Gabriel. "And that too."

Lauren's eyes flickered and a moan passed her lips. She blinked and focused first on Gabriel. Then turned and smiled to Mason. "I'm … still here?"

Mason reached over and clasped her hands in his, then placed a kiss on her forehead. "You can't get away from me that easily."

Just then, his phone buzzed. He wasn't going to take it, but then the ring came into join the vibration. Shelby's ringtone, a sassy little urban electronic tune.

"The whole family ..." Lauren whispered, her lips dry. Gabriel understood and went to get her a glass of water from the bathroom sink.

Mason accepted the Skype call and held the phone up so they could see each other.

"Mom!" Shelby's voice. "You look ..."

"She looks great," Mason said, sliding his head into view, resting it on the pillow beside Lauren's, after first glancing in her soft eyes and feeling the pull, feeling the incredible loss he would have experienced if those eyes had never opened again.

"She does!" Shelby added. "Glad you're up, Mom. And ... no bad effects? Everything ok? I was so worried, no one was telling me anything!"

"Sorry, sis." Gabriel came out and set the glass in Lauren's hand, helping it up to her lips. "I didn't return your call, didn't want to say anything until we knew for sure."

"So you let me assume the worst."

"Again, sorry."

"It's all right, kids. No bickering." Mason took the cup away after she had gulped down almost the entire thing.

"When can she get out?" Shelby asked. "I want to come, want to stay with you and help out. This shouldn't have happened!"

"You're needed in London," Gabriel snapped back. "Just a little longer."

"Why?"

"Yeah, what are you doing there, sweetie?" Mason glanced at Gabriel. In light of everything else he had just learned, now he wondered if Shelby was in danger. He had no idea what she was working on or what it involved. If it put her in danger, he would never forgive Solomon, or Gabriel.

"Just some more weather research. Stuff about crops and early history and meteorological trends. Speaking of historical stuff, Mom said you got my paper? Did you get a chance to read it?"

"I did," Mason said, noting Gabriel narrowed his eyes at him. "Interesting stuff, honey. Well written. You should get a great grade."

"Hope so."

Mason smiled at Shelby. "And uh—about the other thing ..."

On the screen, Shelby held up a finger quickly, and gave a little shake of her head.

"What other thing?" Gabriel leaned in to look at the screen.

Mason tilted the screen so he could have Shelby's full attention. "Just that I love you, and am so proud of you." His mind whirled, thinking about the thumb drive. He had to let her know he didn't open it, but wanted to if he could get the password. It must have been something she thought he would know if she had included it. Something personal.

"Love you too, Dad. And all of you. Even you, brother, *twin*."

Gabriel smiled. "Back at you, glad you're doing great and the cure worked. Finish what you're working on and come home soon. You're not going to want to miss what's coming."

"And what is that?" Mason asked.

"Big things," Gabriel said with emotion in his voice, as if he had just solved world hunger. "We just heard.... Solstice won the contract with the WMO."

"Wow!" Lauren said.

"Yes, it was unanimous."

Mason nodded. "So Solomon returns triumphant, and we'll have access to the world's databanks, servers and all the meteorological information we could ever want."

"And," said Shelby, doing her best to feign excitement, "the weather satellites."

She let that hang out there, and Mason got the emphasis, if Gabriel didn't. "Yes, those too, it's a huge win. I actually have to step out for a second. Got a call about it, I'm sure." Gabriel got up and went for the door, and Mason leaned in.

Quietly he said, "Shelby, the other item in the package, the thumb drive … I know you didn't want me to see it, but if it's important …"

She again held up a finger. "Not important, Dad." She said it, but her head moved up and down, indicating the opposite. So she was concerned that this communication wasn't secure. Someone could be—or was—listening in. "Just some pictures of me on a hike, no biggie." She shook her head. "Hey maybe if you're bored, go take a look. I was embarrassed and not sure at first, but now … yeah, I *need* you to see it."

"Great." *Understood.*

Lauren looked from Shelby to Mason, and her eyes hardened. She knew something was up, but Mason ignored her. "Okay, honey. I may have trouble with it, you know me and those things. I never know how … to open them."

Shelby laughed, nodding. "You'll do fine. Remember … when I was a kid? You always knew how to fix things. Like you did with that dollhouse of mine." She let that hang out there. "You'll do fine," she repeated.

Dollhouse … Mason thought back. Remembered the little plastic toy thing, a castle of sorts for her princesses. But he couldn't remember if it was ever broken. Maybe that was the point …

Shelby blew a kiss. "For you Mom, and one for you, Dad. Take care, and call me when you're home!" She signed off.

Mason put down the phone, and met Lauren's eyes.

"What was that about?" she asked pointedly.

Holding up a finger, Mason stood and looked out into the hallway. He could see Gabriel standing there talking to someone. But not on the phone. Taking another step to the side, Mason could just make out the figure—an old man. Hunched over a bit, gray wispy hair barely covering his skull. His eyes hooded and pale. He shook Gabriel's hand profusely and then patted his shoulder, turned and left.

Mason cleared out of sight before Gabriel could turn around. He returned to Lauren's side. "Quick, what was the name of Shelby's dollhouse?"

"What?"

"Her toy thing—that plastic monstrosity we got her for one Christmas. She called it something."

"Oh, right. How could you forget? Her favorite movie you too used to watch together."

"Lord, how did I forget?" *Here's looking at you, kid.*

"Casablanca."

After that, it was all Mason could do to hold back his impatience, to act interested in Gabriel's questions and to pay attention to Lauren and see to her needs, when all he really wanted to do was get into his computer, insert the thumb drive and see what it was that had Shelby so excited—and scared.

But it was if Gabriel knew something was up and wouldn't let him be. "Maybe I'll stay," he voiced over a yawn. "Long day, and I can just pull up one of the chairs here. You and I, Dad, we can chat all night, catch up, braid each other's hair...." He laughed, smoothing his hand over his bald head.

"Nice thought, Gabe but don't you have something to do? Don't we all?" Mason clicked on the TV's volume, where he had seen the news (the real feed this time, not ... whatever that had been before). He wondered fleetingly about the Haitian, and if he would, in fact see him again; but now wasn't the time to think about it.

The news segment launched right into a special effects demonstration of Solstice's technology in action—an impossible-to-follow conglomeration of graphics and arrows and vectors, all leading from data servers and weather gathering techniques to data-crunching computers and analysts doing their thing, to satellites and radar dishes all across the globe, all seamlessly working together to blanket the earth in one comprehensive sphere of predictive behavior, foreseeing everything from jet stream flows, earthquakes and major weather systems down to local precipitation and humidity levels.

"That's big news," Lauren said, and Mason noted that Lauren had opened her eyes and groggily focused on the screen. "Solstice ..."

"Yes, Mom." Gabriel leaned in and stroked her hair, keeping his eyes on Mason. "It'll mean big changes for us. For everyone, in fact. One day, the world will look back on this moment and call it a major turning point."

For the better? Mason wondered, but remembered to play along. "I'm still not privy to all the details, but anything that can help tame the chaos of Nature and save lives in the process is okay in my book."

Gabriel smiled and all three of them watched the screen, where Solomon stood at a podium, head down, appearing humble while the head of the WMO spoke, enthusiastically describing this new partnership that will be to the benefit of all the world, extolling the generosity and far-reaching vision of Avery Solomon in sharing this technology with the United Nations.

"So what are the next steps?" Mason asked Gabriel. "How do I fit in?"

Gabriel kept stroking Lauren's hair, and now she was fading again as the news dealt with deeper applications of the technology, and Solomon began to speak, fielding questions about the process, about unfettered access and about security concerns, all which he addressed handily.

"You fit in where we tell you to," Gabriel said with emotion. "And when it's time. Until then, you can catch up on the new technology, and read patent cases and—"

"Bullshit."

Lauren was definitely out and overmedicated if she didn't respond to that, and Mason was glad.

"What?"

"Come on, you didn't bring me on so urgently just to read up on patent cases or stand around all day in scenic groves marveling at the waterfalls. What do you need me for? If your computer programs are so incredibly precise, then why me?"

Gabriel stood up, shaking his head. "Fine. Okay, they still want the human element. You're still … ugh don't make me say it."

"Say what?" Mason frowned. Was he playing him? Building up his ego, or was this real? If not, Gabriel was acting really beyond himself.

"That you're good. You're … the best. You can see patterns that computers and satellites miss. We still need that. Your weatherman's intuition. Whatever it is, you have it. And we still need that."

Mason was silent, thinking.

"Like I said, Dad. It pains me to say it, but you know it's true. I've always been proud of you. Of what you do. I've just never … quite been able to say it."

"You didn't want to say it," Lauren whispered, her eyes still closed, but her lips curled into a smile and she sought and squeezed Mason's fingers. "Told you. Knew he still loved you."

"On that note," Gabriel said, stretching, "I think I'll reconsider. A real bed sounds good about now. Will leave you two lovebirds to hold down the fort here. And you …" He pointed to Mason. "See you bright and early, or whenever that turns out to be for you. As you heard, we've got a lot of work to do."

As he left, Mason got up to shut the door and lingered a moment, watching his son—the boy he now realized was lost to him completely—catch up with the old man from before. The old man who put his arm around Gabriel, and the two of them walked down the hallway into the flickering light and beyond.

Mason shut the door, turned and heard the satisfying sound of Lauren's deep breathing that would soon turn to snores.

It was time.

He reached into the closet for his laptop bag.

But first, he let his fingers caress the smooth ivory of the staff he had hidden in the back.

This be yours now.

Mine, he thought, and fought back a chill.

He had no idea what that meant.

But as he reached into the bag, opened the laptop and inserted thumb drive, he had a feeling he was about to find out.

Book 3

Chapter 1

olomon sent his limo to pick up Mason at the hospital in the morning. They were keeping Lauren in for observation one more day, and she insisted he go back to work. She promised to get plenty of sleep, and spend some more time Skyping with her daughter and relishing in the sound of her voice.

Mason left her in good hands and stepped out into the parking lot to wait. His attention immediately focused on something else: a line of police tape around a battered mini-van that looked like some giant had stepped on it. Frowning, Mason recalled dimly hearing a car alarm last night.

Right after the Haitian left.

He continued to stare at the shattered windows and the dented roof, and then looked over to the lawn, to a burned section in the grass.

Feeling an urge to go over there and investigate further, he almost didn't hear the door open or notice the black limousine idling right in front of him.

"Mace," said the familiar voice inside. "Won't you join me? I figured we could do our part for the world's fossil fuel consumption, and carpool." Solomon's face appeared in the light as he leaned forward, all smiles.

Mason forced one of his own and joined him inside.

Whatever Mason was expecting, it certainly wasn't small talk. Solomon seemed to be full of it, discussing everything from the personalities of some of the WMO members to the colors of the hotel rugs to the inadequacy of the wine list in the restaurant. It was almost as if he purposely avoided talk of Lawton, of the tornado and what he must have known Mason did next. The lack of confrontation was just fine with Mason for now. He was still pondering what was on the thumb drive, and glad for the avoidance of other issues.

In fact, he had thought of calling Shelby right back and asking if the drive might have been corrupted somehow. All it had was a single file, called "WatchMe.avi." And when Mason clicked it, up came a sequence of kaleidoscopic imagery mixed with soft flute-like music. Ambient and pulsing, with jagged lines and weird geometry, figures and three-dimensional planes, all forming sequence after sequence of mesmerizing sensory stimuli.

Mason let it run, staring at it, feeling pulled in, lulled by his own lack of sleep and exhaustion over the past two days, but also strangely drawn to the imagery in a way he couldn't explain.

In any case, it stopped after about five minutes, and then started up again in a continual loop. He let it go all the way through again, then gave up. His eyes were sore and he had an odd feeling like vertigo, and then it was enough. He didn't need that right now.

He'd have to call Shelby and get to the bottom of this, but in the meantime he'd fall back on more conventional means to understand what was going on. And to fulfill his promise to the stranger last night, the Haitian who seemed to know more about him and the state of events than he was letting on. Jack seemed to be part of some larger group, a group at odds with Solomon and his leadership.

What did it all have to do with the farmhouse that Solomon was avoiding, even now, all these years later? For that very reason alone, Mason was tempted to go right to it, admit where he'd been and call Solomon out on it. Ask that he explain his past. If indeed he was the young boy, then who was this Palavar? And just what did that drawing represent—the boy with the knife, and the sacrifice on the altar?

Mason scrutinized Solomon as he spoke, still lost in the past. And he decided. Screw it, he'd try something. Not the whole truth, but enough to get himself off the hook and hopefully allay Solomon's fears so that he would trust Mason again.

He cleared his throat and jarred Solomon in mid-sentence, where he'd been digressing about predictive capabilities of unified satellite data and global weather patterns.

"I'm sure you know," Mason said quietly, keeping his eyes fixed on Solomon's, "I was doing some research on my first day, and came across a rather unique weather situation documented back in 1980. In Kansas."

Solomon licked his lips, never blinking. "Yes, interesting that you stumbled upon this so quickly on your first day."

"After Lawton, I apologize but I wasn't in a good frame of mind, you understand. Completely thrown by my errant forecast. That and nearly getting killed by a freak tornado kind of messed with my head."

"So you took a drive."

"I did."

Solomon reached out and let his fingers settle on his gnarled wooden staff leaning against the door. "And how was the visit?"

It was Mason's turn to lick his lips as the limo stopped at a red light. Outside, the sun peeked over a line of trees and attempted to push through the tinted windows. "Well, the drive was uneventful, and the site—a farmhouse—long since abandoned. Not sure why. I just thought I'd see it firsthand."

"That's why I like you Mason, you're very hands-on. Not content with backroom research or trusting someone else's reporting. So, anything of interest on your inspection?"

Mason let out what he hoped was a convincing sigh. "I don't want to say it was all a waste of time, but something odd definitely happened there. Something out of the ordinary, I just don't know what."

"Tell me what you saw; maybe I can fill in the gaps."

"I was wondering if you could," Mason said, scratching his neck. "You see, there were these signs up from the Department of Agriculture, and access to the farmhouse was chained up, the doors all locked."

"Hmm, interesting."

"Yes, and the more I researched the place, I wondered if maybe I could put the pieces together and get a sense of why that area saw so much tornado activity and strange weather, and yet the farmhouse came out unscathed from it all."

"It is a meteorological conundrum, I grant that. So did you turn up anything in this research of yours?"

"Only that the farm was owned by one Louis Palavar, who made a fortune in commodity futures, making huge bets on crop failures and drought-impacted prices."

"Another interesting tidbit."

"Yes, and the government seemed to take an interest in his land, bought him out but then never did anything with it again. Afterwards, Palavar went on to make a name for himself and several more fortunes in Hollywood. But still, it all began in Kansas, and I began to conclude that maybe back then he possibly had some sort of … weather manipulation technology."

"Ah, now we come to it." Solomon's eyes lit up.

"Yes, we do." Mason crossed his arms, leaning back as the limo sped up. "You see where I'm going with this, in light of what happened in Lawton, and on your company rooftop."

"I'm not sure I do," Solomon said, lowering his tone. "Are you implying that artificial means were employed in both cases to achieve the forecast predicted? Now that would be something for sure."

"It would." *Time to wrap this up and get on with it,* Mason thought. "I'm not sure what I'm saying, I'm only speculating that at least with Palavar and 1980, I believe he may have been experimenting with early weather mod techniques. Cloud seeding was an early attempt by the government to cause rain. Weather cannons, not unlike what ski resorts use now, might have been used with some sort of variation. I saw a road that could have been a runway for a small plane that he could have used to spray the clouds and lower atmosphere with nitrous particles or other chemicals, stirring up the currents and creating conditions ripe for tumultuous weather in the area.

"The timing fits. That was about when the government started using such techniques at home and abroad. Project Baton, then Stormfury. Hurricane relief and prevention were the aims, but the same concepts could work with tornadoes and rain production."

Solomon nodded. "I see. So you think maybe this Palavar fellow developed such technology, perfected it beyond what the government was doing...."

"Or they bought out his ideas."

"But maybe first his science got a little out of his control. The tornadoes, the destruction ..."

"... and the sparing of his home at the last minute," Mason added. "It all points to him being in control of the weather, or at least, regaining control in time to save his home and anyone in it."

"Ah. And did you learn anything more? Did he live alone? Have a wife ...?"

Mason shrugged. *Got to be careful here.* "Nothing on that. Alone as far as I could tell."

"Ah." Solomon nodded thoughtfully. "Makes sense. Lonely mad scientist type. Fascinating work, Mace."

"It is fascinating. But is any of it true?"

"Which part?"

"The weather technology part." Mason thought for a moment as Solomon made no motion to interrupt. "Oh, I know the government attempted a number of weather control projects. Most, like Baton and Stormfury, ended in failure or at the least, inconclusive results not statistically different from natural processes."

"True."

"But there's no denying some success. Farmers have used cloud seeding in cases to help end droughts. Hail cannons were used to break up hail and save livestock and crops."

"Also true."

"And there have been military uses. Vietnam. Operation Popeye, I think it was, 1967 until 1980."

"Nothing to do with spinach," Solomon said, licking his lips.

"No. Again, cloud seeding in Southeast Asia, Laos and Cambodia, trying to increase the monsoon season, which apparently it did by over a month. Higher rainfall, slowing down trucks and convoys, battering the enemy formations …"

"One success, at least. But really, rainfall is a parlor trick, nothing more."

"Seems a pretty good one to me. And the best we've got, and have ever managed. Unless you give credence to the wilder conspiracy theories about the HAARP array facility in Alaska."

"Ah yes." Solomon let out a chuckle. "Dozens of patents on weather control technology using microwave radiation and other techniques."

"Countries all over the world accusing us of using it to cause environmental nastiness. So, do you believe that technology can do what they claim? Is that something like what Palavar had, and if so … has it been modified by Solstice?" Not hearing an answer, Mason let the pause drag out.

Solomon looked out the window, his eyes losing focus. "Do you know what some claim about Genghis Khan?"

Mason frowned again at being taken off topic. Solomon had an infuriating way of doing that, but Mason decided to play along. "That half of the world's population carries his genes because he was such a promiscuous conqueror?"

"Yes, but also—"

"—that a group of so-called psychics are out looking for his legendary tomb and a crapload of treasure?"

"Yes, that too. But I am talking about some of the descriptions of his military conquests. Specifically how he overwhelmed larger forces."

"Wasn't it through sheer ferocity? And cavalry, he was among the first to use mounted forces. That, and superior cunning and military strategy?"

"All of those things, surely, but other accounts have it that before many of the battles, Genghis, who was not only commander but a priest-king, would take to the mountains much as a shaman, and invoke the spirits to provide assistance."

"Assistance in what form?"

Solomon kept staring out at the sun. "Accounts claim that the formerly clear skies would turn pitch black. Wind and thunderstorms would appear out of nowhere. Massive lightning strikes struck the land. Hailstones the size of small boulders rained upon the enemy, ice and sleet wore them down and then fog occluded their vision so that by the time the Mongol forces rode down upon them, they were as good as defeated."

"That," said Mason, "I didn't know. You sound as though you believe it."

Solomon was silent for a moment, then finally turned his attention away from the sun. He faced Mason and smiled. "We're almost at Solstice. I have much to share with you about the New York trip, and the subsequent conference in Zurich. We have big, big things ahead of us. Much as you shared with me, there are things that will open your eyes in the days to come."

"And this technology?" Mason asked. "Is weather control part of it? Please, you must see how it all seems to me. I'm one of the best meteorologists in the country. That's why you said you brought me on, and yet … to be this wrong? I know nature is unpredictable and always has the last laugh, but usually it's within reason and afterwards I can see the signs I missed. But lately … I have to believe there may be another cause."

"A man-made cause? You think perhaps we took and improved on Palavar's technology—if he had such a thing?"

Mason shrugged. "*Occam's Razor.* Simplest explanation is usually correct. Either that, or you guys have some powerful sorcerers in your employ, doing rain dances and human sacrifices to the gods."

Solomon nearly choked out his laughter. "Oh, now that would be something, wouldn't it?"

"But you know about Palavar," Mason said directly. "I know it's not unfamiliar to you."

"No, of course not. Such a famous event in meteorological history." Solomon clasped his hands together. "Of course we studied it, just as we studied another close call involving a tornado that happened some years earlier."

Mason's mouth went dry. "Which one?"

"Oh, a certain traumatic event in Indiana. A young boy asleep when a Class Five tornado ripped away half his home and swept his parents away into the sky. A boy, orphaned in an instant."

Mason trembled. "You knew that about me too. I'm sure Gabriel told you."

"He filled in some gaps. Listen, Mason.…" Solomon leaned forward and set a reassuring hand on Mason's arm. "We picked you because you are the best, yes that's true. But also because you are emotionally invested. You want what we want."

Revenge? Mason almost said. "And what is that?"

"A way to control the uncontrollable. And, perhaps to mimic Prometheus in some ways."

Mason frowned. "Sorry, my Greek mythology is a little rusty."

"The titan who stole fire from the gods and gave it to mankind. The ultimate gift to take us out of the clutches of night and cold. Imagine such a gift at such a time when the world was clothed in fear and darkness."

"Ah now I remember. Wasn't he punished for his generosity by being chained to a rock and having his liver chewed out by giant birds every night?"

Solomon smiled and patted Mason's arm. "Exactly. He made a sacrifice. The ultimate sacrifice, in fact. A common theme in myth and religion. Salvation granted for others only through great personal sacrifice."

Mason nodded, his head suddenly spinning with remnants of Shelby's kaleidoscopic program on the thumb drive. And again he thought of her paper, of the druids' sacrifice in Anglesey. And again he thought of how Solomon had just cleverly deflected his questions on weather manipulation and technology.

He would have to wait for those answers.

But that was okay. He had done what he needed to do—got himself off the hook and convinced Solomon that he was no threat. He hadn't let on that he knew Solomon had been with Palavar, or that there was an altar and a human sacrifice, and that if there had been technology, it had been superseded by a boy who at least believed he had the power to control the fiercest aspects of nature.

It was all coming together, and Mason had bought himself the time he needed.

"Let's continue this discussion soon," Solomon said. "But now, time to get back to work and earn that big salary." He grinned and opened the door, letting in the bright sunshine and the symphony of birds and insects.

"We're here."

Chapter 2

Down in the Star Chamber, Mason stopped to check out the state of the world as revealed by the huge screens. A greater number of Solstice employees were in the area, manning their stations, staring at the screens or engaging in private conversations and analysis. Near the center of the western section Mason found Gabriel. He was walking away, rather intent and with a frustrated look on his face.

"Trouble in paradise?" Mason asked, looking over his son's shoulder at the likely source of his concern—Annabelle. The girl was flushed, refusing to look up, just throwing herself into some project on her screen.

Gabriel shook his head. "Nothing to worry about. I heard you had a luxury ride in to work this morning."

"I won't get used to it. Still, it was nice to spend some time clarifying things with our boss."

"I'm glad for that. Speaking of whom, I've got to run to a meeting with him."

"I'm not invited?"

Gabriel smiled. "Not yet. Be grateful. Not everything we do around here is fun."

Mason glanced around at all the overwhelming stimulus, and then back to Annabelle, wondering what Gabriel did to ruin that for now. "So, son don't you worry about your mission?"

"What are you talking about?"

"Look around," Mason said. "All this, and the deal with the WMO. You're no longer the outcast, the rebel with a cause. Now, if all this works the way you intend it to, if you start saving lives and giving away all this amazing foreknowledge about weather patterns, controlling nature for once instead of the other way around, well ... don't you see what will happen?"

Gabriel just stared ahead.

Okay, don't take the bait. I'll continue. "Your mantra of climate change. The political and social movement, being on the right side of history against the evils of overpopulation, pollution and resource plundering."

"What about it? None of that changes."

"Doesn't it? I would argue the opposite. That your movement was making good progress, that as long as the these disasters kept striking home and hurting regular people where it counts—in their wallets as well as in their homes—then you had a swelling of support and eventually all that pressure would result in the global change. But now," Mason pointed to the center screen, the largest, showing an interconnected series of satellite dots around the representation of the earth, all transmitting data and presenting schematics and specs, "all that goes away. If this all does what Solomon claims it can, then the world has a safety net—one that will just make everyone feel that much better about driving their SUVs and cranking up their furnaces and drilling for those fossil fuels."

Something flickered, dark and treacherous, behind Gabriel's eyes. "It changes nothing," Gabriel said through grit teeth. "And that's not what will happen. You'll see. The world has its own timetable, and the day of reckoning won't be delayed."

Mason smiled back. "As long as it waits until the younger generation inherits the mess." He clapped his hand on Gabriel's shoulder and walked passed him. "Don't be late for your meeting."

Twisting away, Gabriel stormed off without a backward glance.

As he left, Mason returned his attention to the main screen, studying the information on the satellites, analyzing their positions, seeing something familiar. It tugged at his mind, much like the program on his laptop. So much so, seeing the configuration, reading the statistics that scrolled by, not quite understanding any of it, but still …

"Amazing, isn't it." A voice at his side. She'd been standing there, he wasn't sure how long. "Annabelle?"

"Hi, Mr. Grier."

"Please, call me Mason."

"I feel strange about that."

"Well, whatever makes you comfortable. And sorry I couldn't help notice, you and Gabriel …?"

Annabelle looked down. "He's driven. Sometimes. And he makes sacrifices for this work. He …" She shook her head.

"I know," Mason said. "Believe me, I'm his father and I haven't been able to reach him for years. I was just hoping we'd have another chance, but you're right. He can be very focused on things that I would say are not the things that really matter." He looked at Annabelle. "Losing sight of personal connections and imagining a greater responsibility that can never be achieved isn't a good thing. I've wrestled with that balance myself."

Annabelle nodded. "In your career, always looking out for the community. Like a doctor caring for everyone else but himself and his family."

"Exactly." Mason sighed. "So, what do you do around here? And for that matter, what do I do? What should I be doing right now?"

Annabelle let out a laugh, relaxing around him now. "Well, that's a good question. Actually two questions. I … I serve in whatever way I can. Solomon recognized my skills and brought me in to complement some of the others, including Gabriel. And I've held my own."

"You must be good, then. Surely you had some competing offers?"

She looked up sharply, then glanced around, and when she spoke again it was with caution. "Of course I did. There was some serious competition when Solomon first made his move to set up

Solstice as an independent company under his leadership. A lot of us … had choices to make."

"And do you feel you made the right one?"

"Sometimes," she said, but her eyes were red and trembling, Mason noticed as she looked up again at the satellites.

He decided to change the subject. "These satellites … I'm wondering, I mean I know the big push for Solstice was access to the WMO's global network. The land and sea based weather centers, the servers and data centers. But the focus here I'm seeing seems to be on the satellites. Do you know why?"

Annabelle shook her head. "I'm thinking that's probably what they're talking about now in that meeting. And you asked earlier about your role. I think whatever they're deciding, whatever this all has to do with, they need you for the next step."

Mason looked back at the screen. "Do you have any idea what that might involve? I mean, I know they said they wanted me for the human element—my intuition, my skill at reading the data and coming to a gut feel conclusion."

"Yeah that sounds right."

"Does it?" Mason shook his head. "I'm not sure." Mason thought for a moment. *She knows. More than she's saying. Maybe she's been told to keep it a secret. Or more likely … she's scared.*

That was it. He could hear it in her voice.

"I don't know," Annabelle added. "Well, I need to get back to work. You should head to your office. I'm sure there will be an email or an assignment or something. That's how it usually works."

"Yeah I'll do that. But first …" He thought of something. Lowered the strap of his laptop bag and took out the computer. "Let me show you something."

He set up at her station, and after checking around first to make sure that creepy Victor guy wasn't around, Mason started up the program. Annabelle seemed nervous at first, and didn't act too interested, but as soon as the kaleidoscopic swirling lines and geometric spinning figures took over the screen, she leaned in, enraptured.

After a minute, she started to nod.

"I see it now. It's a subliminal program."

"Huh?" Mason squinted and moved his head in and back. "Like one of those 3D pictures where you stare long enough and finally see an elephant riding a dolphin?"

"No, I've seen this before. I was a psych major, and I researched some techniques involving therapy for deep-seeded repression. Things like this program here often helped break through mental blocks."

She looked up at Mason. "Where did you get it from?"

Mason started to tell her. She had that expression, and her tone seemed genuine, but still, she was Gabriel's girlfriend. Or at least, had been up until recently. And she was a Solstice girl. He didn't know how loyal she was. Better to be safe—and maybe he could get something out of her in the process. He thought up a quick lie.

"It was on the laptop when I got it. Part of my orientation, a list of files to open and run. Most of the others were weather installation programs, password setup kind of stuff, but this …"

Annabelle still had a perplexed look on her face. She stared at the patterns a little more, and just as Mason watched and started feeling lightheaded again, she nodded. "I would suggest, then, that you take this back to your office and keep studying it."

She said it confidently, but her tone had changed. Mason could tell she was reverting back to loyalty mode. Convincing her that Solstice wanted him to have this "memory-block" eraser thing made her go with it. Just trying to be helpful, he imagined, but he also sensed possibly a hint of some concern for him.

"It works on the subconscious, so it might help you relax and access that intuition Solomon wants you to develop."

"Yeah. That's probably it." *Actually, I'm sure that's not it.* Mason blinked and resisted the pull of the shapes and twisting lines, and for a moment he almost saw words in the mix of weird geometry. He shook his head. *Whatever it is I'm supposedly blocking, Shelby knows about it. Have to talk to her first.*

He reached for his phone. "I'll get going then." He closed the laptop and stepped away.

"Hope it works," she said with a nervous smile. "And good luck with everything."

Mason nodded and looked back up at the massive screen and all the other ones surrounding it. The satellite orientation around the earth again triggered something, a memory, an image, and with some difficulty he put out of his mind all the other weather-related imagery and news and statistics crowding the screens.

He took a step back, still studying the main viewer.

Annabelle had taken notice. "Mr. Grier? Something else I can help you with?"

"Just … the way the satellites are set up is interesting."

"Oh that's not all of them," Annabelle said. "I noticed too that there were fifty that we now have access to, but Solomon had the engineering team only activate these twelve as the ones to provide coverage and data access."

"That doesn't make sense," Mason said. "More data is always preferable to less. And I'm sure there are whole areas of the globe not covered by just these twelve, so I don't understand why—"

Then he remembered. *The orientation of the stones drawn on the wall in Palavar's upstairs bedroom. Around the altar. Around the sacrifice. Weren't there twelve there too?*

Mason's blood chilled.

It was the same configuration.

He tried four times from his office to reach Shelby, but the calls only went straight to voice mail. On the next try, the call was interrupted. It was a number he recognized as the hospital.

"Mason," Lauren's voice. "I'm calling from my room."

"Good to hear your voice." Mason leaned back in the chair and diverted his eyes from the subliminal program to the side wall, to the view of the serene mountains and streams. "How are you feeling?"

"Like that time at Gabe's little league practice when I took a baseball to the head."

"Oh jeez. That bad?"

"Worse, actually but I'll manage. Listen, I'm calling because—and I'm sure this is just crazy—but I wanted to talk to you, hear your soothing voice after the awful dream I just had."

"A dream?"

"Yeah, probably just from lack of sleep and all the medications and everything's that's happened, especially with the fright over Shelby, but … Oh god Mason it was so terrible."

She had his attention now. "You can tell me if it will help. I'm sorry I'm not there with you; I figured you'd be sleeping most of the day. If you want, I can come right back."

"No, it's no problem. I'll be resting, but I just wanted to tell someone. Shelby … I tried to call her because it was that raw, that disturbing."

Mason waited, and for a moment he imagined the faux sky dimmed, the lighting shifting despite no clouds in the virtual sky.

"I was in a field, or a forest," Lauren said. "But not in my wheelchair. I was standing, and at first I was thrilled by it. Feeling my bare feet on the grass, wriggling my toes in the earth. But then I realized the dirt was full of worms, and bugs and maggots."

Mason trembled.

"But the worst was that I walked through them, squishing them and kept going, toward a circle of people. Twelve of them, I remember. All wearing hoods and carrying weird old sticks. I walked, in a daze, into the circle and saw …"

The room darkened further, and the images flickered and Mason almost dropped the phone as he stood up and gaped at the change. He was in the forest she was describing. Larger than life figures moved past him under a canopy of braches and leaves, all scattering when they hit the overhead tiles of the regular ceiling, but even that solidity seemed to be losing cohesion as she spoke.

What the hell is happening? This can't be a projection or wall simulation.

He reached out to touch the nearest body—but that's when he saw the altar up ahead. The white stone slab set upon two square blocks. And on it …

"Oh Mason, it was Shelby. And she … she was screaming. This figure stood over her with a bloody knife."

Mason saw it, as if her words conjured the imagery through his eyes and projected them on the screen.

"He stabbed her, Mason, again and again. I screamed and tried to run to her, but now the ground was full of snakes, and they locked my ankles in place and held me down. Shelby … she turned her head.…"

And she looked right at Mason, with eyes free of pain and a broad smile as if to say: *I wanted this. I went willingly.*

The figure with the crimson knife lifted his head, and looked in Mason's direction.

"Her killer, he looked right at me Mason, and he—"

—*pulled back his hood.* Mason gasped and now he did make contact with the wall and everything blasted to white, but not before he saw the face behind the hood.

"—it was Gabriel."

"I've never had such a vivid dream," Lauren said after her voice calmed, after several more deep breaths and after Mason tried to convince her it was normal.

"Everything that's happened lately, Gabriel at this job, the way they took Shelby to administer the cure. You're going through exactly the same sort of mental reasoning I am." Mason spoke gently. "Your dream—nightmare really—is what we were both fearing inside, that Gabriel had some ulterior motive behind all this. Given Shelby's research and her studies, which I'm sure she's shared with you, it's more than understandable that your mind came up with this, mixing everything together as it did."

Mason sat down, still trembling, staring in disbelief now at the pure white walls. What had made the image change? What brought about the end of the projection? Was it all in his head?

While he talked, he searched for a switch, a lens or a projector. If there wasn't any, then it had to be built into the wall's surface itself. Outwardly opaque, but maybe with hundreds of thousands of microcells that with the flip of a switch could carry a projected set of pixels from within.

"I know," Lauren said. "I just felt without a doubt when I woke up that something was terribly wrong. I've been calling Shelby non-stop. There's no answer."

"I know, I tried too." He pressed his hand against the wall, then tapped it. *Maybe it's a Clap On?*

"I'm really worried, Mason."

"I'll get a hold of her. Call the London Solstice office—"

"Yes, do that! I should have thought of it."

"Okay, give me a minute and call me right back."

"Don't forget, my love. They're coming back with more meds and I'm sure I'll be out for awhile this time."

"I will, and I promise, I'll be there this afternoon, when you wake up."

Her voice cracked a little, finally breaking under the stress and the weight of everything she'd been through. "You've always kept your promises."

"Well—"

"No, you have. And you don't know how much that has meant to me. How much *you* have meant to me. To stand by me through everything I've put you through."

Mason looked away from the wall. His mind settled and as he was about to respond, his vision settled on the laptop program just as it started up again. It tugged at his mind, clouded his thoughts and suddenly he was staring at the weird geometry and the flashing bursts and now he was seeing other things.

Windmills, cornfields, a pair of giant willow trees.

He blinked as he heard Lauren's voice. "Mason?"

"Hang on, I … I'm sorry, love. I heard you and I—wait, I have a beep. It's …" He looked at the screen. "It's Shelby! Hold the line." He pressed the switch button. "Shelby?"

"Dad. Listen I don't have much time. I know you and Mom have been calling. I'm fine, heading home in fact. I'm in Chicago."

"What?"

"Yes, Solstice doesn't know. I … I just felt I had to be home. For Mom."

"Oh, honey. She's okay.…"

"But mostly, for you."

"Me?"

"Dad, the program. I can't say much more, and don't talk. If you're in your office, they may be listening."

"Who? Honey, what are you talking about? I wanted to ask about that because I know what it is. Or at least, what it's supposed to do."

Silence for a moment on the other end. "If you know that, then you're close. Listen, I don't know what you're going to remember.

Not exactly. But I do know that it's something buried deep, something they don't want you to access."

"What? Shelby …" He was struck again by how suddenly her voice had changed, and how he was beginning to forget what she had even sounded like before, with her impediment. It was like talking to someone new, but someone he had known all his life. "I don't know what you think it is I need to—"

"Don't say it."

"Revisit," he said, hoping that synonym would suffice. "But trust me, I have nothing. I'm not sure where you've got this information about me, but I would know if—"

"No, you wouldn't. Whatever was done to you, it was done deeply, and powerfully. You have no idea. But you will if you keep watching the screen. And do it while you're relaxed. Or as much as you can be. But I was calling to say maybe you should wait. That's why I'm coming home."

"What do you mean?"

"The more I thought about it, the more I realized that the people who told me about this program, the ones who convinced me that you were being used and needed to have your memory restored … the more I realized you might not be able to handle it alone."

"I'm not alone, and—what people are you talking about?"

"Dad, they said they tried to contact you. Some were killed, one might have gotten through, although you might have thought it was a dream."

Mason's blood chilled again—and suddenly the wall behind him lit up and he was back in the serene world of mountains, streams and blue skies.

"Honey, I—"

"Don't talk. Listen, please. They told me another member of their group, a team that opposes Solomon and what he's got planned, she was the one that slipped you some other information. Something vital you needed to understand. So I don't know if you followed up on that…."

"I did, but I don't understand it all. Not yet."

"No, you won't, Dad."

"I actually don't understand any of this."

"You won't, not until the program finishes on your mind."

"But I don't believe—"

"It doesn't matter. Listen, you must have doubts. You must realize they wouldn't go to these lengths just because you're a good meteorologist."

"Good? I thought I was the best?"

"Whatever, it doesn't matter. They don't need a forecaster or an analyst. They need something else from you, something only you can give."

"What is it?"

"We'll find out together. I have some ideas, some theories that I've come up with after all that research. I sent it to you so if I'm right, then you won't have such a hard time believing me."

Mason rubbed his neck. "Then now I'm really baffled."

"Just wait. Turn off the program and wait for me, I'll be there in six hours. Turn it off. I looked into the process some more and I fear that once the blocks crumble, it won't happen all at once. You'll start getting flashbacks. You'll think maybe they're hallucinations. It might be terribly confusing."

Mason shook his head. "I really can't believe any of this right now."

"It's okay. Maybe … maybe get out of Solstice. Get to the hospital, you have the perfect excuse to be with your wife. Don't give them—even Gabriel—an opportunity to sense there's anything wrong. I'll be there, and together we'll find what you've got locked away."

"Gabriel? Do you think—?"

"Don't say anything. And yes, I think he's in this up to his neck. As much as that scares me, we know how my brother is, and I'm worried he's been brainwashed."

The hood, pulled back … Gabriel's grinning visage over the bloody knife …

Shuddering, Mason asked: "So you believe these people? This other group?"

"I do, Dad, and it really scares me. If what they've told me is true. So please … They're about to announce my flight, please turn off the program and wait for me."

"All right, all right. I promise, but before you board, call your mother. I'll give you the number."

"Okay, is she up?"

"She is, and very worried about you. Don't ask, just call and reassure her. Let her hear your voice."

"I will, and thanks. See you soon, Dad."

She hung up, and Mason swiveled in his chair, turning away from the sprawling natural vista that somehow, defiantly, existed despite his efforts to find any projection device. He reached for the monitor, about to shut it off when the program ramped up to its grand finale of pulsating lights, flashing words and now—images that he could see more clearly.

Were they hidden there all along? These snapshots of cornfields, of stormy skies, of young willow trees, a windmill and …

A stone circle.

And a tornado in the hazy distance, approaching over the wind-blown corn stalks.

Palavar's farm.

Mason realized it with a start, just as he turned and saw—

The walls were no longer serene, no longer projecting mountains and sun and lush forests.

The walls—the floor—the ceiling. Everything had changed. He was no longer in his office.

He was in Kansas.

He dropped to his knees as the chair, his desk and the computer vanished into the shadows of a looming willow tree and a section of large white boulders arranged in a circle.

—around the altar.

Wrestling with complete dislocation, Mason tripped and fell backwards in a sudden gust of wind. He landed on something hard. Lifted his head and saw two immense tornadoes slamming down into the fields, scattering husks and leaves and dirt and rocks in every direction as they bore down mercilessly toward him.

They came at a summons, it seemed, rushing toward their master as if they were dogs hearing the dinner bell.

Their master—an unlikely one, a small figure in a hooded grey sweatshirt.

A small boy. Who turned, just as the tornadoes ground to a halt behind him.

A wide grin on his face, the freckled boy with the crisp green eyes lifted a huge, sharp knife.

Chapter 3

ason tried to scream but his voice was lost in the whipping winds and the howling anguished cries from the restrained tornadoes, as if they were being tormented, demons summoned from the depths of Hell and then restrained in powerful magic circles.

It's not real, not real, not real. Just walls and projections! Just my mind—

But then the child opened his mouth, and a deep voice came out.

A voice that was familiar and chilling, but overly welcome at this point.

It was Victor's voice, and just hearing it broke the spell, or the virtual projection, or the madness or whatever it was.

The storm world faded and then exploded into white light, and immediately returned to the plain walls and the silent office room.

Victor stood where the boy had been, looming over Mason. The enforcer turned sideways and noted the computer monitor and the running program. He looked back to the walls, eyes narrowing, and then he lifted his phone to his lips.

"Sir? I have him." Victor stared now at Mason, curled up on the floor where just moments before he had believed himself lying on a stone altar.

Victor continued. "I've confirmed what Annabelle told us, it looks like some kind of memory-unlocking program. He's accessed it.… Yes, definitely. *He knows.*"

He wasn't sure when exactly the succession of flashbacks stopped, or if they ever really did. Images kept breaking through into reality, tearing through the fabric of not just the walls and the ceiling, superimposing storm clouds and cornfields, willow trees and eldritch standing stones in the place of other mundane objects, but also supplying olfactory sensations and tactile elements. He heard the frenzied winds flaying through the stalks, felt the debris striking his face and smelled the crackling ozone in the air.

A low humming chant issued from the hooded boy's throat.

That child, those pale green eyes at last disintegrating and blossoming into a bright sunburst. And striding out of the light came Solomon, and those same pale eyes coursed with powerful adult energy.

"Welcome, Mason. This is not how I intended it, but you have come to this stage on your own accord. And now there is no longer any need for secrecy."

Mason groaned, holding his head. He tried to get up but felt the strong arms of Victor behind him, aiding and then leading him to a stone wall. What he thought was a wall, but actually a *menhir*, one of twelve immense misshapen boulders, narrower at the top, and moss covered on one side.

"Where am I?"

"Welcome," said Solomon, "to our Inner Sanctum."

"The walls——?" He squinted, and could only see blackness at first with small pinpricks of light. "Stars …?"

Solomon nodded. "Wait a few moments and you'll witness the heliacal rising of Sirius over my left shoulder, close to the center stone. The alignment will be precise, at dawn, and our time will be at hand."

Another flash and the section of reality to his left shifted to the roof of Palavar's farmhouse, and the windmill spinning out of control, sparks flying from its gears. Then, like a camera viewpoint, it tracked downward to a ring of stones, and a bloody body writhing on an altar.

The face on the body was blurred out, even as the view magnified.

Solomon noticed, then lifted his eyes. "Ah, so there *are* still some secrets left."

"What are you talking about?" Mason gathered his energy, shook his arm free of Victor's grasp and pointed at the image. "What is this? How are we seeing it? Where are the projectors?"

Chuckling, Solomon reached for his staff and pointed it at Mason. "He doesn't know yet who he is," he told Victor. "Close, but Palavar's mental wipe went deep. You're still working through it, aren't you Mason?"

Shaking his head again, Mason looked back to the young body on the altar. The blood, the little hands on his chest. Hard to see with all the debris flying around, but the wound …

And then it hit him. The image flickered, went out and Mason reached down, lifted his shirt.

"There it is," said Solomon, the tip of the staff now pointing at the vertical scar just above Mason's navel.

Mason backed away, stumbling hard into another stone as Victor and Solomon looked on, amused.

"Not possible," Mason stammered, shaking his head. "I remember…. I remember…."

The background flickered again, and again images appeared. *A different tornado, ripping open an entire wall, scattering toys and clothes, a Tonka truck sailing into the maelstrom. And the same young boy as on the altar, sitting up in bed, screaming as shards of wood ripped around in the cyclone's wake. One jagged sliver whipping across the void as the tornado stormed off, carrying its precious offerings.*

Young Mason looks down and sees the sliver in his gut, protruding from the flesh as a trickle of blood seeps out.

It's there one moment—just as he remembered....

But then gone the next. His torso—clean, unbroken skin. It was never there.

The image vanished, replaced by the quiet stars, cold and heartless.

"You remember," Solomon said, "what you were meant to. But tell me, what do you recall of the events after that? Of your foster care? Who were you staying with?"

Mason clenched his eyes shut for a moment. "I remember as much as any five year old kid. Which isn't much. A little house in the suburbs of Indiana. A brother named Jack and a little cocker spaniel named Alfie."

"Let me guess, Dad was a truck driver, Mom stayed home and fed you peanut butter sandwiches and let you watch cartoons all day until school. And then after age seven, you went to the Morrises in San Diego, a nice rich childless couple who showered you with attention and money for school and encouraged your interests in weather and science." Solomon came closer, and behind his head, a faint view of a spinning galaxy took shape, framing him with a divine cosmic halo.

"I don't understand," Mason said in almost a whimper. "The Morrises were great. I remember all that."

"Clearer than you remember the earlier couple?"

"Of course, but I was younger then, and traumatized by the tornado and losing my parents. Of course everything was hazy."

"You weren't in Indiana."

"I was."

Solomon smiled and again pointed at the scar.

"You weren't. Strings were pulled, and a certain affluent landowner from Kansas took a striking interest in you after your survival at the hands of that tornado. You were special, and he wanted special. He saw potential in you, a chance to mold you into something." Solomon raised his head and looked up, blotting out the galaxy's light.

Mason's throat tightened, but he spoke anyway, giving up now any further attempt at deception. It was over and he was lost. "It was you," he said. "In the sweatshirt."

"Yes."

"Wielding the knife."

"Yes."

"You … had the rocking horse in the basement. The first room at the top of the stairs."

Solomon inclined his head, a little surprise in his eyes. But he gave a nod.

"You …" Mason let it roll of his tongue. "Were my brother."

"At last," Solomon said, spreading out his arms—and the staff along with it. "He remembers."

"But how …?"

Mason held onto the solidity of the white stone and focused on its granular streaks and multiple fractures as a sign of truth. Although at this point, he didn't know anything anymore.

"You're wondering how you can trust anything now, aren't you?" Solomon made a motion to Victor and the man nodded and made his way out into the shadows and through a door that closed promptly, returning the room to the semblance of a moonless night on an ascended peak close to the infinite sky.

"How is any of this happening?" Mason made an agonized face. "Hallucinating. I have to be. Drugged?" He thought of the Amazon jaunts Solomon boasted about and the rare plants and roots they had found. The ingredients that cured Shelby might have had cousins that were in the LSD family and acted on his brain. That was the only solution.

"It's one possibility," Solomon agreed. "Another is that your mind is just powerful enough to project what it's envisioning externally. But not in the reality sense that you think. In fact, you have been projecting into the minds of those around you."

"What?"

"Exactly the reverse of how we set up your office, for example."

"What do you mean?"

"There are no projectors, as you've discovered. No hidden technology or plasma modules or microfibers. You saw what we wanted you to see. And I needed to learn if you had the same ability, to project what you wanted others to see."

Mason blinked at him, and for a moment he had a vision of ancient moors, and hooded figures making the Romans see armies where none existed. "I don't believe it."

"You don't have to. Just like you don't have to believe that multiple tornadoes can converge on one spot, as if summoned from another dimension."

Mason took a deep breath. Had to steady himself again. He looked upon Solomon with new eyes. The scales were off. "So, brother. Assuming I believe that this Louis Palavar took me in as a foster child and I lived on that farm, then you …"

"Another stray." Solomon sighed. "You and I, we share a great many things. Including a tragic end to our parents. In my case, not just mom and dad, but two older sisters as well, caught in the crossfire."

"What happened?"

Solomon leaned on his staff and he closed his eyes.

"Best if you see it firsthand. Sit back, relax and enjoy the show."

Spinning little wheels over pavement. A baby carriage on its way through a park. Mother and father each holding a handle. Beautiful sunlight in the long blonde curls of twins, skipping ahead toward a playground.

The sound of the girls' footsteps drown out the crying, wailing of the baby boy. Fierce green eyes squint against the glare.

"Put the visor down," the mother insists.

"We're almost there," says dad. "Just a minute and we can put him in the shade.

"But he's miserable, it's right in his eyes."

"He can take it. Jesus Christ he'll be fine."

"I can't stand the crying, you didn't hear him again last night."

"What can I say? I sleep like the dead."

"Bastard."

She pushes faster, and the carriage shifts, the sun spears brighter into the child's eyes and the wails intensify to a fever pitch and all of a sudden …

The clouds devour the sky as if dumped from a massive funnel. In seconds the park plunges into shade and the winds pick up, swirling at first and then driving hard from the north, gathering speed.

"What the hell?" the father says, and then louder: "Girls! Girls! Get back here, run to the car!"

The last part is lost in a peal of thunder that sounds as if a war has just erupted in the skies.

Hail the size of fists begin to pelt the park. They hear it first as the great chunks of ice slam into the metal slides and the bars of the jungle gym. Then the plunk-plunk-thud against the earth and the pavement.

But the rest is devoured by screams and cries of pain.

"RUN!" the father yells again, but then immediately falls to the ground, slamming his forehead against the concrete path, and his dazed eyes lock on the green of his son's. The baby carriage, overturned, provides the only respite from nature's onslaught as hailstones bounce off the rims and the protective side covering.

Other screams eventually dwindle. Someone's crying, whimpering and calling a name, "Avery ..." but even that silences with another thwump sound and a squish like a hammer bursting a melon.

The baby ... silent now, just blinks at his father, even as the hailstones keep battering his body and crunching his skull. A huge gash in his dad's forehead keeps pumping red. Blood runs into the rainwater that has started to fall like a wave of archers' arrows, cleaning up after the stones have done their job. Drenching, washing the world clean.

Eventually, the baby sighs. Snug in his restraints, Avery Solomon closes his eyes and drifts to sleep.

"After that tragic little story hit the news, people were drawn to the miracle baby that had survived such a horrific event. Donations flooded in and my grandmother was grateful, but she was old, with one foot in the nursing home."

Solomon smiled wistfully as the room returned to its nocturnal components and the visions—either in Mason's head or still projected somehow, he couldn't understand which—dissolved. Mason still leaned against the large stone, looking about for a chair, anything to rest on. He only found the altar in the center, and the light hitting it revealed just enough of traces of red to give him the chills. *Had they already done sacrifices here? What the hell have I walked into?*

And more: *What was Gabriel a part of? How deep did this occult shit go?*

Solomon had his back turned now, and began pacing. "Keep listening Mason, I'm getting to the part about you."

"Oh good," he replied, forcing dialogue, if for nothing else, to keep grounded and not leave his mind adrift, dangerously close to going over the edge of the earth.

"So that's when Louis Palavar entered my life. A tidy sum he paid to my grandmother, along with promises of visitation and constant updates ... of course which never happened. She was dead within a month."

"Sorry."

"Things happen. Anyway, that's how I came to the Palavar ranch. And for a time, it was just me and my new 'father.'"

"What did he want with you?"

"Same as he wanted with you," Solomon replied without turning around. His head was inclined up at the stars and the faint galaxy above. "We were—are—like lightning rods. There's a power within us, an affinity with nature that goes beyond natural selection, beyond luck or just karma. You hear of people who can sense changing air pressure in the bones, an advancing thunderstorm in their sinuses. But others, like us—it's more than that. We are part of a long history of men and women. In the past we would have been called sorcerers, shamans, medicine men or magi."

"Druids," Mason whispered, and Solomon's eyes widened.

"Ah, so you're not completely clueless."

"I didn't say I believed any of it. All those people—just like the rainmakers in the dust bowl or snake charmers at the circus, they played on people's gullibility. Their needs. They used some general forecasting ability, modest sensibilities of rainy seasons and typical historical behavior. Red sky at night sort of proverbs, that's all. Spoken in the right way, with ceremony and maybe some animal sacrifice, and your followers are suddenly in awe of your powers." Mason shook his head. "It's not all smoke and mirrors, but as Arthur C. Clarke said: 'Any significantly advanced technology is indistinguishable from magic.' Just keep the advanced tech—or knowledge—away from the common folk and they'll believe in wizardry. Or druidism."

Solomon gripped his staff and turned, displaying it for Mason. "You're not wrong. But you're not entirely correct, either. Palavar showed me that, and showed you too, before you forgot."

"I don't—"

"Remember, I know. But we learned, you and I. Especially what we could achieve with the right tools." He hefted the staff, admiring every nook and twisting grain of wood. "The way to harness that power."

"Wait," Mason said. "Back up for a minute. Palavar brought you there, adopted…. Why? Because he thought you, even as a baby, had this innate power over weather?"

"A dangerous power, but something, for sure. He wasn't positive, but the signs were there. A sudden violent storm out of the thin air, one that I alone survived. It could have been dumb luck, the way the carriage fell and protected me, but it could have been more. I was under extreme stress, I'm told. Reacting to my parents' emotional state, and furious with how they were ignoring me."

"You were a baby, for god's sakes."

"Exactly, not knowing any better. Trying to influence the world and get what I want, when normally the only way was through tears."

"So okay, Palavar thinks you can do that and wants to what, train you? Or keep you out of the way so you won't harm anyone else?"

"Both, for sure. There on that farm, away from the greater population … my outbursts, if they stirred up the weather again, could only damage the land or some cows. But it was also … a time of testing."

"What do you mean?"

"Palavar was … not a nice man. At least, not outwardly to me. You see, he had to develop my powers, had to use me to see if I could do it again, and to what extent. And what could be controlled. To achieve that, he … beat me. Abused me.… The torments …"

For a moment, the side wall melted away into a snarling visage of a middle-aged man with a rugged beard and blazing eyes … and a belt gripped in a fist that drew back and swung down … again and again.…

The scene melted away, back to the serene circle of stones.

"It worked," Solomon said. "My pain, my frustration and anguish … You saw, in your research …"

"The tornadoes, the wild weather over several years."

"I brought it all, yes. Not too extreme at first. At first, it was thunderstorms and hail, wind and lightning. But oh, we harnessed it."

"How?"

"Palavar … he was no ordinary man either."

Mason frowned, and a flash of light in his mind lit up that familiar cottage in the mountains, then it was gone—and he was grateful that none of that showed up on the walls. He felt sure it would give away something Solomon shouldn't know about Mason's knowledge.

"He belonged to an order. He wasn't the leader yet, but he would soon rise to that position. With my help. With *our* help."

"I'm completely lost," Mason said, feeling suddenly weary beyond belief. He thought of Lauren, of Shelby, and suddenly wanted nothing more than to be as far away from this place as possible. He thought of Channel 7 and Pamela and wished he was still at his old job, thinking about nothing more complicated than the latest prevailing wind speeds.

"Look," said Solomon, and the walls shifted again, and this time the circle of standing stones had transplanted back into the earth at Palavar's farm, in the same configuration that Solomon had drawn on the wall in his bedroom.

Eight figures wearing white robes and hoods …

"A KKK rally?"

Solomon laughed. "Notice the different hoods? And belts made out of mistletoe, with holly wreathes around their necks? No, quite a different group here."

"Druids, then."

"From a long and noble line, tracing back to the Celtic traditions and the—"

"Time of the Saxons and the invasion by Rome."

Solomon nodded approvingly. "So you paid attention in some history classes! Not just a science boy, after all. Does this look familiar?"

"What do you mean?" Mason asked, even as the hairs at the back of his neck were standing up.

"It does, doesn't it?"

"A drawing, on the wall upstairs in his farmhouse."

Solomon let out a chuckle. "Knew you'd seen that. It must have pulled at your subconscious."

"Why? Why would something you drew have made an impact on my mind?"

"Because I didn't draw it."

Mason blinked. *And the images flickered. Remained, but the viewpoint pulled back—up and back, through an upstairs window to where two boys were crouching, peering out through the glass, watching the ceremony outside. It was dusk, but still light enough even though there were torches beside each stone....*

And a body on the altar.

One of the boys pointed and the other nodded. He went for his crayons, looked out the window, then started to draw....

"That's how we learned," Solomon said. "From the council, gathered here at Palavar's request. He had something to show them, after all. The power of nature, harnessed by two new recruits. He offered to train us in the old ways, just as he was trained, and as most of them were. It's a long tradition, and without such training ..."

"You make it sound like Jedi school," Mason said. "And he's Yoda?"

"Something like that, only we weren't the ideal students."

"What do you mean? And what, for that matter, did we learn? Assuming I believe I was there with you. You could be making all this up. Hypnotized me maybe, into believing it. My mind ... it's ..."

"Believe what you want," Solomon said. "You were there, because that's how you got that scar." He pointed past the scene now, where the boys were frozen in time, again looking out the window, down into the clearing where a young woman was voluntarily stepping through the circle, shedding her robe and lying naked onto the white slab. She spread out her arms and then crossed them over her chest as one man—Palavar—came forward. Raising up a knife ...

The image dissolved as he brought it down in a graceful arc, and again Mason and Solomon were alone in the dark.

"We learned," Solomon said, "what he didn't want us to see. Secrets we weren't supposed to know until much, much later. Up until that night, we had been mere tools for him to experiment with.

We were lightning rods in the purest sense, and he used us to call down all sorts of weather. To improve his crops, to cause drought and tornadoes, to wipe out competing farms ... We gave unwilling support, but we were just as guilty."

"But ... if he was such a hotshot druid as you claim, and if they really have these powers over nature, why did he need us?"

Solomon smiled. "Fair question. But the truth is that just like the forecasting you did at Channel 7, magic is no different. You can't do it alone. Especially as the stakes get higher and the results you want are bigger. To reach farther distances or impact whole sections of the country and not just a local park where you're having a picnic ... then you need help." Solomon walked to the altar and set his staff upon it.

"You need ... sacrifice. Blood, especially. Sometimes it's antecedent to the effect you want, other times it's promised in return for what you're asking for. Or perhaps it's the release of energy at the moment of death that does it. The sacrifice of one so connected to the natural energies of the world could certainly buy up enough potential that he who wielded the knife could control greater outcomes and call upon greater sources of energy."

"Now you're losing me."

Solomon shrugged. "It doesn't matter. You weren't lost back then. In fact, it was all crystal clear. After that sacrifice, the one we just witnessed, we saw a tornado the likes of nothing since. The druids, with Palavar at the center of the circle, summoned that demonic thing out of thin air, spun it around like a top, dressed it up in lightning, then sent it on a massive killing spree where it decimated eighteen counties and tore up half the neighboring farms.

"So after that, after Palavar and his pals recovered and slept and drank and had some all-night parties, you and I ... we saw the writing on the wall, quite literally. We put two and two together and came up with the idea that one of us, like a fattened cow, would be sacrificed next."

"Was that it? Was that why he wanted us?"

"Perhaps," Solomon said. "But it was too early. I found that out later. For the sacrifice to work, for it to really have power ..."

"It had to be made willingly by the victim."

Solomon again looked surprised. "How did you know that?"

Mason licked his lips, thinking of how not to give away Shelby's theory. He pointed at the section where the images had been. "The clearing, that woman. Unless she was drugged, it looked like she was a volunteer."

"True. We didn't know it at the time, but she was. A martyr for the cause. Maybe brainwashed, or maybe Palavar had some leverage over her. I'm not sure. But she did it for him, for them. And you saw what happened."

"Okay, saying I believe all that? What are you getting at? What does any of this have to do with Solstice, with me, with … whatever you've been trying to do at the UN? Why do you need me?"

Solomon turned and leaned against the altar.

"I'm sad you can't just accept that I wanted a reunion with my childhood playmate. My friend and my one-time brother."

"Reunions aren't my thing," Mason said. "And I doubt they're yours either. Especially after you tried to kill me."

"Did I?"

Mason lifted his shirt partway. "Remember this?"

"I do," said Solomon, "but I also remember I wasn't the one to give it to you."

"What the hell do you mean?"

Solomon shook his head. "Do I have to show you? Or can't you remember? Aren't the blocks gone yet?" He suddenly picked up the staff, took a step and slammed it down on the floor, creating a crack like a peal of thunder … and a flash of light—

And Mason was lying on the slab under the dying sunlight peeking through the gently-waving willow branches. Young Solomon approached, a scared look on his face under the hood of his sweatshirt as he held out the knife—hilt first.

Mason took it, and turned it around. Held it with both hands, pointing at his stomach. He nodded to Solomon, took a deep breath …

And plunged it down.

Chapter 4

You can choose what to believe, Mason control four of the wildest, but the truth is that you have within you the power to be like us."

And, saying that, Solomon backed up and raised his staff, and suddenly there were seven others in the room. All wearing grey suits. Three women and four men, each standing by a stone. Each wearing holly wreaths around their necks and holding staves.

Solomon took a deep breath. "You lack our training, but the power in you is vast, intense and dangerous. You unwittingly called it upon your family as a boy, with tragic results."

"What?" Mason's head swam with the implications and the sudden guilt. *Was he right?*

"It would have been much worse later, especially in puberty, had Palavar not found you and worked with you and—failing you, as he realized when he found us in the circle, you bleeding out and me trying to summon and control four of the wildest cyclones at the same time ..."

"No...." Mason shook his head and held his stomach, feeling the renewed pain. "But I survived, I ... remember."

A flash, and Palavar was there, his hands bloody and also full of dirt and some sort of green leaf, stuffing everything into Mason's wound and muttering words of ancient power over him, barely making himself heard over the shrieking winds and the competing tornadoes pounding and demanding tribute.

Palavar stepped away from Mason, the wound patched, the blood flow ceasing.

"The sacrifice is incomplete!" he shouted—to Solomon, to the skies. And he bent low and raised a staff and stepped onto the altar, straddling Mason as Solomon cowered on his knees. The four tornadoes rocked and flayed and spat up chunks of earth. Palavar switched directions and raised his staff.

It looked like he was wavering, losing strength. His staff cracked down the middle.

"No …"

Just then, others came running out of the farmhouse. A young black man with dreadlocks, a pretty brunette, a blond man with a long pale face and spindly arms, several others. They spread out quickly, dodging debris and struggling to see through the stinging wind and dust, but they managed to get in position around the altar, and a sort of luminescent green haze formed from around the stones, connecting side to side, then diagonally and forming crisscrossing lines of shimmering power that built and built and suddenly exploded backward.

Every druid was bathed in emerald energy, and their eyes glowed like miniature green suns.

And Palavar stood tall, absorbing that power.

His staff healed and reformed and then he swung it in a huge 360-degree arc and it was as if he had reached out an impossible distance and struck the eye of each cyclone in turn.

One by one they shattered and exploded, fizzled and died out, scattering into a wind that went nowhere.

And then he collapsed, along with the others.

Solomon alone stood in the circle looking upon them all, and then turning his attention to Mason, seeing his chest rise and fall slowly although his eyes were closed.

Ever so slowly, Solomon moved closer and reached for the staff in Palavar's grasp. Touched just the edge of it before it was snatched away.

Palavar sat up and gave him a sneer full of fury and malice, and then slapped him with the back of his hand so hard the lights went out for a long, long time.

◌

"You were healed," Solomon said as the images faded one last time. "And when you regained consciousness, you were far, far from Kansas."

"But … I still don't remember how."

"In reality, he worked on you for three weeks. Keeping you drugged, sedated while he tinkered in your mind. Creating images like we've been doing here. Over and over, reinforcing memories that never were. Giving you a past you never had, writing over the real events of the past two years, just like you do when you record over existing songs on a cassette tape."

"But the initial ones were still there, somewhere."

Solomon nodded. "Palavar called a vote, and you were out. Too dangerous to be trusted, too powerful to be trained successfully."

"But if I had really done … that …" Mason pointed at the wall again. "Tried to sacrifice myself … Wasn't that what they wanted me for?"

"Yes and no." Solomon sighed. "In the end, no one wanted to relive what had happened. We were too young for that sort of sacrifice. Nature … the energy our forefathers thought were gods … it didn't want the blood of kids. Souls not developed enough yet maybe, or else it's the free will factor that's most important. And at that age, it's just not there. In fact, it's almost a sacrilege to attempt it. That's what we discovered."

"So I was cast out."

"Yes, but he didn't send you out without sufficient guarantees. He toned you down, so to speak. Made you much more mellow a fellow, if I might take verbal license."

"To stop me from what—more inadvertent tornadoes?"

"Emotional states can be tricky. We don't know what exactly causes such outbursts, but you are obviously deeply in tune with meteorological conditions." His eyes twinkled. "And, some might even say, your forecasting ability is so uncannily good as to indicate that maybe you have a hand in *making* the weather rather than merely predicting it."

"That's ridiculous."

"Is it? After everything you've learned about yourself and others today?"

Mason was silent, still absorbing it all; but like an over-soaked sponge, he had no room left for another drop of unreality. Instead, he looked around at the others, settling on Solomon, and brought the discussion back to ground. "And you remained with him?"

"Palavar still wanted a pupil. Needed a successor. Apparently you can't be an arch-druid without some apprentices in tow. Doesn't look good on your resume."

Mason cocked his head. "And is Gabriel your ... apprentice?"

Solomon smiled. "Now we get to the good part."

"What's that?"

"Your children."

Mason bristled. "What about them? Gabriel I understand. He's cut from the same mold, with the same intentions, but Shelby ... Why her?"

"Because," said Solomon, "they're you're children. Because sometimes it's hereditary. And because of what happened on that Colorado highway when you weren't there. The freak storm, Lauren's accident ..."

"You think ... it was Shelby? That she did what you and I had done as kids?"

"Either her or Gabriel." Solomon shrugged. "We'll never know, but what I can tell you is that if one has it ..."

And then Mason remembered. The legends, the talk with Pamela about the most powerful shamans and magic users, always being ...

"*Twins ...*"

Mason advanced on Solomon, fists clenched. "This is far enough. You've threatened my daughter, kidnapped her—and yes, cured her, but now I have to wonder. About Lauren, about the timing of her hemorrhage ..."

A restraining hand caught his shoulder, making him wince in almost debilitating agony. Victor had returned, and pulled him back, holding his arms in check. Not that it mattered, Mason was going nowhere.

Solomon took his place at the cornerstone, near the head of the altar. "Don't be alarmed. The time for sacrifice is not upon us yet.

We have another day until the Solstice. Until the alignment and the reckoning will come. For more than two thousand years we druids have worked behind the scenes, guiding humanity, striving to allow it to coexist in a natural world where it had no right to belong."

"No right, according to whom?"

"According to our weaknesses. Our genes. The only thing we have going for us is stubborn perseverance. We get knocked down by a volcano here, a tsunami there, hurricanes, earthquakes and firestorms, lightning and tornadoes. Brutal ice and persistent subzero temperatures or non-stop heat waves. And then the survivors get back up and we do it all again. Rebuild on the same shore or at the foot of the same volcano, expecting different results this time. Yes, it's insanity, and that's what humanity is. Certifiable. And yet …" Solomon looked around at the smiling faces. "We support them anyway. We do what we can, always from behind the scenes. It's been our way for millennia. Never gaining credit, and sometimes rightfully so. For we haven't always acted in the best interests of humanity. Sometimes, civilizations just had to go."

"And you're saying you helped?"

"We can't claim complete credit, but yes. The Mayans. The Aztecs. Egypt even, going farther back. It once thrived in a lush climate at the banks of the Nile, with steady rainfall and abundant crops. Easy enough to shift them out of such a zone, to bring the drought, spoil the earth and poison the air. Civilizations like theirs had run their course, and much like today, the world's so called great powers have run amok, unchecked in their greed. They have become too arrogant, believing themselves above nature. The earth isn't their plaything."

Sounding just like Gabriel. No wonder he's found a kindred spirit. "And so you're going to knock them back down to size?"

"More or less. It's past time, and would have happened years ago if not for … divergent feelings on the matter from some of our members. Those with much less daring visions."

"Palavar?" Solomon asked. "Is that what happened?" *A coup …*

"He was old," Solomon said. "And had nothing left to give to the cause but his blood and his … staff." Smiling, he held up the arch-druid's weapon of choice.

"He didn't think big enough, content to mold the impressionable young minds with Hollywood drivel and Twitter feeds and other social media claptrap. As if that would stop the juggernaut of devastation, deforestation, and resource destruction the world over."

"I thought all that global warming stuff was political bullshit to you?"

Solomon shrugged. "True, in the overall scheme of things, Nature will win out and man will go the way of countless other extinct species, but I would be negligent in my role as caretaker if I didn't do all in my power to … hasten things along. Wipe the slate clean, if you will."

"And what is it this time? Let loose the tornadoes and the hail, your own unique dogs of war?"

"Think bigger. As you've seen in the past few weeks, it's already begun. We've softened up the world, set the primer, so to speak, with tsunamis and hurricanes, earthquakes and violent storms. The sacrifices have been taken and the stage is set for more. Appetites have been stoked, and the main course is ready."

Now the images formed, the earth in the air over the altar, with twelve red spheres circling it, getting in alignment….

Just like the standing stones.

Mason saw it now. "So we are here to finish the job, and you think these satellites will direct what … your energies and powers?"

Solomon smiled. "I don't *think*. I know what they can do. Magic, sorcery … it's all indistinguishable from advanced technology—or from bits and bytes. Ones and zeroes. We upload the code in the same way we'd chant over a geographical position, the same way the druids of old focused their efforts on a cloud or mountaintop, or how Genghis Khan sent storms upon the enemy. Only now, with this technology and our strongest magic, we can do it on a global scale."

"Eat your heart out, Genghis." Mason motioned with his chin to the altar. "And am I to be the sacrifice again?"

Still smiling, Solomon said nothing.

"I won't do it willingly, not this time," Mason said. "I'm not some five year-old kid anymore."

"No," Solomon agreed. "Now you're a husband. And a parent."

And there it is …

Mason swallowed hard. "Shelby …"

"And your dear wife. You were right of course." Solomon waved his staff and the section over the right shoulder vanished, like a planetarium surface, creating an image of a familiar hospital room where nurses rushed in, and Lauren was there, convulsing in the bed as the monitor spiked out a warning in a high pitched alarm.

"Lauren!"

The image vanished, replaced by an airport lounge, where Gabriel and three men in black coats approached the arrival gate, zeroing in on Shelby, who had just deplaned, still with her headphones on, oblivious to her welcomers.

The scene vanished, leaving Mason to lower his head in defeat.

Solomon let out a sigh. "I think you'll do the right thing. The only thing."

The others turned and began to file out of the room. Victor released Mason. Solomon followed him out. "You'll have plenty of time to think about it when you are locked in here. One more day, Mason, and it will all be over. Do what you must, and your children, your wife—they'll all be cared for, ushered into the next golden age of humanity. Down in our bunker in the lower levels, the members of Solstice I've handpicked … we will emerge and start again upon a world wiped clean of corruption, a world restored to natural order."

With that, he left and the door closed in, seamlessly blending with the night, and the cacophony of insects and the wind rose and sang as one as Mason fell to his knees and turned onto his back, staring up at the heartless constellations.

Chapter 5

He wasn't sure when he finally found sleep, but it came and it tugged at his thoughts and his memories, and teased out dreams and recollections, swirling both into one tapestry that was indistinguishable as either.

Sleep came, and like he had just boarded a subway train; the doors closed and whisked him to the next stop. Only this time, he wasn't a passive passenger. He thought about Central Park, and the feeling was the same. This was no ordinary dream. It was controlled and lucid, and the more he focused, the more real it seemed until when those doors opened and he stepped out, he knew exactly where he'd be.

Exactly the destination he expected.

The hospital. A dimly lit hallway. Intensive Care sign on the walls. He walked briskly and directly, reading the names outside the doors. Passed a couple of nurses on the nightshift, but no one seemed to notice him.

Am I really here? He wondered about it, but not too hard. He felt the connection was tenuous at best, and thinking too much on it would be like the moment you realize that you are dreaming, and promptly lose control and wake up.

At the same time, he felt sure that he was here, if for no other reason than the Haitian had told him: *Your spirit be walking mighty far, my guess is, by your bare feet and the twigs stuck between your toes.* Mason just didn't know how to control it, although he felt he was doing just fine now. As for other people, he had the sense that they didn't see him, although they might if they looked just in the right light, or out of the corner of their eyes.

He wasn't about to test that theory though. Especially after he found Lauren's room—and found that she wasn't alone.

He almost went in through the open door to throw his arms around her and hold her hand, but held back at the threshold. At first, it seemed she rested peacefully, her head bandaged, eyes closed, tubes up her nose, but something bothered him. Something about the chair by her bedside. The room was dark and the shadows thicker on that side, but still … he saw the chair was empty one moment, and occupied the next. Like an image in a novelty lenticular photograph, the old man in the dark coat was there one moment, gone the next.

Mason focused and found the angle where the man remained. He seemed bored, like he was on guard, performing a menial function. A black cane-staff rested against the chair, untouched as his hands were occupied, a bag of peanuts in one as he greedily stuffed handfuls in his mouth, chewing with loose dentures in a salt-riddled mouth.

Mason backed out slowly after checking on Lauren once more, seeing the monitors, watching the rising and falling of her chest.

Sleep well, and dream of pleasant days ahead. When this is all behind us.

He backed up, about to turn the corner—

When the man in the chair snapped his head around. Eyes widened and found him and he stood in a cascade of falling peanuts and cracked shells.

He opened his mouth, dribbling crumbs, and reached for his staff.

Mason felt a wave of power and energy rippling from the aged man, far in excess of the impression he gave off. And Mason had no intention of feeling anything further, already desperately sure he had given away everything.

He closed his eyes and stepped back one more step—into the waiting train. The doors slammed shut just as the snarling, twisted old features rushed toward him, and he was gone.

Not back to Solstice. Not yet. Not if he could still maintain this dream-astral-projection state. Whatever it was, he had to check on Shelby. For this feat, however, it was a little more difficult than he anticipated. Not only did logic and reason slip and threaten to pull him from the dream. *How is this happening, how can this be real?* Those questions were put aside in favor of impressions about her location, about finding Gabriel.

His mind drifted, his thoughts roamed from the airport to the surrounding areas, and settled on a speeding black limo. Watching from a hawk's eye view, Mason wasn't sure if this was real time, or had happened already. He followed it, zooming in, moving closer, dropping.... Until it parked at a large abandoned lot in front of a warehouse with broken windows and rusted gutters.

Mason paused, and as if waiting for assurance, storm clouds suddenly rolled in. They converged from east and west like opposing vanguards of their respective armies. Slowing, the clouds finally twisted and churned together directly over the warehouse.

She's in there, Mason thought. *And she's not the only one.*

He forced himself down, in through the roof, and confirmed that time here was far from linear. He settled through the superstructure and found himself on a metal walkway over the warehouse floor. Shelby sat directly below, and Mason could see she had her wrists tied behind her back. The warehouse itself was a wide open space, a few pillars supporting a secondary level of metal frames and shelves. Otherwise, the ground floor was just dust and debris, some crates and empty barrels in a corner. Bird nests and broken windows decorated the upper level.

Victor stood in the background, his bulky frame almost blocking out that of the limo driver's. Two other well-dressed associates from Solstice were there, discussing plans with each other. Nexus and Remulus: Mason recalled meeting them in the grove the first day, and now had the impression they were far more than they seemed. Apart from the muscle and the added security, there was one other person in the large space.

Gabriel.

He faced Shelby, holding his staff. His bald head glinted in the overhead lights that flickered and pulsed. Shelby's hair lifted and flew in front of her face and the other two men turned and approached.

Mason debated.... Could he get down there and do something? Every cell in his body screamed that he should be down there helping his daughter, but at the same time he knew it would do no good. He wasn't strong enough. Just a fledgling with this power, unsure of his wings or how to use them, much less how far they could take him. And he had the sense that the display down there—and the drama show up in the skies—was just that. A show. A reaction of the two of them together.

How much did Shelby know, Mason wondered, about herself and her abilities? Obviously it was partly genetic, partly learned. Gabriel had extensive training from a master druid. Shelby ... he guessed her background was more trial, error and spontaneity.

Whatever was going on down there, Gabriel seemed to be winning. With his free hand, he warded off Victor and the driver as if to say *I've got this.* And he did. Soon, Shelby tired, the breeze died and she lowered her head, hair falling over her eyes.

Gabriel muttered something that carried through the acoustics, "Sleep and behave. Or we'll be forced to knock you out." Then he turned away and took his cell phone out and started to make a call.

Seeing a chance, Mason thought of something. Just a gesture, but he had to let her know that there was hope, and to hang on.

He thought hard and focused ... On a crack in the masonry between her feet, right where she was looking ...

Can I do this? He thought it even as he learned the answer. Felt a power source nearby—whether it was in the air itself, or from the churning convection event in the sky above, he wasn't sure. Or maybe it was from Gabriel and Shelby themselves—there was something he plugged into like an outlet, and it gave just enough current to fuel his thoughts.

He sensed the dirt and debris just through the crack, deep down under the masonry slab. The old earth lying dormant. And he teased it, nourished it with a tender touch of energy, found and molded a kernel of biological material. Conditioned it, then set it free.

And he watched it grow. A tiny green stalk at first, just peeking through the crack, then ascending and twirling a little, rising about four inches.

Shelby's head moved slightly. Lifted and her shoulders tensed. She watched just as Mason did, watched the bulb form, grow, then open. Four gentle bright yellow petals unfolded, revealing a darker stem in the center, surrounded by eye-like dots and a smiling coloration.

It was Shelby's favorite flower, growing up and all through high school. If a boyfriend didn't bring her Black Eyed Susans, he might as well turn right around at the door. Mason still remembered slipping a corsage on her wrist for the prom after her thoughtless date had arrived without one. Then Lauren took a million pictures of the two of them before they let her go.

Shelby saw it and she looked up, turned her head around. Gabriel's back was to her and the other men were still in a discussion in the other part of the warehouse, looking bored.

Look higher, Mason thought. In another moment, she did. It took a couple long seconds and again Mason wasn't sure if he was visible in this form or if he was really here in some alternate sense. But her eyes swept back and forth, and then settled on his location, and her mouth opened wide.

Mason put a finger to his lips, and then spread out his hand as if to say, *Wait. Sit tight. I'll be back.*

With help, hopefully.

She nodded, then put her foot—reluctantly—over the flower to hide it. Mason let himself go, just as reluctantly, his heart swimming in guilt for leaving her. But he did it, and pulled himself away.

No train this time; it was more like just a shift in scenery.

An uncontrollable, unplanned shift. Maybe it was still that nebulous power he had tapped into, or some sort of natural energy line, but it suddenly and sharply whisked him away like an undersea current. Swept down in an undertow, then hurled a great distance away.

And suddenly he was somewhere else....

Chapter 6

O n a well-worn path in a wooded realm, a hazy sun rose, peeking between the snow-capped trees like a curious newborn stag.

Mason followed the path as it traveled over a gentle hill. He followed it as a carefree hiker or latter century explorer, his mind clear and his thoughts oddly free of distraction. Just taking in the magnificent scenery, the sloping terrain, the majestic sequoia trunks and extensive foliage. The sounds of the forest, the animals and insects, the cool northern breeze through the branches …

The breeze that died completely within a few more yards as the shadows deepened and the land sloped into a steeper decline, warming slightly until the recent snowfall melted and revealed the ground cover of twigs and leaves, roots and rocks. Moss encroached in the congealing shadows and the trail vanished. Mason stopped, frowning. He scratched his head and wished for a walking stick or a staff of some kind. Seemed he was sorely unprepared without one. Not only unprepared, but also … lacking the invitation he needed to proceed.

He squinted and tried to peer through the darkness ahead. Somehow he couldn't make out any features or distinctions in the forest, no sign of the trail for sure, but also a layer of mist had moved in and clouded the way ahead. Only, Mason wasn't sure if the clouding was in reality, or just in his mind. His temples throbbed and his eyes hurt as if he'd just woken from a night of hard drinking and dehydration.

There was something he had to do. Something in there, farther along the now-nonexistent path. He looked back over his shoulder. Even the sun was afraid to go any further; it had descended and pulled a layer of earth over its eye, darkening the world even more.

Undeterred, Mason walked straight down into the spreading darkness that rose up to meet him, into the mist that sent out a cool, clammy embrace. He walked and walked, until the footing became knotty and treacherous, until he couldn't see even his hand in front of his face. The world had become shadows and fog. No up or down, no sense of reality in any direction. For all he knew he could be heading straight off the edge of a cliff.

He had to stop. Stop and think....

Where am I? What am I doing here?

He thought and thought. For a long time, until he feared he might have even been here for hours, days. And if he thought about it some more, the days would turn to weeks, months. Years.

This was no ordinary mist, no ordinary forest.

Despite that realization, he clung to one thought in the formless nothingness, the mist that had gone through his nostrils and ears into his mind, obscuring all:

I am no ordinary man.

He had something to do. Something to find. He thought again, pushing the mist aside with a gentle breeze.

And in his clarified mind, swept clear of clouded debris, he saw the image that had flashed in his vision earlier, during his meeting with the Haitian—a familiar landscape with a snow-capped mountain in the background, only now he saw it from an eagle-eye view. He rose up, through the green ceiling, higher and higher, ascending up above the air currents and gracefully soaring into the sunlit realm, where light still held its own dominion.

Regaining purpose was difficult with such majestic power and control over the winds and the air, swooping and climbing, but he brought his sight back down and peered across the sea of green. Back and forth until he found what he was looking for: a lone clearing in a patch of thick trees. Nothing more could he see, as the area stubbornly refused to resolve itself, as if it were a satellite photo blurred out by government security teams before it could be shown to the public.

In a flash, he was back on the ground, back in the dark and the mist. But this time, he returned with a sense of direction.

He was close. He just needed a little help, a little assistance in finding the way.

A little … magic.

His eyes closed or opened; he couldn't tell. Mason reached out and shuffled his feet until his fingers contacted something. Bark, sharp thick wood with rough edges and deep creases. He reached up and down, almost caressing the tree like a lover, until he found an off-shooting branch.

Too fresh, he went on to seek another, and another and then found one. Nearly dead, brittle and if not diseased, at least ruined enough that it wouldn't grow any more. He found the base, and with both hands, snapped it free.

In the darkness, he estimated the size of the branch. A little too long for his purposes, he set the bottom edge down against the ground, and using his foot, broke a section off to make it a manageable size. Held it up, then moved his hands up and down, breaking off odd shoots and old sapling branches. His skin was cut, bleeding and smearing his blood on the wood—which, he imagined, might only make the magic more powerful.

Then he was ready.

It wasn't the ivory staff he was given back in the hospital, the one he still needed to retrieve when the time came, but for now, this would do.

He held it up, not sure what to do or how to proceed. He only knew that this was right, this was the missing piece. This was the invitation he had been lacking.

Holding the makeshift staff with his right hand, he aimed it toward the darkness and let the mist curl all around it, and then he focused on the staff, focused all his thoughts and energy.

He thought of Shelby and of Lauren. He thought of the sun, its energy and power, and let the feeling of warmth and intensity of illumination gather in his arm and travel up to his hand.

And he spoke, deciding to call on his rudimentary knowledge of Latin, if only to make it seem more realistic. *"Lux in obscurum!"* He said, pronouncing the words with care. A little "light in the darkness." That had to work, he hoped.

Nothing happened.

He shook the staff, and kept holding it aloft until his arm started to hurt. He waved it around, then sighed. *Harry Potter never had this problem.*

He stamped it on the ground and again raised it up. *"Lux in—"*

The world lit up all at once, in a blinding sphere of light, banishing darkness and bathing the forest in a dazzling light that Mason couldn't bear. He dropped to his knees, eyes clenched and still writhed in stinging pain, his eyes watering.

What the hell …?

Slowly he opened them, peeking and seeing that it wasn't his staff making any sort of guiding light, but the sun itself, which had risen higher and now shone through a huge pocket in the trees, banishing the shadows and lighting up the world with the strength of a desert sun.

He gripped the staff and stood up, wobbling, just as a wind flowed down the hill, this one cool and caressing, smoothing away the sweat from his brow and—as his eyes cleared and focus returned—scattering the mist and clearing away all obstruction.

He blinked several times, and then shifted and walked three paces to the right—to again set his feet upon the well-trod path that had been so close all this time.

He curled his toes, flexed his fingers around the bloodied staff, which now looked more knotted and rugged, like a walking cane should, and he set himself down the path, around a winding trail that took him through a serene forest, into a grove, and to the very doorstep of a quaint and wondrous cottage.

Inside, once he let go of the shamrock-shaped handle, the quaintness ended and the horror began. It looked like an epic battle of the elements had recently occurred, complete with fire and ice; earth and vegetation, lightning and wind. Mason choked on the smell of burnt flesh, gagged on seeing two frosted, preserved heads not-so-cleanly decapitated and resting against a blackened wall.

Great vines hung lifelessly from a scorched ceiling in a rounded chamber with the remains of what looked to be a massive oaken table and a shattered grand piano. A place of meeting, a place of power. Decisions were made here, Mason thought. Powerful decisions. In this little room, this cottage in the heart of the forest with the majestic mountains and the crisp natural air among the ancient woods.

Half the table had been blasted into oblivion and more blood and gore decorated the back wall, which somehow still stood, although cracked and shattered in places. The eastern windows were all broken but covered now with newly-grown vegetation, providing a modicum of shade, like drawn curtains for modesty.

Or shame.

Three statues stood amidst the carnage. Three bodies—two men and a woman—encased in clear, thick ice.

It was toward these figures that Mason drew near. Without a doubt, he had come for them. He set a hand on one, the nearest— the woman. Red hair, pale features and a long flowing thick dress. Mason couldn't understand why these ice blocks hadn't melted. The air was certainly colder in this vicinity, but it felt as if the cold was being generated by the individuals inside the ice rather than from any outside source, maintaining their own condition indefinitely.

It made no sense, but nothing about this magic did. Mason's hand trembled, and his staff twitched and seemed to heat up, as if some internal mechanism sensed a need and generated its own power. He could feel a tremendous sense of energy flowing all about this cottage. Sensed it even as he approached, in the grove outside. Situated on a powerful location, maybe an underground source of energy, a sacred native Indian site for sure, located and co-opted by the druids for their meetings or conventions, or whatever went on here.

Whatever the history, Mason was out of time. He had come for these people. They had been imprisoned, and the others … by the gruesome evidence here … had been killed. Mason could only surmise that Solomon's was the hand behind all this, and that these three refused him, spurned any alliance, and he had left them behind, neutralized for the time being.

Whatever his reasons, any enemies of Solomon's had to be friends of Mason's at this point.

He touched his staff to the ice, just under the woman's eyes, and watched the surface start to melt.

Two minutes later, his feet were wet, but not much progress had been made. The ice was too thick, and his slight heat generated from the staff wasn't doing much.

He backed away, held up the staff and tried another bit of Latin: *"Ignis!"*

Nothing. *Come on,* he thought, imagining burst of flame shooting from the staff. A fireball, or something.

"Flamma! Incendia?"

Again, nothing happened. Frustrated, he looked around for an alternative.

A minute later he had a little woodpile created and piled around the statue. Broken bits of the table and walls, chair legs and backs. And a plastic bottle of candle oil he had found in one of the cupboards in the next room, along with a box of starter matches. After drenching the wood, he dropped a match and backed away.

Suddenly he felt like a priest of the Inquisition, about to burn a suspected witch.

God I hope this works, and I don't kill her … assuming she's even still alive in there.

He hadn't even thought of that yet. Without air, without food or water for days … Were they still alive? He had assumed this was like a suspended animation thing. In fact, he was somehow sure of it, despite all logic. They were imprisoned only.

In any case, he was about to find out.

The block of ice, encased now in flames up to her shoulders, began to melt. The fire licked and drank, and kept melting despite the flow of water upon the base ... it was enough. In fact, too much.

A scream, and the remaining ice around her head shattered, and Mason had just enough warning to turn and duck, or shards would have torn through his skull. He heard a wet flopping sound, then a rolling and screaming and something battered the floor and walls. The smell of burnt hair and flesh assaulted his nostrils, and he turned—just as the dark shape with literal fiery red hair stood from a wet crouch.

Her gown flowed and swirled in a sudden breeze that extinguished the flames, and as Mason watched, the burnt skin on her legs and face miraculously healed over. Emerald eyes sought him out, and her mouth twitched into a hideous snarl.

She raised her hand and made a flipping motion.

Mason's feet launched off the ground, upending him. He struck his head on the floor, then he was thrust up to the ceiling, flattened on his back as she strode beneath him. She took deep breaths, hand still raised, keeping him pinned, as she looked back to her fellows trapped in the ice.

Fingers to her lips, she blew two kisses in their direction.

Mason could feel the edges of that gust of heat from the ceiling. Her breath carried the intensity of a volcanic steam blast, and within seconds, the two statues were thawing.

Satisfied, she turned her attention back to the ceiling, and as soon as she heard the stamping of wet feet and the breaking of brittle ice behind her, she spoke to Mason.

"And what exactly are *you*? Somehow you found our location. No easy feat for a commoner, much less a practiced druid. Which would indicate you are far more advanced that you seem."

A gnome-like man appeared at her side, smoothing his balding head and wringing out his cotton shirt. "Angelica? What have we here? Is this our rescuer?"

"That remains to be seen, Morris. He found us with what must have been ancient magic, yet had to resort to common fire to melt ice."

"Sorry," Mason stammered, fighting the pressure against his chest holding him in place. "I was kind of rushed for time."

"I see that." She cocked her head, then glanced at the next friend to appear at her side. "Belgar? Are you reading anything from this one?"

Belgar, with his canine-like jaws and hooded eyes under overgrown brows, sniffed the air, then growled. "I get the scent of Solomon on him."

Morris's nostrils flared and he scuttled back, finding his own staff and raising it up. "End him, now."

"Wait," Mason cried. "I came to help you."

"Why?" Angelica asked.

"The Haitian … he said …"

"Jack?" Belgar tensed. "Where is my friend?"

"I don't know," Mason said honestly. "But please … let me down. If you would stop Solomon, then we are on the same side. And …" he spoke slowly and forcefully, "…we don't have much time."

Angelica frowned, looked out the window, then up as if peering through the roof itself.

"It is almost the solstice."

"Dawn is coming," Mason said, "and with it, the end of everything. I don't know if we can stop it, but I know for sure I can't do it alone."

Angelica lowered her arm and Mason fell, catching himself just at the last moment and getting a foot down to break his fall. He stumbled, then stood, facing them.

"What's he planning?" Morris asked timidly, and Mason feared for a moment that this motley assemblage had a less than zero chance of doing anything. If they had been so easily incapacitated before, what help could they possibly be now, when Solomon had full power and a veritable army at his disposal?

"Can I tell you on the way?" Mason asked. "He's got my wife and daughter. And I—I think I'm to be the sacrifice that starts all this. I don't know how I can refuse."

Angelica looked him over, her eyes softening. "We'll get to that, but first … we may have underestimated you."

"How do you mean?" Belgar asked, sniffing the air again. "Oh … I see now!"

"What?" Morris asked.

"It's him, but it's not him."

"A nice trick," Angelica said. "He's split himself, and only few can do so." She stepped closer, standing a few inches over Mason. "Perhaps that's why your strengths are more limited and you can't manage simple tasks. You're not whole in this place."

"I … guess not." Mason frowned, and for a moment, the other position snuck in, superimposing itself over this reality. The circle of stones under Solstice headquarters, the dark room and the night sky. He was still there, curled into a ball, propped against a stone, to all the world asleep.

"How did he learn this?" Morris asked, his voice full of respect and wonder. "That's a power reserved for later instruction by the arch-druid himself. Only Solomon advanced enough under Palavar's tutelage to perfect it."

"There's more to this one than we thought," Belgar said, echoing Angelica's earlier observation. His tanned face and sun-drenched features exuded the scent of beaches and coconut breezes. "Who are you?"

"Just a weatherman," Mason said. "Oh, and I recently learned I had spent some time with Solomon as a kid. I lived with …"

He paused, looking back to the shattered section of the conference table and the blast radius of scattered blood and remains.

"Palavar?" Angelica whispered the name. "It has to be."

Mason nodded. "I believe so. My memory …"

She held up a hand. "Enough. We understand. And now we understand why you're the sacrifice."

"It can't happen," Belgar said.

Morris stepped forward, his eyes darkening, fists clenching. "No. We … we can end it now."

Angelica held up a hand. "Don't think that."

"What are they talking about?" Mason asked, stepping back.

Morris cleared his throat, aiming his staff. "Sorry, but I'm talking about the greater good here. I'm sure you're a nice enough fellow, but if you're to be sacrificed and if by so doing, your death brings about the slaughter of billions on this planet, well …"

"I get it," Mason said, nodding.

"Kill him now," Belgar said, his voice cracking. "And Solomon's plans go up in smoke."

"I don't know about that," Angelica said. "He may have an alternative."

"Maybe," Mason said, "but also don't forget, I'm not really here."

"Ah, damn it." Morris set down his staff. "I keep refusing to believe you can do that."

"He's right," said Belgar reluctantly. "Kill this one, and the other will still live, maybe in shock for a bit, but that's it."

"No," Morris agreed. "We'll have to kill that one too." He smiled as Angelica swatted him with a look.

"Stop it. We're going to work together."

"And only kill him," Belgar said, "as a last resort."

"Fine," Mason said. "But now …"

"Yes, we have to get you back." Angelica took a deep breath. "And to stop your voluntary completion of the sacrifice, I imagine we must remove the leverage Solomon has on you."

Mason nodded.

"Your wife and child." Belgar found his staff and fit it in a strap behind his back. "First order of business. Rescue mission."

"Just my style," Morris said. "Like the old days!"

"What old days?" Belgar fired back. "We've never done anything like this."

"Well, not us, but you know—stuff we've read about. Back in the day. The Celts, the good old druids and the ancient battles …"

"Nostalgia later," Angelica hissed. "Stay focused. But before we go, let's give our new recruit here a little crash course."

Mason trembled. "Uh …"

"No," Angelica insisted. "You've got the basics and a good sense of things, but the memory wipe clearly went deeper than you realize. And I'm sure Palavar didn't directly share any of the good stuff with you. How you picked up what you did, must have been from sheer proximity."

"Or luck," Mason said.

"Whichever. If we're to go into battle, you have to be ready."

"Oh, okay—" Mason started, but then the three of them converged on him, staves raised.

And his crash course began.

Chapter 7

wo hours later he was back in the circle at Solstice, waking as if from a long and grueling dream that had left him anything but rested. He woke to the stars and the shimmering galaxy, and the bright star Sirius edged toward the tip of the cornerstone, directly opposite where he had been trussed up and resting uncomfortably on his side.

Mason's wrists burned and his ankles chafed above the socks where Victor had inelegantly fastened the plastic cuffs. Returning to this position, merging back with this version of himself, Mason was again surprised that he had managed the split, and that his dream self—or whatever that was—hadn't felt this pain and itching and he hadn't been wrenched from the dream.

He groaned and tried to sit up. Questioning that sort of phenomenon in light of all he had just seen, done and learned in the past two hours almost made him break out in a chuckle. What stopped him was the realization that he wasn't alone.

None of his new friends could do what he could in this sense, so they were coming—but using more conventional modes of transportation. They would be a few hours, and he had been instructed to sit tight in the meantime and not make a move on the hospital or the warehouse until he got their signal. They had a plan, and a good one, but still, there was a lot of time until it could begin. A lot of time for something to go wrong.

Mason hoped he'd be left alone here until the sacrifice, or the ceremony, was to begin. Apparently that wasn't the case. A figure stood in the shadows beside one of the stones, just outside the circle. Slender and thin, she spoke in a voice as distant as the stars, but much less cold.

"Where were you, Mr. Grier?"

Into the pale constellation's light, she emerged, pulling back the grey hood from her face, letting the auburn curls drop below her shoulders. Her eyes were red and her expression pale.

Mason shifted, trying to use the rock for leverage and to sit up. "Annabelle?"

She put a finger to her lips. "I'm not supposed to be here. But I think it's safe. Victor is with Gabriel somewhere out there...." She waved a hand haphazardly toward the region of Orion in the night sky. "And Solomon is firing up the troops in an all-out gathering in the lobby. The ceremony ... at dawn, it will be up there, you know. Not here."

"What?" Mason looked around. "I thought this was it. It's perfect. It's—"

"Artificial. Too many layers of earth and substructures between us and the ground floor, the sky and the wind and the elements." Annabelle shook her head, wistfully looking up at the stars. "It's a beautiful representation, but it's only in our minds. Not a worthy ceremonial site by any means. But upstairs, the grove there was converted directly from an old shrine, a burial site and sacred offering zone used by the natives for centuries. That's where it has to be done."

Mason cursed himself for shortsightedness. He had prepared for this to be it. But really, they could improvise. And upstairs made access for his friends a little easier. Maybe things were starting to go his way.

Only, the "army of employees" up there was unexpected. At most, he figured they'd have to face a dozen druids down here, not hundreds up there.

His spirits sunk again.

"Why are you here, Annabelle?"

She knelt near him. "It's Gabriel. And Solomon, and ..." Lowering her eyes as if feeling unworthy of the cosmic lights above, she shook her head again. "It's not the dream I had, not the one I followed and believed in all my life." She met his eyes reluctantly. "You know what they're planning?"

Mason nodded. "Somewhat. It has to do with the satellites. Using them to transmit magic in the form of codes and data, transmitting energy and directing it against the earth. I'm not sure exactly how it will happen, or what they're going to stir up...."

"*Stir up* is a very apt phrase," Annabelle said. "Do you know the prevailing theory on the Pre-Cambrian extinction, what they call—"

"The Great Dying?" Mason licked his dry lips. "Where ninety-eight percent of the world's species were wiped out? It wasn't asteroids?"

"Not that time, although scientists fought long and hard to find such evidence. That would have been vastly preferable to the alternative."

"That something terrestrial—and repeatable—caused it?"

"Exactly."

"It will be a global coordination of multiple factors to create an unstoppable greenhouse extinction event. Focusing on the Arctic ice shelf and the Siberian permafrost layers that have trapped gigatons of methane below the surface. Normally the methane is vented in slow processes of gradual erosion, taking centuries at least, and in that time the effects are minor."

"But you're going to speed it along?"

"Earthquakes and direct heat and convection directed at the highest concentrations of methane deposits, all designed to release just enough into the atmosphere."

Mason shook his head slowly, even as he saw it materialize on the screens behind her. A shattering of glacial fields, plumes of gas venting through enormous cracks as the land beneath was rent and the deposits pulverized and released. "A methane pulse." He reviewed what he knew about the gas. "Methane is seventy times more potent a greenhouse gas than carbon dioxide...."

"And methane has another benefit."

Mason nodded. "It's easily broken down in the atmosphere, only having an effective life of what—ten years?"

"Twelve maybe, but whichever, it's perfect. Sure there will still be lingering effects and damage, and the higher than ideal temperatures, but our more powerful members can easily restore the balance in a short time. We'll all emerge from the bunkers, our children grown, and we'll inherit a world swept clean of filth and corruption. *Tabula rasa*, a world ready for us to restore, to tend and cultivate with new seeds and farms and forests …"

The screens all dissolved and images surfaced now of sprawling lands of greenery, enormous trees and verdant fields.

"Some of it has already begun," Annabelle said. "Solomon's people around the globe have been aggravating the weather, going wild as it were, given near free creative reign to cause chaos in whatever form they choose."

News screens appeared in the sky behind her, materializing as if they'd been there all along and only just found power. Mason watched, trembling as the weather channels delivered on the wild global weather: snow storms in the southwest had traffic piled up for miles, and no-travel alerts existed in four states; blinding rain drenched London and Paris, where buses were swept away in flooded streets that looked more like Venice; monster winds ravaged buildings in Tokyo. On and on it went, with satellite maps of huge swirling storms battling it out in the skies, blotting out the oceans and devouring the land.

"Phase One is finished. Phase Two … after the ceremony, will release the methane, and very quickly the atmosphere will heat up exponentially."

"Can they really do it?" Mason wondered.

"We can," she whispered.

Over her shoulder, another satellite map of the world materialized, with red dots appearing over the arctic, then expanding out in pockets throughout the atmosphere, as the world was a snow globe filling with blood.

"And that's not all of it," Annabelle said. "You're probably so terrestrially-minded that you don't pay attention to the other important factor impacting our weather. Something that doesn't easily figure into the models or if it does, it's rarely understood correctly."

The earth map vanished, replaced by a huge, seething ball of reddish-yellow. Our sun, spitting out coronas and swirling gasses.

"Solar radiation," Mason said in a whisper.

"Yes, and tomorrow morning at six twenty-seven Eastern time, we are predicted to be caught in a massive geo-magnetic storm from a solar flare that occurred six and a half hours ago." She took a deep breath. "We all knew about it, expected it and prepared for it."

"How could you know about it?" Mason wondered. "Solar flares aren't predictable in any sense other than relying on models that say we haven't had one in three years and we usually average that many, so we're due."

"That's right," she said, "but we knew. Trust me, we knew."

Mason swallowed hard at the implication. *They caused it? Either that or they divined it, saw into the future.* He'd go with that. The alternative was too much, even after everything else he had seen.

"So this solar flare—it's an X20, intense enough to exaggerate the usual infrared radiation that passes through our atmosphere. It warms the land, then gets irradiated back, and now—absorbed by the cloud cover, the CO2, the water vapor and methane. All the greenhouse gasses stirred up in massive quantities. The radiation trapped and absorbed and ..."

"Used to exponentially heat up the earth and the oceans, further accelerating the release and transmission of the methane into the atmosphere." She sighed. "The air will turn to choking gas, crops will wither and in the oceans, plankton will die out. Starting with the bottom of the food chain on up, every species will be locked in a fight for survival. And as for us humans, millions will die in Phase One, but by the second week of Phase Two, when scorching temperatures, combined with the poisonous atmosphere and stifling drought and starvation take hold, billions are going to perish. And it won't be fast or pleasant. We are entering another mass extinction phase. A Great Dying the likes of which the world hasn't witnessed for two hundred and fifty million years."

Mason cringed, closing his eyes. He didn't want to see anything of the sort up on those virtual screens.

Annabelle wasn't finished yet, however. "And one more thing, the solar flare will also knock out most satellites over the western hemisphere. So no cell phones, no GPS, no extensive communications arrays or low-earth orbit analysis. Relief efforts will be hindered, global coordination near impossible."

"But wait, if it knocks out the satellites, won't that disrupt the ceremony?"

Annabelle shook her head. "The satellites will have served their purpose before the flare's impact is felt, before the solar wind strikes."

Mason opened his mouth, then thought, his mind calculating. "How long before?"

She shrugged. "Not too long, twenty minutes maybe? Solomon has it all worked out to the minute, I'm sure." She hugged her shoulders and started rocking. "It's too much. I wanted to send a message, a strong and irresistible message. But I wanted ultimately to work within what we have, not destroy everything and start over." Her eyes watered and lips trembled. "I like what we've done as a race. Sure, there have been huge mis-steps and sad eras in human history, but I like our culture. Music and arts, heck even TV. I love *Mad Men*, and that adorable *Frozen* movie...."

She started to break down. Turned and leveled a hard look at Mason.

"And your son ... he's not what he claims to be."

Mason nodded slowly. "I'm sorry."

"He's killed. Offered sacrifices without the victim's consent."

Mason's mouth dried up and his blood ran cold.

"Cheated and lied. It's all about power and control to him, nothing more. Not change, not ..." She shook her head.

"Annabelle. Help me."

She looked up. "I don't know how, or if it would do any good."

"You told me earlier that you had ... competing offers?"

She frowned. "Yes, but those ... dried up. No longer there even if I—we—wanted to reach out to them."

Mason shook his head. "Not entirely true." He motioned with his chin and she glanced up, at the blurry images overhead in the stars. Three faces moving in succession.

Annabelle's mouth went wide. "Morris, Angelica ..."

"And some righteous lord named Belgar. Former friends of yours?"

Annabelle swept her hand up overhead, and smeared the images away, dissolving it like an ephemeral mosaic. "They live?"

"Yes, and they need our help. Annabelle, before your colleagues move me upstairs and the ceremony begins, can you do something for me?"

Mason thought for a moment, going back to the initial plan— the plan that with this new information had been thrown into disarray. It was no longer enough to stop the ceremony. Billions might be ultimately saved, but millions and millions were still doomed, and for those that survived, earth would become a living nightmare.

It wasn't going to work.

Chapter 8

In the recovery ward at San Diego General Hospital, Mason appeared as before, stepping out of a dream. This time closer to Lauren's room, but not too close. It was nearly 4:00 AM, less than two hours away from dawn.

And the start of the end of the world.

He had to move fast, but first he had to hope the others were here. No time to tell them of what he had learned, but there was nothing else for it; this part of the plan had to stay the same. Lauren and Shelby needed to be freed. There was no way he was going to kick off an environmental apocalypse, but he couldn't take a chance that anything could happen to Lauren or Shelby.

First things first.

He headed down the hall, into the main processing and waiting room, where a lone TV displayed more weather-related news. This one a local broadcast, his former Channel 7 News, with his stand-in, Rebecca Montross. She looked haggard and exhausted as she pointed to the map of the local counties, all swirled with high concentrations of clouds and precipitation. A flashing red ticker at the bottom proclaimed a storm watch for an unheard of four inches of snow, with icy road conditions and a city-wide state of emergency.

Mason passed in front of Lauren's room quickly, looking only out of the corner of his eye, taking in the room in a glance.

No one there. At least not in the chair. The creepy old man could be around the corner or by the head of the bed, but Mason couldn't tell. He glanced around and noted he wasn't alone: three nurses and an assistant behind the counter, one who peered up in his direction, then looked away.

A commotion down the hall caught their collective attention.

Mason took a second to take it in. It must have looked to the nurses as if someone had opened all the windows in the wing. Papers and boxes were flying about, slapping against the walls and swirling around. Snowflakes rushed inside, along with a howling wind.

The diversion had begun.

Mason waited by the side of the door, pressed flat against the wall. Sure enough, with a flourish of his black trench coat, the old man—who Angelica had told him was named Niles Stanwick—rushed out in a near gallop unseemly for his age. Three bounds and he stopped in a crouch, staff extended lengthwise as he scanned the hallway, and sniffed the air.

"Tildershines," he spat. "I smell your foul English cologne from here."

A stairway door opened, and the half-sized druid emerged, wobbling unsteadily but grinning ear to ear. He winked at Mason, then gave Stanwick a look of disdain. "Hello Niles, you're one to talk, what with the stench of the grave about you."

"You shouldn't have come alone."

Morris grinned. "Who said I did?"

Mason slipped around the doorframe and into Lauren's room, glancing back once before edging out of sight, just long enough to see the flowing brown and red embroidered robe glide into view from the opposite direction. Angelica floated in through a patient's window, and with a wave of her vine-encased stick, the nurses and the orderlies froze in place.

Lingering a moment, Mason felt the pull to join them, but the beeping of Lauren's blood pressure machine pulled him from the fixation. He turned and rushed to her side.

Still out, calm and serene, thank God. She was sleeping soundly, eyelids flickering. He pressed his lips against her forehead, smoothed her hair and stepped back.

A scream, and a blast of something rocked the floor just as Mason felt another rush of cold air burst into the room. It fueled his legs and in seconds he was at the closet, tiptoeing, reaching inside, way back … Reaching …

"Looking for this?"

The bathroom door had been ajar, and now it kicked open, and a pale-faced young man stepped out. Mason recognized him as being one of the members of Solstice, had seen him taking tea and relaxing in the grove.

Only now, his expression was anything but serene.

He held Mason's ivory staff in his left hand, another in his right.

Apparently, Old Man Stanwick hadn't come alone, either.

The training still fresh in his mind, training done mostly without a staff to harness the natural surrounding energy, Mason feinted left then rose up and lunged. The kid—for he was barely over twenty as far as Mason could tell—reacted in surprise at the aggressive move and lifted a staff.

Fortunately, it was Mason's and he grabbed it as he knocked into the adept and smashed him back into the bathroom.

A surge of energy rolled wavelike up Mason's muscles, into his shoulders and neck, and then he willed the force back down with all his fury. The kid screamed as if he'd picked up a scalding hot pot's metal handle, and let go. But he had the sense to push Mason off and then strike with the other staff.

Mason blocked it, surprised at the speed of his reaction and the burst of lightning that scattered along the connection at the same time. He fell back though, stumbled into the room and struck the edge of the bed.

A glance out the door was enough to show Angelica pinned against a wall, giant vines holding her wrists and Stanwick advancing on her, staff outraised. Morris was on his knees, recovering from an assault, his head bleeding. Snow and ice swirled around the three of them, with swaying vines and sharp branches breaking through the ceiling. Mason couldn't figure out who controlled the vegetation, but he didn't have a chance to consider it.

A blast of searing hot wind struck his eyes, spun him around and held him in place to witness a wall of locusts converging on Lauren. Huge wriggling insects scuttled over one another, about to reach her hair, fall into her eyes, climb onto and chew the wires.

Horrified, Mason struggled to break free, about to use the staff and try calling out a gust of wind....

But then he blinked. Took a deep breath, and squeezed harder, his fingers feeling the calming ivory touch, the soothing cold that erased the mental fog of heat and oppression.

A veil lifted from his eyes—a veil of illusion and nightmare. He peeled away the entire scene of illusionary locusts and scattered it like a bad page out of a book gone wrong. And with one fluid motion, he turned and swung out like a major league batter, high to low, stepping into the swing.

Crack! He connected hard with the side of the adept's head, crushing into the temple in a bone-fracturing sound. Lights out, the kid dropped and fell hard, face first.

Chest heaving, his mind still clearing, Mason gave another glance to Lauren to reassure himself she was safe. He planned on rushing out to help his new friends, but he saw her eyes flicker, then open.

He rushed to her side.

She wasn't awake, not completely. Out of focus, her pupils contracted slightly. She turned her head toward him, licked her lips and spoke. Barely audible, Mason had to lean in to hear.

"Dreaming," she said, *"of the sun."*

"Honey, don't stress. Just rest."

"Shining so bright, so so bright ..."

He stroked her chin, and her eyelids fluttered again, struggling to stay open.

"Burning … the sunlight. Burning …"

Her eyes closed and her chest exhaled slowly.

"…all the trees and the vines, everything, burning all the green …"

"Lauren?"

She was out, and just then he heard a choked cry from the hall. Galvanized, Mason turned and jumped over the kid and raced out of the room.

He skidded to a halt on an icy floor, almost falling. Staff raised, he was ready to do what he could to try to turn things around for his new friends, but he found he was too late.

The hanging vines, it seemed, had indeed been in service of the diminutive Englishman.

Old man Stanwick was currently hanging upside down, ankles encircled by the thorny appendages. His staff lay on the ground below, broken it two. Blood dripped on the frosted floor, seeping from the open wound in his chest, from which his decrepit old heart had just been torn free.

Still beating, the organ sputtered, pierced on a vine waving slowly in front of Morris's face as he shook his head and turned it a little to look in Stanwick's eyes.

"Sorry old chap, looks like you won't be needing this any longer. And … ah, there you are Mr. Grier!"

Stanwick's fingers stopped twitching. A second later, the vines tugged and up the body and heart went up through the open ceiling tiles, which promptly slid back in place. Morris stamped his staff and the ice on the floor melted, swirling with water that washed out the blood, then simmered, boiled and evaporated, leaving behind nothing but shiny floors that looked as if they'd just been washed.

Mason whistled. "You sure clean up nice. Where's Angelica?" He glanced at the wall free of scorch marks, dust and gore, and saw no sign of her.

Morris smiled as he put his staff behind his back. "Change in plans, my friend! She was never here."

"What do you mean? I saw her, she came in, charmed all the nurses, then … she was pinned to the wall."

"You and Mr. Stanwick both saw what I wanted you to see." Morris beamed as if to say, *Damn I'm good*. "Distracted him into thinking she was the greater threat, as if bigger is always better, regardless of gender." He shrugged. "Anyway, while he was busy with her, I took care of him."

Mason nodded appreciatively. "So she's ..."

"Heading to the warehouse with Belgar. We believe that might be a tougher test, and involve both of them to pull it off without alerting Solomon."

"I better get there," Mason said, glancing back toward Lauren's room. But first, he looked around the lobby. Four nurses stood like statues, wobbling slightly, their expressions locked in terror and disbelief. "What about them? Don't want this story hitting the Internet."

"I got it," Morris said, approaching the first pair. "They'll wake with a minor headache but no memories of all the fun."

"Wait," Mason said quickly. "There's another one to take care of." He thumbed over his shoulder, and Morris took a peek in Lauren's room.

He whistled jovially like a leprechaun. "Damn, you do learn fast! Nice work. All right, go, I got this. Clean up duty, all I'm good for."

"And Lauren ..."

Morris's eyes softened, and it almost looked like he'd cry with a sudden sense of empathy. "Don't worry about the lass. I'll stay and stand guard. No harm'll come to her. You just do your thing."

"I'll try," Mason said. "And thanks."

He closed his eyes, and as soon as he thought about Shelby, he opened them—and found himself transported into the midst of hell.

Chapter 9

Fire, ice and wind battled it out on the warehouse floor as Mason arrived, anchored on the walkway again above Shelby. She was still tied to the chair, cringing as debris hurled around her. Barrels were flung into the air, crashing down near Belgar who dodged one, then another, then leapt into the air and tossed a barrel back toward the two well-dressed druids near the entrance. One dove out of the way while the other tried to block the projectile only to have it explode like a powder keg. Fire swept over the wall behind Belgar, unraveling like a crimson carpet.

Mason shouted a warning and leapt down, forgetting for a moment the height. But it didn't matter, for an updraft seemed to catch him and deposit him with just the right poise, landing on his feet behind Gabriel, who spun and momentarily lost control of his fire attack. Belgar turned and slammed his staff against the floor, spreading ice and bitter wind back upon the fire and snuffing it out. He turned—and another blast of wind-riddled insects swirled at him from the surviving druid.

Taking it all in, Mason had barely a second to register that someone else was up on the walkway at the other end. Someone taking aim with a much more conventional weapon.

Mason shouted, "Belgar, above you!"

But then Gabriel made a motion with his hand and the sound waves compressed back to him, echoing Mason's words as if through a deep pit, and then into a tunnel of water.

"So, Dad. You made it to the party after all. Found your invite, and your … true nature. A little late, I'd say, but it's finally good to talk without all the lies."

Mason focused, pushed and gripped his staff tighter, then spun it and felt the encircling waves of energy dissipate, and potency returned to his lungs.

"I may be late, Gabriel, but I'm not sure you're done with the lies." He glanced sideways to Shelby, was about to call out to her but noticed that she was behaving strangely. She seemed focused on Belgar, straining, her face turning red.

A shot rang out and went wild as the walkway bent and tilted in the same moment Victor pulled the trigger.

Gabriel flinched but didn't look back. "It's all too late, Dad. Whatever junior magic tricks you've learned in the past few days, it won't amount to anything. I've had years of study, and I'm just one of a hundred other followers. True believers." He shook his head. "You can't stop us. You can't even get in the way."

A burst of lightning came from the ceiling and struck the metal ledge just as Victor leapt off it. Mason watched as if appreciating a good action scene from a movie. He marveled at Victor's landing, but then realized he hadn't been Belgar's target. The entire walkway collapsed in a storm of sparks, and one huge section slammed down onto the remaining druid who had no chance for escape, splitting his skull and burying him under twisted, lightning-riddled metal.

"Don't you know?" Mason asked over the carnage. "I'm the sacrifice. Without me, you've got nothing, so I'd say I can more than get in the way."

Gabriel laughed. "We have Shelby."

"Take a look around, son. You've lost."

Belgar made a motion with his staff and Victor's feet left the floor as a wind burst tossed him up and over Gabriel and Mason and pinned him against the nearest wall.

Gabriel hissed, stamped the floor with his staff, then spun in an arc, flipping something into the air, then striking it with the staff. At first Mason swore it looked like a small hand sized Nerf football of some kind, but then he realized it was brittle, white and full of holes.

A honeycomb. It burst apart when struck, and a horde of wasps roared out toward Belgar, who immediately spun himself around like a figure skater, causing a whirlwind as he spun faster and faster.

"Thought you hated bees," Mason said. "I remember when you got stung on your sixth birthday and you swore you'd never go outside again."

Gabriel turned to him and his lip twitched. "I'm not a kid anymore."

Belgar's cyclone spun faster, tossing off the attacking wasps, and then he stepped free and smoothed back his hair, smiling. He raised his staff.

Gabriel turned away from his father again and was about to conjure up some new effect when the ground at his feet cracked opened and fingers of roots and clay reached up to grasp his ankles and pull him down. More roots emerged and encircled his body, up to his neck.

Belgar sighed as he fixed a few more errant hairs. "That should settle things down for now."

Feeling like he had done nothing to help, Mason approached his son where he lay squirming and struggling.

Belgar cleared his throat. "Don't make me cast a silence spell on you, kid."

Gabriel cursed him. "I'm no kid, and ..." He gripped one section of the root and squeezed, causing it to smoke and sizzle.

Mason reached out with his staff and let the ivory tip press against Gabriel's cheek. "Son. Enough. Stop and listen."

The smoke fizzled as Gabriel's fingers lightened up. "I've nothing more to hear from you."

"You never did listen," Mason said, nodding first to Belgar and checking on Shelby, who still sat motionless. *Where's Angelica?*

"But listen to me now, Gabe. I respect your mind, and I've always respected the hell out of your courage to stand up for the things you believed in, but this ... this isn't the way."

Gabriel sneered. "Let me go, I'll show you the way."

"Yeah your way. Billions of people wiped out? All of civilization—everything we've ever done as a species to pull ourselves out of the chaos and survive—gone. Is that really what you want?"

"It's what has to happen," Gabriel spat. "Balance, restoration of—"

"Bullshit," Mason hissed as Belgar came closer, towards Shelby. He hoped his tone had the desired effect, and from the look on Gabriel's face it did.

"I know this isn't you. Your mother and I, we always feared you'd been brainwashed or something. Where's the cute, happy kid we raised? The one that loved animals and TV and games and the one we had to yell at to throw his trash in the garbage and be considerate?"

Gabriel said nothing, just writhed and struggled against his bonds. He looked over to his sister as if for support, or to lash out, but she still seemed unresponsive.

"I grew up," he said through clenched teeth. "And no matter what you hoped for me, Shelby was the one you really wanted. Hadn't planned on twins, did you? She was the good one, always the fighter, always the happy one. She walked through the snowstorm for help, she braved the cruel world to save your wife."

"To save you too. Or did you forget that?"

Gabriel laughed, then choked again on the roots cutting into his neck. "I'm beyond saving. But the world isn't. That's why this is so important. I'm doing something—"

"That will destroy all the very people you once wanted to save! Do you think Shelby will be fine? Your mother?"

Nodding, Gabriel spat it out with difficulty. "They'll be fine. We have plans for them."

Mason sighed. "Solomon and his Noah-esque dreams to repopulate the earth?"

"Of course. The right caretakers, the right plan. A destiny that will lead us not only into a new Eden, but a golden age."

Mason shrugged. "Not sure that's going to happen. Might have to settle for silver." He lowered his head, and thought of something. "But I don't want to give up on you. Yes, Shelby made a great sacrifice going for help to save you both, but you did something just as important."

"The hell are you talking about? I sat there and huddled in the car seat trying to stay warm."

Mason dropped to one knee, looking into his son's eyes. He shook his head and smiled. "No, you stayed with her. You gave your mother comfort through her injuries and her fear. She told me you sang to her. Held her hand and sang...."

Gabriel's eyes clouded and bubbled slightly as he looked back. His lip quivered.

"It was *you*," Mason continued, "that saved your mother. Just as much as what Shelby did, maybe more. You have an empathy others lack, it's still inside you. I know it is. You can't do this. You can't want this ... this suffering on a scale billions of times worse that what you endured in that car. You saved her then, but you also saved yourself." Mason stood up, sensing a change suddenly in the air.

"Do it again," he started to say—when the roof tore open and a roaring cyclone slammed down with a force that shattered the remaining windows and rocked the foundations.

Belgar was there one moment, tossed away the next, a blur of arms and legs flung far into the depths of the warehouse. Mason might have heard a bone-crunching impact, but couldn't be sure. The wind and the howling field of air and debris, the proximity to Gabriel and Shelby ... he couldn't see, couldn't hear.

But he could just make out a form in the twister. The narrow cyclone writhed snake-like, undulating to an unseen flautist's melody, then it scattered, leaving behind a man in a clean-pressed suit. Emerald-green tie matching his eyes. Solomon stepped forward, walking with his staff as a cane.

He quickly noted the surroundings: Mason staggered, recovering; Gabriel struggling but restrained; Shelby still tied up; Victor injured but gaining his feet ...

Solomon made a motion with his staff and Gabriel's confining root turned immediately to dust and blew away. Quickly rising, Gabriel lowered his head. "Thank you, the elder druid was—"

"—not acting alone," Solomon said, narrowing his eyes.

Mason regained his balance and his grip on his staff. He figured Solomon was talking about him, and readied himself, even though he knew his training was no match, not yet and not in this limited split spirit state. He might have to beat a hasty exit, but he waited, wanting to give Shelby a chance, and attempt one more time to free her. He looked at her again, at the same time Solomon did, and he figured it out too.

"Gabriel, I'm surprised at you," Solomon said. "Surprised you didn't see it. Training has apparently been amiss. And what have I always said? It's the minor details that, if missed, can ruin the best laid plans."

"What do you mean—?" Gabriel started, but then the air behind Solomon shimmered. He leapt back and hurled a bolt of swirling fire at Shelby.

"NO!" Mason shouted and raised his staff, but he knew it would be too late. Cringing, he watched helplessly, but in the next instant he was utterly surprised as the fireball crunched into an invisible convex shield.

Shelby stood up, easily slipping through her bonds, and her appearance changed, morphing at once into someone taller with red hair cascading around her shoulders and her woodland robe unfolding over the other clothes.

"Dear Angelica," Solomon said. "Thought that was you. What, lending aid in hiding? Ingenious I suppose, and enough to fool my adept here."

"And your other lackeys," Angelica said, raising her staff. She glanced at Mason: a concerned look that said: *be ready for anything.*

Anything, unfortunately, didn't include more conventional attacks. A sideways look and nod from Solomon and a gunshot rang out behind Mason. He flinched and ducked, but saw Angelica wince and drop after spinning with the bullet's impact. It struck under her left arm and might have punctured her lung, it was hard to tell with the robe. But she went down, still gripping her staff.

She screamed out a word and a cascade of lightning bolts rained down through the open roof, blasting the floor and branching in all directions.

Mason stood his ground, wincing as Gabriel and Solomon ducked and leapt out of the way.

Victor, however, wasn't so lucky. One blast struck a metal grate then ricocheted and slammed him back twenty feet into a wall. When he finished jittering, he fell to the floor with a heavy thud, still groaning as smoke issued from his nostrils.

Mason's attention darted around the chaos. Solomon and Gabriel were crouching, shielding themselves and firing off their own volleys of ice and fire. Vines erupted from the floor and the walls and Angelica knocked them back as she half-ran, half-stumbled away, toward where Belgar had landed.

Mason knew she could heal herself and Belgar, if given a chance. So he had to act, and act fast. And there was still the matter of Shelby. *Where was she?*

As if reading his mind, Gabriel scoured the warehouse floor, then settled on a collection of barrels. He raised his staff and a mini-cyclone formed, racing toward them.

Mason moved, aiming his own staff and concentrating. He saw the inside of the whirlwind, felt its eye, and mentally went in and just gripped it hard, twisted and broke it apart. Gabriel howled in frustration as his cyclone broke apart, but its finale still had enough gas in it to scatter several of the empty barrels, revealing Shelby crouched behind them.

"Dad!"

"Shelby, here! Run!"

She got up and raced to him, but a block of ice fell between them like a huge frozen curtain. It dug into the concrete, spewing up chunks of rock. Mason struck it with his staff, and with satisfaction he saw it turn brittle, red, and then burst inward with a sloshing liquid sound.

Only, Shelby was no longer behind it.

She was in the air, lifted by a twisting stalk of vegetation like something out of a fairy tale. Solomon stood nearby, moving his hands, guiding the vine. It brought her high and then down, right over him and then released her.

Solomon caught her and brought her down to his side, then motioned to Gabriel.

Behind them, Angelica came out of a doorway blasted through an inferno of smoke, flame and ash. Belgar had an arm around her shoulder and limped ahead, but his eyes, like hers, reflected the flames and magnified them with greater intensity.

Solomon, however, had what he wanted. "Sorry to cut this short, everyone. But dawn is only minutes away. And we have a world to end."

Mason raised his staff, just as Angelica and Belgar did the same with theirs. They had a shot, still, but Shelby was in the way. Was there a chance to just hit Solomon and free her? Everything was unraveling, and unless they could get her free, it was over.

"Don't try it, Dad." Gabriel grinned through bloodied lips.

"It's over," Solomon added, as if reading Mason's mind. "Your friends won't reach us in time, even if their help could actually do anything. And you … you Mason, are late for your own party. Come back now or …" He squeezed Shelby's throat with his left hand, just hard enough to cause her to cry out.

As Mason moved, about to rush them regardless of the consequences, Solomon stamped his staff on the ground, and the same twister that deposited him here moments ago reached in and stabbed down like a god-like finger. It plucked Solomon, Gabriel and Shelby from the floor and whisked them away with a roar and a blast of wind.

Mason was left wobbling in a dying, acrid breeze, the smell rekindling all kinds of childhood flashbacks now. He pushed them aside, and opened his mouth to ask Angelica what now, but suddenly his connection to this location trembled. His whole body and mind shifted, his voice failed, and everything blurred.

"… pulling you back," Angelica said.

"… don't give in," Belgar shouted. "At the sacrifice. Fight it, fight …"

But then they were gone, and he was waking, back at Solstice.

He was in the elevator, jarring back in time with his other self, reuniting in one body. A hooded man nearly a foot taller than him reacted fast, reaching out and snagging the staff from Mason's hand while he was still disoriented.

"I'll keep this for safe keeping," said the voice under the hood. He turned and reverently lowered his face as the elevator continued its ascent, rising with six other hooded, faceless druids who had Mason surrounded.

Rising to the rooftop grove, to wait for dawn's kiss and the start of the ceremony to end the world.

Chapter 10

Despite the violent weather surging around the rest of the state (and the world), the conditions at the top of Solstice HQ were cool and crisp, with a southwesterly breeze driving over the trees, low humidity and a chill that would soon give way to normal temps in the '70s. Any other day in any other part of Mason's life, and he would have confidently predicted all of that, plus abundant sunshine and more of the same for the next couple days.

But today wasn't any other day.

Today was, quite possibly, the last normal day anyone would see for a long time.

He stepped out through the elevator doors and closed his eyes at first, breathing in the potpourri of scents: lavender and jasmine, holly and mistletoe, ferns and violets. It brought back an immediate memory: hand in hand with Lauren, walking into a greenhouse to pick out flowers for their wedding.

Breathing deep, he wondered if with this new power he might be able to transport himself there, even across time, back to the innocence before any of this began.

Something jarred him, and he realized it was his own ivory staff, used to herd him out into the morning air and towards the congregation.

More than a hundred druids gathered solemnly around and between the stone dolmens. He saw a main block lying horizontally over two large squat stones. An altar that hadn't been here on his earlier visit when he first met with Solomon, and he wondered if— no, he knew it now—it had been here the whole time, hidden from his mind.

It had all been here, ready for him. He saw now the deep crimson stains on the altar and sensed that all these stones exuded a sense of great age, as if plucked from primordial quarries, hewn from the same megalithic strata trod upon by ancient dinosaurs, and he imagined fossilized jawbones and claws embedded still into the rock.

Mason's legs almost gave out as he stumbled ahead and through a section of the crowd that cleared the way at his approach.

He heard a soft humming, then realized it was chanting. Faces turned to him, expressions full of reverence and awe, tear-streaked features overwhelmed by the sheer epic nature of the moment and their part in it all. They looked upon him as the ultimate martyr, Mason realized. The perfect sacrifice, a willing conduit of energy, about to release his soul through pain and suffering, all to cleanse the entire world.

Some people reached out to touch him, as if feeling him in the flesh would part some element of the divine, of his magical essence, and grant them an iota of the courage he was about to display.

Mason wanted to tell them how wrong they were, how disappointed they would be when he refused, when he turned the tables on them and brought this whole charade crashing down.

But then the crowd thinned, his progress slowed and he was there, in the clearing with the altar and the eight black-clad druids, hoods removed, waiting for him.

At Solomon's side, between the master and his pupil Gabriel, Shelby knelt with her wrists bound, eyes red, a curved knife to her throat. Gripping the knife—Victor, head bloodied and looking a lot worse for wear, but nonetheless back in his role and just as menacing.

Mason knew there would be no disappointment for this congregation.

They had him, and he would do what was required if Shelby could live.

There was no other choice. The world outside faded in his mind. Perhaps it didn't exist and never had. Maybe, like the rooms downstairs and the views and the scenery on the walls, everything else was just illusion. The world was much smaller than anyone thought, the universe nothing but a black dome and twinkling electrical lights.

He had to think that way, anything else would be to invite madness and the crushing weight of guilt. If he just thought of Shelby and Lauren, even Gabriel, and reduced the world to those terms, he could act. He could sacrifice himself. *What parent wouldn't do the same for his children?*

He could do this. There was no other way.

Solomon stepped forward to greet him and he raised his ancient staff. The crowd quieted as Mason was finally left to his own motion, and the others stepped back and the circle reformed. He looked up, refusing to make eye contact with Solomon. Or Gabriel or Shelby for that matter. Not yet. First, he took in the sky, the dull metallic blue that turned azure and violet, and then black farther west, over the swaying canopy of treetops. Stars still burned through the black shield in that direction, before yielding to the soft and overpowering glow spreading like a virus from the east.

A loud stamping thud brought Mason's attention to the ground. To the staff base Solomon had thrust against the ground. Immediately the earthen floor smoothed over, replaced with a virtual viewpoint again, this time a representation of the earth seen from space. With an arrangement of satellites blinking with red lights, larger than scale, surrounding the globe in their strategic positions.

"It's time, my friends." Solomon spread out his arms. "All our hard work and patience has led to this, the morning of the true Solstice! The final solstice of this age of corruption. Just as the curtain fell on the old age of Rome when it dared destroy our groves, invade our lands and disrupt the cycles of nature with greed, so has this world's occupiers gone much farther in their travesties. And we, as caretakers, have been far too complacent. Far too passive. We bear the responsibility for this state of decay, for this imbalance."

Now Mason did look up, meeting the eyes of his son. And for a brief moment, Gabriel caught his glance, and the fire in his eyes faded slightly. His will cracked and Mason saw the first possibility of doubt cross his features. Then it was gone and Gabriel nodded his head like the others, and resumed that disconcerting low humming.

"It all ends today," Solomon continued, turning his attention to the west, and the congregation followed his eyes, watching over the rooftop and over the rolling hills and forests of bristling leaves, to the spreading glow of the rising sun.

"Our age is at hand. And the new world, a new life, begins as it always has. With a sacrifice, with pain and sacred death. For only through this act of ultimate sacrifice can the world be renewed. All the world mythologies have recognized this fact, and today we merely set foot firmly in the prints of our predecessors."

Solomon withdrew from his robes the large curved ivory blade. And all the druids reached up to replace their hoods and face the altar. The chanting increased, the humming drowning out the insects and the morning song of the birds.

In the pause, Gabriel turned to Mason and spoke. "Is the sacrifice prepared?"

At his side, Shelby whimpered. She struggled and tried to rise, but another hand pressed her shoulder and kept her down. Mason looked and saw under this shorter druid's hood—it was Annabelle.

And she met his glance—and through a scared but confident expression—winked at him.

Mason's heart skipped. Had Annabelle succeeded? And more importantly, could he trust her? In a moment, it wouldn't matter. The die was cast, and he had to trust her. Had to trust in the balance, in nature, and hopefully in a God that wasn't yet prepared to wipe out his creation.

Solomon stepped forward and handed the blade, hilt first, to Mason. "Now is the time," Solomon said just above a whisper. "Fulfill your destiny. Finish what we began as innocent children."

"That was a game," Mason said. But he took the knife. "A game that nearly got us all killed."

Solomon gave him a smile. "We were saved for greater glories." He bowed and backed away a step, then motioned to the altar.

"Dad, no …" Shelby began, but then the big man put a hand over her mouth.

Mason felt a wind pushing him toward the altar until his legs brushed against the powerful stone, and a momentary image flashed through his skull: the farmhouse, the willow trees swaying in the rising wind, the immense tornadoes dropping like funnels from the sky.

He closed his eyes and shook away the image, just as the warm breeze tugged at his wrist and seemed to lift it. Was he moving on his own? Was any of this really voluntary?

A scan of the crowd: Annabelle giving a nod to someone across the circle; other figures moving slightly as if jockeying for a better position of the coming ritual; Gabriel stepping back, turning pale, the only one besides Solomon not to draw his hood; Shelby crying, shaking her head, struggling against her wrist-bonds and Victor's strong hands.

Below his feet, the earth's image hung, a perfect blue-green orb of symmetry, majesty and diversity five billion years in the making. A living, breathing, feeling entity shining bright in the void of chaos. The satellites glowed and sparkled, and data points, numerals and text scrolled faster under each one. *The transmissions have begun,* Mason realized, as the servers downstairs received and transmitted a different sort of data stream—Solomon's self-described energy-as-indistinguishable-from-magic transference.

Mason raised the knifepoint to his chest. *Now or never.*

The sun cleared the edge of the trees, and its warming glow washed over his temples, his eyes and his lips, and glinted off the blade. He pressed the tip against the edge of his shirt and moved it aside to rest against the flesh, just above the heart.

With a smile to Shelby, he nodded, ostensibly to Solomon, but really to Annabelle.

Just flip the knife and throw it. That's all it would take. That and a lot of luck in his toss and the hope that Solomon wasn't ready. Now—

"Wait!"

Solomon raised his staff, and the chanting halted. Annabelle froze, mouth open. Gabriel and Shelby looked up, confused. Solomon extended his free hand and the ivory knife tugged in a sudden gust filled with sparkling tinges of electricity that made Mason wince and release his grip.

The blade spun and flew into Solomon's grasp. He stepped forward. Never taking his eyes off Mason's, he held out his staff, and placed it firmly in Mason's open grip.

"This is yours now. You've earned it."

His smile was warm and inviting. "Much better, you'll find, than that temporary ivory stick you've been carting around."

"What—?" was all Mason could manage, his head spinning. The sun continued its rise, but still hadn't fully pulled itself from its blanket of trees. And the visuals on the satellites below their feet flickered as the transmission faltered; lines of code blinked as if in standby mode.

Murmurs rushed through the crowd, but Solomon was quick to quiet them. With a powerful leap he landed on the flat altar stone, towering over Mason and the others. And he let the rising sun, nearly half-free now, fall upon him until he was bathed in an angelic glow.

He held the knife high, and the glow extended to the blade and sparkled along its edge, setting it ablaze.

"My brethren, this one has passed his final test and has proven himself worthy. Brothers we were once, and none is more suited to assume the mantle of leadership in my wake."

Mason caught the look on Gabriel's face. He had no idea any of this was coming, and seemed to have trouble registering just what was happening, the same as everyone else in the crowd.

Solomon spread out his arms, and as the fire spread from the knife down his arm, setting his robes ablaze, Mason realized the truth.

And realized that they were all too late.

Mason was never intended to be the sacrifice. He didn't have that kind of power, the energy that Solomon needed. Didn't have it. Not as a kid, and not now.

But Solomon, as arch-druid, leader of his people and caretaker of the natural world, surely did.

He gave one last smile to Mason, a smile of triumph. A smile punctuating a lifetime of ambition. "I consecrate myself to the world, and now you, dear Mason, can start anew."

"No!" Mason shouted, the objection echoed by Gabriel who rushed forward. But they were both met by a blast of heat and wind, knocking them back just as Solomon, engulfed now in flames, turned the blade and plunged it into his own heart.

The building shook, buffeted by a blast of downward-spiking energy and met with tumultuous winds battering it from every side. Torches blew out, hoods flew off and people screamed.

Solomon burned.

A pillar of writhing flame on the altar, his motions slowed, arms waving as he tipped backwards, then he righted himself, dropped to his knees and continued to burn.

Mason looked away from Gabriel and met Annabelle's eyes. He shook his head in utter dismay, but shouted, "Do it!"

And she complied, giving an order, at once obeyed. Two dozen men and women in the crowd rushed ahead and engaged the front line of Solomon's druids, incapacitating and attacking the inner circle. Shocked and confused by their master's sudden turn of events, awed by his personal sacrifice and the epic scene before them, those druids involved in maintaining the ritual and surrounding the altar were suddenly overwhelmed by the interlopers.

Annabelle had accomplished what Mason had hoped: she used her previous connections, having almost joined the "enemy." Sought out those remaining white druids, those in hiding who had understood what Solomon's ascension truly meant for the destiny of the planet, those who still resisted the plan of global rebalancing. She had brought them in, simple enough, blending with the others in the confusion of the mass ceremony.

She would have acted earlier, and if Mason had been the intended, this all still could have been prevented. The ceremony disrupted, the plans derailed.

But this …

Mason couldn't take his eyes off the smoking, melting mass of flesh and cloth on the altar. Solomon's cries were full of agony, yet he still roared in triumph.

He's not dead yet, Mason thought, and held onto that thought, just as he held onto the arch-druid's staff, and looked away from the burning sacrifice to the ancient branch in his hands.

He raised it up, feeling the old wood vibrating with energy, picking up like a lightning rod on the elemental power coursing through the winds and the rising sun and the energy of hundreds of druids all in one location. He glanced around, saw sporadic fighting between those who had cast off their robes, revealing green garments beneath, and those still with the grey and white, struggling to regain control. Annabelle in the thick of things, and then Victor … Aiming with his gun.

First things first. Mason casually pointed the staff at Victor, then flicked it slightly. Just with a thought in mind, he shifted the winds, swept under his arms and made the first gun fire up harmlessly to the sky. Victor's head snapped around with a look of surprise that turned to pure anger.

But Mason wasn't wasting any more time with him. Another flick of the wrist and a vine shot up and over the side of the canopy, spinning and narrowing and then, bursting right through Victor's chest. It grew spiny appendages on the other side, popping through the branchlings covered with his blood.

Victor looked down, mouth open and bubbling red, had a moment to cry out, then he was yanked backward as the vine curled, bending like an archer's bow, then snapping as it flung Victor high into the air and over the side of the building.

Gabriel watched all this in shock.

Mason pointed his staff at the burning, moaning body on the altar.

"It's not yet too late. Gabriel, help me stop it."

"What do you mean?"

Mason focused, holding the staff now in both hands and approaching the altar. "Lend me your energy."

Gabriel shook his head, wobbling uncertainly on his feet, but someone pushed by him, someone running up to Mason's side. Shelby held her wrists out, still bound, but splayed her fingers and touched the great staff just above Mason's hands.

"Do it," she whispered. "Think of ice, and …"

"Got it," Mason said, lifting one of his hands and placing it around hers. "Saw what this can do up in the woods a while back."

Come on, he thought, and visualized cold. Just as he was thinking bitter snow and arctic breezes, suddenly the fire swirled and smoked and sputtered, and icy flakes attacked the ash and consumed the smoke. Over the blackened, fused skin and clothes, the melted flesh and exposed bones, one oozing eye, green as a jade bauble, settled on Mason.

"You …" was all he managed before a cyclonic swirling of frost encircled Solomon's body, weaving around and around like a spider's web or cocoon, faster and faster, then solidifying, hardening and then … clarifying.

Mason exhaled, his breath fogging the air, joining with Shelby's, as they both looked upon the block of ice encasing Solomon.

Gabriel stumbled forward, hands on the altar gingerly, unsure if they would burn or freeze. "Is he—?"

"Alive," Shelby said, shuffling closer, peering at the green eye in the ice. "But just barely. We got to him in time."

Mason licked his lips, then looked up at the sky and back to the treetops where the sun had just cleared the makeshift horizon. Then back down to the satellites …

They were still shining red. Still receiving transmissions sent minutes ago. Still transmitting data to each other and focusing the energies of the sacrifice and the ceremony. Below, the earth spun and directional beams of energy focused down upon the Arctic....

And as Mason focused, the earth expanded rapidly, spinning, and like a camera zooming in, the vision focused on site after site after site.

Volcanoes bursting and bubbling over, monsoons slamming into high rises, tsunamis gathering height and speed, racing towards shorelines like monsters released from the depths; arctic ice shelves breaking free and plummeting through melting strata, venting poisonous methane clouds.

"It's begun," Mason whispered dryly. "We couldn't stop it."

Chapter 11

Gabriel tried to reach his boss encased in the ice, and Mason couldn't imagine the emotions going through his son's thoughts right now, but he also couldn't imagine much of anything at this point.

He had failed. The world was in the throes of transformation.

Annabelle and the other druids had subdued those who had offered modest resistance, but it hadn't taken much effort. Their will to fight was gone, and Solomon's people, the loyal employees of Solstice, now watched the images on the projection below the altar. Some turned their attention skyward, where the winds had at last brought menacing storm clouds. Only these were far from natural, full of lightning sparks and churning flames under their bellies as they raged toward a collision with another front descending from the east.

The building shook again and a monstrously cold wind roared through the trees and up to the rooftop.

The elevator doors opened, and out raced Angelica and Belgar. Both were limping, still in the process of healing, but they were energized and ready for a battle that had passed without them. "So it's true," Angelica said over the wind. Her attention went from Solomon, where she took grim satisfaction in his current state, back to Mason, and the staff.

She lowered her head in reverence, mimicking Belgar's motion, and Mason raised the staff. "Please, it's not like I did anything for it."

"You've earned it nonetheless," Belgar said, then eyed the vision of the earth below his feet. "Now, what about this mess?"

"It's too late," Gabriel said, his back to them. Still staring at Solomon, he shook his head. "It wasn't supposed to be this way."

Mason moved toward him. "It was, Gabriel. It always was his plan; you were just never in on the whole thing. He used you."

Gabriel's right hand clenched and he pressed the staff against the altar stone, mumbling some words.

"Gabriel?"

Shelby reached out to him, moving in front of Mason, and for a moment in a clearing before the clouds completely blocked out the sky, there was a low angle where the sun shone clear and bright—perhaps the last time it would be seen for a long, long time. Shelby's face glowed and her hair seemed to dance in an angelic aura, and all at once, Mason remembered the hospital … Lauren's dream.

Burning … the sunlight. Burning … all the trees and the vines, everything, burning all the green …

The wind buffeted him and drowned out the crowd's murmuring. Mason's eyes widened as he focused on the satellites on the projection below. Focused, and remembered …

"Shelby!"

She spun her head around, Gabriel forgotten for the moment. "What?"

"I have an idea." He motioned to Angelica and Belgar, then shouted to Annabelle. "Re-form the circle, fast!"

Mason made a motion with his fingers, pointing at Shelby's wrists, and the bonds broke apart into a dust that blew away at once. She flexed her hands, and suddenly Mason's old ivory staff jumped into the air and settled in her grasp. Smiling at her, he nodded to his side, an open niche in the circle being created by the others.

She took her spot and now Mason stood tall, at the corner-stone, with more than twenty druids spread out in a circle before him, and more joining ranks behind them. It seemed like they all knew what to do. Several concentric circles, everyone touching the shoulder of the one in front, and the front line holding out their hands toward the altar, and then skyward, mimicking what Mason was doing, aiming his staff up to the swirling clouds, and beyond.

"Not much time," he spoke so Shelby could hear.

"Gabriel?" He called out to his son, who now just seemed empty like a deflated doll. He sagged to his knees, forehead against his staff, still resting on the altar stone. The altar itself was wet, the block of ice surely melting, but not fast enough for concern.

"Leave him," Annabelle said, at his right. She stood next to Belgar and opposite Angelica. "Whatever you're planning, do it fast."

Shelby pointed her staff's bottom edge to the image of the earth below, where the blues and greens were being devoured by dark masses of grey-black, a chaotic, crawling mass of clouds filled with sparking lights and flares of crimson.

"How can we stop this?"

"With the weather," Mason said, closing his eyes. "Think larger, think higher. Focus on the atmosphere, on ..."

"The solar wind!" Shelby yelled. "Space weather, geomagnetic storms ..."

Mason recalled everything he knew about solar radiation, flares and the constant flow of radiation particles bombarding the earth from the sun, the varying intensities of the geomagnetic forces surrounding the earth and trailing it, leading into the atmosphere and causing coronas and auroras. The very radiation that heats the earth and is trapped by the clouds and greenhouse gases ... Solomon had done his part to release massive amounts of methane and CO_2 and water vapor, hoping to trap the existing heat and intensify it, causing a runaway greenhouse effect that would cook the planet and boil the oceans and kill off most of the species on the surface.

Tremendous damage had been done, but it wasn't finished yet and what was to come would be infinitely worse.

Mason clung to two shreds of hope. The first was that the methane pockets were being released slowly, the glaciers thick and the permafrost was still heating. Stopped soon, the worst effects could be mitigated.

And the second—the sacrifice wasn't complete. Solomon still lived.

To stop the energy flow and the continued weather-cycling, they just had to break the circle up there. Break the satellite's connection.

Or knock them out altogether.

He focused and projected what was in his mind over the visuals of the earth on the floor. The sun appeared, up close and personal. A seething, churning mass of fiery power, rippling with blazing heat and—as they watched, shooting off a sunspot, a massive solar flare that created a looping burst of plasma. A coronal mass ejection of extreme size and power.

"The sun!" Mason yelled. "An X-twenty class flare was expelled three days ago. Most of its impact wasn't felt here as it wasn't directly facing earth, but we caught enough, and are still in the trail of the geo-magnetic storm it produced."

His eyes swept over the crowd.

"We are going to do to that storm exactly what you've all been doing here on earth. Terrestrial or space, it makes no difference. We are the caretakers of the earth, and its weather is more than just what happens under its atmosphere. To fully control it, we have to expand our minds, expand the limits of our jurisdiction."

He pointed his staff skyward, challenging the writhing, battling clouds. "This is our dominion! We control the earth, the moon, the very sun."

Both hands now on the staff, he closed his eyes and felt the energy rippling through the old wood, collected from the surging power of every soul on this rooftop, collected from the fears and dreams and thoughts and wishes of everyone so deeply connected to the earth and the air and the elements, in turn fueling their magic.

It coursed through his muscles, his veins and bones. Galloped through the neural pathways in his brain and intensified. And now the entire floor of the rooftop balcony faded away, replaced by the stars and the great ball of the sun, blasting out its plasma storms, a wind that seethed in different wavelength filters, roaring and twisting, swirling and gaining down upon the tiny planet.

The planet with its own magnetic shield that vainly fended off the surging storm, deflecting huge swathes of driving particles and shimmering streams of energy.

Mason concentrated, and felt the entire congregation merging as one, standing fast against both winds now: terrestrial and solar, being in two places, above and below the fray.

He gathered the solar storm's energy, tweaked its trajectory, felt its power and almost ran fleeing from its sheer godlike strength. He felt like a gnat beneath its foot, but raised up his hands anyway to catch and redirect the behemoth's weight and force, shifting it ever so slightly.

A minor change that, at such distance to the earth's atmosphere, was enough.

Ordinarily, with monitoring of the sun's flares for X-Class eruptions, terrestrial satellites had time to take measures to turn the sensitive equipment away from the onslaught of the impact. But this time, there had been no need, and the satellites lay unprotected.

Seven of them over the western hemisphere, among the hundreds of other satellites not controlled by Solstice.

Collateral damage for sure. But these seven ... Mason focused harder and then let his mind relax, and just rode the wave of the solar wind, feeling it roar at over a million miles per hour, surging with all the power and energy of supercharged plasma particles.

He exhaled and watched now as the impact occurred, and again the image on the floor switched to the earth itself, with the blinking satellites in the druidic formation.

Four sparkled, vibrated, then went dark. Three more quickly followed. The lines of energy intersecting the globe fizzled, retracted, then withdrew.

Mason sighed and lowered his staff, as the congregation did the same. Wide-eyed, they watched the floor, then turned their eyes skyward.

The clouds still surged and battled, but all at once, their fury seemed to abate, their ferocity dropping by visible degrees. Like soldiers whose commander had just fallen in battle, they lost the will to fight and gave in to the winds that turned a notch warmer, swirling and blowing in an extreme southward path that began to scatter the thicker masses.

Mason watched as a patch of blue appeared, one that expanded and spread, trying to gently muscle in on the territory ceded by the storm clouds.

And almost immediately, something else formed in the clear sky: an undulating ribbon of light, multi-hued, an extensive and exquisitely beautiful aurora that Mason knew would continue for hours, given the strength of the flare and the storm raging in the ionosphere.

"Did we do it?" Shelby asked hopefully.

Mason looked back to the image of the earth, with its areas of gray starting to dissipate and break up, revealing areas of green and blue beneath. He shuddered to think of the terrestrial damage, the lives lost in the past few hours across the world, and he knew soon they would have to connect to the news services and survey the damage. There would be questions and demands, riots and hopefully—a coming together of the world in new and more cooperative ways. But for now, all he knew was what he told Shelby as he squeezed her hand.

"I think so. The world—all of us—we have another chance."

She was about to say something more as she squeezed his hand back, but a cry from the altar shattered the moment.

Gabriel stood up. His staff was ablaze, and he slammed it down—right upon the block of ice. Whether in frustration, anger or out of some hope to free Solomon, Mason wasn't sure. The staff struck and an immense blast of heat and flame tossed Gabriel back into the crowd.

The ice block shattered all at once, exploding outward in a burst of arms and legs.

Another cry arose, inhuman and primordial, full of pain and screaming at the very depths of nature. Solomon slid off the altar, fell on his blackened knees, then somehow got up.

Nothing was recognizable from his features except that one green eye, dripping out blood-red tears over burnt, hollow cheekbones and scorched teeth. A blistered tongue slithered out and muffled words struggled to form, sounding like occult obscenities.

Solomon reached out his hand. And the staff in Mason's hand trembled, started to pull away. But Mason held it tighter, wrestling it back, as his feet slid.

And all at once, a swarm of bugs flew up from the cracks in the roof and under the vegetation. Locusts, wasps, flies and beetles of all varieties. Rising up in an undulating cyclone, twisting horizontally, then arching and dropping—over Solomon.

He looked up, and that one eye widened, then flashed back to Mason in surprise.

It was as much a surprise to Mason as well. "Not my doing," he said over the buzzing and clicking and fluttering of wings. Mason had a sudden flash of a memory—back to Palavar's farm and the interruption of the sacrifice ... and the extreme reaction nature took when denied....

Solomon made to lunge, to throw himself across the roof onto Mason, but his legs never completed the motion. The plague of insects met him at once, covered him like a complete glove, every last stray bug searching for purchase, some spare bit of cooked flesh to chew and consume.

And they were hungry.

The crowd murmured, some cried out and others looked away. But still others, like Angelica and Belgar and Shelby all watched in grim satisfaction as the insects had their fill. Efficient, fast, unyielding and brutal, they devoured Solomon like tender meat, saving nothing for leftovers, and cleaned the bones. Then they scattered up into the air and back under the tiles, leaving behind a bleached skeleton that tumbled upon itself and collapsed into a heap.

A lone insect remained, hovering, fluttering over the remains. A dragonfly, yellow and red. Engorged. It alighted on Solomon's skull, cleaned its wings fastidiously, then darted off.

"It wasn't me," Mason repeated hollowly, this time to Gabriel who had staggered out of the crowd now, then stood still, frozen himself in shock and awe.

And for a moment, Mason saw it clearly again: the dragonfly, just as he has seen others just like it before, on his first day. That first morning down in the grove greeting him, and then again, here on the summit, when the insect had hovered around Solomon. Only now, Mason was sure it hadn't appeared for Solomon at all, but for him. It was a sign, repeated now. And Mason knew, knew without any reservations, what his totem was to be.

But that could wait. Now …

The winds continued to blow and swirl, and the clouds continued their gradual retreat. Somewhere a bird was chirping, and somewhere the sun shone through, competing with the beauty of the scintillating aurora.

"He didn't follow through with his sacrifice," Gabriel said quietly, head down. "And was punished for it." He gave a sideways glance to Mason, and the implication was there.

"Just as I was," Mason said. "Although not as immediately." *Nature was patient with me, claiming its due much later.*

Shelby squeezed his hand.

But Gabriel had other ideas. Scanning the ground, he found what he wanted, rushed forward and plucked the ivory blade from the ice shards and paused only to look into the empty eye sockets of Solomon's skull. Then he put the blade to his own neck.

"The circle still demands blood, and it shall have it."

"Gabriel, no!" Mason took a step, then stopped as Gabriel pressed the blade deeper, drawing a line of red. "No more sacrifices, no more blood."

"I can't escape it," Gabriel insisted, looking up at the clouds, then down at the image of the cloud-riddled earth. "All this … everything that almost happened. My fault, I encouraged it. I wanted it. I would have reveled in the destruction of so many…."

"Gabriel, we can sort it out. We can—"

"No, I'll never forget. Never live past it. I almost killed you, Shelby … Mom …"

Mason lowered his head. But Shelby stepped closer, reaching out to her brother. "Don't do it. I've only just found you again, Gabriel. And I have a feeling you and I—we're going to be needed."

He frowned at her.

"We're twins," she said. "And I've never felt complete unless you were at my side. Together, here at Solstice, we can do something real. Still accomplish something to save the world, but in our own way. Join me…."

Gabriel's eyes watered in anguish. He bit his lip, chewing it almost, but his hand didn't waver. "I can't…. Can't ever forget. I—"

Suddenly, he froze in place, hand trembling, but lowering slightly. His eyes darted back and forth, and saw Angelica circling around, standing in front of him. Annabelle stepped forward and joined her, as did Belgar.

"No more blood," Angelica said. "The Arch-Druid has spoken, and we agree." She flashed a smile from Mason back to Gabriel. "And as for your memories. If you truly wish to forget, well … we can help with that."

Gabriel blinked, tears spilling on his cheeks. He gave a look to his father, and Mason realized what they were proposing could work.

"I had it done," Mason admitted. "And a pretty good job Palavar did on me. If you can do it," he said to Angelica, "without being so invasive or all-encompassing …"

She smiled back. "Just a few bits here and there. Memory modification really, rather than eradication." She cocked her head, as if peering into Gabriel's mind. "He's got all the right motives, just the means to achieve them … well, we can tweak what he remembers about his role. Make it much more passive. Nothing that will stand out in conflict with actual events, so the blocks should stay in place."

Gabriel lowered the blade and let it fall. He reached out and took Shelby's hand. "Do it, and let's get on with our lives."

"And go see our mother," Shelby said. "We have a lot of catching up to do."

Mason exhaled and looked up, following the expanding aurora now as it stretched over the brightening sky, serving as a barrier of sorts to the clouds, sending them back and establishing dominance.

CHAPTER 12

Four days later, Mason finally had his chance to address the United Nations. The Assembly Hall had a makeshift ceiling, still very much a work in progress, and one that promised to be even more costly and beautiful, artistic and expensive at the same time. The lost delegates had been replaced, plaques to their memories suitably placed in prominent position marking their service and dedication. The mood was somber, yet bustling with activity. Press from all the major news stations were in attendance, and Mason had to sit through over two hours of updates from member countries.

There followed the litany of misery, the I-told-you-so's from global warming alarmists, and a quick tally of the dead and missing, of the countless hundreds of billions in damage so far. The great screen behind the podium showed a collage of disaster sites, of floods and coastal cities leveled, of villages still burning with volcanoes smoking in the background, of forest fires still ablaze, valleys still flooded, farms with crops frozen under thick ice. Arctic glaciers cracked, but not melted, permafrost still holding over most of the area.

Third world countries were hit hard with the after-effects of disease and starvation, and their plight was all the more difficult since the industrial countries were dealing with their own widespread damage and reconstruction. Emergency funds were used up, and now charities were being funded from private institutions and organizations from around the world.

It was an amazing coming together of people joined in one common experience, one brutal and nearly fatal attack on the complacency so many had enjoyed for so long.

Whether or not it was enough to shake up the population and force behavioral changes was anyone's guess. Teams of scientists spoke for and against the causes of all this meteorological mayhem, the opposing side winning some logic points stressing that no climate models assuming man-made carbon emissions, even at extreme levels, could have ever produced the kind of simultaneous global effects that had ravaged the world for over a week.

But all agreed that the world had, almost miraculously, been given a reprieve. Religious groups of all faiths banded together, insisting that God had spared them after coming close to re-enacting the Flood; others were extremely disappointed, believing the Rapture had at last been at hand, only to have deliverance snatched away at the last moment.

Mason endured it all, watching with impassive enthusiasm, sitting between Shelby and Lauren. He knew Shelby was paying rapt attention, amazed at the connections and the implications. She had to be overwhelmed, being in the thick of one of the most pivotal moments in human history. A turning point for sure, something that would stick in our collective memory for generations, and would certainly inspire some major changes. If not purely in the economic sense, then certainly in the sense of increasing what had been noticeably lacking for the past century: awe and humility before nature.

And when it was finally his turn to speak, and he joined the senior members of the WMO, Mason reiterated Solstice's potential for easing these crises, lamenting that his company had been brought on too late to help, and also had to deal with the untimely death of their CEO and a large reorganization in his passing. He promised to pull back on the requests for unlimited access to various data, at the same time making their own data and findings more accessible to the world community. And in light of the satellite disruption that had taken out communication and cellular service for thirty percent of the globe, and which had only recently been restored, Mason offered to sell (for a very economical rate) a new solar storm predictive algorithm and program that promised to increase warning time and more accurately predict the severity of solar flares.

He closed by thanking the WMO and the nations of the world, who had come together in shared experience of near annihilation. It was a humbling moment, an event that bonded humanity as one, showed our weaknesses and highlighted our strengths: compassion, charity and courage. He was confident that together they would rebuild and strengthen and prepare for ways to ward off or at least mitigate future damage.

Stepping down to cheers and respectful handshakes, Mason joined Shelby and his wife, taking Lauren's hand as she stood—on her own—smiling. She walked gingerly, leaning on the old weathered staff. She seemed to draw energy from it, and with every step her back seemed to straighten and her legs wobbled only slightly, looking to all the world as if she had never had anything seriously wrong.

"Well that wasn't so bad," Lauren said.

Shelby stifled a giggle as they walked through past the other rows and out into the hall, where Mason finally took a deep breath. He hugged Lauren, and then found Gabriel waiting for them around a corner. He had several other Solstice employees with him, including Belgar and Angelica—newly appointed board members.

"Ready for a trip?" Angelica asked.

Lauren looked up at Mason. "You really have to go?"

"London," Mason said. "Yes, the duty apparently of all us arch-druid types. Got to pay homage to where it all began, do the state tour and visit the shrines."

"Don't worry, Mom." Shelby hugged Mason's arm. "I'll show him around and keep him safe. No sacrifices, no tornadoes."

"I'll hold you to that," Lauren said. "And Gabe?"

Gabriel shook his head. "Not me. Someone's got to stick around and hold down the fort. Helping get the satellite data restored and weather stations back online around the world, implementing some new software."

Mason smiled. It had been almost a week, and no ill effects yet on Gabriel. The memory modification seemed to have worked. He led Lauren out into the bright sunshine where there were just a few hints of darker striated clouds to the east. The air was full, hazy and warm, with a light breeze coming in over the river.

"What do you think?" Lauren asked as she got in the limo and looked up at the sky. "Weather forecast?"

Mason smiled and kissed her. "Excellent chance of continued sunshine and mild temperatures through Thursday. Although, I've been known to be wrong. From time to time."

She handed him the staff. "Keep this, then. Just in case you happen upon one of those times."

He gripped the staff, and felt its coursing power. Felt the wind stir and ripple around him, the air fluctuate and the earth tremble in deference.

"Don't let it go to your head," Shelby voiced with some concern.

"I won't," Mason replied. Then, out of habit, he signed: *Still my girl?*

Shelby grinned a big grin, all teeth and gums. She signed back, just as fast: *Always,* then pulled him along. "Let's get to the airport. Gabriel, you coming to see us off?"

"Not yet," he said. "I'll stick around and see if the press has any follow-up questions I can help with. Have yourselves an uneventful trip."

Mason paused at the door, turned back and approached Gabriel. Looked into his eyes, then reached in and gave his son a large hug. One that was returned.

"See you soon."

Epilogue

abriel made it to the roof of the nearby apartment complex twenty minutes later. Nearly out of breath, he took a moment to compose himself before approaching the hooded figure standing near the edge. The figure was squat and shorter than him by a foot, but still, dressed in the darker grey robe and leaning on a twisted knotty staff of cherry wood, the druid seemed full of confidence and power.

"I received your message," Gabriel said as the winds picked up. He looked out over the street, past the buses and cabs, to observe the new construction on the UN dome, and the intensity of the sun glinting off the metal framework. "But I don't understand. Who are you, and why couldn't I speak of your request for a meeting? Why all the secrecy?"

A slender hand rose and pulled back the hood, revealing a curly mass of red hair. The short, solid woman turned, revealing hauntingly attractive features. "You will have all the answers, in moments. Once I remove the memory blocks."

Gabriel opened his mouth, about to protest, but then the light in her eyes—bright and fiery—stopped him cold. And he stood motionless as she approached, raising the staff that glowed and pulsed like a light from a miniature sun.

"I'm Lady Sunfire, young man. And you … you are the key to restoring your true master's vision, and restoring the balance."

"But—"

"Quiet now," Sunfire said. "Clear your mind and focus on the light. This will take but a moment. You will remember, and together we will forge ahead with what must be done."

Gabriel tried to shake his head, tried to back up. This wasn't right. He was doing great things, reshaping the world, working with his father and sister. *That* felt right. Nothing else mattered.

"Oh, but it does," the elder druid said, as if she had read his mind. "And when you remember what was taken from you, I will show you new ways of exacting revenge. After all," she said it with a twinkle in her eye and smirk to her lips. "Your father showed me the way. It's my namesake after all, but the solar weather is the key. Sunfire indeed!"

With that, she stamped her staff on the concrete floor and said: *"Remember!"*

About the Author

David Sakmyster is the award-winning author of more than a dozen novels, including *Jurassic Dead* and *The Morpheus Initiative*, a series featuring psychic archaeologists (described as "Indiana Jones meets the X-Files"). He also has an epic historical adventure, *Silver and Gold*, the suspense novels *Crescent Lake* and *Blindspots*, and a story collection, *Escape Plans*. His screenplay, *Nightwatchers*, has been optioned for production. Visit him at

www.sakmyster.com

Other WordFire Press Titles by David Sakmyster

Escape Plans

Our list of other WordFire Press authors and titles is always growing.
To find out more and to see our selection of titles, visit us at

wordfirepress.com